W9-BCL-239

3/6/14

120-1917

HAYNER PUBLIC LIBRARY DISTRICT
ALTON, ILLINOIS

OVERDUES .10 PER DAY. MAXIMUM FINE
COST OF BOOKS. LOST OR DAMAGED BOOKS
ADDITIONAL $5.00 SERVICE CHARGE.

DEMCO

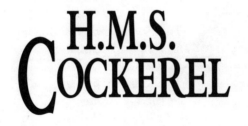

H.M.S.
COCKEREL

ALSO BY DEWEY LAMBDIN

The French Admiral
The King's Commission
The King's Coat
The King's Privateer
The Gun Ketch
For King and Country

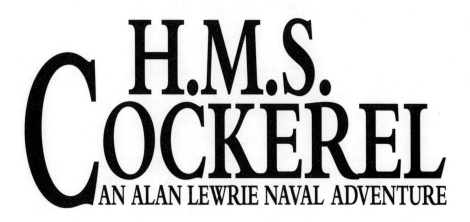

H.M.S. COCKEREL

AN ALAN LEWRIE NAVAL ADVENTURE

DEWEY LAMBDIN

DONALD I. FINE, INC.
New York

HAYNER PUBLIC LIBRARY DISTRICT
ALTON, ILLINOIS

Once again,

For my father,
Lt. Comdr. Dewey Lambdin, USN

With thanks to:
The U.S. Naval Institute for many reference works;
MacKenzie of the Maritime Information Centre, at the
Iain National Maritime Museum, Greenwich, England:
To Doug Cantrell at Nashville Tech Community College for his
excellent map of Toulon;
To Genevieve and her books *Merde* and *Merde, Encore*
where I garnered such wonderfully feelthy phrases;
and thanks to Genoa and Foozle, who cat-napped long enough
for me to get a good day's work in, now and then.

Copyright © 1995 by Dewey Lambdin

All rights reserved, including the right of reproduction in whole or in part in any
form. Published in the United States of America by Donald I. Fine, Inc. and in
Canada by General Publishing Company Limited.

Library of Congress Catalogue Card Number: 94-061909

ISBN: 1-55611-446-X

Manufactured in the United States of America

10 9 8 7 6 5 4 3 2 1

Designed by Irving Perkins Associates

This novel is a work of fiction. Names, characters, places and incidents are either
the product of the author's imagination or are used fictitiously. Any resemblance
to actual events, locales, organizations or persons, living or dead, is entirely
coincidental and beyond the intent of either the author or publisher.

ACP-6045

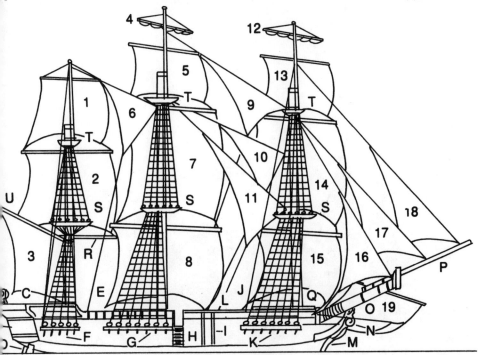

Full-Rigged Ship: Starboard (right) side view

1. Mizzen Topgallant
2. Mizzen Topsail
3. Spanker
4. Main Royal
5. Main Topgallant
6. Mizzen T'gallant Staysail
7. Main Topsail
8. Main Course
9. Main T'gallant Staysail
10. Middle Staysail
11. Main Topmast Staysail
12. Fore Royal
13. Fore Topgallant
14. Fore Topsail
15. Fore Course
16. Fore Topmast Staysail
17. Inner Jib
18. Outer Flying Jib
19. Spritsail

A. Taffrail & Lanterns
B. Stern & Quarter-galleries
C. Poop Deck/Great Cabins Under
D. Rudder & Transom Post
E. Quarterdeck
F. Mizzen Chains & Stays
G. Main Chains & Stays
H. Boarding Battens/Entry Port
I. Cargo Loading Skids
J. Shrouds & Ratlines
K. Fore Chains & Stays
L. Waist
M. Gripe & Cutwater
N. Figurehead & Beakhead Rails
O. Jib Boom
P. Bow Sprit
Q. Foc's'le & Anchor Cat-heads
R. Cro'jack Yard (no sail fitted)
S. Top Platforms
T. Cross-Trees
U. Spanker Gaff

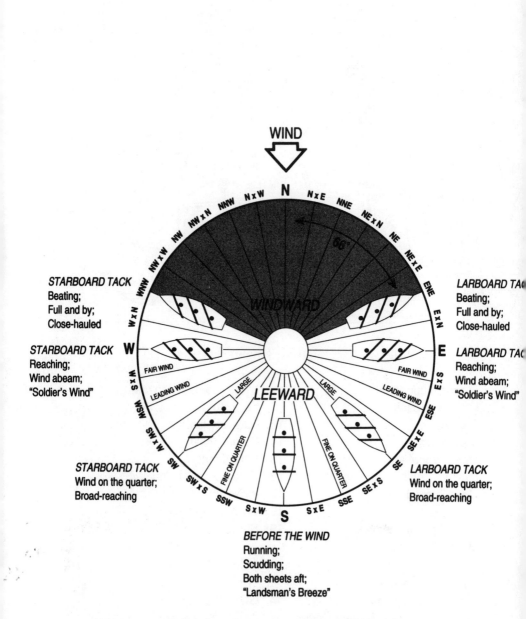

POINTS OF SAIL AND 32-POINT WIND-ROSE

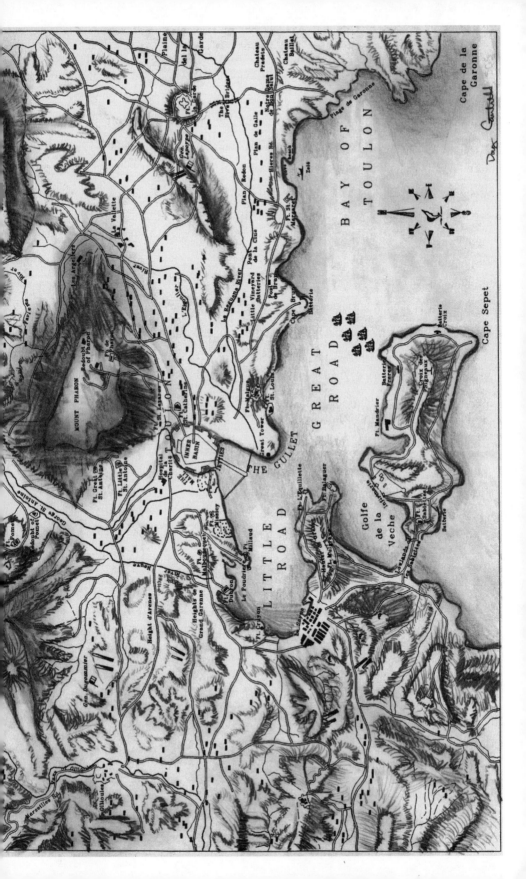

Book I

Quid faciat laetas segetes, quo sidere terram vertere, Maecenas, ulmisque adiungere vites conveniat, quae cura boum, qui cultis habendo sit peccori, apibus quanta experientia parcis, hinc canere incipiam.

What makes the crops joyous, beneath what star, Maecenas, it is well to turn the soil, and wed vines to elms, what tending the kine need, what care the herd in breeding, what skill the thrifty bees—hence shall I begin my song.

—Virgil
Georgics, Book I, 1–5

CHAPTER 1

"Ooh, sir, wawtch out f'r the . . ."

Wherever I go lately, Alan Lewrie mused, rather resignedly, I seem to be arse-deep in shit. Oh, well.

He waved off the towheaded young "daisy-kicker" at the Olde Plough-man Public House's hitching rail, who stood with silent offer to towel the offending matter from his glossy top boots.

"No use, lad." Lewrie said as he swung up into the saddle. "There's plenty more where I'm going."

"Oh, aye, sir, so they *be!*" The lad chirped, letting go the reins he held. Lewrie dug ha'pence from his wash-leather purse and flipped it to the daisy-kicker, who whooped with glee, as if the coin were the first he'd ever earned, as if Lewrie did not reward his chore each time he departed from the Olde Ploughman.

" 'Ta, yer honour, sir!" The boy called as Lewrie turned his horse west on the High Street. " 'Night, Squire Lewrie!"

Lewrie touched the wide brim of his hat with a riding crop in reply as he clucked his tongue and kneed his mount to a brisk walk.

Squire, Alan sighed with a snort; not *exactly* true, was it? Squires were freeholders who rented land to others, while he was only a tenant, a rent payer himself. Now if I sublet, he thought: perhaps to a well-off hermit (and *was* there such a creature as an eremite with the "blunt," he wondered?) who wished half an acre down by the creek, where he could pile himself up a grotto and become Lewrie's tenant. Performing, perhaps, the odd Jeremiad—thrice on Market Days—talking in tongues or dancing like a Dervish, or old Saint Vitus, would I then be a squire at last? Or even *less* welcome in the parish? Might be worth doing, at that—it'd drive Caroline's uncle Phineas batty!

His horse paced through the village of Anglesgreen, heading west for the vale between the rolling hills, hooves clopping on the icy earthen

3

road, as candles and lanterns were lit in the windows of the homes alongside, and lights were extinguished as shopkeepers at last shut, after long hours of sparse winter trade. Very few villagers were out now that the brief stint of cloud-occluded sun had all but gone, and the winds blew foul and cold. Without the casual labourers of the sowing or harvesting seasons, Anglesgreen was an even more tedious and empty a place than ever he had experienced, now Christmas and Epiphany were come and gone. And cold. As cold as Parish Poor's Rate charity. And about as unattractive.

Arse-deep in it, he told himself again, glum with rum and ennui. Up to my nose in acres of it . . . and that, so *bloody* boresome!

There were, to Alan's lights—much like the descending levels of Hell in Dante's *Inferno*—distinct gradations to the shit existing in the world. And the quality and quantity of it a body had to abide. Uncle Phineas, his lessor, for instance; his eternal, sneering, stultifying monologues, his miserly few suppers or "dos" (which formed the bulk of a bleak Lewrie social life)—now *there* was shit from the lowest Nether-Pit itself! And totally unabidable, in quality and amount.

In contrast, the literal item (such as the horse droppings he'd just stepped in)—some of those he didn't mind half so much. Horses were noble beasts, beautiful in form and motion. Their stalings *were* abidable, for they bore convivial folk together, astride or by coach, eased a traveler's burden, pleased with their speed, heart and endurance, livened hunts, fairs, social occasions . . . or elated one with the order of their finish at a race.

No, truth be told, Alan Lewrie, like all good English gentlemen, rather *enjoyed* horse poop. It had a redolence of hospitality, of congeniality, of freedom, excitement . . . and far horizons!

The by-products of the lesser beasts necessary to a farm, though; even his inept, clueless style of gentleman farming, of which folks said he did little but raise his hat—now they were odious in the extreme. He knew little after four years, and was forced to depend upon the knowledge of Governour Chiswick, his brother-in-law, or to the vile old Phineas Chiswick; they both dropped their jaws and whinnied at his questions, making him feel as out of place, even after four years of applying himself, as he had aboard *Ariadne* back in '80 on his first day as a callow midshipman.

Or, even more discouraging, to have to "talk things over" with dearest Caroline in private, being coached on what orders to give that particular day to the few permanent farmhands, or the hired day workers. To be such a humble know-nothing in his wife's eyes!

Truth be told again, Alan Lewrie thought the life of the rural gentleman farmer stank, in more ways than one, no matter it was the fondest wish of every successful man to make his pile, get acres, and aspire to the squirearchy. It was . . . shit! Of the most unabidable sort! And fast as he strove to shovel it away, here came more.

His sheep, for instance. He squirmed on the cold saddle as he contemplated them. The farm (the *rented* farm, he reminded himself) was awash in the smelly things—most of Surrey was these days—unutterably stupid, messy, foolish . . . and shit-bedaubed. Even a goat could manage to keep a reasonably clean nether end, though they did stink like badgers.

Swine—there's chapter and verse for you, too, he thought. And chickens! Lord, what a fetid reek the henyard bore. It was a wonder a self-respecting fox would have a go at 'em, 'thout holding his nose! And cattle, I *ask* you, he grunted, his neck burning with revulsion. Fat, shambling, lanky-hipped, floppy beasts, capable of veritable *broadsides* of loose, flat, disordered ordure, shot off by the barrico, whenever and wherever they wished. Stinky his city of London might be, brassy and corrupt a warship might become, but it was never a tenth as bad as a working farm. Sweet as hay and clover were in the spring, the gardens' romantic aromas, soon as one inhaled a restoring lungful of bucolic bliss, here came some reek from things best hung in the curing house as *meat*, revolting one! Or plopped all over one's best pair of top boots.

It was tempting to think that now his Granny Lewrie had passed to Her Great Reward and had left him quite well-off in her will, he and Caroline could move to London, and use the farm as a spring and summer retreat; hire an estate agent to look after it for them. It did, in spite of his ignorance, turn a pretty penny or two, enough to qualify him as a voter. Then he could nod and smile on his rare visits, chortle over the books when they showed profit, and call out "Carry on!" to some experienced and knowledgeable underling, leaving him leisure time for horses, for amusements. For a *real* life!

Lewrie hitched his heavy wool cloak closer about his neck as he rode near the Red Swan Inn. Late as it was, as close to suppertime for the revelers inside, whom he could espy through the cheery diamond-paned windows, there was quite a merry crowd gathered there. A fair number of horses were hitched outside, blanketed against the cold, under the now bare but towering oaks. The richer patrons had theirs temporarily stabled in the warmer barn behind. He thought he spotted Governour's tall gray gelding, and beside it, two hunters he knew as belonging to Sir Romney Embleton, Bt., and his whey-faced son Harry.

Now there's shit for you, Lewrie thought with a rueful grin. For a mad fleeting moment he thought of going in the Red Swan for a stirrup cup of hot gin punch, or a mug of mulled wine to warm his journey home. Just on a lark, to see the looks on their phizes for daring to show his own in the more refined, high-gentry squire-ish Red Swan!

For just a moment, he envied his brother-in-law Governour, too. He was married to Sir Romney's daughter Millicent, long before Lewrie had come to Anglesgreen and wed Caroline, upsetting all the plans of seven years before. Governour and Millicent could socialize when and where they might. Bad as blood was between Lewries and Embletons, and because of them between Chiswicks and Embletons, Governour had welcome still at Embleton Hall, and at all the parish and county's doings. Though it was sometimes a *trifle* thin. His and Caroline's, however, was nonexistent. And looked fair to being nonexistent far past the advent of the coming new century.

Truth, even further, be told, since they'd returned from the Bahamas in '89 when his last ship *Alacrity* had paid off in Portsmouth, they'd been treated bad as leprous Gypsies by those locals who walked in dread of Embleton disapproval, or fawned on Embleton largesse. Considering Embleton influence over the area, it was a wonder the Lewries even had benefit of clergy at mossy old St. George's. And with rural social life revolving 'round the local fox hunt—and that hunt's Master of Hounds none other than Sir Romney—they might as well have been turbaned Turk horse thieves for all their welcome.

Well, not by all, Alan qualified, as he drew his horse to a halt at the turn-in gate. The hot rum punches he'd downed through an afternoon of war talk and genteel arguing at the Olde Ploughman were working on him something hellish, and the idea of riding in to 'front the bastards direct was rake-hell, damme-boy appealing. No, not all treat us shabby, he snorted. There were a few of the minor gentry, the younger folk, and most of the common sort who thought the Lewrie saga romantic beyond words, and sympathized with them in their banishment.

Lovely and sweet Caroline Chiswick, the poor Loyalist *émigré* home after the Revolution, being "buttock-brokered" by her Uncle Phineas to wed rich, so he could get even more acres by her, her parents almost helpless in their penury to help her. Four suitors: two very old widowers and a sheeper-tenant—all vile beyond belief—and the Hon. Harry Embleton, an MP and heir to untold wealth and power, and next-door acres, the most favoured.

Then, along came Lt. Alan Lewrie, RN, and swept her away. Not only rescued her, but came within a hair of dueling Harry for her!

Well, it never came to *that*, Alan gloated, warmed against the cold as he savoured that long-ago triumph. Harry learned we'd posted banns, and went lunatick at a fox hunt. Took a whip to my treed cat, took his whip to *me*—'bout as public as it gets! And I flattened his nose and made his bung sport claret. Make matters worse, he goes and whines to Caroline 'bout her choice, goes off again, calls her every vile thing he had in his little mind, and damned if *she* don't whip him 'cross the field with her reins, too! Bang on his busted nose in front of damn near everyone in Surrey that matters! Lord!

Ah, well, he shrugged, that was a bloody good day. Just didn't think I'd end up paying for it the rest of my natural life. Going on now a full seven years, and time hadn't mellowed any of the participants. He had to give the Embletons credit—they could hold a snit as good as he could.

And there was no sense in stirring the pot up further. Or in being seen as he was at that moment, sitting slumped and indecisive, like a beggar too fearful to knock for pittance at the back entrance of a rich man's manor.

Devil with 'em, he sneered as he turned the reins and clucked his tongue once more, urging the horse with his heels to an easy canter. The gelding knew the way as well as he; on past the Red Swan and a new bank of row houses, onto the Chiddingfold Road, west along the stream, thence over the wooden bridge to Chiswick lands, his rented corner of them, and home.

Where there's a better sort of welcome waiting, he grinned.

CHAPTER 2

" 'Ave 'at owf in a tick, sir," his groom told him as he alit in his stable yard. Bodkins took the reins and tied the horse, then knelt with a rag so Lewrie could prop his boot on a wooden bucket. " 'Ere ye be, sir . . . good'z noo."

"Thankee, Bodkins," Lewrie replied, free at last of rank goo. "Be sure he gets a good, warm rubdown. 'Tis a fearsome cold night."

" 'At I will, sir, never ye fear," the groom said. " 'Ere, Thomas, me lad. Untack 'e master's horse."

It was a fine new stone stable, attached to the older thatched-roof house that now served as the carriage house for two coaches; one light and open for good weather, and an older, boxy enclosed coach. Lewrie petted and fussed over the gelding before the stableboy led him away for his well-deserved oats and rubdown. Lewrie crossed the stable yard, sure that his workers had shoveled before dark, sure he would encounter no more messy surprises lying in wait, on past the hulking older "wattle and daub" original barn where the products of the farm were stored to tide him, his kith and kin, and his beasts, through the rest of the winter.

Uncle Phineas had leased them, and that quite grudgingly, 160 acres, a corner of his vast holdings at the foot of his lane, like a gatehouse to the manor proper. But it was close to the village and the Chiddingfold Road, and quite handy. A sheeper had been renting when they left in '86, but it was vacant upon their return. Acreage enough to run a middling flock of sheep, a few beef cattle and dairy animals, swine, goats, turkeys and chickens, with orchards and grape arbors enough for the home-farm to feed quite well. There was enough cleared land for a decently profitable crop of wheat and hay in addition to the sheep, with wood lots, kitchen gardens, access to three creeks and several sweet wells. Hops and barley gave them home-brew beer, and they were awash in preserved fruits.

The new house, though! The old thatched-roof cottage had been a two-story, smoky, bug-infested horror, and, since wages and construction materials had been quite low, they had run up a presentable new stone and gray brick Georgian house, for about a quarter of what a London manse its size might have cost. It gave Alan pleasure to know that it was as fine as anything Governour in his new wealth had built, or as uncle Phineas's gloomy old red-brick pile. The perverse old bastard would not part with land permanently, but had been bludgeoned into a long-term lease which would expire long after he did, so Alan had no fear of losing his £800 investment. And it made Phineas grind what few teeth he had left in his head, so it was more than worth every penny.

They had a slate roof as tight as a well-caulked and coppered ship of the line, and enough fireplaces to keep it snug and cozy on all but the iciest nights—windows enough, too, to keep it breezy and well lit in the warmer seasons. Fashion had demanded, and with Granny Lewrie's last bequest the Lewries could afford, a Palladian facade for the center hall, in imitation of Inigo Jones.

He stopped to admire it in the lantern light, taking cheer at the sight of amber-glowing windows and fuming chimneys confronting the frigid night. Even coming from the rear, between the now bleak kitchen gardens and the ornamental flower gardens and shrubberies on the west side near him, it was imposing, big as a brig!

The central hall jutted towards him, which held the kitchens, the still rooms, butler's pantry, storerooms and laundry facilities. Just off the kitchens, they had a private bathing room, with a marble tub big enough for two. Nearest him, too, was an intimate dining room where they most often took breakfast, or dined *en famille*, overlooking the cheery ornamental garden that was Caroline's pride. Nearer still was the library and music room, and his private study, in the front of the house, adjacent to a receiving parlour just off the foyer and its cloakroom. The hall was tiled and paneled, with a broad staircase which led up to a landing, and another pair-of-stairs. And beyond in the east wing was a dining hall and main parlour *almost* big enough to host a middling-sized guest list for a dance. Unfortunately, that was little used so far—one needed guests who'd accept one's invitations. So furnishings beyond bare bones were far from complete.

Over his head in the west wing was the nursery, the childrens' small bedrooms and the governess's quarters. Over the entry hall was their own spacious bedchamber and intimate study (actually, Caroline's sewing room, so far). There were three more bedchambers for guests in the east wing—once again, vacant and unused. Hopefully, once the last Lewrie was out of "nappies," they planned to convert the nursery into a classroom for a private tutor, with lodgings in the east wing.

"I'm home!" He called out hopefully as he entered through the garden doors to his cozy study. He sailed his wide-brimmed farmer's hat at a wall peg and shrugged off his cloak, draping it over a wing chair near the cheery fireplace. Warmth was what he wished that instant, the Fires of Hell if he could get 'em. He raised the tails of his coat and backed so close to the hearth that his heels were almost between the firedogs.

"Didn' 'ear ya come in, sir," Will Cony said, entering from the central hall. " 'Spected ya through th' front, I did. I'll take yer things, 'ang 'em up f'r ya, sir. Aye, *'ere's* 'at ol' cat, Pitt, sir!"

The grizzled old battler shambled into the room, stalking slow and regal. William Pitt the ram-cat was getting on in years, spending most his days lazing in windows or patches of sunlight, but he still ruled the farm with fang and claw, and even the dogs slunk tail-tucked in terror when he was out and rambling.

Pitt's haughty entrance was disturbed, though, by the arrival of his middle son Hugh, who darted between Cony's knees, leaped the cat, and dashed for him, whooping like a Red Indian. Sewallis, his firstborn, entered behind him. William Pitt, outraged and his dignity destroyed, turned, raked the air in Sewallis's general direction, hissed and moaned before hopping up on his favorite wing chair to wash furiously. And Alan noted that Sewallis shied away from the cat, giving him a wide berth. That was all he had time for before Hugh tackled his leg, howling a greeting.

Alan laughed and reached down to pick him up, to lift him over his head and give him a light toss, making Hugh shriek with joy.

"There's my bold lad!" Alan rejoiced. "There's my dev'lish man! What mischief you been into today, hey?"

"Pwaying, daddy!" Hugh wriggled as he shouted his reply.

"Good Christ, you're in that much trouble again? I surely hope *not*! Oh, *play*-ing, you mean, ha ha. And here's Sewallis. Come here, my boy. How was your day? Been keeping your brother out of scrapes?"

"Yes, father." Sewallis replied with his usual reserve. He cast a wary look over his shoulder in Pitt's direction to determine how safe movement might be, then dashed with unwonted haste as Lewrie held out his arms. The boy came to him dutifully for a more sedate welcome-home hug, and a kiss on the forehead.

"Good to be home," Alan told them both. "Cold as the Devil out tonight."

"Wa' yoo bwing me, daddy?" Hugh coaxed in an almost unintelligible voice. He was only three, and still having trouble pronouncing his "R's," so much so that even a doting daddy, who should have been familiar enough with baby talk, had difficulty understanding him. The boy's eyes gleamed, sly with expectation, clinging to Lewrie's knees, his tiny fingers beginning to probe all the pockets he could reach.

Thievery, Lewrie thought: runs in the family, don't it. Boy has a promising set of careers open to him, long as he doesn't get caught. Few years practice, though . . .

"Why, I brought myself, boy!" Alan chaffered, kneeling to eye level with them. "You don't get a pretty or a sweet *every* time I ride to town, do you?"

"Yess, ah *doo!*" Hugh hollered.

"A body'd think I had to bribe you lads for affection."

"No puddy?" Hugh gaped, beginning to screw his face up for a heartfelt bawl of disappointment. This was betrayal at its blackest.

"Don't be a baby, Hugh, 'course he did." Sewallis chid him with a very adult-sounding touch of vexation.

Alan glanced at his eldest. Both the boys were "breeched" in adult clothing: stockings, shoes, breeches and waistcoats, shirts and stocks, their baby hair grown long enough to be plaited or drawn into a man's queue. But Sewallis suddenly sounded so very mature for his tender five years. Always had, Lewrie realized. Even young as Hugh, the boy had always been aloof, quiet and reserved (call it what you really think, dammit!)—*timid*—with none of the neck-or-nothing exuberance, the silliness or the folly of a normal boy. Scared of the cat? And for God's sake, he hardly ever goes near the damned pony I got 'em. A Lewrie afraid of a horse? An *Englishman* shy of a horse!

"Of course I brought you something," Alan announced, "just as Sewallis said, little man. Can you keep a secret?"

Hugh agreed with a firm nod as Alan peered into corners, like a housebreaker unloading his ill-gotten gains in a slum alley, an eye out for the previous owners.

"Rare treats," he promised. Hugh was giggling now, dancing in impatience and wonder. Sewallis . . . well, he was a little wide-eyed, but ever the little stoic. "I made an arrangement with a pirate and a smuggler, lads. Fiercest, meanest set of blackguards you ever did wish to see. Off they went, far as the East Indies. Down to *Malabar*. Oh, 'tis a mysterious, fearsome place—elephants, and snakes thick as my legs, heathen princes and headhunters. The pirate, he took 'em, and the smuggler, he got 'em out, one step ahead o' the headhunters. Then six months at sea on a tall 'John Company' ship they came, all the way from pagan Hindoo India. 'Round the Cape of Good Hope, over to the Argentine and the Plate for a slant o' wind—"

"Mister Lewrie—oh, excuse me." Mrs. McGowan, the cheerless governess, had entered the room. She didn't approve of parents and children mixing except at teatime, perhaps after supper for an awkward moment or two of stilted conversation. Certainly not of parents who really wished to spend time with their children.

"Firewood and water, then off to St. Helena, the crossroads of the Atlantic, m'dears. Thence 'cross the Westerlies, daring all the French privateers, to Ushant. Up our good English Channel, into the Pool o' London up the Thames. From mysterious *Malabar* . . . a delight fit for the mighty Moghuls themselves!"

He reached into his tail-coat pocket as the boys fidgeted.

"And here they be—cinnamon sticks!" he cried as he produced them, to howls of rapture and leaping, clutching little hands.

"Oh, sir," Mrs. McGowan simpered. "You'll spoil their supper. La, I do allow you cosset these lads something sinful. Come along, Sewallis, Hugh. There's good boys. Wash up and dress. Sweets later, *if* you're good. Waste no more of your father's time. Mister Lewrie, sir, mistress says to tell you that table is set, and you may sup as soon as you've washed the road away. Come, lads. Now."

"No, now!" Hugh demanded petulantly, but it was not to be. He saw his treat tucked into Mrs. McGowan's apron pocket. Lewrie stood, with none of the magic of the moment left but the stickiness of the cinnamon sticks on his fingers. And feeling as ordered about as the boys did as they were chivvied off.

"Well, damme," he groused, returning to the fireplace for a warmup. "Ain't this my own house? Ain't they my own lads, to cosset as I wish? Cosset 'em? Aye, damned right I will. And how dare that . . . that hired bitch gainsay me, hey?"

Cony only shrugged in reply. "Got water'n towels laid out, sir. Bit of a wash afore supper?"

"I suppose so, Cony," Lewrie huffed. "Damn my eyes, but there's a hellish lot of . . . domesticity about these days. Aye, I'll come up. I'll be a good boy. Ain't we all learned to be such . . . *good* lads!"

"Ahum!" Cony coughed into his fist to hide a rueful grin of sympathy. "Aye, sir."

Alan paused in the central hallway, though, peering at the two portraits hung there side by side; his and Caroline's. His had been done in '83, just after the Revolution, when he'd been a twenty-one-year-old lieutenant. Caroline's had been painted by a talented (but annoying) artist in the Bahamas, just after they'd arrived in 1786, when she was twenty-three, and a newlywed.

Early morning tropical light, with her lush flower garden and the impossibly emerald and aquamarine waters of East Bay, which had fronted their small home as a backdrop, she in a wide-brimmed straw hat and off-shoulder morning gown, her clear complexion and her hazel eyes bright and dewy as West Indies dawn, and her long, light brown, almost taffy-blonde hair flowing carefree and loose, teased by the ever-pressing, flirtatious trades . . .

Had Caroline changed? Not in features, so much as . . . she was still lissome and slim, no matter birthing three children. She still rode almost every day, walked the acres, kept active as so many sparrows. Oh, there were laugh lines now around her eyes and mouth, more than before, her graceful hands and fingers sparer of flesh. Where, though, had *that* Caroline gone, he wondered?

And for himself, well, like it or not, not a fortnight before, on Epiphany, he had gone over the edge. He was *thirty*! Middle-aged, and Caroline soon to follow by spring.

As if I don't have enough complaints, God help us, he thought.

He felt vaguely queasy and unsettled at the fetching of such a prominent seamark. Like espying the peaks of Dominica, which signified arrival on-passage to the Caribbean, yet knowing that whatever West Indies port of call one was bound for, no matter how joyous the passage, was no more than a week's sailing downwind. And no beating against the inevitability of those insistent Nor' East trades had ever availed.

Lt. Alan Lewrie, RN, peered out at him from the picture with a hopeful grin, the hint of devilment in his eyes that were gray or blue by mood. Shiny, midbrown hair, sun-bleached to light brown and curling slightly at the temples and forehead, yet drawn back into a proper seaman's plaited pigtail, lay over the ears and tumbled over the uniform coat's collar. It was a youthful courtier's lean face he saw, though tanned by blistering sun and sea glare beyond a courtier's fashionable paleness. And the slight hint of the vertical scar upon one cheek—the result of a duel for another girl's honour, a girl now long gone, in point of fact— the artist had wished to suppress that, but Alan had been quite proud of his disfigurement at the time and insisted it be rendered exactly. Just as they had disputed the teeth-baring grin, too; English gentlemen were supposed to be sober and dignified in life, and limned so in portraits for posterity.

Yes, he'd wash up, he decided, taking the first of the stairs. And see if he, at the advanced age of thirty, even slightly resembled the young "sprog" he used to be.

Thirty, Jesus, he thought! And he used to spurn women who had gotten a little long in tooth. If only he'd known then in his feckless days what he knew at present!

There, he thought, almost satisfied. His reflection didn't vary much from the portrait downstairs after he had washed and toweled.

Much, he amended.

He'd been eating well, and even with rugged, outdoorsy country pursuits he was not *exactly* the lean-cheeked courtier of his youth, nor so pale as a titled lord. But it was near enough.

Cony finished brushing his coat and waistcoat and he redonned them. He'd slipped out of his top boots and exchanged them for a pair of indoor shoes, little more than soft-leather pumps, more like womens' dancing slippers than anything else. Insubstantial though they felt, they were all "the go" lately.

Standing well back from Caroline's dressing mirror, he perused his form as well. He *had* been eating well, after all, though there was no snugness to the sewn-to-be-snug, buff-coloured suede breeches beyond what fashion demanded. His bottle-green coat and waistcoat sat well upon him, he thought—though they *were* new, run up before Christmas, so what comparison would they be?

Well, there's my uniforms, he sighed, almost relieved.

They'd changed the Regulations for Sea Officers' dress in '87, whilst he was overseas, and though he'd gone on the half-pay list as soon as *Alacrity* had paid off, he'd faced the expense of meeting the new dress regulations so he could call upon the Councillor of the Cheque each three months, about the time of the quarterly assizes, to prove that he was alive, that he still possessed all his requisite parts, that he was eligible for future sea duty, and to collect what was laughably termed Half-Pay. He'd just come back from the Admiralty in London, just before his birthday, and his uniform had fit him admirably well.

Damme, though . . . He frowned, lifting his coattails to study the heft and span of his buttocks. Hmmm . . . ?

"Supper is served, sir . . . mistress," Cony announced at last, as the rum punches at the Olde Ploughman threatened to consume his stomach lining.

"My dear," Alan beamed, rising to greet Caroline as she swept into the smaller second parlour, where he'd been kicking his heels.

"Sorry, dearest, but I simply had to stop by the nursery to look in on little Charlotte," Caroline smiled in reply, coming to his arms for a welcome hug and an affectionate, wifely, kiss. Alan took her up off her feet, unwilling to let a pat and a peck on the lips suffice. Children be damned, servants be damned, he thought, I want a proper welcome!

"Alan!" Caroline chid him, but not sternly at all as she gave him what he demanded. He could hear Hugh blowing indignant bubbles of revulsion as they kissed again.

"Nothin' to sneer at, Hugh," Alan chortled softly as he let her go at last. "Take my word for it."

There was a rare light in Caroline's eyes as she knelt to give her sons a peck, too. "Ah, little Hugh. What? You'll flinch from my kiss? And Sewallis, our little angel! That's my little man, *you'll* not wipe off your mother's affections."

"And how is Charlotte?" Alan asked as he offered his arm to lead Caroline into the informal dining room.

"Simply perfect, of course," Caroline chuckled, filled with a maternal warmth. Baby Charlotte, named for her maternal grandmother, was barely twelve months old and still nursing.

Soon to stop, please God, Lewrie begged silently. No matter they could afford wet nurses, no matter how unfashionable for English ladies, Caroline had insisted upon it with every child, months and bloody months of nursing! Months and months of baby talk, billing and cooing between swaddled babe and doting mama, and God help the man who interfered or tried to conduct an adult conversation. Alan espied a tiny, darker damp spot on her demure woolen bodice—a dottle of lovingly egested milk, and noted the flush of pleasure she usually bore after a feeding.

Hugh made another blubber-lipped sound of disapproval as he was helped into a chair by the governess.

"You'll appreciate girls in your own time, me lad," Lewrie cautioned him. "Even a little sister."

He pulled out Caroline's chair to seat her at the foot of the table, saw Cony and Mrs. McGowan get the boys placed, and took his own seat at the head. Before he could unfold his napery, out rushed a maid with a steaming tureen of soup, and Cony was uncorking a bottle of hock with a cheery "thwocking" sound.

"Hearty chicken soup, with a dash of tarragon," Caroline announced, urging them all to dig in. "Takes the winter chill away. *Out* it goes . . . then *up*? 'As a ship goes out to *sea*, so my *spoon* goes out from *me*'! And young gentlemen *never* lean over their bowls, do they, Hugh?"

Hugh gulped what looked like a heaping shovel-full into his greedy maw, hunched over his plate with the spoon held like a ladle in a clumsy little paw. His cheeks puffed out like a squirrel's as he tried to swallow, and a line of creamy soup frothed between his lips. Followed a second later by the entire mouthful, since it was so hot. He began to fan, buttock-dance on his chair and bawl.

"*Small* sips, that's the way, Hugh. Lord . . ." Caroline sighed, rising to rush to his side to sponge him down and comfort him. "See how Sewallis does it? There, there, Hugh, you're not hurt. Take a sip of water, *there's* my little baby . . ."

Oh, for God's sake, Lewrie thought, eyeing them. One son prim as a parson, one looking like he'd just spewed a dog's dinner, and a dowdy wife! A matronly wife! Definitely matronly.

Well, she is a matron, ain't she, he qualified to himself. A young'un, thank the Lord. Seven years wed. Bloom off the rose, and all that. Still, she wore a fiercely white, starched mobcap, with her hair up and almost hidden beneath it; a heavy old woolen gown drab as a titmouse, with wrist-length sleeves and a high-cut bodice, totally unadorned by even a hint of lace; a pale natural wool shawl over her shoulders which plumped and disguised even more of her youth; and a bib-fronted, slightly stained dishclout of an apron, useful during child-rearing of an infant still incontinently in nappies, but Lord!

And that baby talk—*all* the time, he thought, feeling guilty and disloyal, comparing his (mostly) delightful wife to the fetchingly handsome girl she once had been.

"I'll take them, ma'am," Mrs. McGowan volunteered from the kitchen doors, summoned by the noises. "La, they're too excitable for a sit-down supper. Not utensil trained, neither. Come, boys? We'll finish supper in the kitchen. Let mummy and daddy eat their meal in peace, and you may see them later, before bedtime."

"Perhaps that's best . . ." Caroline surrendered, though she did cock a chary eyebrow in the governess's direction, and furrowed her forehead in what Alan had long ago learned was simmering vexation.

"Good soup," Alan commented a minute or two of weighty silence later. "Meaty. And the tarragon brings out the flavor wonderfully well. As do all your spices, dear."

"I'm pleased you're pleased with it, love," Caroline smiled in reply, though with half her attention on the feeding noises from the closed kitchen doors.

"About Mrs. McGowan . . ." Alan posed in a soft voice. "I'm not entirely happy to have our own lives ordered about so. We are not her favorite sort of parents, and—"

"I have noticed," Caroline sighed between dainty spoonfuls. "I will speak to her. If she cannot alter her ways, well—"

"You are mistress in your own house, dear," Alan comforted her. "And a damned fine one, I assure you. I will not have your sensible ways upset, nor you distressed, by a mere servant."

"Thankee, Alan," Caroline beamed at him this time. "I promise I will speak to her."

"*Damned* good soup," he commented again, raising an eyebrow. "Too bad little Charlotte isn't ready for soup such as this. Think of what she's missing, poor tyke. Why, it may be a week or two more before she's even able to take mere gruels and paps, d'ye think, dear?"

Tell me I can have you back, hey? he pleaded, with the merest sign of innocent inquisitiveness on his phiz. Once Caroline put a child on a solid diet and left off nursing, he could play once more with those twin peaks of his delight. Once, that is, she stopped producing milk. He'd rushed it the week before, and still felt embarassed by the almost perverse, cloyingly sweet taste of mother's milk which had flooded his mouth in the throes of passionate foreplay.

"Oh, I think more than a week or so, Alan," Caroline told him, colouring herself at the memory. "Perhaps another month. She *will* take tiny spoonfuls of thin paps now, but . . ." Caroline shrugged in explanation, which was no explanation at all, save for the heavy way her breasts brushed and lifted beneath her prim bodice. Nursing was a very private pleasure—almost as good a pleasure as *me*? Lewrie wondered. It seemed so. Domesticity, he groaned to himself, keeping his face bland as he hid behind a sip of hock. Ain't it *grand*, thankee Jesus!

"And how was the village?" Caroline inquired, changing the subject deftly.

"Quiet as usual. Same old complaints. Same old faces." He grimaced slightly and laid aside his spoon. Caroline rang a tiny china bell for the soup to be removed and the mutton chops to be fetched in. "Talk of the French. Bags of it."

"Anything new?" she asked, frowning.

"Fear, mostly. Even the tenant farmers are getting worried all that levelling, Jacobin talk about equality will come here someday. Now they've murdered their king and queen—"

"Perhaps it'll die out, like Nootka Sound," Caroline prayed. "A great deal of commotion, then. It's been ten years since America went the same way, and nothing's come of that," she stated, to reassure them both. "Englishmen aren't as crazed as the French, thank God, nor as empty-headed as the Rebels were. There's nothing wrong with *English* society needs changing! Let the whole world turn upside down, we'll be here, season to season, sane and orderly, as usual."

"We may, dear," Alan countered gently. "But the Germanies, the rest of Europe . . . First the Colonies went unhinged, now France, and as bloody as you could ask for. Didn't call it the Terror for nought, y'know. There were no aristocrats to butcher in the Colonies, and a fair number of them were Rebels to start with . . . My pardons."

Caroline's brother George *had* been butchered, by Chiswick relatives in the lower Cape Fear of North Carolina. And that pregnant woman murdered in her bed Alan had discovered outside Yorktown, before the siege set in, her unborn babe pinned to the log walls with a rusty bayonet!

"First the Colonies, then France, God knows where next—not England, o' course," he reiterated after a bite of succulent mutton chop, heavy with hot mustard, Navy style. "But if this plague spreads, how long before we're alone in a sea of hostile Republicans?"

"Pray God it will blow over like a summer storm, then," Caroline shuddered, all but crossing herself. Cony fetched out a bottle of burgundy, more suited to mutton, to replace the lighter hock. "And if you are called back, well, it would not be for long."

Nootka Sound, '91: an incredibly petty spat between Spain and England over fishing and furs halfway 'round the world on the grim and forbidding coast of America, almost to the Pole, almost to northernmost Asia! The Fleet had been called up to prepare for war, ships laid up inordinary had been refitted, and new construction begun. Alan had spent six weeks in active commission, first officer into a 5th Rate thirty-six-gun frigate upriver at Chatham, before saner and cooler heads prevailed and the whole business had deflated like one of those frogs', Montgolfier's, hot-air balloons.

"Another Nootka Sound, I'm certain, dearest," he promised her.

Their bedchamber was snugly warm, and Alan Lewrie was fighting the urge to yawn, to succumb to sleep—hoping for better things to do in the shank of a cold winter evening. They'd finished supper, taken the boys into the small parlour and let them prate, babble and play as wild as they wished for an hour before shooing them off to bed. Alan and Caroline had played a duet, a medley of reassuringly old country ballads—she on her flute, he on his cheap tin flageolet. Years of practice, and he still sounded so terrible he would not play for any guest. She'd beaten him four games out of seven at backgammon and finished the bottle of claret with him, flushed with victory, liquor and so much happily domestic contentment that she'd quite forgotten her previous worries.

The cook, governess, maidservant, his man Cony, the scullery wenches and the rest of their burgeoning household were all now belowstairs or tucked away in their garrets. Caroline was seated before a mirror at her dressing table, mobcap and dowdy woolen apparel gone, replaced by a flimsy dressing gown. Her hair was down and loose, long and shiny as she slowly and methodically brushed it.

Lewrie was under the pile of coverlets and quilts, with the steamy clothes-iron heat of the recently removed warming pan under his buttocks and back. The fireplace glowed cheery and hot across the chamber, its amber dancing flames reflected into the room by a brass backplate, throwing shadows on paneling and wallpapers.

Beneath his fine linen nightshirt he was happily encouraging a cockstand.

He smiled in eager anticipation, admiring her reflection in the mirror as she smiled a pleased and secretive smile to herself. She posed her hair, arms lifted, exposing a graceful neck and slim arms, slim back shifting beneath her silken gown. She went back to stroking her hair, underbrushing now, with her head cocked over to one side. In her mirror, shadow breasts rustled against silk, fuller and heavier, so very much more promising than when she was girlish.

When they'd met in Wilmington, North Carolina, during the evacuation, she could not have weighed eight stone sopping wet, and that with half a dozen petticoats. Slim and coltish, still—not the usual apple-dumpling matron, after all. Perhaps a half stone more, Alan wondered? Just the slightest bit fuller in hips and upper thighs—but it was such succulent, acquiescent, *yielding* and secret excess. Sweeter, softer than ever before, as soft as gosling down.

His fingers began to twitch with a life of their own as he contemplated the butter-softness of the luscious bottom he'd soon be stroking.

"Not much needs seeing to tomorrow, I fear, dear," she said to him, colouring a little as she saw his intent, reflected gaze.

"Muck out, feed the stock," Alan yawned, jaws creaking in struggle against it. "Have the beef cattle driven to the stockpens. Not a morsel of pasturage left for 'em. And we don't wish to risk any spring calves, if the weather turns off colder."

"You're beginning to anticipate a farm, after all," she replied with a light chuckle, but it was very matter-of-fact. As if sensing that she'd been too blunt and critical of his farming skills, Caroline crinkled her large hazel eyes at him via the mirror, pursed her lips and blew him a distant kiss across the bedchamber.

"After four years it's about time, don't you think?" he said, shifting under the covers. She was smiling that particular, that secret, heavy-lidded smile—it promised to be an intimate evening indeed! "Like the Navy, knots an' ropes," he rambled on, putting his hands beneath his head on the pillows, thoroughly at ease now. " 'Cept for the bosuns who'd flog my bottom raw if I got things wrong. Thank God. 'Can't birth a *lamb*, Mister Lewrie? 'Pon my *word*, sir! No way to bind a *sheave*, Mister Lewrie! Bosun, dozen o' y'r best, at once, sir! Bend over, kiss the gunner's daughter, Mister Lewrie!' Or is it the *farmer's* daughter, hmm?"

Caroline giggled, then went back to stroking her hair, humming a tune to herself, almost crooning. "Oh," she paused. "We're invited to a game supper at Governour's and Millicent's. Friday night. He bagged a stag, and it should be well hung by roasting time."

"And Uncle Phineas and his dull compatriots will be there?" Alan frowned with displeasure. "Dear as I love well-hung venison . . . Pity he didn't bag Uncle Phineas. Might be too tough an old boar to chew, though."

"We're to bring a covered dish," Caroline went on, resuming her stroke. "I thought a dessert would be best from us. Hmm?"

"A tart fruit jumble, that'd go well with venison," he suggested, stifling another yawn. "Something half wild, like that red-currant preserve you put up in the fall."

"Mmm, yes, that might do main-well." She put aside her brush and bound her hair at last into a long, single tress. She rose from her dressing table, let the dressing gown fall open over her bedgown and crossed to the fireplace. William Pitt, their ancient tawny ram-cat, lay stretched out on the narrow padded bench in front of the fire like a rather large orange-coloured plum duff. He was whimpering and grunting in his sleep. Caroline touched his grizzled head and he woke enough to look up, thrust the top of his head against her hand, and turn over to lie facing Lewrie, all four heavy paws together as he stretched. The one good eye regarded the bed. The stubby tail curled lazily as he recalled how cozy-warm it was to sleep with humans on cold winter nights.

Not tonight, you little bastard, Alan gloated at him.

Caroline blew out the last remaining candle and came to the high bedstead, slowly undoing the fastenings of her dressing gown, shrugging it off her shoulders to puddle at her elbows. Her hips swayed in the flickering amber darkness. He put out a hand to her.

And little Charlotte took that exact, and unfortunate, instant to wake, either wet, hungry, lonely, bored or terrified—perhaps a combination of all five—and began to bawl her little head off.

Even in the near dark Alan could see Caroline's face go empty and vacant, then vexed, then subsumed with worry, and after that she had no more thought for her husband than she might for the Man in the

Moon. With frantic, matronly haste she did back up her robe and was out the door and down the hall for the nursery.

"Bloody . . . !" Alan Lewrie groaned in a soft whimper, head back on the pillows in sudden defeat, though still up on his elbows in welcome. "Bloody Hell!" he moaned, collapsing.

"*Marrrh*," William Pitt announced in a grumpy, closed-mouthed trill as he hopped up on the foot of the bed, as if he had known how the evening would fall out. He padded slowly up the covers, tacking cautiously around the slowly sinking seamount of his master's fading tumescence, and flopped himself sideways against Lewrie's upper chest, leaning his whole, and not inconsiderable, weight against him. Pitt's good eye regarded Lewrie with commiseration, his one undamaged ear gave a tiny twitch and he yawned again, as close to a grin as felines may essay, baring his remaining teeth and mismatched fangs. One heavy, round paw, big as an unhusked walnut, reached out and patted at Alan's chin, claws nicely sheathed, to give comfort. And to demand some for himself.

Lewrie slid an arm down from inside the warm, recently inviting covers to pet him and scratch the top of his head, the shaggy ruff of fur around his thick neck.

"You knew, didn't you, Pitt?" Lewrie whispered, resignedly. "I wish to God I knew how you do these things."

"*Murpphh*," William Pitt harrumphed, beginning to purr loud and rattling, like a bilge-pump chain. He closed his eye in bliss.

At least *somebody* 'round here's blissful, Lewrie thought. And most uncharitably, too.

CHAPTER 3

Breakfast was a rushed affair; strong cup of tea, leftover mutton chop and burned toast. The household was a veritable babble of activity, of sound, and Lewrie needed time away from it. That and the reek of soiled nappies. Charlotte was being her usual incontinent self, Hugh had suffered a tiny "accident," no matter he was supposedly breeched and past such. Thankfully, it was the washday, and once Lewrie returned from his morning ride across the hills, the aromas of steam, boil-water, soap and starch, and hot irons would have conquered, for a time at least, the winter-pent aromas of sour milk, soiled swaddles and progeny poop.

He had one foot in the stirrup, crouched for the leap, when a voice interrupted him. It was Cony, calling his name, standing in the kitchen door, waving something at him.

"Bloody . . ." Alan sighed, hopping on one foot to clear his boot toe from the stirrup. "*Now* what?" he demanded of the frigid morning. It had *not* been a good evening. He had struggled to stay awake until Caroline might return from the nursery, but it had taken what seemed like hours until she had quieted little Charlotte enough to allow the governess to finish the ministrations. She had slipped back into bed with him, her skin cool against his toasty warmth, and had snuggled close, kissed him a time or two with a weary, acquiescent, wifely absence of passion, gently puffing her lips with her mouth ajar against his throat in utterly stupefied slumber not half a minute later.

And had risen to her great joys of domestic duties before Cony had fetched him his first cup of tea!

"Letter f r ya, sir," Cony told him as he tromped through the kitchen garden. "They's a messenger come with it, down from London. In th' kitchen, warmin' 'is backside f r now, sir."

Lewrie turned the packet over and sucked in a cold breath of chill country air as he beheld the blue wax sealing wafer, with the fouled anchor beneath the crown. ADMIRALTY.

"War wi' th' French, I wager, sir," Cony declared as Lewrie broke the seal. His man was all but hopping from one foot to the other in rising excitement. "Ever'one knowed h'it wuz a'comin'."

"Thought the old fart'd retired by now," Lewrie commented, as he noted the inscription below the message. A harried junior clerk had penned the bulk of it, but for the prim signature of the first secretary Philip Stephens at the bottom. He'd been first secretary to the Admiralty since the year Lewrie had been born.

20 January 1793
Admiralty, Whitehall
To Alan Lewrie, Lt., Royal Navy
Sir,
My Lords Commissioners for executing the Office of Lord High Admiral require your most immediate attendance upon their Lordships. You are charged and directed to . . .

"Well, damme." Lewrie breathed again. The chill settled lower, into his stomach, not just into his lungs. "Bodkins, put Anson back in his stall. I'll not ride today. Do you fetch out the closed coach, though. It's . . ." He drew out, opened, and peered at his damascened watch. "Nigh on seven. I wish to depart for London by ten."

"Yessir." The groom nodded, touching his forelock.

"Be it war, sir?" Cony inquired anxiously.

"No mention of it, Cony. Yet. Something that smells nigh to it, though. I'll see that messenger now. Do you look to my chest, see what's wanting. You know my needs well as any by now. And lay out a uniform for me. I'll be up directly."

"Aye, sir," Cony agreed, touching his own forehead in a lank-fingered salute of old habit. "Uhm, ya wish me t' be goin' wi' ya, up t' London, that is, sir?"

"Yes, Cony. At least to London." Lewrie smiled, though a bit grimly. "Once I'm assigned a ship . . . well, that's up to you. I allow you may be very helpful to Mrs. Lewrie about the farm. Farming's what you know best. What you enjoy most?"

"Uhm, yessir." Cony shrugged.

"Estate agent . . . overseer . . ." Lewrie rambled on as they entered the warm kitchens, where the maids and scullery wenches walked small about the elegant but threatening stranger down from London. "No need to take you off to sea. And there's Maude down at the Ploughman, is there not?"

"Uhm, yessir," Cony blushed, grinning a little. The publican of the Olde Ploughman was getting on in years, and his pretty little spinster daughter Maude was of marriageable age. Mr. Beakman was now a widower, had no sons interested in inheriting the public house, and both father and daughter were fond of Cony. Almost everyone in Anglesgreen was. He'd make a fine partner in the business, and a knacky publican later. Whichever way he jumped, he'd land on his feet.

And do it on dry land, if he has any sense, Lewrie thought.

"I'm Lewrie, sir," he announced himself to the stranger. "You will wish a quick reply to carry back?"

"That would be welcome, sir," the functionary nodded. "Though I've several more officers to call upon about Chiddingfold and Petersfield before returning, sir. The paper work, you see, sir—"

"Quite," Lewrie grimaced at the necessity, and made the messenger grin, too, in recognition of the volumes of correspondence government seemed to generate over trifles. "Come to my study so I may scribble you something suitable. Bring your tea. I've some brandy there. A dollop'd thaw your bones, I wager?"

"Oh, aye, sir!"

As they left the kitchen for the central hall, Lewrie espied Caroline and the boys. She stood trembling, with a wild cast to her expression, with the petulant, whiny children tucked into her skirts. They couldn't know what was transpiring, surely, he thought. But it was plain enough to them that something momentous was being played out.

"Alan . . . dear," she called after him, clearing her throat, but almost in a whisper. He thought to pause, to speak a few consoling words to her, before joining the Admiralty messenger in the study. It was her furrow and her frown that stopped him. Almost accusatory, it was, the vexed look Caroline might bestow upon an unruly boy as a warning that further such behaviour would call down chastisement.

"I'll be with you shortly, dear," he said, instead.

"Is it war?" Alan asked after he had closed the double doors upon the rest of the household.

"Not yet, sir." The messenger scowled, busy at the wine cabinet. "But they've been calling officers and warrants back for weeks, now. I heard tell the 'Press has been warned. Just in case."

"Doesn't say much for me, then." Lewrie forced a chuckle. "I was one of the first returned in '91."

"Our Lords Commissioners never released some of those called in over Nootka Sound, sir. The Fleet stayed at least quarter-strength since, once the Terror began in Paris. Uhm, hah . . . you see, sir, you are most certainly in the *lower* half of the lieutenants' list, so if we are at quarter-strength, d'ye see—"

"Lower third, or lower, actually," Lewrie scoffed, sitting at his desk. "February of '82." He laid out a fresh sheet of vellum, a pot of ink (black, preferred), and took a small penknife to the nib of the nearest goose quill.

He got through the date and his local address, the address of authority, and his salutation. Then sat, quite nonplussed, wondering exactly what the Devil he would say to Our Lords Commissioners.

Milords; bugger off. Perhaps?

The Navy had not been his career of choice; he could thank his father, far off in Bengal with the East India Company Army, for pressganging him into service, for he should have inherited the money from Granny Lewrie long before. He had never been what one might call your truly *glad* sailor. Thirteen years of his life he had given the Fleet (not without much real choice, truth to tell), nine in active service, midshipman to lieutenant—and these last four "beached" on half-pay.

He thought the French had a particularly apt word for these four years—they usually did, damn their troublesome, rebellious eyes: *Ennui.* Boredom and isolation. Shunned, and out of his depth. And as anchored as Ulysses in his dotage.

Without a war (and it was now certain one was coming, in spite of his assurances to dear Caroline), what would his life hold for him? More of Anglesgreen, still a leper to his neighbours, until such time in a misty future, when he had outlived Sir Romney and Uncle Phineas, and the grudge had faded out? Harry would inherit, become baronet, marry some unfortunate mort, and let it go at last? Lewrie *might* become a proper squire then, with owned, not rented, acres, have right to hunt and fish his own lands, instead of waiting to be asked by others' charity; some stooped and graying rustic with a fund of tedious yarns, and hair growing from out his ears, with a nose that bowed in low *congé* to his departing teeth! A well-respected, cackling bore, no matter that he bored his audience at the Red Swan at last, instead of the Ploughman.

And whilst there'd been war with the French, as tall frigates prowled like tigers in the night, bright-eyed and hungry to claw at each other, as line-of-battle ships formed to bellow, to make or break history, he would have been nothing but a spectator, and one far back in the cheap seats, too! He would *farm*, hey! Read the news down from London, in the

Naval Chronicle, brandish his walking stick and "Huzzah!" each victory . . . or write scathing letters to the *Times*.

Caroline needed him, though, would prefer this time . . .

He shuddered with revulsion at the image of his respectable civilian future—Caroline or no.

No, like his father, Sir Hugo St. George Willoughby, of the 4th, the King's Own, now of the 19th Native Infantry, had said to him once, after they were reconciled in the Far East . . .

Damme! He realized, shivering again, recalling the details of a half-abandoned past. They had been arguing in a seething tropic rainstorm, hot as shaving water. It was at Bencoolen, on the Malacca Straits, ready to sail for the Spratlys, just my tiny ship and his regiment, to fight more pirates than the New Forest has nuts! Beat the bastards, too . . . oh, didn't we *just*! Oh, it's all moonshine, this death or glory chatter. Yet . . . !

Lt. Col. Sir Hugo had said: "Might not have been a *glad* soldier, boy . . . but I became a good'un." Or something like that.

Growl he may, but *go* . . . aye, he believed he would. There would not be a second asking if he turned the Admiralty down. His place on the list would be scratched out, his commission thrown over.

Alan Lewrie might not have been a gladsome tar, either, but he knew in his heart that, by God, he'd become a damned good Sea Officer. And there would be no peace for his already restless soul if he didn't take the King's Shilling and serve, just one more time.

"Y'r pardons, sir," Lewrie said, as if coming out of some trance. " 'Tis been so long since I had to pen an official letter, formalities quite escaped me. You've found the brandy, I trust?"

"Rum, sir," the messenger replied quite happily, baking before the morning fire, his large mug of laced tea in his hand. He had not taken the slightest notice that Lewrie might have been delaying, dithering or hesitant to accept the possibility of an active commission. In fact, what delay he might have at last noticed he would have liked, so he could warm himself against another cold ride and make free with Lewrie's fine, sweet dark Jamaican rum.

"Rum for me, too, it seems. 'Clear Decks And Up Spirits,' seven bells of each forenoon," Lewrie grunted with guilty pleasure as he put the finishing touches to his note of acceptance. He shook sand over it and blew on the ink so it would not smudge. He folded it carefully and applied candle wax to form a seal along the outer fold.

"There you are, sir. I expect to be in London by nightfall, and in the Waiting Room by tomorrow morning."

"Then I shall keep you no longer, sir," the messenger stated, finishing his laced tea with a gulp, and stuffed the precious note into a hard dispatch case, where fully two dozen more were already crammed, then bowed a swift departure.

Lewrie went to his wine cabinet and poured himself a glass of dark Jamaican, inventorying the study for items to take along. Would he get a ship of his own this time—something small, like *Alacrity*? Wine cabinet, fold-leg desk, caddy for tea, coffee, chocolate and sugar, extra chest yonder . . . pewter lanthorns down from the garret, just in case. Ferguson rifle there, the fusil musketoon, too, and—

No, he thought, taking a welcome, and bracing, sip. I'll go a lieutenant still, most like. Dog's manger of a cabin in the wardroom, not room for much beyond a sea chest, and little else.

He held the small glass of rum up to the firelight. It was almost opaque, and the alcohol fumes wafted the sweet, lush, adventurous scent of far-off West Indies molasses about his head, rife with promise of potency and over-the-horizon, beyond-the-sunset, larger-than-life adventure. Excitements! Honor and glory be damned.

He took another sip, savouring the rawness of the rum's bouquet. Soon it would be passer's-issue rum, cheap pop-skull, the weary seaman's anodyne. With the rum, he could almost begin to sniff a whiff of ocean. The hemp and tar, the steep tubs and the fat used for slush on running rigging, the iodine tang of open, rolling seas, the fresh-fish aromas of storm wrack and the tidewater mildewed mustiness of harbourside, of hot sand and kelp baking under a cruel sun on distant strands, and the dank-cave breath of a ship, wafting up through limber holes, and carpenters' walks from below—unwashed men, paint and wet wool, old cooking greases, of seasoned oak and sweating iron artillery.

Caroline, he thought, at last. What to say to her? Sorry, dear, but I'd crawl to Whitehall on my knees to escape the boresome shit my life's become? Dear as you are to me, dear as Life is with you and the boys, it isn't you—'tis me?

He tossed off his rum impatiently, steeling himself for the hurt words he was sure would come. He set the glass on the mantel, reached up and took down his sword—not a proper officer's straight smallsword but a hanger, a slightly curved, single-bladed hunting sword, much like a light, elegant cutlass. It had stayed hung there for years, far out of reach of inquisitive little hands. There was dust on the royal-blue leather scabbard, and it had not gotten the strenuous attention their tableware did from the maids. He ran his fingers over the slightly tarnished silver lion's-head pommel, the dark blue hilt wrapped in silver wire, the belt hook on the chase, the front and side handguards formed like argent seashells.

He half-drew it to test its edge against a thumbnail. But it was a Gill's, a fine blade, and had lost none of its keenness. No matter how long it had hung, neglected and idle.

BOOK II

Nee vero ipse metus curasque resolvere ductor, sed maria as-
pectans "heu qui datus iste deorum sorte labor nobis!"

Now verily did the leader himself forget all fears and cares,
but gazing on the seas, "Alas," he cried, "how hard a task is
here set us by heaven's will!"

—VALERIUS FLACCUS
Argonautica, Book IV, 703–705

CHAPTER 1

If great London also bore loathsome reeks of its own particular devising, at least they were urbane and cosmopolitan. And Lewrie, in his mounting excitement to be returning to the city of his birth, and gateway to the wider world beyond, took no notice of them. Farm lands and villages got closer together, villages became towns, until once they had passed Guildford, the conurbations crowded each other until they seemed one vast burgeoning of the capital, brimming over with bustling enterprise, like a boiling pot.

Lodging was almost impossible to find. All the coaching inns were full, as were the private residences which would let rooms, and the use of the parlours, to guests. Sparsely furnished rooming houses were out of the question. Even those dubious "rooms to let"—which usually signified hourly rates for the sporting crowd—were taken by officers of both Army and Navy being called back to their colours.

They finally alit upon a hideously expensive posting house just before dark, after hours of rumbling through the streets. It was near King's College and Somerset House, on Catherine Street, just off the Strand. Being a posting house, though, accustomed to travelers who came to town in their own coaches, it could be expected to be clean and quiet enough to suit the most fastidious high gentry or titled visitor, and set a decent table.

At twelve shillings sixpence a day, it ought to, Lewrie carped, to himself; that's more'n twice my active-commission lieutenant's pay!

They.

Caroline never failed to amaze him. Where he had expected the tears and recriminations of an abandoned wife, accusations of running away from familial responsibilities . . .

Damme, she was packed herself and ready to travel near as fast as I was, he thought admiringly. Babes bustled off to Granny Charlotte and off we jounced! Himself, Cony, Bodkins as coachee, Caroline and her maidservant, all jumbling together as the closed coach clattered over winter-hard roads so crossrutted they were fortunate to still have a collective tooth in their heads!

Once settled, Lewrie wrote a letter to his solicitor, Matthew Mountjoy, to make arrangements for Caroline's, and the farm's, allowance whilst he was at sea. He also penned a note on his account with Coutts & Co., bankers, for ready funds, and future drafts to be sent overseas; all of which Cony would deliver on the morrow.

Then a quick, quiet supper and up to bed, so he would be well rested for his appearance at the Admiralty. He donned his nightshirt and slipped into a warm bedstead, wondering how often in future he'd have the luxury of retiring completely undressed, of enjoying a full night's sleep, instead of two-and three-hour snatches between crises. Wondering what sort of ship he'd be assigned to . . . a frigate was his dearest wish. How slow and cumbersome a 3rd Rate ship of the line is by comparison, how plodding and dull, and . . . hello?

Caroline snuffed the candles (beeswax, a round half-dozen to the room, and each charged for what three would cost in the country!) and slid in beside him. Her head found its usual resting place upon his shoulder, her arms encircled him as he extended his right arm to nestle her warmly close. The light, citrony aroma of freshly dabbed Hungary Water enveloped him. Caroline slid one hand up his chest to his neck, to the back of his head. With sinewy strength, she turned his face to hers and their lips met in the dark as she grappled him nearer, as she slid upward, as she cast a slim thigh across his lap. Seductively, yet fiercely, her kisses searing and intense as sobs.

"I could not let you go away," she whispered in a raspy breathlessness, "with last night your remembrance of me. God knows how long you'll be gone, or how soon . . . how little time we . . . !"

All said between long, searching, open-mouthed kisses, breath hot and cow-clover musky, her soft, smooth flesh flushed and warming as Alan slid her silk nightgown to her waist to fondle, to possess that peachlike bottom, that butterfly softness of her inner thighs, that fount of all pleasures . . .

With almost frantic impatience, Caroline sat up on her knees and one arm and shucked her nightgown, tossing it to the four winds. Reached down as though to rip his bedclothes high enough away, to lean down over him, take his hands and guide them to her breasts as she pressed her mouth to his once more, her tongue almost scalding.

"All night, I swear it!" She almost wept. "All the time they give us!"

"God, I love you, Caroline!" he muttered as he took hold of the up-swelling of her hips to guide her down to meet him. "I love you!"

"Oh, Alan, dearest . . . I love you!" she vowed. "Love me now, I beg you! *My* remembrance! Ahhh, yess!"

S'pose they'll not see me *that* early, he most happily thought; God, I can get a whole *day's* sleep in the Waiting Room, more'n like!

Even at half past six of the morning, London's streets were thronged with mongers and their wares fresh from the market, waggons and drays, livestock, weary prostitutes and pickpockets, revelers on their way home to bed, shopkeepers and clerks on their way to work. The bulkhead shops were already open, as were the greengrocers and butchers. Coal-heavers were out, houseservants or valets to fetch their masters' or mistress's breakfasts from ordinaries or taverns. It was quicker for Lieutenant Lewrie to saunter down Catherine Street, cross the busy Strand, with a trained ear attuned to the rude cries of "Have care!" or "By y'r leave, sir!" of coachees, careening waggoners, or sedan-chair bully bucks. To stand still, dumb as a fart in a trance, even on the footpaths, was an invitation to getting trampled. And take a boat to the Admiralty.

At the foot of the bank where Charing Cross ended there were stairs to the riverside—slimy, mucked and erose, and worn down by long us-age. As soon as he was spotted, the cacophonous din set in, reminding Lewrie of a hunting pack who'd cornered the fox.

"Oars, oars!" cried the boatmen. "Scullers, scullers, sir! Tuppence!" countered those with smaller dinghys featuring a stern-sweep as pro-pulsion.

"Oars," he answered back, scanning the flotilla and selecting a bullock of a fellow, who sported the crossbelt, brassard and coat-of-arms of the Lord Mayor.

"Whitehall Steps . . . sixpence, sir," the fellow nodded as he boarded the small craft. "Tide'n wind be fair 'is mornin', sir."

"Hard not to tell," Lewrie commented as he settled himself on a forward thwart, his coin out and ready.

"Aye aye, sir," the man crinkled a sun-wrinkled smile as he shoved off and shipped his oars in the tholepins. "Young man wearin' King's Coat . . . canvas packet unner 'is arm . . . well, sir!"

"You were in the Navy?" Lewrie asked.

"Both th' las' wars, sir. Landsman . . . ord'nary'n able seaman . . .'en gun cap'm . . ." he related between powerful strokes, seated to his front, knee-to-knee with Alan. "Quarter-gunner . . . Yeoman o' th' Powder 'fore 'twas done. Now 'ere come another war. Y'r welcome to it this time, sir. You an' all t'other young'uns. War 'fore th' week's out's my thinkin'. Can't 'llow th' frogs t'spread 'eir pizen f'r long. Folks is stirred up enough a'ready, sir."

"By levelling talk?" Lewrie inquired. His stretch of Surrey might as well have been in China, for all the rumors that missed him.

"Thom Paine, sir." The old gunner beamed, tipping him a wink. *"Rights o' Man.* Correspondin' societies. That Thom Hardy feller an' all? Price . . . Priestley . . . dissentin' an' such. Learned t' read in th' Navy, I did, sir. Time on our hands so heavy an' all? 'Nough t' know all them Friends o' the People societies' penny tracts is trouble. Wrote in th' same words'z anythin' wrote in France. 'At spells rebels an' combinations, sir. With so many folk outa work, an' wages so low when ya do get work, well . . .'ear tell they've plotted secret committees, gone right over t' Paris itself!"

"Widespread, d'ye think?" Lewrie asked, morbidly intrigued.

"Not so much yet, sir. N'r by hard-handed men, d'ye see? Give 'em time, though . . . never thought I'd see 'at 'Yankee-Doodle' madness took up in a *real* country!"

"But it doesn't upset you enough to . . . volunteer, I take it," Lewrie said with a knowing smirk.

The waterman tapped the brassard on his chest which protected him from the Impress Service, and tipped Lewrie another and equally knowing wink. "I ain't *thet* stupid in me old age, sir!"

He paid off the waterman at the foot of Whitehall Steps, amid a swarm of other boats, of other officers reporting for duty. A walk up Richmond Terrace to thronging Whitehall, a stroll of about one hundred or more yards north up Whitehall, and he was there, before the curtain wall with its columns and blank stone facade between; before the deep central portal which led to the inner courtyard, beneath the pair of winged sea horses which topped the portal.

Admiralty! What a leviathan one single word implied. Ordnance Board, Victualling Board, Sick and Hurt Board, boards for control of ship's masters, of petty officers with warrants, of officers from lowly midshipmen to fighting admirals, port admirals, the Impress Service, HM Dockyards . . . cannon foundries, clothing manufactures, pickling works for salt beef and pork, huge bakeries for untold tons of hard biscuit. And rope, tar, seasoned timber, paint, pewter messware, iron and bronze nails, pins and bolts, the copper industry for clean bottoms and defence against teredo worms. Sailcloth, slop clothing, leather works, sheath knives and marlinspikes, forks to cutlasses and boarding pikes . . . taken altogether, the needs of the Fleet, and the myriad of suppliers, contractors, jobbers—and thieves—who filled those needs, the Royal Navy was the single largest commercial enterprise in the British Empire. Which meant, of course, the civilized world. And one single word—Admiralty—spanned it all. Just as the Royal Navy would soon span the globe, the most efficiently armed, supplied and equipped military organization known to man. The enormity of the endeavour made even a cynic such as Lewrie take pause.

Until he got to the door, of course.

"Lewrie?" The long-term tiler sighed with a weary, frazzled air as he scanned his admittance list with one arthritic finger, and applied the other index finger's horny nail to ferret between mossy teeth. "Y'r *sure* they wish t'see ya, then, sir? However d'ya spell that? Doubya-Arr-Eye-Eeh, is it?" The tiler seemed offended that it wasn't some simpler name, perhaps. Or perhaps he was disappointed he had no wisp of fatty bacon left to suck on. Whichever it was, he made an open grimace of disgust. "Aye, y'r *listed*," he announced at last, almost grumbling with outrage to find Lewrie's name. "Go 'long in, sir. Take a pew wi' th' others, God help ya."

"You have no idea when . . ." Lewrie began, after heaving a tiny sigh of frustration, anxious to know what hour, or which day, his appointment might be.

"Run outa ideas, summer o' '78, sir, when I took this position," the tiler shot back impatiently. "There's one lad, midshipman he was, was three full year warmin' 'is backside in yonder. Will-ya-not-go-*in*, sir-there's-a-horde-o'-others-waitin'-you-next-yes-*you*, sir!"

Lewrie stifled his retort, knowing it would do him no good, or even begin to penetrate the querulous tiler's thick hide. He entered, left his cloak with an attendant who was even surlier than the tiler, and "took a pew" in the infamous Waiting Room.

Early as it was, all the chairs, benches and sofas were taken by commodores, by post-captains, by commanders. Lowly scum such as he had perforce to stand, and in the draughtiest corners at that, as far from the fireplaces as rank and dignity would allow.

So much for a long nap, he sighed to himself. Without children to cock an ear to, he and Caroline had spent a night so passionate it rivaled their first days together as man and wife. And they had gone far past the point at which they might usually crash to sleep in utter exhaustion.

He no longer held that thirty was *exactly* the dotage he'd feared. Truth to tell, he was quite proud of himself and his prowess, his endurance. But he was now paying for it. Once still, and hemmed in in the frowsty-warm Waiting Room, he was almost asleep on his feet, held up by the press of other nodding men's shoulders.

Except for the boisterous, Old Boys' Day jocularity which the rest displayed; the hummumm of an hundred men conversing, punctuated by cock-a-whoop laughter, calls of welcome, the "damn my eyes if it ain't . . . !" greetings of shipmates long separated, whether they'd despised the person greeted or not, after three years' commission elbow to elbow. And the clatter of scabbards as both clumsy and adroit slowly paced the room, tangling and untangling, taking or giving way. He dry-swabbed his face, shook himself, and made his way towards the steamy aroma of hot tea, gladly willing to kill for a cup.

"Mister Lewrie, sir!" cried a cheerful voice.

"Damn my eyes," Lewrie called back, "if it ain't Hogue! A commission officer, now. How d'ye keep, hey?"

"Main-well, sir," Lieutenant Hogue blushed. "And you to thank for my promotion, I learned." His former midshipman was aglow with fondness.

Damn right you should thank me, Lewrie thought smugly.

"Did it yourself, sir," he pooh-poohed, though. "Your service did it. When they gave us *Culverin*, and we fought the Lanun Rovers in the Far East." Lewrie took care to say that loud enough for others. The Waiting Rooms were no place to show lickspittle meek before one's peers. Now there was almost war with France, their covert work could be revealed. "Put paid to Choundas and his pirates. Where are you bound? Do you know yet?"

"Third Rate 74, sir," Hogue boasted. "Only fourth officer, but . . . I'm off to Chatham on the next diligence coach. And you, sir?"

"Just arrived, so I've no idea yet. Time for tea, though, my lad?" Lewrie offered. "Warm your ride in the 'rumble-tumble,' hey?"

But Lieutenant Hogue had no time. And, an hour later, there was one more old acquaintance; Railsford of the old *Desperate*, a captain now.

"Damn my eyes if it isn't Lewrie, ha ha!" Captain Railsford cried, pumping his hand vigorously. "Heard about your last commission. The very merriest time you must've had in the Bahamas . . . all those pirates? Me? *Hydra*, down to the Nore. Finest frigate ever I laid my eyes upon. Damme, wish I'd known you were available, I'd have requested you. But, I already have a first lieutenant. And you *are* getting senior-ish."

"Oh, well. I understand completely, sir," Lewrie grinned back, though he was crestfallen. Another three years under Railsford, fine seaman, well-disposed friend and mentor, would have been a joy.

"And Captain Treghues, sir?" Alan asked, merely from curiosity.

"Inherited the title last year, I believe. Married well, too, into the Walpoles. Cadet branch, but . . . !" Railsford enthused. The Walpoles were one of the Great Families, who pretty much ran England through influence and married-in minions. "Got a seat in Parliament out of it, too. Capt. Lord Tobias Treghues, Baron. Sure to make rear-admiral soon, with those connexions."

"Is he still . . . ?" Lewrie simpered, screwing a knuckle to the side of his forehead.

"Occasionally daft as bats? Hmm, let's say, now he's risen so . . . a *tad* eccentric." Railsford chuckled softly. "And that only on odd *humid* days. Well, my fondest wishes for your continued good fortune, Lewrie . . . but I must dash. Write to me."

An hour, another slow circumnavigation of the Waiting Rooms (and two cups of tea) later, still with no seat, he ran into another "old shipmate," of a sort.

"Sir George," Lewrie said hestitantly, anxious though he was to see a familiar, if hated, face. Sir George Sinclair was now a rear-admiral. He turned a hostile, aquiline glare on the interloper who'd *dare* trifle with his valuable, and selective, attention.

"Alan Lewrie, Sir George. *Desperate*? Antigua . . .'80 . . .'81?"

"Ay, yes." Sir George replied frostily, his eyes glazing over with sublime disinterest. "I remember you." It sounded more like a threat. "Still *at* it, are we, Lewrie?"

Alan imagined he could hear talons being stretched, hard chitin claws being honed. "Uhm, aye, sir."

"And you recall my nephew, Forrester, do you not?"

Oh, damme! Lewrie sighed, defeated and eager to run. The round post-captain hovering over Sir George's shoulder was that selfsame porcine glutton, that bane of his midshipman days, Francis Forrester. He hadn't gotten any trimmer. But he *was* a post-captain, despite his being dense as a kerbstone. It helped Lewrie's flagging confidence to recall that his fellow midshipmen had once painted Forrester blue as a Druid, and pissed in his shoes at every opportunity. Forrester's expression, however, told Alan that *his* memory of his days in the cockpit berths was just as keen . . . if not quite so fond.

"*Much* senior, are you, Lewrie?" Forrester grunted.

"Bottom half, I would imagine, sir." That "sir" was wrung from him with the greatest chagrin. Last he'd seen of Francis, he'd been a paroled prisoner after Yorktown, exchanged on the *Bonetta* sloop to New York, his career in pieces. God, how he'd risen, though!

"Eminently employable, then," Forrester beamed with sudden joy. "Do you not think, uncle?"

"We *shall* keep you in mind, sir." Sir George vowed.

Jesus, kill me now, and have done, Lewrie prayed! Anything but their clutches! Anything!

"There's Bligh!" someone breathed behind Lewrie's left shoulder, quickly followed by a stifled giggle of mirth. "Poor old fellow," someone else more charitable commented.

He was a little fellow, nothing like the tragic hero he'd been proclaimed when he'd first reached England after the Mutiny. Nothing like the ogre he'd lately been portrayed, either. Despite his recent, and calamitous, downfall in popular opinion, he still drew his throng of admirers. Lewrie joined them. It was a *slow* morning.

"Read your book, sir," Lewrie toadied, all but simpering. "God, I wish I'd but known you might be here this very day, sir . . . I'd have fetched it along so you might have inscribed it."

"Kind of you to say so, sir. Quite," Captain Bligh replied, a trifle dubiously, a trifle shyly, half-expecting he was being made the butt of a jape.

"Bad timing, I gathered, sir," Lewrie went on. "Having to wait so long at Otaheiti for the breadfruit plants' growing season. Well, what crew *wouldn't* go stale on one, I ask you."

"Delivered properly this time, sir," Bligh declared, firmer in his convictions, now that he saw he still had some admirers. "In *Providence*, a proper ship, an Indiaman."

"Pity, though," Lewrie shrugged, "Captain Edwards and *Pandora*. Had their Lordships ordered things the other way 'round . . . you to go pursue your mutineers, Edwards to fetch the breadfruit . . ."

Capt. Edward Edwards, a taut hand if ever there was one, who made Bligh's easygoing (though unpredictable) ways seem like a saint in comparison, had apprehended several mutineers left behind when the *Bounty* sailed off for parts unknown. But Edwards had piled *Pandora* on the coral reefs of Endeavour Straits, and had lost her.

"I predicted dire consequences, ya know," Bligh almost preened by then, feeling more comfortable among sycophantic curiosity seekers.

"*Told* 'em Edwards did not know the navigation of Flinders Passage in the reefs, of Endeavour Straits. Excuse me, sir . . . but you are . . . ?"

"Lewrie, sir. Alan Lewrie."

"Ah, yes. Well, thankee for your kind opinion, sir. Thankee kindly," Bligh bobbed with a shy smile.

"I suppose you must be going, sir, I will delay you no longer. Off to a new command, I trust?" Lewrie fawned.

"Good day, sir," Bligh snapped suddenly, turned on his heel, and departed in a frosty, insulted huff.

"Bloody hell!" Alan muttered to himself in confusion.

"I shouldn't worry over it much," an unfamiliar lieutenant told him in a whisper. "The court martial only hanged three out of ten and let the rest off, lenient as possible, didn't they, now. Read Edward Christian's *Minutes of the Court Martial*, and the scales will balance. Fletcher Christian's brother, don't ye know?" the man sniggered. "The First Lord, Lord Chatham . . . I'm told he's issued word he'd only award Bligh with a ship should Hell freeze over. Won't even give him the time of *day*, is the rumor! No berth to be had with him. Thank the Good Lord."

"So I've . . ." Lewrie sighed with a wry grin at his toadying.

"Right. Pissed down his back for nought," the other chortled.

"An occupational hazard of ours, though. Is it not, sir?" he posed with a sardonic lift of one brow, to cover his chagrin over being so toadying. And so obvious at it.

"Oh, it is, *indeed*, sir!" the other officer agreed heartily, equally taken by the drollery of it all. "Hypocrisy in the service of one's career is no vice at all. One must simply be aware of when, and most importantly, *to whom*, one is the canting toad. Will you take tea with me, sir?"

By late afternoon, the Waiting Room was just as crowded, though at least a third of its denizens, who hid their impatience (or their dismay) behind poses of bemused boredom, stoic sternness or glum patience, were new arrivals. And Lewrie's name still had not been called. Fearing he'd miss his grand moment to ascend to the Board Room, or at least receive his orders in writing from a harried clerk, he had not even dared take time away to dine, not even as far as the inner courtyard, where one might buy dubious victuals off vendors' carts beyond the curtain wall and portal. His innards were growling by then, much as they had when he was an underfed midshipman. And the gallons of tea he had taken aboard! When a secretary at last announced that the day's business was at an end, he forgot dignity, and notions of rank, to outrun half a dozen dozy post-captains to "the jakes," where he passed water prodigiously as a cart horse, for a rather *long* time.

Tomorrow, he told himself, as he plodded, swell-footed after standing since breakfast, for Whitehall Steps and a boat back to his lodgings. Tomorrow'll be my day.

CHAPTER 2

The Admiralty's letter had been penned on the 20th, and Lewrie had received it on the 22nd, arriving in person on the morning of the 23rd. Yet, by the morning of February 1, his "tomorrow" had yet to come. To save money, they had removed to Willis's Rooms, in New Bond Street, down at the fashionable end, closest to his old haunts around St. James's. Closer by road to Whitehall, too, so Alan could hire a one-horse hack to and from, for less than his ferryman cost daily.

He was completely fagged out, again, of course. Caroline had delighted him with yet another night of honeymoon passion, and that after a public-subscription ball at Ranelagh Gardens; a night of fine food, music alternating between patriotic and lushly romantic, and an almost palpable aura of frenetic enthusiasm. Young men in uniforms had suddenly sprung from everywhere, and young ladies to match, torn between tears of separation and last-opportunity wantonness.

Caroline had come down to their common parlour in a new ball gown, a caprice of the times, like some Grecian goddess sprung from the frieze of a precious, ancient urn. Her gown was closer fitting, almost a sheath, with fewer petticoats, and scandalously hemmed *above* the toes, almost to her ankles, with an artfully ragged turn-back to reveal the lace of one petticoat. Her waistline was very high, her bodice low-scooped to reveal *décolletage*, sleeves short and gauzy, all but baring arms and shoulders. And about her neck she wore a red-velvet riband choker. What fixed his intense, open-mouthed stare was her hair—it had turned into a tangled nest of Medusas, tousled, ratted, snarled and dangled in crimped ringlets.

"What the *blazes*?" he'd gawped. Caroline had turned herself into a cross between a Dago peasant and a Covent Garden whore who'd had a rather hard night of it!

"All the rage," Caroline had chuckled, pirouetting for him. "It is 'à la victime,' dearest. Like the French aristocrats in the tumbrils going to the guillotine? The riband . . . for poor, beheaded King Louis and Marie Antoinette. You . . . you do not care for it?" She asked hesitantly, losing her gay demeanour and her confidence.

"My word!" he gasped. "It's so . . ." He had been about to say that he did not, in the *least*, care for his wife to go out so scandalously attired, sure she would be hooted, and dunged, by the Mob. Yet seven years "Active Service" with her, standing "Watch-And-Watch" on their quarterdeck, warned him he'd crush her if he told her what he really thought. Hoping such clothes were indeed "all the rage," he decided to brazen it out and agree to deem it Fashion.

And . . .

Damme if she *don't* look fetchin', like a whole new woman, Alan had thought; fetchin' enough to *eat* . . . on the *spot*! Wanton, bold and brazen. Always been favourites o' *mine*, God help me. No sober-sided matron tonight! Aye, I think I do like it, after all. Brand new, as smart as paint . . . an' triced up like a present, to be unwrapped.

"Caroline!" he'd said at last, beaming forced, but total, approval. "It's so different, *you* look so . . . ! So deuced handsome. Lovely! Surely, I'm the luckiest man in England tonight. Gawd, come 'ere, you. Let me shew you how much I adore it. So artfully . . . uhm, artless!"

And to the titters and blushes of the house staff at Willis's, her maid's and Cony's smiles, he had taken her in his arms and given her a long, rewarding kiss, right there in the public rooms.

And his fears had been groundless. At the ball, there had been ladies, some with barely a jot of Caroline's sublime face and form, in à la victime mode, some carrying it so far as to look as bedraggled as Irish peasants. And flesh; more flesh bared that night by younger ladies (and high-priced courtesans) than a man might see had he owned a "knocking-shop," all of which inflamed Lewrie's lustful humours.

They'd drunk Frog champagne as if it were a patriotic duty to expunge the last trace from the British Isles, danced together round after round, had circulated 'round the rotunda, talking too loudly, laughing too gaily, greeting old acquaintances. And had gone home, after a midnight collation, for that longed-for "unwrapping."

"It's war!" The rumour began, just about eleven in the morning. The traffic in messengers through the lobby and foyer, up the stairs to the

Board Room and offices, increased; and those couriers sent out with dispatch cases and bundles of papers were in more haste than was their usual wont. Elderly Admiral Howe made an appearance, almost arm in arm with Lord Chatham, the First Lord, on the way upstairs, whispering and frowning grave, dyspeptic stoicism.

"It's war with the Frogs!" Hopefuls began to gossip, breathless with barely subdued excitement, their eyes bright as famished hounds at the prospect of scraps.

"Heard the latest?" one boasted, as if he had. "France marched into Holland yesterday. Their ambassador's packing his traps. We'll declare by midafternoon. War at last! Employment at last!"

"No, no . . .'twas Austria," decried a second officer, refuting that round of news when it got to him. "Prussia, Naples . . . that last decree from Paris, 'bout supporting republican insurrections anywhere in Europe . . . they're all coming in as a coalition, 'cause of that."

"Did they march into the Austrian Netherlands yet?"

"It'd be about time, should you ask me. There's their General Coburg, with a *real* army . . ."

"Finest in Europe," opined several together.

". . . sitting on their hands nigh on a whole year," continued the speaker, "feared of a tagrag-and-bobtail horde o' Frog peasants—led by former corporals, so pray you—'stead o' kickin' their arses out o' their territories a week after the invasion."

"*We* should have declared when France took Antwerp," another anonymous strategist declared strongly. "Why, we might as well give up the Continental, *and* the Baltic trade, else. What's next on the Frogs' menu? Amsterdam . . . Copenhaven . . . Hamburg?"

Finally a commodore, fresh from the seat of power in the Board Room, came down the stairs, and was almost mobbed for information. He held up a hand to silence their fervent queries.

"The true facts which obtain, sirs . . ." he announced solemnly. "Very early this morning, His Majesty's Brig o' War *Childers*, standing off-and-on without the harbour of Brest, was fired upon by French batteries. Word has reached us by the semaphore towers that she was struck several times by heavy round-shot. *Childers* will come in, to display her damage, and the French round-shot . . . in her timbers, and upon her decks."

"But, *are* we at war, sir?" several officers demanded.

"Better you should ask of Lord Dundas, or Lord Grenville, for that, sirs," the commodore rejoined, snippish at their lack of deference to a senior officer, and their lack of decorum. "The Secretaries of State, and the Foreign Office . . . our Sovereign and Parliament, will best answer."

The commodore glared them to silence, harumphed a last broadside of displeasure, settled his waistcoat, and stalked away to gather his things.

"It's come!" Alan Lewrie muttered to himself, feeling a thrill run up his spine to be *there*, on such a momentous occasion. Secretly pleased, though, to know there would be no more indecision, no more delays. Soon he would be aboard a ship again. The time for half-measures and tentative mobilisation was ended. "By God, it's come!"

"It's war!" a lieutenant nearby cried exultantly, lifting his arms in glee. "Glorious war, at last!"

Lewrie cocked his head to peer at him searchingly, as he and his compatriots pummeled each other on the back and chortled happily. Of course, he was very young, the lieutenant, he and all his fellows in badly tailored, ill-fitting "pinchbeck" uniforms. His sword was a cheap Hamburg, not even ivoried or gilded, with a brass grip sure to betray him and turn in his grasp were his palms ever damp.

Second or third sons, the honourably penniless, with no means of livelihood but the sea, and warfare. For these desperately eager young men, peace had been a death sentence, stranding them miserly and sour on half-pay and annual remittance, perhaps, of less than fifty pounds altogether. But war, now . . . !

Prize money, full pay, loot from captured ships, and a chance to practice their sea-craft, to gain advancement . . . to be *noticed* at last. Weaned as they were, as Lewrie had been, on personal honour, on "bottom" so bold they'd dare Death itself to display gay courage, risk life and limb for undying fame and glory . . . or *fall* gloriously at the very moment of a famous victory . . . well, now!

Surely, Lewrie thought; the fools *must* recall the dangers, the fevers . . . the rancid food, foul living conditions . . . storms and peril! They weren't ignorant midshipmen, starry-eyed and joining their first ship! They'd gone months without a letter, years of separation, seen shipmates slaughtered, scattered in pieces like an anatomy lesson at a teaching hospital, hopelessly wounded men passed out the gun ports alive to clear the fighting decks, dead sewn up in shrouds . . . or the permanently crippled amputees, the blind, the . . . !

'Course, there's more'n a *few* thought me perverse, for sneerin' at death-or-glory. No one, in his *right* mind, goes out of his way to die a hero, does he? 'Leastways, I didn't. Not to say that Fortune didn't have her way with me, whether I wished or no. I mean, dead is *dead*, for God's sake, and what's the bloody point of . . .

"Lewrie?" A voice interrupted his fell musings. "Would Lieutenant Lewrie be present? Alan Lewrie, Anglesgreen, Surrey . . . ?"

"Here!" Lewrie shouted in a loud quarter-deck voice, putting aside all his foul, ungentlemanly, un-English sarcasms and forebodings at once. "Tomorrow" was here!

"The Deputy Secretary, Mister Jackson, will see you upstairs, Lieutenant Lewrie," an old and ink-stained senior writer informed him. "Would you kindly step this way, sir?"

George Jackson, Esquire's offices were a smaller adjunct to the First Secretary's, on the same floor as the Board Room. Lewrie presented himself, fingers twitching to seize the packet of orders which would be his passport. His Fortune.

"Your servant, sir," Lewrie coaxed, to gain the man's notice.

"Ah? Lewrie, well," Jackson said, barely looking up from the burgeoning mounds of documents on either side of his tall clerking-desk, behind which he slaved standing up. He looked down immediately, though, to cluck his lips over an ineptly turned phrase, perhaps some ink smudge, or a clumsy or illegible example of penmanship. "I have your orders, sir. Hmm . . . these, aye."

"Thank you, sir." Lewrie beamed, accepting the folded sheaf of vellum which one busy hand extended to him. He opened them eagerly, to see to which ship, what sort of ship, he would be assigned.

"Bloody hell?" Escaped his lips as he beheld the concise words. "Excuse me, Mister Jackson, sir. There must be some mistake. I'm for the *Impress* Service? *Me*, sir? 'Mean t'say—!"

"You wish to question the wisdom of our Lords Commissioners, do you, Lewrie?" Jackson countered quickly, rewarding him with a tiny *moue* of disgust.

"Sir, I'm not so old I *dodder!*" Lewrie rejoined with some heat. "My sight is excellent, I've all my limbs . . . I'm sound, in wind and limb! Hale as a dray horse, sir. With all my teeth, which is more'n *some* may boast! Sir, the Impress Service is for those who—"

"If we're not at war with France this very instant, young sir, we shall be by nightfall," Jackson fussed, giving Lewrie only half of his distracted attention. "No, no. Redo this section before . . . this whole page, in point of fact, before it goes to Mr. Stephens. Now, Lewrie . . . should there have been an error, which I most surely doubt, you may correspond with us from your new posting to amend it. Prevail 'pon your patrons to write us . . . but *at* this instant, we need to man the Fleet. The bulk still lies in-ordinary, and must be got to sea! Orders have come down for a *hot* 'press,' Admiralty Protections to be waived, and that requires the most immediate reinforcement for the Impress Service. Else merchant seaman will escape our grasp, and England's 'Wooden Walls' will continue to languish for want of hands! I do not originate orders, Lewrie, I only inscribe them and pass them on. Bloom where you're planted, for the nonce, hey?"

"Sir . . . Mister Jackson, I implore you," Lewrie continued, in a softer, more wheedling tone of voice, striving to sound reasonable . . . though what he wanted most at that moment was to leap across the desk and strangle the frazzled old fart. "There was a term of service, in the Far East, a covert expedition . . . '84 through '86. Notice was put in my packet to the effect that I was unemployable. To disguise my absence, so I could pose as a half-pay officer with no prospects who took merchant service. Were you to but look, sir . . . perhaps that is still in there, and influenced my assignment . . ."

"I am aware of that service, sir, and I was most scrupulous, at the First Secretary's behest, to expunge your file of any false information, and to include a true accounting of your deeds, as soon as you paid off. *Telesto*, 3rd Rate eighty-gunner . . . Captain Ayscough. And, I also vividly recall your most gracious reception in the Board Room by Admirals Lord Hood and Howe, and Sir Philip Sydney. February of '86, was it not, sir?" The Deputy Secretary fussed, proud of a memory as finely honed as his master, Philip Stephens. "I recall, too, that you received an immediate further active commission to the Bahamas, your first true *command*, did you not, sir? Hardly a sign of official disapproval, surely. There, d'ye see?"

"Good God, though, sir . . ." Lewrie shivered.

"Do you object strenuously enough to *refuse* an active commission, Lewrie," Jackson cautioned with a grim, reassessing stare, "we shall needs select another officer. I might imagine an hundred men would leap at the chance. And you may continue to wait belowstairs. You are not so senior, or renowned, I must advise you, that a refusal now might ever lead to an active commission dearer to your heart. It is customary to demote truculent officers to the *bottom* of the List. Or strike them off altogether. It is your decision. Well, sir?"

"No, sir," Lewrie all but yelped quickly. "I shall not *refuse*! It's just . . . it's just . . ."

"Needs of the Sea Service, sir," Jackson concluded with a prim smugness. "Which do not, of necessity, happen to coincide with yours. And, we note that you are a married officer, sir. Surely your wife . . . and children, I note as well . . ."

"That's not a handicap like being lamed, or . . . surely!"

"More like an *excess* of limbs than the lack, Mister Lewrie." Jackson took time to form a labourious jape. "You know the Navy has a chary opinion of the zeal of a married officer. Now, we *are* quite busy, and you have taken more valuable time than I should have given you. Will there be anything more you wish of me, sir?"

"Uh, no, sir. I suppose not." Lewrie sagged, completely defeated. And burning at the unfairness of it, the peremptory treatment . . . and the utter *shame* of it! "Good day to you, sir."

He bowed himself out, staggered down the hall, down the stairs, to the Waiting Room to gather his boat cloak. And reread what seemed a cynical boot up the arse.

"Mine arse on a bandbox!" he muttered bitterly. He wasn't even to go near a *real* naval port. He'd expected the Nore, downriver near the mouth of the Thames and the Medway; to Chatham, perhaps. Or south to Portsmouth and Spithead. Instead, he was to report to the Regulating Captain of the Deptford district, just below London Bridge and the Pool of London. Deptford, hard by Cheapside, Greenwich Hospital and infamous Wapping. He seriously doubted if a single whole seaman, with *any* wits about him, would be found there after the morrow. Not after word of a "hot 'press" made the rounds!

"I mean, if one's going to pressgang, at least one could have a post worth the trouble!" he sighed. From what he knew of the nefarious ways of Deptford dockyard officials, there'd be five thousand men with Protections by sundown (with a pretty sum in those officials' pockets, too) and the "Wapping landlords," the crimps, would sell a corpse to a merchant master before they'd ever aid an Impress officer. Navy bribes could never rival civilian.

"Dear Lord . . . is it too late to catch up with Sir George and 'Porker' Forrester?" he wondered as he pocketed his hateful orders and went out into the inner courtyard. "They mightn't be too bad."

CHAPTER 3

"Mi'ng arf on a . . . !" Lewrie cursed as he struggled to rise, running a tongue over his teeth to see if they were still all there. He tasted hot blood, coppery-salty; could almost smell it, like the damp winds off the Thames. "Get th' baftuds!" he roared to his "gang" as he got to his feet again, knocked down with a (fortunately) empty chamber pot swung at his head by a desperation-crazed sailor just off a West Indies trader.

It had sounded like a mischievous lark when they'd set out on their raid earlier in the evening. Surround a ramshackle old lodging house converted to a sailors' brothel; confer on the sly with the old Mother Abbess who ran it, so she could sell half a dozen or so of her worst-paying customers, who had taken the place over as a refuge, into the hands of the 'Press; creep up on them as they were well engaged with girls, passed out drunk or asleep, and take them in a well-timed rush.

"'Ere's yer hat, sir," Cony offered.

"Phankee, Cony," Lewrie attempted to reply. "Bu' where'f me head?" He was only half-jesting, as his vision swam.

"Split yer lip, sir . . . looks worse'n h'it 'tis."

Whores were shrieking, furniture banging, the pairs-of-stairs thundered ominously, making the thin lath and plaster partitions judder like the old pile was about to come down about their ears. Harsh male voices roared defiance on either side, with the occasional cry of a man getting the worst of some encounter. Truncheons beat a meaty tattoo, punctuated by the sound of a door being smashed down.

A shadow flitted past Lewrie's notice from one of the rooms, loomed up in front of him. It was a sailor, a teenaged topman by his build. He gave a great gasp as he realized he'd dashed the wrong way, skidding to a halt with his mouth open to cry out.

"In th' Kinf's name!" Lewrie shouted first, bringing his truncheon down to *thud* on the lad's shoulder and neck. The fellow dropped like a meal sack.

Damme, but that felt good! Lewrie exulted to himself.

"Oy, min' me furnishin's, yew!" the Mother Abbess commanded as she lumbered her bulk up the stairs. "Gawd, one o' me very *baist* fackin' cheers smashed! Ahh, shut yir gob, Helena! Stewpid bitch!"

A spectacularly developed young whore, all poonts and angular curves, was wailing her head off, garbed only in a thin, open, man's shirt. Lewrie stopped to judge her performance for a stunned moment.

"Clumsy bastits, take *keer*, will 'ee, now!" the barge-shaped Mother Abbess carped. "Nought woz said 'bout trashin' me place, sir! Fiffy poun' damages, ye done, if it's a fackin' farthin'!"

"You wished them out, ma'am," Lewrie commented, spitting in a corner to clear his mouth. "You should have liquored 'em better, 'fore we came. They'd have gone easier."

"Liquor 'em, hah!" the old whoremongress cackled mirthlessly. "An' thaim 'thout tuppence betwixt 'em? *Free* gin, it'd been, an' 'ey'd a got suspaictin'. Helena, will 'ee *stop* 'at caterwaulin'? Ye ain't hurted. Hesh, hesh'r ye will be!"

The dark-haired girl hiccuped to sudden silence and leaned on the broken jamb of the door to her grubby little cubicle. Perhaps because of her mistress's harsh glower, and her pudgy shaken fist, sign of a sound thrashing later. Perhaps because the sounds of melée diminished at last, with only the odd *thud* now and again, or a heartbreaking groan or two of pain.

"Ah, there ye be, sir," Lewrie's burly bosun's mate reported as he rumbled down the passageway, dragging a squirming sailor under his arm in a headlock. "Got 'em all, we did, sir. Eight hands, t'gither. All prime seamen. Oh, make 'at nine, sir. See ye got one, too!"

"Lemme go, ya bastard!" the "prime seaman" in the headlock hissed. "I gotta p'rtection! A 'John Comp'ny' p'rtection!"

"Now what's a West Indian trader called the *Five Sisters* doing with an East India Company Protection, hmm?" Lewrie smirked. "And how recently did you buy it? Wasted your money on a forgery, if you did. There's no protection covers you. Face it, man . . . you're took fair."

"Sir, f'r God's sake!" The man wriggled to face him, looking much like a beheaded victim under the burly bosun's Henry-the-Eighth-ish armpit. "Frigate stopped us down-Channel, soon'z we wuz in Soundin's. Took twelve hands . . . put eight Navy aboard t'work her in. We anchor in the Downs, befogged, an' a Nore tender takes 'nother eight! An' only lef' us four t'do their work!"

"An' how many volunteered, hmm?" The bosun purred, lifting the man almost off his feet, forcing him to look up at him awkwardly.

"Well, half o' 'em, th' firs' time, an' . . . three th' last," the seaman confessed sheepishly, then found some courage. "But that'z coz they'd been took, no matter, an' least if ya volunteers, ya gets the Joinin' Bounty, an' yer pay gets squared, on th' spot, see—"

"Then why not emulate them, and volunteer yourself, not sneak about?" Lewrie asked him. "Don't you wish to serve your king?"

"King George ain' off'rin' twenny-five guineas th' man, f'r a roun' voyage, sir. Hoy, yer right, sir! I'm a volunteer, sir!"

"Much too late f'r that," the bosun chuckled, shaking his whole frame, and jiggling the reluctant sailor with him. "Matey," he cooed.

"Bloody . . . !" Cony whispered under his breath. "Twenty-five *guineas!*" Those were royal wages, and the war not even barely begun!

Of course, it was suspect whether those merchant masters and ships' husbands who offered such royal wages would ever pay up, for many were happy to see the Navy press their hands before putting in and paying off. In some cases, they even connived at it with Impress officers who'd tip them the wink, for a bribe, and certify that all wages were accounted for, up to date of impressment. And Navy hands had to be put aboard to assure that a ship had enough hands to reach harbour; what amounted to free labour. It was a wonderful bargain.

Lewrie had a chary eye for the Mother Abbess of the brothel, too. Twenty-five guineas, these last fortunate sailors had pocketed, yet now they were so poor they "hadn't tuppence betwixt 'em"? Quim and gin, room and board, with perhaps more, paid the woman to shelter them before *Five Sisters* was laden and ready to sail, with a midnight dash from whorehouse to the docks at the last minute . . . a fee paid too, perhaps, for "long clothing" so they could do their dash without being recognised as sailors. *And* the forged protections . . .

And, Lewrie realised, she'd just made an additional ninety shillings from his own pocket, as the bribe price for revealing them!

They must have been too noisy, demanding, or upsetting . . . or had spent too freely too quickly. Else, she'd have been glad to have merely stripped them of their last farthing before turning them out her door and waving her fond goodbyes. Else, she might have simply sold them to merchant-ship crimps for more money. There must be some small measure of revenge being exacted, if she'd stoop to a Navy press-gang in Wapping.

"Any commotion in the streets yet?" Lewrie asked, going to the door to Helena's squalid little bedchamber, and reaching past her for a fairly clean towel with which to dab his damaged lip.

"Nary a peep, sir," the bosun assured him. "I'd 'spect ev'ryone about'd admire t'get a good whorehouse back in service."

"Yes, it does seem to cater excellent wares," Lewrie chuckled, still looking at Helena. The girl glanced down, fetchingly shy, then back up; a bolder, practiced "come-hither" twinkle to her eyes.

" 'Ere, lemme tend yer lip, sir," Helena cooed, taking the towel and dipping it in a water basin. "Can't let a fine gen'lm'n such'z yerself leave our house lookin' bedraggled, can we, now?"

"Get 'em in irons, bosun, and we'll be on our way, before the situation, and the neighbourhood's mood, changes on us." Lewrie said.

"Ya gotta go s' quick then, sir?" Helena pouted playfully.

"I, uhm . . ." Lewrie sighed. It had been six weeks since he'd reported for duty at Deptford, six weeks since Caroline had departed for home and the children, torn in two by her affections and duties. Helena was a wonder, compared to her drabber sisters in the knocking-shop, most of whom could only look delectable to men who'd been six months on-passage, and had no taste to begin with. Helena was young, not over sixteen or so, not so coarsened by the trade, and . . .

And his man Cony, who had so inexplicably insisted on volunteering, in spite of the obvious advantages and comforts Anglesgreen afforded him, was practically breathing over his shoulder. Anything Cony might see would be sure to find its way to Caroline, sooner or later . . .

And there was the threat of the Mob. Other sailors might see them, and drunkenly decide to brawl to "liberate" their fellow tars. Civilians full of anger, or boredom, who'd raise the hue and cry, and set upon *them*, the brutish instruments of oppression by the national government against their local. Englishmen, being enslaved by other Englishmen! It would be too much, and the only voice those prickly, pridefully inde-pendent locals had was the Riot.

"Some other time, perhaps?" Lewrie promised vaguely, tipping his hat to her. She curtsied to him quite prettily, spreading the bottom hems of her shirt, her only garment, like the heavy skirts of a ball gown, which rewarded him with a disconcertingly pleasant view.

"Let's go, bosun . . . Cony," Lewrie coughed regretfully.

"Come back, do!" the girl whispered as the others preceded him to the stairs, reaching out her room to cup his face in her hands and kiss him with a deep, if lying, passion. "An't been with a *real* gen'lm'n, not workin' 'ere, sir. An' *la*, I'd admire ta!" She teased in a small and throaty tone.

"Christ on a crutch!" he could but moan.

* * *

"Doubt they spoiled yer beauty, Lewrie," Captain Lilycrop told him after their surgeon's mate had attended his hurt and taken a stitch or two in his upper lip. "An' ye done good service this night, damme'f ye haven't. So, take cheer," the old man comforted, offering him an ancient leather tankard full of light brown ale.

One of the few delights (admittedly perhaps the *only* delight) of the Impress Service was serving under his old captain from the *Shrike* brig again. Lieutenant Lilycrop, now a lofty post-captain, had lost a foot and shin at Turk's Island in '83, just weeks before the peace, and the end of the American Revolution. He'd lost *Shrike* to Lewrie, too, when Admiral Hood had appointed him to take her over. But Hood had also promised to stand patron to the tarry-handed old Lilycrop, perhaps the oldest, and most without patronage, Commission Sea Officer in the Fleet, until that time.

Lilycrop's hair was thinner, just as cottony white, but better dressed these days; his pigtailed, plaited seaman's queue, which had hung to his waist, was now neatly braided, perfectly ribboned, a fitting (and more fashionably short) adjunct to the awesome dignity the old man exuded in his heavily gold-laced captain's "iron-bound" coat. His breeches, waistcoat and shirt front were snowy white, not tarry, tanned or smudged by shipboard penury. He now sported silk stockings (one at least), an elegant shoe with a solid-gold buckle, and his old straight, heavy dragoon sword had been replaced by an almost gaudy new blade and scabbard. And his pegleg was a marvel of ebony wood inlaid with gold and ivory dolphins, anchors, crossed cannon and sennetlike braidings as intricate as ancient Celtic brooches.

Exquisitely tailored he might be, but Captain Lilycrop was still the solid, roly-poly pudding, with a stomach as round as a forty-two pounder iron shot. And nothing could be done about that Toby Jug of a phiz, all wrinkles and creases; though his face was now wracked by good food and drink, not sun and sea. The same merry brown eyes lurked and gave spark deep within the recesses of snowy brows and apple cheeks. The same old Lilycrop, thank the Good Lord.

"Near thing, e'en so, sir," Lewrie commented, rotating his neck and shoulders. "God, what a shitten business. The Mother Abbess . . ."

"Old Bridey?" Lilycrop snickered, rubbing a thumb as thick as a musket barrel alongside his doorknob of a nose. "Well, what could she do? They were 'skint'—eatin' th' ole mort outa house'n home—an' rogerin' like 'twas their private rooms. Bridey, well . . ." Lilycrop sighed, sitting himself down near Lewrie. "Aye, I know she looks thick as a bosun, an' fierce-faced'z th' Master at Arms, but 'tis a fearsome trade. Knew her o' old, I did. Just made topman, I had, Lord . . . fourteen'r so . . .'bout when Noah was a quartermaster's mate . . . hee hee!" the old man recounted wistfully. "First *man's* pay in me pockets, first *seaman's* run ashore. No more ship's boy. An' I run inta Bridey. 'Nother knockin'-shop, no so far from where you an' th' lads were t'night. A rare ole time I had with Bridey. Couldn't o' been a quim-hair older'n fourteen herself back then, oh, she was a *rare* Irish beauty . . . all ruddy hair, blue eyes, and skin'z pale an' soft'z cream! 'Course," Lilycrop harumphed remorsefully, "I was a diff'rent sort myself back then, too. We kept in touch, Bridey an' I."

"So tonight was more a sort of . . . mutual favour, sir?" Lewrie inquired.

"She needed p'rtection, I need seamen," Lilycrop shrugged his assent. "An' I drop by, now'n again, visit her establishment. . . ."

"Just to keep your *hand* in, sir?" Lewrie snickered, though it hurt a bit.

"So t' speak, young sir," Lilycrop wheezed. "Bridey allus did treat her girls better'n most, got th' handsomest. An' treated her oldest'n best customers t' th' finest her house has t' offer. Did ye do her much damage?"

"Some, sir. Nothing too sore, I suspect, but—"

"Got her ear t' th' ground, Bridey does, Mister Lewrie," the old man snorted, coming up for air from his ale tankard like a seal blowing foam. "Bridey'll be back in business t'morro' night, but I s'pect she'll come 'round here, all blowin' an' huffin' 'bout her damages. She'll demand th' Crown square it for her . . ."

"Make you several attractive offers, sir?" Lewrie smirked. The smirk was easier on his lip than the full-mouthed grin.

"Oh, indeed!" Lilycrop beamed like a beatific cherub, and sucked air through his teeth in expectation. "Like I say, she's some damned handsome quim in her stable, oh my, yes! An' a poor ole cripple such'z myself can't do 'em *that* much harm, th' little darlin's . . . anyways, I 'spect, like I said, that she'll have more trade f'r us. I've expense money 'nough t' cover half o' her damages, an' she can make up th' overage. But, she'll whisper th' name an' th' address o' sev'ral more bawdy houses an' hideaways, where seaman're t' be found. An' put some o' her new competition's noses outa joint, inta th' bargain. Oh, 'tis a grand bus'ness, th' Impress Service, Lewrie! A *toppin'* bus'ness!"

It was for Lilycrop, at any rate. And, as Regulating Captain for the Deptford district, *he* didn't have to risk life and limb out in the streets, either! He had his lieutenants to do "the dirty."

And he was finally making himself, in the twilight of his naval career, a truly princely living. Lewrie hadn't dared to probe into another officer's affairs—a friend's affairs—but he *had* seen Lieutenant Bracewaight's ledgers a few days after reporting for duty. They'd shared a brace of wine bottles at their rendezvous tavern where they both lodged, and Bracewaight, he of the missing hand, the eyepatch and the wooden dentures, had left them open when he jaunted out back for the "jakes."

Still carried by the Navy Pay Office as a half-pay officer with a disablement pension, plus Impress Service allowances and subsistences, the swarthy swine was making fourteen shillings sixpence *per day*—more than a senior post-captain in command of a 3rd Rate!—*and* with travel and lodging reimbursed on his own say-so, *plus* the bonuses paid—five shillings for each raw landsman volunteer signed, up to ten shillings for each ordinary or able seaman brought in, by hook or by crook! And Lewrie rather doubted if Captain Lilycrop was maintained *per diem* in any less fashion, or denied any bounties of recruitment.

So far, up until that evening, that is, Lewrie had been spared the sordid side of the press. He'd run the tender from Deptford Hard downriver to the Nore, full of hopeful innocents or gloomy experienced seamen. He'd set up shop, to assist the other officers, at rendezvous taverns up and down the river; the Horse & Groom at Lambeth Marsh, the King's Head at Rotherhithe, and the Black Boy & Trumpet at St. Katherine's Stairs. They'd lay on music, hornpipes, beat the drum, and go liberally with rum and ale. His "gang" was half a dozen swaggering Jolly Jacks, True-blue Hearts of Oak, as gay and "me-hearty" as any gullible young calfhead could wish for. They were full of a fund of stories, chanties, japes and cajolery. Enough cajolery that many disappointed landsmen, many a young lad, *had* enlisted. And real, tarry-handed tarpaulin men, experienced sailors, *had* joined the Navy during those recruiting parties. Like the men pressed at sea off the *Five Sisters*, they at least had a chance to claim the Joining Bounty, and go with a pack of their old shipmates, instead of being shoved into just any old crew. They might return to a warship they'd served in before, with an officer they trusted! Navy work might not pay as high as merchant, but the crews were much larger, so the labour was shared out in smaller dollops. The food was regulated in quantity and quality, and in the Navy at least, they could complain, within reasonable bounds, if it wasn't. And there was the liberal rum issue, too!

And there was the excitement, the danger and the glamour of it all, for sailors and landlubbers alike. For many, it was a means of escaping their dreary existence. Boredom played a part, as did failure at trade or domestic service, as did poverty. For many farm labourers, enlisting in the Navy meant freedom from the narrowness of rural life, the mindless drudgery, the uncertain nature of putting food in one's belly—and the uncertain nature of the food itself.

And more than a few volunteers were running away from shrewish wives, demanding sweethearts they hoped to jilt, too many children at their ankles, or lasses turning up "ankled" and suing for marriage.

Well, perhaps the Impress had more than a few sordid sides, Alan had to admit. At those same jolly recruiting fairs, he'd seen masters connive to offer up their apprentices, to ship them off to sea so they would be spared the expense of feeding and clothing them, then register their indentures at the Navy Pay Office so they could draw off the impressed apprentices' pay! He'd seen rivals in love, or those selfsame jilted young girls, get their own back by whispering the location of a prime hand. Unhappy wives could find a way to pack off the brute who beat them once too often. Relations, usually in-laws, could rescue their family's good name, and their daughter or niece, from a marriage or engagement to someone unsuitable, if he was sound enough to man the tops of a fighting ship, or pulley-hauley in the waist.

And there were the lads, bastards like himself, who'd proved to be an embarassment. Putative fathers would bring them 'round, tip the recruiting officer the wink, and leave them gamely weeping as future cabin servants, powder monkeys or landsmen. Mothers, who had too many mouths to feed as it was . . . widows who might get their new man to marry *if* the brat was gone! . . . or wives who wished to dally without testimony from sons to unwitting, or absent husbands and fathers . . .

And, there were the raids on taverns, brothels and lodgings, like the one they'd pulled that night. That took a different "gang," with no need for Jolly Jacks and "me-hearty" True-blue Hearts of Oak. *Cudgels* of oak, more like!

The brutal fact was that there were a myriad of landsmen, but no surplus of seamen, and it took at least a third to a half of a crew of a warship to be made up of seamen, if she had a hope of getting to sea and surviving once she'd made her offing. Englishmen would not tolerate conscription for any military service; that smacked of brutal central government oppression. The only way left was the 'Press. And only seamen were liable to be pressed . . . supposedly. Though many innocent civilians caught in the wrong place at the wrong time were swept into the tenders. Yet the Press was so opposed by local magistrates, and the courts deluged with wrongful-taking suits, the Impress Service so thinly manned, that they could never "sweep the streets," as the public's popular image held. It had to be done with craft and guile. With stealth and speed, in the dead of night.

"So you expect another raid soon, sir?" Lewrie asked at last.

"T'morro' night, I'd wager, soon'z Bridey whispers a few words in me shell-like ear, hee hee! An' ye done well, so I've a mind ye'll go on that'un, too."

"Of course, sir," Lewrie sighed. "Uhm, have any letters come?"

"Nothin' from yer good wife t'day, Mister Lewrie," his superior grunted. "Aye, if a feller's goin' t'commit th' folly, then I give ye points f'r good taste, me lad. She's a living', breathin' angel, Mistress Lewrie is. Even finer'n all th' others I saw ye squirin' in th' West Indies. An' they was *mighty* fine."

"I was hoping the Admiralty—?" Lewrie prayed.

"Nothin' from them, neither. Oh, I know ye b'long at sea, an' it rare breaks me heart t'see ye took so low, Mister Lewrie," Lilycrop commiserated, topping up his ale. "I've wrote meself. Locker, down t'th' Nore . . . Jackson an' Stephens, an' Admiral Hood, too. Nothin'z come back t'me, official, so far, neither. Did get wind o' somethin', though . . ." Lilycrop frowned.

"Yes, sir?" Lewrie sat up hopefully.

"Member how ye used t'speak about politics so glib, Lewrie?"

"Aye, sir?"

"Well, from what I gather, unofficial-like, 'tis petty politics holdin' ye back. Some rear admiral, name o' Sinclair?"

"Oh, shit. I knew he hated me more'n cold, boiled mutton."

"And, there's another . . . some retired rear admiral. Not on any board, but he has lots of patronage an' influence . . . man ye crossed in the Bahamas, I hear tell."

"Commodore Garvey?" Lewrie gasped. "He's Yellow Squadron scum! How could he sway my appointment?"

"Aye, that's th' name," Lilycrop nodded between healthy swigs. "Rich as Midas, I hear, tied t' all th' nabobs in th' City. *Civilians* don't know Yellow Squadron . . . nor what it means. They retire a fool'r a cheat, they bump him in rank, 'stead o' cashierin'r court-martiallin' th' bastard, an' he's Rear Admiral o' the Blue, respectable-lookin'z anythin'. Rumour is, ye exposed 'im, him an' a pack o' thieves, your last commission. An' now he's thick with th' thieves *this* side o' th' ocean who liked th' old way o' Bahamas dealin'. High-placed thieves, too. That means under-th'-table, petticoat talk . . . rich City society wives'n mistresses with th' ear o' Navy Board wives'n mistresses. I 'spect that's why ye sat these last years on th' beach t'begin with."

"My God, I never thought . . . !" Alan exclaimed. Of course, the last few years ashore, I didn't give a further Navy career the time of day, he confessed to himself. Show up at my door, back when we'd first started, and I'd have run the bastard through who'd have sent me back to sea so quick!

But now there's a real war . . . ! He sighed, squirming with impatience to do something more meaningful than coshing drunken sailors on the head and dragging them off by their ankles.

"Fear nought, me lad," Lilycrop cautioned. "Corral enough men, ye'll get yer ship. Look at Bracewaight. There's rumours he'd done an arrangement . . . he fetches in 200 seamen, they give him an active commission. One-handed'r no, he's still a *dev'lish* sharp scaly-fish, an' just as wasted here'z ye are. There's a midshipman, down t' th' Nore, braggin' that his hundredth recruit'll fetch his lieutenantcy! 'Course, he's a high-up Dockyard sea-daddy f'r a patron, I'm told."

Two hundred pressed men, Lewrie almost gagged? At the rate I'm going, that'll take 'til next Christmas, and how long'll this war last?

And with just whom, exactly, did one make such a Devil's bargain?

He vowed to "smoke out" Bracewaight at the first opportunity. And write yet another pleading, weekly letter to the Admiralty.

CHAPTER 4

Old Bridey, the Mother Abbess, must have had decades of hard be-grudgements to work off (or far costlier damage done to her establish-ment), for the next few days, and nights, were filled with raids.

The Impress Service dealt with deserters, both those who ran delib-erately and stayed away, and those who "straggled." There were some who'd run, intent upon life-long escape from Navy service. And there were some who volunteered over and over again, collecting the Joining Bounty, then taking "leg-bail" to enlist under another alias. Their raids netted about a dozen of the worst offenders, and put the fear of capture in many others.

Then, there were the "stragglers." These were seamen who had missed their ship's departure, gone on unsanctioned "runs ashore" on a whim, gone adrift from working parties intent on a stupendous drunk, a mindless rut, with no thought for the morrow. Or long-term sailors with good records who'd been granted shore leave, but had been robbed or otherwise "delayed," who had a mind to rejoin, and were anxious to go back aboard. Hands didn't exactly join the national war effort, didn't sign up to fight "For King and Country"; they wanted to be aboard, and gave their primary loyalty to, specific ships and crews. Fellows from the same neighbourhood or village, the same shire, friends (or people they felt comfortable with). And the Impress Service was their clearinghouse.

Men who'd been put ashore sick or hurt into Greenwich Hospital, but had recovered, They were particularly vulnerable, for they owned pay certificates, or solid coin for once, and there were many jobbers and "sharks" who preyed upon them to buy up their certificates for a pit-tance, then turn them in at the Pay Office for full value. And get the released hospitallers drunk, penniless and desperate. Desperate enough to fear returning to the Fleet, and sign aboard a merchantman or pri-vateer.

So some of their raids were in the nature of rescue missions to reclaim those befuddled men before worse befell them; the Navy "getting its own back."

Tonight it was to be deserters, the genuine articles this time, not stragglers, and the "gang" was the round dozen of the toughest of hands. True deserters would face punishment, and would fight like a pack of badgers to stay free.

Their hideout was above an "all-nations," a dramshop serving a little bit of everything, at the back of a winding mews of dockyard warehouses. It was a mean and narrow building, dwarfed by the height of the warehouses, hard up against a blank brick wall which separated it from one of the worst "Bermudas" of Wapping, a slum so gruesome and crime-ridden, and its lanes and alleys so convoluted, that their escape from any threat would be assured, if they had warning.

"One door art th' back, sir," the crimp whispered in Lewrie's ear, his breath as foul as rotting kelp. "Winders'z bricked up, 'cept fer that'un ye c'n see. Winder Tax," he shrugged. "But I'd s'pect 'ey got 'em one jus' boarded over, 'bove th' wall, sir."

How Lilycrop, or Bridey, had talked the crimp into aiding them, Lewrie could not fathom. Crimps usually were in competition with the 'Press. The Navy had to use their own gangs, for locals stood a fair chance of being found beaten to a pulp, or dead, if they were spotted helping round up people for the Navy.

The old Mother Abbess, Lewrie decided, leaning away to escape the stench, must know where he buried the body! Took his clothes, too, no doubt; the crimp's body odour was, if anything, even more loathsome than his breath! He smelled like a corpse's armpit!

"Down to the end of the mews, bosun," Lewrie instructed, after giving it a long look. "Two hands atop the wall, either side of their bolt-hole window. You've placed two more at the back entrance?"

"Aye, sir. Snuck 'round a'hind th' warehouses."

"One to stop the front door, once we smash in."

"No need fr 'at, sir," the crimp muttered, producing a sack of tinny, clanking objects from within his greasy coat.

"You have a key?" Lewrie goggled.

"Manner o' speakin', like," the crimp chuckled softly, thumbing through a set of picks and tiny pry-levers, selecting them by feel in the dark, foggy gloom. "Best lock's on th' shop side, not th' stairs door. Been in afore, I has, an' nary a drap'd I get, th' knacky ol' whore-son!"

"Let's go, then," Lewrie murmured, changing his grip on his truncheon. They flattened themselves against the front of the warehouses, vague darker shadows in the night, in single file. Alan gave the dramshop another squint as they got closer. There was one door to the alley, offset to the left of the storefront, and the window, or bulkhead bay, that formed the majority of the narrow building's face, was tightly sealed by large barred shutters.

"I gets 'is lock t'op'm, sir . . ." the crimp informed him in a gay, professional afterthought, " 'Ey's a door t'th' right, 'at's th' shop. Pair-o'-stairs onna lef' . . . that's y'r pigeon, sir. Up ye'll fly. I'll be waitin' backit th' corner. Ah, tha's me darlin'!" he wheezed as rusty tumblers clicked. A light thumb on the latch, and it was open. "Wait!" The crimp drew out a small flask of oil, and atomized the hinges of the door with as much loving care as a woman might, to apply her favourite, most alluring scent.

"On y'r own now, sir," the crimp bowed, and lightfooted his way to the far end of the alley, farthest from observation.

"We'll creep, far as we may, men," Lewrie ordered. "First sign of alarm, though, we go like blazes. Lanterns hooded, 'til I give the word. Right?"

They slunk into stygian blackness, feeling softly with toes for the first step of the riser, groping for a railing that was not there. And measuring the height of the subsequent steps, and their depth, one cautious tread at a time. Nine men, including Lewrie, his bosun and Cony, all trying to breathe, to climb as silently as possible; though to Alan's ears, they made as much noise as a like number of grunting, rasping hogs in that narrow, airless passage.

Lewrie held up one hand to warn his gang to pause for a moment, so he could listen. He thought he heard soft murmurings, a snatch of throaty laughter from above. Unfortunately, his men couldn't even see their hands in front of their own faces, much less his, so all he did was bunch them up to a chorus of grunts, subdued yelps of surprise, of awkward feet thunked on creaking boards, and the thud of truncheons on the peeling plaster walls.

"Hoy, wazzat?" came a cry from above.

"Go!" Lewrie screamed, almost on his hands and knees to grope upward quickly. "Lanterns! Go!"

There was a hint of light, so he could espy a tiny landing and an array of doors at the top of the steep stairs. One of them opened a crack, spilling more light, right ahead of him. Lewrie scrabbled to his feet and dove for the door, crashing into it before the people behind it could close and lock it. He stumbled through at waist level, avoiding the slash of a jackknife above his head. Before the assailant could slash again, he was brought down by a truncheon smashing on his arm. The knife dropped from his numb fingers.

"In the King's name!" Lewrie howled, lunging at the startled young sailor on the cot before him. He used his truncheon like a pike to knock the breath from the lad, and curl him up like a singed worm around his bruised stomach, gasping for air.

There was more ruckus from the center room, as its denizens discovered that their escape route through the boarded-up window which let onto the stews was filled with pressgang hands.

"Jeez-*us*!" the bosun exclaimed with disgust. "Bloody . . . !"

"Got *these*, sir," Cony told him. "Christ!"

Lewrie turned about, taking his eyes off the younger sailor for a moment. His assailant was knelt on the floor, against the wall near a wardrobe. Cony and two more hands were already binding him in irons. Oh, he was a sailor, no doubt about it; tattooed and sun-baked, a ring in his ear in sign he'd survived a sinking sometime in his past. And as grizzled and stocky as a longtime bosun's mate. His clothes were sailors' "short clothing" and purser's slops—though the man was now bare-arsed nude, still sporting the remains of a prodigious cock-stand.

"Oh, bloody . . ." Lewrie muttered as he grasped the situation. He turned back to the younger sailor and ripped the filthy linen sheet away from him. He too was naked.

"Please, sir!" the lad whimpered, looking up with pleading in his large, doelike eyes. Except for the usual ruddy sailor's tan, he was . . . pretty; pretty as some biddable young miss! "Please, sir!" he begged again, almost fluttering his lashes in hopes he could stir pity. "Warn' wot ya think, sir, I swears it! Warn' my fault, sir!"

"A Goddamned sodomite!" Lewrie almost gagged.

"Don' take me, sir . . . they'd flog me somethin' awful. They'd *hang* me, sir! I'm a good topman, sir, see . . . ain't never been flogged? Ain't been no trouble 'board ship, sir."

He reached out in supplication, tears rolling unashamedly down his face, and Lewrie flinched back from his touch, fended him off with the truncheon.

"Don' *never* mess 'board ship, sir," the young seaman began to blubber. "An' won' never 'appen agin, sir. Won' do h'it no more, I swears it. Fell in wif bad comp'ny, sir. Run outa money, an' . . . an' I needed money, sir. Drink an' bad companions, sir! Sir!"

"Irons here," Lewrie barked, snapping his fingers for his men.

"Oh, please mates, don' do h'it! I'll go back, swears I will. Ain't no trouble wif me messmates . . . !"

"Ain't no mate of yer'n, ya bugger," one of the gang growled as he advanced with a set of fetters. " 'Old still now . . . *missy!*"

Lewrie stumped stiff-legged from the chamber, onto the landing, peeking into the other rooms for confirmation. He had not only stumbled onto a nest of deserters, he'd stepped right into a *proper* dungheap.

No wonder they'd run, he thought. Sodomy was one of the few of the thirty-six Articles of War, besides murder and mutiny, the Navy really did hang people for.

"Gawd, sir," his bosun spat, "ain't just deserters. This here be a boy-fucker's buttock-shop. Center room, sir . . . musta been seven 'r eight o' th' . . . *things* . . . t'gither when we busted in, as evil'z . . . anythin'! Not all of 'em seamen, though, Mister Lewrie. Dramshop owner, e'z one, too. Caught 'im in th' front room, we did. Had 'im a lad in 'ere no bigger'n me youngest boy Tommy, th' bastard. Two of 'em'z ship's boys. An' a coupla . . . *gen'lmen!*"

Lewrie took a look in the front room. It was much larger than the other two chambers, part bedchamber and parlour, and quite well furnished compared to the rest. A chubby old reprobate sat unmanacled on the edge of the high bedstead, trying to cover part of his nudity by shrouding his groin with his hands, wide-eyed and high-browed, and striving to appear as sheepishly innocent as a dog might, caught licking the Sunday roast. But cowering up by the pile of pillows, weeping fit to bust, was a cherub of a boy, not over ten years old.

"That . . . suet-arse was buggering that *boy*?" Lewrie demanded.

" *'Pears* he wuz, sir. In bed with 'im, naked'z Adam, anyways."

"You misconstrue, sir," the harmless-looking old bugger began to explain, shaking his head as if it was a very tiny, silly mistake. "I can assure you, sir, you see—"

"Save it!" Lewrie snapped. "Tell it to the magistrate."

The man gasped, paling with dread. Hauled before a court on a charge of sodomy, he'd face hanging for his peculiar tastes. A public whipping, then days festering in the stocks on display at his most hopeful prospect; but subject to the taunts, fruit, stones and physical abuse of the Mob. And few survived that, either.

"Didn' cuff 'im yet, sir . . . bein' a civilian'n all," the bosun commented. The 'Press had been sued before for even laying hands on civilians, no matter how briefly. And the bosun was a cautious, and experienced, Impress man. "T'other bugger'z in 'ere, sir."

Alan stomped to the door of the center chamber. There he saw what he could only construe as the aftermath of a backgammoner's orgy. Cheap, low beds lined the walls, feather mattresses and blankets stood service for the carpet. The room reeked of spilled rum, gin, brandy and ale. Several candles guttered in the corners, so the participants might take pleasure in observing, between bouts. Even by that guttery light, Lewrie could pick out several seamen, and a pair of snot-nosed, shivering ship's boys, from the pasty-skinned, maggot-pale civilians.

One of the civilians—again, unfettered—had hurriedly dressed. His clothes were elegant and expensive—silks and satins, fine-cut figured velvet coat and breeches, expensive shoes, the accoutrements of a courtly salon slug. And a courtier's smug airs.

"I am a *gentleman*, sir," he began, with a sneer at discovering an officer to whom he could complain. "I am a civilian. I am not, nor have I ever been, a sailor, sir. Therefore you have no authority over me, and I insist you let me pass, at once!"

"But you *are* a bugger, ain't you?" Lewrie countered. "What if we just call for the 'Charlies' and hold you 'til a magistrate comes?"

"You would not *dare*, sir," the slim young courtier simpered. "No magistrate would sanction the 'Press in his domain, sir, even were he aware of your presence . . . which awareness I most *sincerely* doubt," the man shot back, sure of his ground. "Show me your warrant, sir, or confess that your actions this evening have no sanction."

Damme, Lewrie groaned; a bloody sea lawyer! And, no, we *don't* have a warrant to show. That's why we were successful tonight. Word couldn't get out, and the streets about weren't warned to expect us.

"I *see*," the slim aristocrat purred in triumph. "So it will be impossible for you to detain me, d'ye see. Nor summon any local authorities 'pon me. Nor hold me 'gainst my will. *You* alone have authority to detain, to lay hands upon me, sir, but your writ does not extend to your minions. And your bullybucks have *already* laid hands upon me, striven to prevent me from dressing, or departing. That constitutes, of itself, a wrongful-taking . . . for which you, and you alone, are liable before a court of justice, sir." He was singsonging with glee.

Damme, he's well versed, too! Damn his eyes!

"And I feel it my obligation to caution you, sir, that I am from a *most* influential and powerful City family. With a circle of friends far more powerful than are *yours*, I'd expect, with legal assistance far beyond *your* miserable purse. You are in difficulties enough already. Detain me a moment longer, and whatever befalls you will be a greater measure of chastisement than *ever* you might imagine. Now let me pass, I say!"

He has me by the short hairs, Lewrie gloomed to himself; all he had said was true. He could be bound up in court for months. Oh, the Admiralty would pay his legal expenses, bail him out of debtors' prison if he lost the judgment, and if the fop demanded a huge settlement. But he'd be out thousands over the matter. And he couldn't risk losing every farthing he had.

"You speak for the others, too, I take it?" Lewrie found spirit enough to sneer in return.

"My dear sir, I care little for any but myself," the man confessed gaily. "These *sailors* are properly in your limited jurisdiction. They and the rest . . . well, it was dull sport, after all. I will take my manservant yonder, and depart. Should you have no objections?"

"Get out," Lewrie grumbled at last. "Get out, and be damned to you, you . . . !"

"Adieu," the elegant young bugger smirked, making a "leg" and sweeping his showy, egret-feathered hat across his breast. "Bonne nuit. Though *not*, you will understand . . . au revoir . . . n'est-ce pas?"

"Sufferin' . . ." Lewrie sighed, slamming his truncheon into his palm, over and over, as the courtier and his shivering "man" departed.

"Aye, 'at stinks, sir," the bosun muttered sourly. "Nothin' ye could do, else. Not with th' likes o' *him*!"

"He left one of 'em behind, at any rate," Lewrie observed, as he walked deeper into the orgy chamber to gaze down upon an unconscious form huddled hard up against a cot.

"Well, 'at'un cut up a bit rough, 'e did, Mister Lewrie. Hadta bash 'im a good'un. Gawd! 'Ese pore tykes. Just babes, some of 'em. Wish we *could* go 'fore a magistrate. Local parish might take 'em in, set 'em right, 'fore they gets buggery in their blood."

"This parish?" Lewrie scoffed, still squirming over his defeat. "What could they do? Already Irish bog-trotter poor. Full of future victims. Can't *have* boy brothels in rich parishes. Like that sneerin' shit, just left? Prays the loudest in his family pew, I'd wager, and plays upright for all to see. Can't take *his* sort of pleasure in a good parish. But that's what the East End is *for*, ain't it?" And I should know, Lewrie shrugged in wry self-awareness. In my early days, I was all over the East End whores, Drury Lane to Cheapside. 'Least, they were *girls*! And I paid well. Full value and more.

"What say we let 'ese litt'lest beggars go, Mister Lewrie?" the bosun almost begged. "Coupla cabin boys, 'eir sort'd not be missed f'r long, no with s'many volunteers. We take 'em in, sir, all they get is caned, then discharged, anyways. T'other tykes, well . . ."

"Aye, bosun, turn 'em out," Lewrie decided, unable to look the quivering, fearful children in the eyes. "Tongue-lash before they go, though. Put *some* fear o' God in 'em. But we take the rest with us."

"Aye aye, sir."

Lewrie went to the last, unconscious, civilian by the cot. He rolled him over with his foot, hoping for signs that he might yet be a seaman, subject to impressment. And his pitifully weak writ.

"Well, damme!" he gasped, as if butted in the solar plexus. It had been years! 1780, if it was a day! That last bitterly cold morning when the naval captain and his brute of a coxswain had come for him, in his father's house in St. James's, to drag him off as an unwilling midshipman. There, lying at his feet in enforced "repose," was the bane of his adolescent life. Even with a trickle of blood at the corner of his mouth, a livid bruise on his cheek and blood matted in his lank, sweaty blond hair, the bastard appeared to be sneering, in truncheon-induced sleep! No, there was no mistaking the rail-thin, haughty, thoroughly despicable face of his half brother Gerald Willoughby. His backgammoning, windward-passage-preferring, butt-fucking sodomite Molly of a half brother.

"Oh, God . . . thankee, just!" Alan whispered with sudden glee.

How many nights he'd swung in his hammock aboard *Ariadne*, his first ship, with silent tears of rage coursing his cheeks, wasting all that precious sleep with schemes of revenge on all who had connived to push him off, a hopeless, clueless victim, to sea.

His father, for Alan's inheritance he'd hoped to steal; their solicitor Pilchard, who'd forged and swindled in the cause; his icily beautiful half sister Belinda, who'd lured him to her bed so he could be discovered "raping" her; even the parish vicar who'd been duped into being witness to his alleged crime.

Most especially, this taunting, cruel, sneering, troublemaking, backstabbing, lying, canting, sneaking, arrogant swine!

Lewrie's ardour had at last cooled, though he had relished news of them. By '86, off for the Bahamas, he'd almost put them out of mind. He did learn, though, that Pilchard had been arrested long before, for forgery, theft and huge debt; and if he hadn't done a "Newgate hornpipe" on the gallows, then he was a prime candidate for the first convoy to New South Wales, now England had once more a place for those doomed to be "transported for life."

Belinda . . . their mutual father'd robbed her and Gerald of *their* dead mother's inheritance, too; run through every penny, and hadn't got his hands on Alan's, so they'd been turned out, penniless. He'd heard she made her living on her back. He'd even seen her listed in the new gentleman's guide to Covent Garden whores . . . a high-priced courtesan, in the latest edition.

Gerald, well . . . they didn't publish guides for what he did. He had survived, after a fashion; toadying, fawning, conniving and scheming to ingratiate himself with every member of his peculiar "tribe" in London, to sponge off others' largesse, so he could still make a grand show about town in the latest fashion, in the best circles. As long as he allowed other men of his stripe to ride him.

Lewrie almost giggled as he took in how low Gerald had fallen in the years since he'd last heard of him. A stupendous comedown, if this establishment was the best he could afford to frequent. Or the meanest strait he'd been reduced to, as a market for his fading wares. Getting buggered for sixpence, instead of guineas.

There was a carefully folded pile of civilian long clothing he took to be Gerald's. Lewrie knelt to examine them. He still sported silk stockings, yes, but they were raveled above the knees and darned where they'd run. His shirt boasted a puffy lace jabot, but the rest, which the waistcoat would hide, was a faded, much-mended horror from a ragpicker's barrow. The seat of his pale blue velvet breeches was worn shiny, his once-elegant satin waistcoat had patches of bullion and silver embroidery missing. And his hat! Gerald had been rather keen on fashionable hats. Gerald's wine-coloured beaver was greasy with too much past sweat, table oils, hair dressing, and stained by overlong exposure to the elements.

Alan poked about until he found Gerald's carefully hidden purse, a worn-bare, figured-silk poke. It held a mere two shillings eleven pence. Prompted by past remembrance, he dug into a cracked shoe, delving into Gerald's favourite hidey-hole, and found . . . a single crown. And this was the top-lofty bastard who'd feared going out of an evening unless he could sport at least fifty pounds! He'd thought it ungentlemanly!

Lewrie stood up suddenly as the lank bastard groaned and rolled his head, exposing teeth grayed by the mercury cure for pox. He spun on his heel and fled the room, before Gerald awoke.

"Bosun," he called, trying to keep his rising malevolent grin in check. "Bosun Tatnall?"

"Sir," that worthy grunted.

"Seems to me there's nought we may do to shut this horror down. Nothing official, that is, but . . ." Alan began, biting his cheek.

"Burn h'it t'th' groun', sir, that'd suit," Tatnall scowled.

"Probably a dozen more like it in spitting distance. But, we could do some real good this night, even so," Lewrie went on. "Can't stay open without its owner, or its star performer up yonder," Lewrie joshed, almost elbowing the man in confidential camaraderie. "Do you not think that old tripes-and-trullibubs would make a fine volunteer, bosun? Once you convince him that joining's a sight better than being hanged for a bugger?"

"Oh, aye, sir!" Tatnall agreed heartily. "An' if the' bugger tries 'is ways 'board ship, they'll flay 'at maggotty flesh off'n 'is bones! Cut a feller soft'z 'im like fresh cheese, 'ey would, sir!"

"Pity about that shop door below, too, bosun. When we left it, it *was* locked, but 'tis a rough location, after all. Pity some criminals from the stew broke in and drank him dry."

"Oh, aye, sir!" Tatnall concurred again. "A hellish pity!"

"I'll speak to that crimp of ours. He must have friends who'd savour a bottle or two," Lewrie snickered. "Take our deserters and the owner to the tender. I'll deal with our crimp, and catch you up later."

"I'll see to 'em, sir, never ya fear."

And I wonder if that crimp knows where a good tattoo artist may be found this time o' night, Lewrie wondered to himself, hellish happy with the evening's outcome, after all.

Bound and gagged, blindfolded, both muffled and disguised by a filthy sheet, Gerald Willoughby could but grunt, squeal and *attempt* to curse as the tattooist plied his skills at Bridey's knocking-shop. The old drab had bales of castoff slop clothing to garb Gerald in, and the crimp delighted in his smart, newly exchanged gentleman's togs.

The tattooist did complain, though, as he laboured over Gerald's pale, hairless and shallow chest, as the whores hooted encouragement to him, at the poor state of his "canvas," at the boot-blacking he had to use; at the weak light and the watching crowd as he strove to complete his masterpiece.

It was rather good, though, considering how Gerald behaved, how violently he struggled against every quill prick, the liberal tots they poured down his maw. The rum won out. Toward the end, his thrashings abated, and he rambled gagged snatches of song, before his lights at last went out, and he began to snore.

And once he was thoroughly comatose, Lewrie, the chuckling crimp and their unwitting accomplice Will Cony, delivered Gerald Willoughby, Esq., into the gentle ministrations of the Deptford district 'press tender. There to sleep off his monumental drunk—there to be sweetly wafted down-river to the Nore as an impressed sailor—there to awaken with a shriek of horror to a new life and trade.

Lewrie was mortal certain Gerald no longer had a single influential or fashionable patron who might spring to his aid, so there could be no hope of rescue from without. And from within, Gerald, garbed in slop clothing, and sporting an especially fine (though new) chest tattoo of a rope-fouled anchor, listed as taken by an Impress officer by the name of Bracewaight, could protest until his face turned blue that he wasn't a sailor, to no avail whatsoever. No, his only hope of escape would be to declare himself for what he was.

But, once 'pressed, he fell under the harsh strictures of the Articles of War, most especially Article the Twenty-Ninth:

> *If any person in the Fleet shall committ the unnatural and detestable Sin of Buggery or Sodomy with Man or Beast, he shall be punished with Death by the sentence of a Court Martial.*

Oh, it would be a fine and manly, though austere, life Gerald would be entering, Lewrie thought smugly. Wind, rain, the perils of the sea, foul food, rancid reeks, stern discipline, days aloft on the yards dependent on fickle footholds, the risks of battle. Flogging.

And the weeks and months spent cheek-to-jowl with hundreds of fit, healthy, lithe young men, cooped up on the gun decks, swaying in a narrow hammock, with not one whit of privacy—living as celibate an existence as so many damned monks!

Or else, of course.

BOOK III

Heu miseros nostrum natosque pateresque! Hacine nos animae faciles rate nubila contra mittimur?

Alas, for those of us with fathers or sons alive! Is this the ship in which we thoughtless souls are sent forth in the face of a clouded sky?

—VALERIUS FLACCUS
Argonautica, Book I, 149–152

CHAPTER 1

"Post nubila—Phoebus, Cony," Lewrie informed his man. "My thought for the day. 'After clouds—sunshine'!"

"Iff'n ya say so, sir," Cony replied, trying to shelter under a scrap of canvas in the bumboat, as Portsmouth Harbour seethed at the lash of a sullen April rain shower.

Bare days after his antic over his half brother Gerald, there had at last come a packet from the Admiralty. Perhaps Rear-Admiral Sir George Sinclair had turned his toes up, or sailed. Perhaps some rumour of Garvey's past dealings in the Bahamas had come to light at last. Or, more likely perhaps, his and Captain Lilycrop's almost weekly letters to far and near had become such a nuisance to some overworked clerk— whatever, Lt. Alan Lewrie, RN, was ordered to make his way to Portsmouth instanter and report aboard the *Cockerel* frigate, a 32-gunned vessel of the 5th Rate currently fitting out, as her first officer.

Even the gloom of a drizzly day could not dampen his appreciation of his new ship as they neared her, nor could spume, mist nor rain detract from *Cockerel's* aggressively angular and martial appearance.

Her lower hull above the waterline was a glossy ebony, as were her bulwarks. Her gunwales were, however, buff-coloured, and gleamed with the sheen of prized ivory, slickened by the rain. The yards on her three towering masts were neatly squared away, of a golden buff from linseed oil or fresh paint where the wooden spars were bared to the gloom; courses, tops'ls, royals and t'gallants all in perfect alignment with each other a'span the decks, and lift lines tugged until each spar lay perfectly horizontal. And not a brace, parrel, halliard or jear hung slack, not a clew, brail or lift line varied from purposeful, straight-line perfection.

There were touches of red and gilt about the transom and the taffrails, the quarter-galleries, windows and ports, and the lanterns aft. There was

71

lavish gilt about the entry port. And what Lewrie could espy of the figurehead, an irate, wing-fanning rooster wearing a golden fillet crown, and the beakhead rails, was liberally coated with gilt paint as well.

"Shiny as a new-minted guinea!" Lewrie muttered to himself as he marveled how devilish-handsome she appeared, as if she was fresh from the builder's yard—or she had a captain who possessed a duke's purse to bring her from in-ordinary, idle seediness to a state worthy of a royal yacht. Her captain had been named in Lewrie's orders as one Howard Braxton; but with no "the Honourable," "Sir Howard," or aristocratic title attached to his name and naval rank, which indicated inherited wealth. Perhaps *Cockerel had* been captained by one so rich, and had been turned over to Braxton entire, he speculated.

Cockerel was supposed to be fitting out, yet to Lewrie's eyes, at last (and grudgingly) experienced with such matters, the frigate's "Bristol Fashion" orderliness bespoke a warship ready at that instant to set sail.

Thankee God, Lewrie smirked to himself with relief; You surely know what a lazy bastard I am. Less work for me, my first week'r so, ha ha! She's better fitted out than any ever I did see!

"Boat ahoy, there!" came a shout from the entry port.

"Aye aye!" Cony bellowed back, shucking his sailcloth cover, and Lewrie shrugged his boat cloak over his shoulders to expose his uniform. Cony held up fingers to clue the harbour watch to the requisite number of sideboys needful to the dignity of a first officer's welcome aboard. Despite the rain, Lewrie undid the chain about his neck and folded the boat cloak for Cony to tend to, so he could go aboard unencumbered by anything that could trip him up, or embarass his first appearance before his new crew. He tucked his hanger to the back of his left hip, and half-rose off the thwart.

Ariadne, Lewrie thought, vexed by the memory of his very first boarding, of being dunked chest-deep, nigh drowned, by the puzzles of slimy boarding battens, algae-slick man-ropes, and a ship rolling her guts out. Thankfully, there was little breeze and *Cockerel* lay still as a patient old hacking mare, gentle enough for a lady to ride. Man-ropes threaded through the outer ends of the battens were red-painted two-inch manila, taut as shrouds in the mainmast chains' deadeyes. And, he noted with relief, someone thoughtful had ordered fresh tar on the battens, reinforced with gritty sand to make a secure foothold.

He scampered up lithely, inclining a bit towards the entry port as the tumblehome of the ship's side retreated inward to lessen the weight of top-hamper and spar deck above her artillery's monstrous mass.

His hat drew level with the entry-port lip as the bosun's pipes began to shrill. Marines slapped muskets and stamped their feet; sideboys lifted their hats, and a Marine sergeant and a Navy officer flourished half-pike or sword, respectively, as he arrived. Lewrie gained the starboard gangway (stepping far enough inboard so a sudden roll wouldn't sling him back where he'd come from) and doffed his own hat.

"Alan Lewrie, come aboard to join, sir," he announced, trying to quash his sudden joy.

"Welcome aboard, sir," the Navy officer said in greeting as he swept his sword down, spun it overhand with a practiced fillip, and resheathed it. "Allow me to name myself, sir . . . Lieutenant Lewrie. I am Barnaby Scott. Third lieutenant." If he'd said his name was Eric the Red, Lewrie would have considered it more apt; Barnaby Scott looked more like an ancient Viking raider (albeit a cleanshaven one). His body was thick and square, saved from brute commonness by his height, which was about two inches more than Lewrie's. Wide-shouldered, thick-chested, bluff and hearty as a professional boxer. Scott's hair was pale blond, almost frizzy, and only loosely drawn back into a seaman's queue that more resembled a horsetail that badly needed teazeling. His complexion was deeply tanned, though sporting ruddier colour on nose, cheeks and forehead. And his eyes were a disconcertingly penetrating watery blue.

"Mister Scott, good morrow to you, sir," Lewrie smiled, taking his hand, which more resembled a bear paw, for a hearty shake. There was no choice about that; Scott did the pumping.

"And you come aboard, sir, as . . . ?" Scott inquired, cocking one suddenly wary blond eyebrow.

"First officer, Mister Scott."

"Thank bloody Christ, sir, and *very* welcome aboard!" Lieutenant Scott beamed of a sudden, and almost mangled Lewrie's hand with fresh vigour.

"Our captain is aboard, is he, Mister Scott?" Lewrie asked, glad to get his hand back at last, with all the requisite fingers.

"Aye, sir, Captain Braxton is aft in the great-cabins. Mister Spendlove?" Scott called over his shoulder without looking.

"Aye aye, sir?" a tiny midshipman chirped as he popped up from nowhere.

"Escort Mister Lewrie, our new first officer, aft so he may announce himself to the captain."

"Aye aye, sir," the fourteen-year-old piped, almost bobbing in eagerness. Or relief, Lewrie wondered? What made his arrival such a *joyous* occasion?

"I'll see to getting your chest aboard, sir," Lieutenant Scott offered.

"Just steer my man Cony the right direction, Mister Scott." He turned to follow the boy to the quarterdeck ladders which led below from the sail-tending gangways to the gun deck.

"Another hand, then? Bloody good!" Scott beamed, cracking his palms together with satisfaction.

Cockerel, like all modern frigates, was flush-decked. Her after fourth was a bare and functional quarterdeck, with no accomodations in a poop cabin. It was broken only by the after capstan heads, the base of the mizzenmast, a double wheel, compass binnacle, chart table and traverse board aft of that, and guns. There were signal-flag lockers right-aft by the taffrail, a hatchway near the stern so her captain had a quick, informal access, and a long coach top, a skylight which fed sun and air below to that worthy's great-cabins, between after hatch and the wheel. On either beam, bowsed up to the low bulwarks, were pieces of artillery; two long six-pdrs. and two shorter-barreled twenty-four-pdr. carronades in both larboard and starboard batteries.

Cockerel's gun deck proper stretched 130 feet from bow to stern, with the bulk of it exposed to the sky in the waist between the foc's'le and the great-cabins. There her main armament nested—twenty-six twelve-pdr. guns, with some aft in the captain's quarters.

Unlike larger two-decked ships of the line, her officers and men did not sleep, idle or sup jammed between the artillery. Frigates had a second, lower deck (confusingly *named* gun deck) below the gun deck proper, for accomodations, with hands forrud, Marines aft of them and the commission and warrant officers right aft, under the captain, in the wardroom. A frigate's captain was the only person to reside on the true gun deck, in solitary splendour of the great-cabins, which were as large as the entire wardroom.

Tiny Midshipman Spendlove announced Lewrie to the Marine sentry on guard without the entry door, underneath the overhang of the quarterdeck's forward edge. The Marine hitched a deep breath, and banged the butt of his Brown Bess musket on the oak planks, then shouted out just what, and whom, dared interrupt their captain's musings.

"Come." A laconic voice was heard from within.

Lewrie entered, hat and orders under his left arm, in past the chartroom to starboard, and a roomy and inviting dining coach which lay to larboard, rich with waxed and varnished table, bulkheads and beams. On a gleaming sideboard there were coin-silver lamps and tea-things, ornate, highly polished brass accoutrements, much like what he had seen in Calcutta or Canton. The dish service was Oriental, too.

He took in the usual black-and-white chequered sailcloth which covered the deck of the day cabin in lieu of formal tiles, and several carpets laid atop it. He'd seen their like before, as well. There were intricately figured trellis-patterned Hindoo and Bokhara, all red and gold and black. And a few pale green, beige or pale yellow Chinee carpets, with their enigmatic glyphs in their centers. To starboard was a seating area, made up of fancy-filigreed Chippendale-Chinese chairs and a real sofa, with ecru silk fabric, and side tables and bookcases of gleaming teak, a large square, glossy black construct he took for a wine cabinet, lightly sketched over with pale gilt scenes. For a moment, he thought he was back in a trader's "hong" in Canton, or his father's luxurious, Grand Moghul of a palace-bungalow in Calcutta!

"Yes?" his new captain prompted at last with some irritation.

"Sir . . . !" Lewrie harumphed, drawing his wits back to the matter at hand, ending his perusal (and rapid valuation) of his new lord and master's private digs. "Lt. Alan Lewrie, sir. Reporting aboard."

"I see," Captain Braxton sighed, sounding a bit put upon. "And you are to be my new first?"

"Aye, sir, I am."

Captain Braxton was seated to larboard, behind a heavy teak work desk, all scrollwork and leaving, inlaid with ivory chips in a "Tree of Life" pattern round the top of the outward-facing sides, and around the edges of the top surface. Braxton rose, careful not to smash his head on the overhead deck beams. Those beams, every exposed wood surface in his cabins, whether permanent structural members or temporary partitions, were highly linseeded and waxed. Where paint did show, it was a pleasing, restful beige. And the traditional blood-red bulwarks below the wainscotting were done in a brighter-than-Navy fiery, Chinee red, too. Against that, the squat black iron twelve-pdrs. seemed drab.

Braxton was about Lewrie's height, in his middle forties, he estimated. His hair was so very curly, short and iron-gray that Alan at first thought he wore a powdered tie-wig. His queue was very short, no lower than the bottom of his collar.

For his age, Braxton appeared remarkably fit, and only just the slightest tad stocky. Most captains in their senior years, once they had gained purses to match their appetites, thickened about the waist. Braxton seemed to have avoided that.

"Your orders, sir," he demanded, creating two deep vertical ruts between his thick, bushy brows. "Take a pew, do, Mister Lewrie."

Alan sat down in one of the comfortable armchairs before the desk, turning to keep a wary eye on Braxton as he paced the cabins and read to himself. His face kept those vertical ruts, making Alan wonder if he always looked so dyspeptic and ill at ease. The Captain possessed a long, square face, with a thin, though jutting, chin. His nose was a weather vane, large and narrow. His eyes were on the small side, however, and set rather close, slightly downturned. And his mouth was downturned, too, to the left side, as he spoke at last.

"Served in the Far East, I see, Mister Lewrie?"

"Aye, sir. Two years."

"Don't recall *Telesto*," Braxton sniffed, dismissively. "Calcutta, Canton . . . 'pon my word, I don't. Held command of an East Indiaman, 'tween the wars. Spent years out there, d'ye see."

"I wondered, sir," Lewrie smiled, hoping to ingratiate himself, "when I saw your cabin furnishings, well . . . it rather took me back, if you get my meaning, sir. Only a China hand'd appreciate . . ."

"Yes, yes," Braxton cut him off.

John Company captain, were you, Lewrie thought. Gad, 'tis no wonder *Cockerel*'s so well appointed. Those buggers make £5,000 for the round voyage! And that's the *legal* sort. Little speculation in opium and such . . . sky's the bloody limit!

"P'raps we'll get on together, then," Braxton continued, still frowning, though. "Navy Board must've taken my experience, and yours, into account, for once. Damn fools."

"As if they intended *Cockerel* to . . . serve in the Far East, sir?" Lewrie stated, striving to cover his sudden qualms.

Oh, bloody Jesus, is that why they . . . ? Off to all those damn plagues an' shit, *again*?

"I *doubt* they've that much sense," Braxton snorted with derision as he came back to his desk, flung Lewrie's orders atop it, and took a seat. "Indian Ocean, China Seas, full t'the brim with Frogs and their proxies. Half the princes, Chink *or* Hindi, eager to revolt. But . . . ! Considerin' the Admiralty's poor parcel of collective wit, sir . . . well, I more expect we're off to Nova Scotia. Beyond orders to outfit and man, I've no word yet where we're bound."

"I see, sir," Lewrie replied evenly, though with a great deal of relief.

"Says you've had independent commands."

"Aye, sir."

"I trust you didn't develop any bad habits, Mister Lewrie. Such as getting so used to doing things your own way, you can't cope with an order." Braxton all but sneered.

"Not at all, sir."

"That was the last fellow's problem, why he didn't last under me. I will not have my orders questioned, ever, I'll tell you straightaway, Lewrie. I've captained a King's Ship, captained Indiamen, before you were 'breeched,' I expect. I will be obeyed. Hear me?"

"Of course, sir," Alan agreed by rote, though mystified.

"I run a taut ship, sir," Braxton informed him. "Officers and men, no matter. I'll brook no dumb insolence, no insubordination. I give a command, an order, I expect 'em to be carried out to my satisfaction, instantly. Can't abide being second-guessed. No schoolboys' debatin' society, no sir, not for me. Not from you, not from anyone. As first lieutenant, you're my voice, my eyes. My whip, if it comes to it. Is that clear, sir?"

"Well, absolutely, sir," Lewrie said with half a grin. "Those all go, pretty much without saying, in the Fleet."

"Good," Braxton nodded, relaxing a bit. "Good, then."

"Might I inquire how long *Cockerel* has been in commission, sir?" Lewrie asked, eager to get on more mundane matters.

"Six weeks," Braxton shot back, sounding as if he was boasting, yet scowling as if it were one of Hercules's Twelve Labours. "And, no thanks to that incompetent *fool*, Mylett. Your predecessor, d'ye see? Slack, idle, cunny-thumbed as a raw landsman . . . how he ever gained his commission, I cannot fathom. Could have been done in four, sir. *Four* weeks, I tell you! Were it not for his dumb insolence, his belabouring of *ev'ry* matter. His idiocy. There's a war on, but Lieutenant Mylett'd not be stirred to energetic action. And obstreperous with me, to my ev'ry instruction! Like it was peacetime, hah!"

"I must say, though, she's . . ."

"Another thing I'll tell you straightaway, Mister Lewrie," the captain grumbled, like far off broadsides. "It is my wish, nay . . . my abiding order, that *Cockerel* distinguish herself in *ev'ry* instance. Sailhandling, gunnery, stationkeeping . . . in action, should it come our lot. *Cockerel* shall be the most efficient command in the Fleet, or I'll crush those who fail her, like cockroaches! And the ones who fail me, d'ye see, sir?"

"Aye aye, sir," Lewrie all but gulped at Braxton's almost fanatical devotion. Damme, he thought; don't think I'm going to enjoy this.

"She will be the triggest vessel, the cleanest, the best!" her captain announced with righteous heat. "Her crew the keenest, officers the most unerring and watchful. Or I'll know the reason why."

"Aye aye, sir."

"She's full of raw landsmen, idlers and waisters. Pressed and turned-over hands. Her professionals've spent too long in-ordinary, too long swinging 'round the best bower-rode at peacetime slackness. Frankly, Mister Lewrie, there're people aboard, commission and warrant, who need hard stirring. They've set too long, like treacle. Mister Scott, that burly popinjay . . . frankly, sir, there're men aboard need a *fire* lit under their fundaments. Too few upon whom I may completely rely. I trust you will be one of those, sir. Indeed I do." Braxton leaned over his desk intently.

"I'm certain you may, sir."

"We shall see, won't we?" Braxton smiled of a sudden, relaxing and turning cheery. "For the nonce, get yourself settled in, make the rounds, get to know the senior people. You'll find my Order Book in your cabin . . . unless Mylett added *theft* to his long list of crimes. You will find my ways demanding, sir. But they are my ways, and they work. As for our needs concerning hands and such, I strongly adjure you to get on good terms with our second officer. He stood in as acting first lieutenant the last week. I'd hoped . . . well. If *Cockerel* is near-complete in her recommissioning, you have his efforts to thank for it. Once we discovered what a total disaster Mylett was. You'll find his insights more than useful."

"I see, sir," Lewrie temporised. Too damn' right, he'd toe the line and walk small about his new captain. But defer to a junior officer? Not bloody likely. "Will that be all for now, sir?"

"Hmm, aye, I s'pose so."

"Then I will take my leave, sir," Lewrie announced, getting to his feet, and almost cracking his unwary skull open on the deck beam directly over his chair. "Bit out of practice," Alan shrugged, turning crimsonly abashed. "Civilian overheads, hey, sir?"

"Hmmmm." Braxton gave him a second, more searching appraisal. And frowned as if he didn't much care for what he saw.

Alan gained the quarterdeck, relishing the cool, brisk dampness of the winds upon his overheated face. He knew that captains in the Royal Navy came in a myriad of forms; and most of those . . . eccentric. But Braxton was a new form in his experience, and he was most relieved to have escaped unscathed. So far.

What a cod's-head's error, he sighed to himself—conking myself addlepated on a deck beam! Like a raw, whipjack midshipman!

Which thoughts made him wonder just how rusty (and treacly!) he really was after four years on half-pay. And what had ever possessed him to thirst for a sea commission. It was Lewrie's curse to be burdened with a *touch* more self-awareness and introspection than the run-of-the-mill Sea Officer. He knew his faults; they were legion. Predominant among them was a fear that he would be found wanting someday, that his swaggering reputation far exceeded the competence upon which such a tarry odour should be based. That he was a thinly disguised sham.

He glanced about the quarterdeck, the wheel, the guns and their tackles. He gazed aloft up the mizzenmast, naming things to himself, recalling the pestiferously quirky terms *real* seamen used. Braces, lifts, jears, clews, harbour gaskets, lubber's hole in the mizzen top, ratlines strung on the side-stays, and . . . and what the bloody hell were *those*?

Tensioning shrouds strung spider-taut from larboard to starboard stays below the mizzen top, they were . . . oh, Jesus! Uppers were called *catharpins* . . . lowers? *Swifters*! Right, swifters. There's a backstay outrigger . . . travellin' backstay? No, breast-backstay outrigger, *there* is the travellin' backstay . . . there, the standing.

Christ, what a dunce you are, you poxy clown! It'll come to me. It'll come, soon as I'm pitched in—I *think*. It had better.

He determined that, in the shank of his first evening aboard, he would, on the sly, swot up on his tarry, dog-eared copy of Falconer's *Marine Dictionary*. Along with the peculiarities of Captain Braxton's idiosyncratic Order Book.

"Excuse me, sir. You are our new first?" another intruded upon Alan's glum musings of disaster.

"Aye," he replied, happy for any distraction at that moment.

"Allow me to name myself, sir . . . Dimmock, sir. Nathan Dimmock," the other fellow informed him, doffing his hat in salute. "The sailing master. Your servant, sir."

"Lewrie. Alan Lewrie, sir," he responded with a like courtesy.

Dimmock was a sturdy fellow, bluff and square, just a bit shorter than Lewrie; soberly dressed in a plain blue frock coat, red waistcoat and blue breeches. Before he clapped his hat back on, Alan saw that he wore his hair quite short, barely over his ears on the sides, with a tiny queue in back.

"Well, Mister Dimmock, how do *you* find *Cockerel*, sir?" Lewrie asked him.

"An excellent *ship*, sir," Dimmock replied. "A most excellently *crafted* vessel, sir."

"Been aboard long, have you?"

"Five weeks, sir, my mates and I."

"So your department is prepared for sea, in all respects?"

"There are some charts I lack, Mister Lewrie, sir, but other than those, *we* are ready, aye."

"But not the entire ship, I take it?" Lewrie pressed, mystified by the stresses Dimmock put on his words. Dimmock all but grimaced, inclined his head towards the open skylights in the coach top, then began to mutter his answer. Lewrie got the hint. He put his hands in the small of his back, and paced slowly away forrud to the nettings overlooking the waist, for more privacy.

"If I may speak plain, sir?" Dimmock grimaced again, as if he were fearful that his words would come back to haunt him, even so.

"As long as you do not speak insolence, sir," Alan chid him in a grim tone. As first lieutenant, he must quash the first sign of any carping or backbiting against his captain, no matter what he thought personally.

"She's a queer ship, sir," Dimmock fretted, with a shake of his round-ish head.

"A Jonah?" Lewrie stiffened. He'd heard of hard-luck vessels, with souls perverse as Harpies, where no sailor'd ever prospered.

"Oh, no, sir . . . no sign of *that*!" Dimmock was quick to assure him. "I speak more of a certain . . . tension, more like. Listen, sir. Pause a moment and give her ear."

Lewrie peeked about, cocking his head to heed any odd sounds, half-expecting some eldritch screech or moan beyond the normal creak of timbers, iron and stays, of masts working with the soft, whispery groans of the damned. But, beyond the sough of the morning wind and the far-off piping mutters of taut rigging, he heard nought.

"Dead silence, sir," Dimmock hissed softly. "No shouting or chaffer-ing. We're still in-Discipline, e'en so, but . . . a crew must make *some* sound, sir. But no. They're below, silent as a pack of whipped curs. And more'n a few already wearin' the bosun's 'chequer.' Hands on watch, hands below, they're ordered to maintain the 'Still.' A dead-silent ship's beyond my experience, sir. And a dead-silent ship's dev'lish queer."

"Not a mutiny plot, surely!" Lewrie scoffed, though he found *Cock-erel's* silence almost belly-chillin' eerie himself. "Six weeks in commis-sion? Hardly, Mister Dimmock!"

"*I'll* not be the one dare to call it mutinous, Mister Lewrie," Dimmock gloomed, shrugging deeper into his coat collar. "Though, do we drive 'em taut as we've done so far . . . tauter'n any ship I've ever been aboard, well. There is the possibility, *someday*, d'ye see, sir?"

"Captain Braxton informed me he's a taut-hand," Lewrie allowed.

"Oh, *aye*, sir," Dimmock sneered.

"Ahum!" Lewrie grunted in warning. "I think we're stretching the bounds of proper discussion too far, Mister Dimmock. Hate him or love him, he is our captain. And he must be obeyed. Chearly. Most of all by his commission officers and warrants."

"And your impression of him, sir?"

"Mister Dimmock, what *I* think don't signify. Now, unless we've pro-fessional matters to discuss?" Lewrie shot back sternly.

"Well, then, sir," Dimmock coloured, huffing up as if stifling a belch.

"You will excuse me. There's to be a flogging at five bells o' the forenoon, so I must go. You'll wish to get settled in. Speak to our illustrious second lieutenant, too. I'm mortal certain you've been bid do so? Mister Braxton?"

"*Captain* Braxton," Lewrie growled between clenched teeth. He had never heard the like from a professional officer. Not even from himself, and Lewrie could backbite and carp with the best of 'em.

"No, sir. Lt. *Clement* Braxton, I meant," Dimmock said, grinning sardonically. "Not Capt. *Howard* Braxton."

"Nephew?" Lewrie frowned deeper.

"His son, sir," Dimmock said with all signs of great pleasure. "Damme, it really does become confusing. We've a Mister Midshipman Anthony Braxton. Now, I do believe he *is* a nephew. And then, there's Midshipman Dulwer. He's cousin to them all, somehow. *And* the captain's clerk, Mister Boutwell. Oh, it's quite the grand family outing, this frigate of ours, Mister Lewrie, sir!"

"Bloody *Hell*!" Lewrie exclaimed cautiously, dropping the stern demeanour required of first lieutenants. "Any more under foot, Mister Dimmock? Mean t'say . . . how far *may* one carry nepotism? How many of the hands turned over with him? Any of the warrants?"

"Ah, now that's the queerest bit, sir," Dimmock sighed. "Captain Braxton's Indiaman? A war declared, soon as he drops the hook, guinea a man Joining Bounty, and all? And nary a hand, nary a mate from his past ships followed him to the Fleet, sir."

"Christ," Lewrie all but groaned. That was *hellish* queer, that a captain could not entice a single tar to serve under him. Even the hardest captains had *some* loyal to 'em! Even the fools did!

"Forgive me for speaking plain for the nonce, Mister Lewrie, sir," Dimmock gloomed. "And that's the last you'll hear from me, by way of insubordination. My word on't, sir. But I thought you had to know. There's good men aboard, afore the mast and in the wardroom. There's many as *could* be good men, given half a chance, and a dose o' 'firm-but-fair' whilst they're learning. But the captain is not the onliest aboard who's . . . 'taut-handed.' Runs in the family, so to speak. They're a hard lot, sir. Ask Lieutenant Mylett."

"Wish I could, sir," Lewrie shivered, though not with cold. "I was told . . . no matter. Mister Dimmock, well met, sir. You understand, I have to make my own way in this. Come to mine own conclusions, not . . . well, not take the word of the first senior warrant I meet. I mean no offence, sir."

"None taken, sir," Dimmock muttered back, glancing about to see if they had been witnessed talking together too long, in too covert a confidence. "I'll leave you to get squared away. At supper, though, to-night . . . I've a brace of French calvados. Apple brandy. Better'n any country applejack you ever swigged. My treat, to 'wet' you into the mess?"

"I should be delighted, Mister Dimmock, thankee."

"And, sir . . . ?"

"Aye?"

"We *all* tread wary, and watch our tongues," Dimmock whispered, though he performed a hat-doffing salute and slight bow, with a smile on his phiz, as if he were imparting nothing peculiar. "It isn't the hands alone who find the 'Still' the safest way."

"I will keep that in mind, Mister Dimmock. Later, sir." Lewrie nodded his head in dismissal, clapped his hands in the small of his back, and paced. He looked below into the waist, where a bosun's mate was braiding a cat-o'-nine-tails, and a sailmaker's assistant was sewing up a small red-baize bag. They looked up at him, as if trying to read his soul, then looked away hurriedly when caught under his gaze. The harbour and anchor watch-standers on deck stood their posts rigid as carved wooden soldiers, stiff-backed and mute.

Those men in working parties, swaying up tuns and kegs on the mid-ships hull skids, heaving away on stay tackles, performed their labours with mere, unisoned grunts, instead of a pulley-hauley chanty or fiddle tune.

Three midshipmen were scaling the rigging of the mainmast, up by the crosstrees, ready to go further aloft. They looked down at him, pausing in their vigourous exercise. Two, fearful; one with the air of a leery customer in a poor tradesman's shop, who'd seen better goods else-where. Lewrie matched gazes with him, unblinking, until the lad's face suffused, and he returned to his instructive "play."

Wull, *stap* me! Alan thought; what the Devil've I got meself into *this* time!

He turned to the nearest gangway ladder, to descend to the waist and make his way below through the nearest hatchway to the wardroom.

Perversely, he began to whistle a gay country air Caroline had played an hundred times, if she'd played it once, on her flute. One he had taught her.

It was familiar to all hands, making a few smile timidly.

The lyrics were hellish vulgar.

CHAPTER 2

Whack!

The bosun's mate ran the braids of the cat-o'-nine-tails through his fingers to unravel them, drew back, took a deep breath, and delivered his next stroke. " 'Leven!" he grunted.

Landsman Preston shivered as with ague, vibrating to the lash of the cat, against the square-cut hatch grating to which he was tethered at wrists and ankles. The skin of his back crawled of its own, goose-pimpling as if to writhe away from the pain. There were red-hot weals diagonaled on his bare back, some broken open and beginning to seep a torrent of crimson tears which puddled in the small of his spine, down by the band of his slop trousers—down by the leathern apron worn by men receiving punishment to protect their kidneys. Landsman Preston was gagged, too, with a leathern strop; something to bite on.

Preston flinched, hunching his flayed shoulders, as he heard Thorne, the burly bosun's mate, suck in his breath as he prepared to stroke again. In the awe-full silence he could be heard to groan.

Whack! Soggier, wetter, meatier, this time.

"Twelve!" Thorne barked, turning away to face the captain above, amidships of the quarterdeck nettings. "Doz'n d'livered, sir!" And Captain Braxton nodded grim approval as he looked down into the waist, with his officers a solid blue wall of agreement behind him, and the Marine contingent, in their best red "lobster-back" coats, with their muskets at the Present at his feet, facing the ship's "people" forrud.

"Another bosun," Braxton snapped with a larboard leer to his lip.

Bosun's Mate Porter came forward, a younger, slimmer man, not as burly as Thorne. He took the cat-o'-nine-tails, knuckled a salute to the captain, and turned to lay on. Porter was a cack-handed man, so the dozen he'd administer would be crosswise to Thorne's.

Porter shook the cat, shook his wrist to flex out any kinks. Shook the cat so blood already drawn wouldn't bind the strands with sticky sera. He took a deep breath, poised on the balls of his feet. Then, displeased with his placement, he took a half-step to his right, and faced a little away from the grating, to open his swinging room.

"B'oony henn!" Landsman Preston could be heard to say impatiently through his leather gag. "Gi' on 'i eet!"

Seamen drawn up by watch divisions shuffled their feet, swayed, and tittered uneasily. Landsman Preston was a game cock, at least!

"Silence on deck!" Braxton shouted. "Silence, the lot of you!" He turned a cold glare upon his first lieutenant, who should have been the first to cry for order. "Carry on!"

Porter shook his wrist once more, drew back, and swung.

"One!" he called in a shuddery voice. "One d'livered, sir!"

Then Two, then Three, in quick succession. Preston barely moved.

"*Put* yer back into it, bosun!" Braxton snarled. "Don't *dust* him! 'Tis punishment he deserves, and punishment he shall have."

"Aye aye, sir. Sorry, sir." Bosun's Mate Porter reddened.

Whack! Much harder this time, Porter almost going arse-over-tit with the effort he put into it. Preston leaped like a touched deer.

"Four! Four d'livered, sir!"

"Ahhh," Landsman Preston moaned, leaning his head against the curved hatch grating which was bowsed upright to the larboard gangway. Perhaps he would not turn out game, after all.

Lewrie sneaked a glance at his Braxtons, father and son, captain and second lieutenant. Braxton the younger had brought Preston up on charges. He'd been owed "gulpers" from Ordinary Seaman Gold's daily rum ration, and Gold'd thought his gulp was more than a tad healthy, so they had snarled at each other. Some elbowing and shoving, a word or two more spoken in anger over the mind-numbing rum, which was the only escape from their misery, their precious elixir. Now both were to be lashed—four dozen apiece.

Had Lewrie his druthers, he'd have given Gold an extra dollop to make it up, then deprived them *both* for a week, with a harsh talking to. Four dozen, he thought excessive, too. Their first fight or trouble, no knives drawn, not even fists swung, really. And Midshipman Spendlove had been there cat-quick, to bark them apart, thrusting his skinny body of authority between them. But Lieutenant Braxton had been certain they'd laid hands on him, ignoring his orders, no matter how accidentally, and had demanded swift and condign punishment. And, as in every instance, Captain Braxton had been more than quick to agree.

Since *Cockerel* had sailed in mid-April as one of the escorting frigates with Vice-Admiral Philip Cosby's small squadron of two ninety-eight-gun 1st Rates, three seventy-four-gun 3rd Rates, and two other frigates, there'd been men at the gratings almost daily—sometimes in twos and threes—and the call for "Hands Muster Aft to Witness Punishment" was now as routine to them as "Clear Decks and Up-Spirits."

Lashes for fighting, as a new crew shook down. For Drunken on Watch, Asleep on Watch, Insubordination, Dumb Insolence . . . which meant they didn't understand a command, or hadn't sprung into action immediately. With more than half the crew complete novices at sea . . . well! Ignorance had become, it seemed, a punishable offence.

On the slow passage escorting the trade from England, past French Biscay ports, where lurked privateers and swift frigates, they had beaten *Cockerel's* crew into a shambling semblance of discipline, had flogged or terrified raw lubbers into *some* sort of seamen. Sail drill, boat drill, gunnery drill . . . Lewrie had run every evolution of proper seamanship until they were a well-trained pack of sailors. Not a crew, though, he thought; that took a confident, shared spirit. And misery and pain were the only commonalities *Cockerel's* "people" had to share amongst themselves, so far. Oh, they could perform any task in the book, lately even to Captain Braxton's grudging satisfaction. But there was something vital missing. As if they were well-drilled puppets in a traveling Punch and Judy, a pack of wind-up German clockwork toys. But they weren't a crew.

Whack!

"Dozen!" Bosun Porter announced, sounding relieved a dirty task was complete. "Dozen d'livered, sir!"

"Very well. Cut 'im down."

"Jeezis!" Preston all but wept as his lashings parted. He almost sank to his knees, wobbly as a sickbed patient. But he waved off those who would assist him, and hobbled away toward the surgeon's mate and his waiting loblolly boys, who would escort him below to salve his hurts with sea water and tar.

He hadn't wept, though it was a close-run thing, and he hadn't cried out. He was still a man grown, and his mates from the foremast of the larboard division could be heard whispering and muttering congratulation as he passed between their tightly ordered ranks.

"Eyes to your front!" Lewrie was forced to bark, feeling greasy as he did so. "Silence on deck."

He cut another glance at the captain, but that worthy was busy. Lieutenant Braxton met his gaze, however, and lifted one eyebrow.

"Ord'nary Seaman Gold!" the captain doomed.

The master-at-arms and ship's corporals led the next man to the gratings, which were being sluiced down with buckets of sea water.

"Ord'nary Seaman Gold, you've been found guilty of violating the Articles of War. Article the Twenty-Third—of quarreling, fighting, or using reproachful speeches towards another person of the Fleet. And of Article the Twenty-Second—of striking, or laying hands upon, person or persons superior to you. For each violation, you will receive two dozen lashes," Braxton thundered. "Bosun Fairclough, seize 'im up!"

A new red-baize bag was brought forward. A pristine new cat was let out of the bag. Each man got his own, no matter how many were to be flogged. Thence to be tossed overboard, supposedly with his sins, once punishment was done. *Cockerel*, ominously, had had to send ashore in Lisbon for a fresh supply of red-baize cloth once the merchant convoy had made port.

Lewrie looked away from the shivering victim, to Mr. Midshipman Spendlove, Gold's alleged target of violence. Tears streamed the boy's face as he stood before the hands of his watch division. And the hands— more swaying, shuffling of feet, more discreet, reproving coughs, and mournful glances left and right at shipmates. A shy, horny hand came snaking from the press of men to touch Spendlove on the shoulder for a moment, to buck up his courage; some older seaman reassuring the distraught lad so he'd show game as Gold, and not shame him.

Whack!

"One," Bosun Fairclough grunted in a rummy, croaking basso. "One d'livered, sir."

"Ship's comp'ny . . . on hats, and *dismiss!*" Lewrie gladly ordered. Gold was made of softer stuff than Preston. He could not contain the pain, and had whimpered toward the end, sobbing aloud.

"Mister Lewrie!" Midshipmen Braxton and Dulwer called for him, scampering aft to the starboard ladder to the quarterdeck. "Mister Lewrie, sir!"

"Aye?" he gloomed, looking down at their eager, intent glares of right-eousness.

"Man for report, sir!" Midshipman Anthony Braxton all but chortled. "We saw it. Able Seaman Lisney, foremast. He laid hands on Mr. Mid-shipman Spendlove, sir."

"Reached out and *thumped* him, sir," Midshipman Dulwer stuck in. "From behind, he did, sir. I saw it, too!"

They were as alike, God help us, Lewrie thought, as two vicious little peas in a pod. Two snapping curs from the same ill-bred litter of pit bulls! Close-set eyes, precociously heavy and thick eyebrows, the same long, narrow, semi-stupid expressions, the same pouty mouths as their elders. The same little points in their middle top lips!

Lewrie stumped down the ladder to them, gathered them close to him by seizing hold of their coat collars, and frog-marched them to the starboard side, between twelve-pounders.

"Now you listen to me, you brutal little gets!" he hissed. "I saw what you refer to, and it was nothing more than simple humanity and compassion. And, were we to ask Mister Spendlove of it, he'd tell us the same. A game, is it, my beauties? Do you earn points on which of you sends more men to the gratings? Or do you keep score by the number of *lashes*? Daily, is it, weekly sums . . . what?"

"Now, Mister Lewrie, sir . . ." Midshipman Braxton dared to interrupt, with a stab at wordly, man-to-man airs.

"Damn your blood, sir!" Lewrie whispered harshly, right in the twenty-year-old fool's face. "How *dare* you take that tone with me! I'll have you kissing the gunner's daughter 'fore you're a minute older, and a full two dozen o' Mister Fairclough's *very* best, those! It is not a *game*, you simpletons. Ship's people aren't dumb animals you can abuse for your nose-picking, arse-scratching amusement!"

"Sir, uncle . . ." Dulwer exclaimed in fear. Or tried to.

"*Captain* Braxton to you, you pustulent hop o' my thumb!" Alan thundered at the fifteen-year-old.

"Sir, the *captain* says we're to be alert for any infraction of discipline. That we're never to allow the hands to get away with one single thing, or they'll . . ." Dulwer persisted, filled with a dutiful but thick-witted indignation. Or as much as he dared.

"Oh, stern duty!" Lewrie sneered. "What a god, that. What cant. They're men, damn your eyes. There's infractions you *must* report, and quash at once. Then there's ignorance, mistakes . . . cock-a-whoop antics hands have always pulled. Always will. And you'd flog for all. And feel so smug and prim doing it, wouldn't you? Use *some* discretion. Learn *some* leniency, or God help you . . . now, or in future. Shit!"

They fluttered their lashes, eyeing their toes in truculent incomprehension.

"I'm *using* the King's English, sirs. Any of this get through those buffle-headed skulls of yours? Shit, no. Get out of my sight before I have both of you bent over a gun. And take your lying packet with you!"

The two midshipmen slunk away, the backs of their necks aflame; though putting their heads together for commiseration. Or for a plot.

"Gawd 'elp us, sir," Cony sighed near Lewrie's elbow once they were out of earshot.

"I don't know why I bother, Cony," Lewrie confessed. "They're so sure of their ground, so steeped in ... Damme, in one ear and out t'other. They'll be back in full cry by the first dog watch, soon'z they get over their sulks."

"They's vicious, sir, no error," Cony agreed, cautiously. "I sometimes wisht I'da took yer offer, 'bout th' farm, sir."

"Hmm?" Lewrie posed, cocking a brow as he turned to his man. "I've been puzzled by why you didn't, Cony. Or take that position at the Ploughman, with Maude and her father."

"Well, sir, y'see an' all ..." Cony blushed, taking a swipe at his thick, thatchy hair. "Aye, li'l Maudie'z a dear'un, but ... they's a lass I wuz more partial to. Maggie, th' vicar's girl's maidservant? Maggie an' me, well, urhm. H'it's a tad complicated, like. Spoonin' Maudie, all but promised, like. An' 'er dad bein' a Tartar, an' all? An' th' vicar, so righteous, too? An' Maggie, urhm ... well, *expectin'*, like. Sorta."

"Sorta," Lewrie nodded, knocked back flat on his heels, and wondering (not for the first time) just how rakehell an influence he had been on his innocent-looking manservant. "Dear Lord!"

"Aye, sir." Cony blushed more furiously, though with a bit of a grin that was only half-ashamed. "Sorta like th' fam'ly way, sir. An' gettin' th' Ploughman, sir. Well, workin' fer ole Beakman'da been ... I ain't cut out t'be no publican, sir, no matter how much it'da paid. Onliest things I know're farmin', an' th' sea. Inheritin' the pub wi' Maudie ... that'd be a hellish portion o' years yet, anyways, sir. An' then they's ..." Cony stumbled to a sober silence.

"Mr. Beakman and Maudie suing you for false promise?" Lewrie prompted, sensing there was more Cony wished to tell. "Maggie's get?"

"Well, that'd be part, sir. C'n I speak plain, sir?"

Lewrie nodded his assent.

"Come down t' marryin', Mister Lewrie, sir ..." Will Cony said, tongue-tied with embarrasment. "Marryin' at'*all*, sir ... well, I seen 'ow things is wi' yerself an' yer fine lady, sir. Well, I figgered a man oughta take a wife, *someday*. But I never figgered they'd be a lot o' joy after, sir. Sorry, Mister Lewrie. I really *am*, sir. I mean, they's some, iff'n ya gets lucky'z yerself, sir. But, they's *such* a portion o' boredom an' all come with h'it. Reason I come away wi' ya, sir ...'sides fearin' Maggie, Maudie, th' vicar an' Beakman ... t'woz fearin' wot come after more, sir."

"It's not *all* boredom and disappointments, Cony," Lewrie told him, wondering how righteous he was sounding, and if he had a right to. "Well, there's good and bad. Good *more* than bad, most times."

"Aye, sir, I seen 'at," Cony countered. "But I seen ya, sir ... a'starin'

offat th' hills, sometimes, like ya wuz lookin' f'r somethin'. An' I didn'
wanna end me own days stuck in Anglesgreen, pinin' meself. Sorry f'r
speakin' plain, Mister Lewrie, but . . . Navy . . . h'it's a hard life, sir, but
'thout h'it, I'da *never* seen New York, n'r China, India, n'r Lisbon, n'r
nothin' grand. After that, sir, Lord, wot's inland an' domestic work got
t'offer? Not that I *ever* . . . ! Ya been a good . . ."

"Never knew you felt this way, Cony," Lewrie said with an assuring
grasp of his shoulder, feeling deserted even so.

"Ya gotta admit, sir, we've 'ad some grand times since we fell t'gether,"
Cony grinned at last, "An' they's sure t'be a portion more 'fore this war
wi' th' Frogs is done."

"So, what do you intend to do, about . . . uhm?" Lewrie posed.

"Banns wuz never posted 'bout Maudie and me, sir. So h'it ain't
'zackly false-promise I done. I've me prize money, me savin's . . . an' a
tidy sum h'it be, sir, after all we been through. Learned me letters'n
sent Maggie a note, an' a draught on me pay t'keep 'er 'til we gets 'ome.
Rent her'n me a cottage, 'cause y'know th' vicar'll turn 'er out, soon'z
she shows. F'r now, though . . . iff'n ya c'n spare me, sir, I'd admire'ta
strike f'r bosun's mate . . . get a warrant postin' someday, make the Navy
me trade. An' do I go back t' Anglesgreen f'r Maggie an' . . . do right by
'er'n our'n, well . . . I'd admire I went some'un respectable, sir."

"First opening, Cony," Lewrie promised, though he regretted the idea
of losing the services of his man after all those hectic years. "I will put
your name forrud, first chance I get. Top captain, for starters, more than
like."

"Gotta crawl 'fore I c'n walk, sir," Cony brightened. "Aye, I 'spects
that'd be best. Mister Scott already 'as me aloft more'n an albatross.
Tops'l yard captain'd suit, f'r starters. Too high'r too quick a jump'd row
t'other lads. An', well, sir . . . they's more'n enough 'plaints t'bite on already sir."

"Ain't there just!" Lewrie agreed sadly. "Off with you, then, you
rogue. And Cony . . ."

"Sir?"

"Midshipman Dulwer is in your starboard watch, on the mainmast.
Watch yourself damn close about him."

"I watches 'em *all* damn close, Mister Lewrie, sir. Way o' life, 'board
this 'ere barge."

CHAPTER 3

Lewrie was required to visit the men's mess daily. Some days, he made it breakfast—today was dinner. The hands dined eight to a mess, on either side of a plank table which hung from the overhead by stout ropes, seated on sea chests or short, hand-crafted stools. With the artillery overhead, instead of between mess tables, they had more elbow room, which was why most sailors preferred frigates. More room to swing a hammock at night, too, even if headroom was a bare five feet.

It was not a happy mess, though, no matter that dinner was salt beef, cheese, biscuit and small beer; not a meatless "Banyan Day," *and* lumpy dogs of pease pudding, boiled in net bags in the steep tubs like duffs, each with numbered brass tabs for the individual messes.

As soon as he set foot on the mess deck, the grumbling and the joshing died away to a low murmur, and men watched him warily, cutty-eyed, as he made his way aft. Hardtack being rapped was the predominant sound.

"Not so gristly today, Gracey?" Lewrie inquired of one senior hand at a larboard table.

"Nay s'bad, sir," Gracey grinned for a moment, wiping his fingertips on a scrap of raveled rope small-stuff, in lieu of napery. "'Tis no more'n a quarter gristle'r bone t'this joint, Mister Lewrie."

"Suffolk don't choke you, Sadler?" Lewrie japed with another.

"Damn-all hard cheeses, sir. Dry'z gravel, but . . ." he shrugged as he masticated thoughtfully on dry, crumbly Navy-issue Suffolk.

"But enough to go 'round," Lewrie prompted. "The 'Nip-Cheese' issues fair portion?" It was a blessing that *Cockerel's* purser Mr. Husie was somewhat honest in his ration issue. Begrudging, but a decent feeder, nonetheless, if one kept a chary eye upon him.

"Fair 'nough, sir," Sadler allowed, just as begrudging.

"No complaints, then?" Lewrie asked, eyeing the nearest tables. There was no familiar response, no chaffering or ironic jeers such as a hearty crew might make to such a leading statement.

"Nuffin' . . ." a young pressed man dared softly, in a bland, innocuous voice. "Nuffin' wif t'pusser, sir."

Damme, I asked for that'un, didn't I?, Lewrie thought glumly.

"Carry on then, lads," Lewrie called with false cheer, as he made his way farther aft between the swaying, rolling tables, beyond the Marines' mess area, to the companionway hatch to the gun deck. He paused once he reached bracing fresh air, cocking an ear to what might be said or done after his departure. The hummumm of low voices resumed, grew slightly in volume, but nowhere near normal level. Nor did he hear any disparaging comments about the ship's officers, or himself most particularly, that old sweats might make. That was some relief, at least. But the lack of humour, of laughter, put him off.

Lewrie ascended to the quarterdeck and took a peek at the compass in the binnacle, and stood with the quartermasters of the watch at the large double wheel as they gently fed spokes to larboard or to starboard as *Cockerel* rolled, heaved and wallowed to a following wind on her starboard quarter, a slow-veering westerly. Somewhere off to larboard and alee was Cape St. Vincent, one of the busiest corners of Europe. Flung far beyond the plodding 1st and 3rd Rate line-of-battle ships of their squadron, *Cockerel* should have seen something. But the heaving, glittering sea was a starkly empty, folding porridge.

"Rudder tackle still working?" he asked Mounson, the senior to weather. "Or are they taut 'nough?"

"Allus works on a leadin' win', sir," Mounson grumbled, turning to squit tobacco into his spit-kid. "Spoke'r two more'n us'll t' larb'rd, I reckon, though."

"Ropes are stretching again. New stuff," Lewrie decided. "I'll send the bosun below to overhaul 'em."

"Anything I might do for you, Mister Lewrie, sir?" Lt. Clement Braxton asked him, wearing a quirky, bemused, only slightly anxious expression on his beady-eyed countenance, as if he were just the slightest bit irked that anyone, much less Lewrie, would find fault in his watch-standing abilities. "Do we conform to your standards, sir?" he all but simpered. It was irksome to Lewrie, but he *was* competent.

"Quiet enough, so far," Lewrie rejoined, biting off the urge to slap him silly. "The merest child could do it. I don't suppose, though, you have inquired about the slackness in the steering tackle, sir?"

"Uhm . . ." Braxton junior stumbled, casting a quick glare at his leading helmsman. "Mounson didn't say anything to *me*, sir, I—"

"That's why one should *ask*, sir." Lewrie replied. "I leave her in your capable hands."

"Uhm, quite, Mister Lewrie, sir," Lieutenant Braxton fumed.

"My compliments to Mister Fairclough, and he is to overhaul the tackle, soon as the hands have finished dinner," Lewrie snapped, going below once more to the companionway, then aft to the wardroom for his midday meal. "Inform the captain," he tossed off over his shoulder.

The wardroom was not nearly as grand as the captain's quarters. There were small, rectangular deadlights in the stern transom, either side of the thick rudder post. Below those windows was a long, narrow settee. On either side were dog-box cabins, temporary shelters framed in light deal, with canvas walls, with insubstantial narrow doors made of shutterlike louvers. There were no locks; commission and warrant officers were supposed to be gentlemen—above stealing or prying. A space long enough for a bed-cot, wide enough for sea chest and bed, and room enough in which to dress—that was their individual portion. That portion was about six feet long and five feet wide for the junior officers who berthed furthest forward around the mess table and mizzenmast trunk; Lieutenant Braxton and Lieutenant Scott, a Marine captain named O'Neal and his lieutenant, Banbrook. Lieutenant Banbrook was the merest child, fair and slight, a seventeen-year-old whose parents had purchased him a commission upon the outbreak of war, and (Lewrie thought) had done so with the greatest sense of relief. All they'd seen him do was rail at Sergeant Haislip and the corporals, flick lint off his uniform, and drink. The Marine captain, O'Neal, a saturnine Belfaster, despaired of the lad ever learning a single blessed thing, and in private referred to Banbrook as "Leftenant Sponge," or "Little Leftenant Do-Little."

Farther aft, slightly (but only very slightly) larger cabins were for first officer, Sailing Master Mr. Dimmock, the ship's surgeon Mr. Pruden, a roly-poly font of what little good cheer their mess possessed, and the "pusser," Mr. Husie. And no purser was ever of good cheer.

"Come and cup a rum of take," Lt. Barnaby Scott offered, lolling idle on the long, narrow settee with Lieutenant Banbrook.

"Hey?" Lewrie gawped, wondering if he'd heard right.

"Or is that a cup of rum, sir?" Scott amended with a befuddled squint. "No matter, there's plenty." He indicated a glistening pewter pitcher on the dining table. "Fresh Vigo lemons, Azores lump sugar in the bottom somewhere . . . touch o' Madeira. And rum, o' course. Have a cup, sir. *I'm* quite took a'ready."

"Bit early in the day for me, Mister Scott."

"For me, too, sir. *Heep!*" Banbrook hiccoughed myopically.

"Pacing yourself are you, I see, sir?" Lewrie scoffed.

"*Heep!*" Banbrook nodded, looking angelic.

"Saving his energies for the ladies, he is, sir," Lieutenant Scott said with a wink. Every now and then, when his faculties had been dulled by drink (more so than usual), the wardroom made Banbrook the butt of their old jokes. They'd sent him capering throughout the ship, the first days at sea, calling for Marine private Cheeks. "Private Cheeks! I say now, Private Cheeks, front and center!" he'd bawled, never suspecting that it was a bugger's term. Banbrook, righteous but reeling, had reported back that Private Cheeks had evidently either deserted, or fallen overboard. There wasn't a sign of him anywhere, though Sergeant Haislip *had* recalled seeing him up forrud, relieving himself on the beakhead rails.

"Pish!" Banbrook snorted. "What ladies, I ask you? *Heep!*"

"Well, hardly ladies, really," Barnaby Scott confided, turning to Lewrie for help. "The first officer knows all about 'em. About the whore transport? I expect we'll fetch her under our lee, oh . . .'bout the end of the second dog? Isn't that *true*, sir?"

"Perhaps not until first light tomorrow, I'm sorry to say," Alan said with a somber shake of his head, which awakened a chorus of groans. "And you know they'll have to service the liners first. They might not put 'em straight to work when we sight her. Might give 'em a morning to rest first." More disappointed groans—even one from Banbrook, who did not yet have the first inkling what they were talking about.

"Whores, sir?" he asked. "*Heep!*"

"Can't allow a new crew ashore in wartime, don't you know anything, sir?" Lewrie frowned sternly. "No, shore leave's out, right out. But a ship will go Out of Discipline, now and again. If she's allowed time in harbour, she'll replenish firewood and water, then hoist the 'Easy' pendant, and out come the whores, or the wives, if she's in home waters. Ever hear the old saw 'bout sailors having a wife in every port? That's where it comes from, Mister Banbrook."

"And you'll note, we didn't stay anchored long at Lisbon, sir," Scott rejoined, weaving the web thicker. "Top you up there, lad? A rum of cup, sir?"

"Believe I shall," Lewrie smiled. "What one in harm?"

"Hey?" Banbrook goggled, trying to decypher the first officer's last statement. He looked down into his full mug, wondering if he had not taken perhaps a *tad* too much aboard. They were beginning to sound . . . higgledy-piggledy. Or something.

"Thank God the Navy's so thoughtful of its people, sir," Mister Pruden confided from his seat at the long mess table. "Better this way.

There's many a Jack been hung for buggery, else. Months and months at sea, without feminine companionship? And, if you hoist the 'Easy' in harbour, why just any old drab may come aboard, and then there's your crew, poxed to their hairlines. No, sir, this is the better way. The British consul at Lisbon will hire the prettiest doxies, get 'em certified by a Navy Sick and Hurt Board *physician* . . . can't expect one surgeon and a mate to do it, y'know . . . contract a ship, and send her out to tag along with the squadron. Then, when a vessel's deserving-like—"

"Or the hands've no fingers left, from 'boxing the Jesuit,' " Alan stuck in, "and can't pulley-hauley any longer."

"Over she'll sail, sir," Scott cajoled, putting a comradely arm about the foxed Marine. "Tippy-toin' under our lee, coy as any minx."

"The hands take their pleasures below, on their mess deck, elbow to elbow. Shockin' t'watch, sir," Captain O'Neal confided to his swozzled second-in-command. "We officers, though, now . . . ah, we get rowed over to the whore transport, d'ye see, lad."

O'Neal was almost cooing in a soft, lilting, more affected Irish brogue, whilst Lewrie had to stuff his fist in his mouth to keep from laughing out loud.

" "Handsomer run o' quim for officers, aye," Scott stuck in from the other side. "Only the prettiest'll do, with the awesomest poonts."

"And in private, in cabins much grander than these, d'ye know," O'Neal went on.

"What . . . *heep*! . . . what 'bout th' 'socket fee,' sir?" Banbrook inquired, eyes round as fried eggs with lustful wonderment by then.

"Why, laddy, that's the best part," O'Neal beamed, though he did bite the lining of his cheek to stifle a hellish case of the sniggers. "You get a guinea ride for ten shillings . . . Navy sports the rest. Just be sure you sign your mess bill, and Mister Husie sorts it all out later."

"Heep!" Lieutenant Banbrook speculated hopefully, fingering his crutch.

"Dinner's on, gentlemen, sirs," the senior wardroom steward sang out as he entered with a tureen of pea soup. Ship's boys trailed him, bearing bread barges of only very slightly weevily biscuit.

"Ah, pea soup!" Lieutenant Scott enthused as he came to the table. "God, there'll be a foul wind from astern this night, I'll wager."

"Do we get long, sir?" Banbrook asked the purser as he took his seat. "Ab . . . *heep*! . . . aboard the whore transport?"

Husie sighed, pulling at his large, though puggish nose, gazing at the expectant, prompting faces of his messmates. Though Husie deplored their high cockalorum, damme-boy antics from the nether depths of his well-ordered, double-entry soul, he felt forced to abet them, just the once, and play up in similar spirit. "Well, d'ye see, young sir . . . much like Marines and idlers aren't required to stand ev'nin' watches . . . one gets what is pretty much, how do you describe your nights off? 'All-Night-In,' so t' speak, sir?"

"Oh, I say!" Banbrook all but swooned. It was hard to tell. It could have been the rum punch. The others cheered Husie for his effort.

"Thought I explained it before," Captain O'Neal chuckled, stuffing his napkin firmly behind the rank gorget which hung high on his chest, below his throat, "Damme'f I *know* just how it slipped me mind, Leftenant Banbrook."

"Ahem," Mr. Boutwell, the captain's clerk, interrupted at the entrance to the wardroom. Boutwell wore his usual well-fed, nose-high and top-lofty superior sneer. "Excuse me, but . . . Mister Lewrie, sir, the captain bids me convey his compliments to you, and inform you that he wishes you to confer with him in his cabins."

"This minute?" Lewrie grumbled, cocking an eyebrow. The pea soup smelled hellish good, and for once they had fresh roast pork to follow!

"At once, he said, sir," Boutwell purred, looking anything but sorry to deprive Lewrie of a hot dinner.

"Very well, Mister Boutwell," Alan sighed, feeling much put upon, and griping in his bowels with dread of another rant from Captain Braxton. "My utmost respects to Captain Braxton, and I shall be up directly."

"Very good, sir," Boutwell replied, bowing his way out.

"Speaking of a foul wind, gentlemen," Lieutenant Scott whispered *sotto voce* once the man was gone, prompting another knowing chorus of groans, or dismal chuckling.

"Mister Scott, I despair of you," Lewrie snapped, putting on his coat anew. "Damme, it's hard enough . . ." He almost allowed his personal feelings to escape, but checked them. "There will be no disparaging remarks in this wardroom, whether I'm present or not."

"Ah, but I was not disparaging the *captain*, sir," Scott gaped in pretended innocence. "I referred to the captain's *clerk*, Boutwell!"

"Just stop it!" Lewrie snarled in exasperation. "I'd admire you save me at least a *slice* of pork. Hot, I s'pose, is too much to ask."

"Might as well not," Dimmock, the sailing master, muttered once the first lieutenant was himself departed. "He never has an appetite after one of *those* sessions, poor man."

"Christ love you, Mister Dimmock . . . but who does?"

CHAPTER 4

"You sent for me, sir?" Lewrie opened, standing before Captain Braxton's dining table. Braxton was having fresh roast chicken from his personal stores which had come off from shore. There was soft bread instead of biscuit, what smelled like a very fruity Portuguese varietal burgundy in his crystal glass; the only common touch was a dollop of pease pudding on his plate. Waiting on the sideboard for later were fruit, a fresh wheel of Stilton, and extra-fine sweet biscuit, with a blood-dark bottle of port breathing for the nonce.

"Yes, Mister Lewrie," Braxton scowled, looking as if Alan's presence put him off his food. He laid aside his cutlery to sip wine as he perused him. "The second officer informs me the steering tackle is slackening. The *steering* tackle, sir!"

"Mounson told me of it, sir. I ordered Mr. Braxton to command the bosun below to overhaul it, soon as the hands have eat."

"You will see to it *at once*, sir," Captain Braxton barked. "We wallow on this following wind and sea. The ropes could part at a moment's notice under the strain. Should she round up or broach-to, we could end up dismasted. And I will *not* see my ship disabled because *you* were *slack*, sir!"

"Sir, the tackle is slack, not chafing or ready to part," Alan defended, trying to maintain a calm, reasonable demeanour. "A spoke'r two slack. And, *should* we have to rereeve tackle ropes, then we have to fetch-to under reduced sail until it's done. For that we'd need all hands, so I adjudged it could wait 'til after—"

"I decide, sir. You do not. I am responsible for *ev'rything* aboard this ship. I will *not* be kept in the dark about matters of her safety, nor grave defects which make us unable to fulfill Vice-Admiral Cosby's orders. You did not see fit to tell me of this defect." Braxton seemed to calm, and

96

got back to mangling a morsel off his chicken breast. "You failed me, sir."

"I instructed Mr. Braxton to inform you, sir," Lewrie replied evenly, stifling his anger, not for the first time, when facing such an irritable, irascible and insecure man. "It appears that he did so. I do not see how I could be perceived as failing you, sir."

There was no discretion for watch officers, or trust in their competency; no freedom to think, or learn, for juniors. Captain Braxton was to be summoned over the most trivial matters, and then took charge from subordinates until *he* was satisfied. Excluding his relations, no one was trusted an inch. It had been a wearying six weeks.

"Do you not, sir?" Braxton drawled. "That of itself is a failure. Of a more personal nature."

"I'll attend to the steering tackle directly then, sir. Will that be all, sir?" Alan inquired, striving hellish-hard for "bland."

"Damn your blood, sir!" Braxton boiled over suddenly. "Do not dare take that tone with me, sir!"

"Sir?" Lewrie gawped in confusion. "What tone?" Damme, I didn't even *half* sound sulky. I thought I covered that well, he assured himself. But then, I've had *bags* of practice lately!

"Your dumb insolence, sir, your *mute* insubordination," Braxton accused, pointing a table knife at him. "Not for the first time, either. That puddin' face of yours, that blank stare . . . Curt and surly you are towards me, sir, and I tell you, I'll not have it!"

"I cannot imagine what you find disagreeable, sir," Lewrie said, flummoxed. "I replied I would deal with the tackle, then asked to be excused to do so, sir. I don't know how *else* one might state—"

"I've given you and your insulting ways just about all the chance I care to, Mister Lewrie," Braxton warned. This time, he confronted his first officer with a loaded fork. "Your eternal sneering, back-talking . . . back-stabbing, sir! As if you and the rest of those idle wastrels think you, only, know best how to command this vessel. I warned, first day, I demand complete loyalty, obedience and support given me chearly, yet I cannot rely on any of you, you most of all! The job's simple enough a fool could grasp it, Lewrie. I tell you to do something, you go and do it, without carping, without questioning. End of story. Yet you continually confront me, you presume to *advise* me! There is one captain aboard, not a damn' committee."

"Sir, I *would* be failing you if I did not relate problems, and exercise my prerogative as second-in-command to—"

"You argue with me, even *now*, sir. The rest of those fools in the wardroom take their lesson from you. The mates and petty officers you poison against my authority."

"Sir, there's not been a single instance—"

"You are all profane, sir," Braxton cavilled on, whacking at his chicken breast and delivering a bite to his mouth. "Wastrels, idlers, disreputable, tot'lly lacking in dedication, common sense, tot'lly without professional attention to duties. Dis*obedy'*nt and truculent . . ."

He even *chews* mean, Alan thought, giddy with carefully secreted rage, as he watched his captain smack and grind, his lopsided little mouth grumbling in slack-lipped petulance, begrudging each crumb.

"You're all soft, Lewrie," Braxton belaboured sourly. "You most of all. Comes of being a married junior officer, I expect. Soft hands and soft head. Too long abed, ashore, whilst better men were out at sea getting calluses. You undermine my authority, attempt to contravene my orders, sow discontent and insolence among the crew. I should sack the entire lot. You, foremost among them."

"Sir, I must protest that I do not any such thing."

"This fellow Lisney," Braxton said, *à propos* of nothing suddenly, cooling quicker than sane people had a right to, as he took aboard more wine. "Who is he?"

"Sir?" Lewrie was forced to gawp anew, off-balance again.

"Lisney! Lisney! Who is he? Damme, sir, you're first officer. Don't you know? Or was he just dropped from heaven, like gull-shite?"

"Sir, Able Seaman Lisney is foretop captain, larboard watch."

Three months in commission and you don't *know*, Lewrie fumed to himself; or don't bloody care, more like?

"He shoved Midshipman Spendlove from behind, I'm told. Yet you refused to credit the report. Suborned two midshipman from doing their proper duty. Let this fellow Lisney get away with laying hands upon a superiour. And kept it from me, sir!" the captain scolded. "One more example of your shoddy, slack and disputatious behaviour towards me and my strictures, sir. More of your softness. Lisney an old schoolmate of yours, is he, Mister Lewrie? A particular favourite?"

"*No*, sir, he is not, but—"

"You know my strict instruction that no common seaman *ever* lays hands on a superiour. If it's nought but a midshipman's jacket hanging on a mopstick, I'll have 'em crawl past, showing proper def'rence. But *no*, you know best, don't you? See fit to circumvent my orders, behind my back, and corrupt two promising young men into *your* sort of officer. And by your inattention to duty, allow the crew to flaunt me. Cock a snook at me, sir!"

"Sir, it was not a shove," Lewrie countered, giving his version of what had occurred, and the "why" of Lisney's gentle touch. He even dared at last to suggest that Midshipmen Braxton and Dulwer were doing it for dumb, brutal fun.

"They don't keep their eyes peeled from a sense of duty, sir," he concluded, breathing high and shallow off the top of his lungs, sure of the tirade to come. By the pose of utter outrage on Braxton's face, he was relating a blasphemy as great as saying King George the Third was a woman in disguise! "They're playing a game, scoring points with floggings and lashes. They take pleasure from the men's pain, sir."

"How *dare* you, sir!" Captain Braxton snarled. "Next you'll say *I* take pleasure in flogging! No, sir. No! It is from a sense of duty, nothing more . . . a grim duty, aye. And I have drilled into them that sense of duty. I want the man on report, Mister Lewrie. And I want Midshipman Spendlove on report as well, for failure to tell me of this fellow Lisney laying hands upon him."

"Sir, it was compassionate. The hands *like* Spendlove."

"And they do not *like* the others?" Braxton drawled, drumming his fingers on the dining table. "What a bloody pity! Those scum are there to do their duty, obey orders, and walk in fear of their betters, whether they *like* 'em or not!"

"That goes without saying, sir," Lewrie dared once more. "But they fear Midshipmen Braxton and Dulwer, sir. The sort of fear that turns bowels to water, and harms the proper disposal of their duties."

"Fear 'em?" Braxton cawed, almost gleeful. "I should certainly hope so, sir. Exactly as I wish. Reason they like Spendlove, he lets them have latitude. Can't bear down taut as he should. Soft. Soft as you and the others. Scott, Dimmock . . ." Braxton waved dismissively. "Even the *bosun*'s gone calf-eyed lately. Well, three dozen lashes to this Lisney, and two dozen on Spendlove's bottom'll take the insolent Jack-Sauce out of 'em."

"You'd decide punishment before a hearing, sir?" Alan inquired, feeling his spine crawl with dread. That would really cause trouble.

"I wish those people on report at once, sir."

"Sir, as first officer, I must advise you," Alan implored. "The ship's people know what Lisney's touch was about. They expect a captain's court to represent even-handed justice. But if Lisney's given three dozen, which is excessive, without a chance to—"

"I tell you, Mister Lewrie," Braxton thundered, "I want those people on report. I give you a direct order, sir. Disobey me at your im-*med*-j't peril." He looked like he was gloating.

"Sir, there must be some discretion allowed me, to sort out conduct which really *is* prejudicial to discipline and—"

"Answer me, you impertinent fool. *Will* you, or will you *not*, put them on report as I order?"

"I . . ." Alan wavered. Christ, *think*, he told himself; not answering *is* insubordination! "Aye aye, sir," Lewrie had to reply. "I will place them on charge."

"Thought as much," Braxton all but sneered over the rim of his glass. "And no more of your obstreperous interceding. I mean to have a first officer who will stand behind me to the hilt, Mister Lewrie. Whether that is you or not, in future, well . . ." he allowed with one more wave of his hand and a grumpy, fussy dissatisfaction.

"Sir, I can't stand mute if I think an injustice is being done."

"And I am ordering you to do so, in future, *Mister* Lewrie. What think ye of that?" Braxton coloured quickly. "Damme, you'll not play Fletcher Christian with me, sir! I'll dismiss you at once!"

"I do nothing of the sort, sir!" Lewrie paled. Captain Braxton had just all but accused him of mutinous behaviour! "I do say though, sir, that punishment in this instance may run counter to your intent, that it might be prejudicial to good order. The final decision is up to you, sir. But as your deputy, I must be allowed to advise . . . aye, to intercede; or at least ask for leniency, sir. I must do everything in my power to present you a well-drilled, disciplined and seaworthy ship and crew, sir. And I think I've done that. But when events happen that might upset that good order, it's my solemn duty to apprise you of such, sir."

"I'll not play a chuckleheaded, gullible Bligh to you either, Mister Lewrie. Oh no, I'll not, you mark my words!" Braxton warned.

"Sir . . ." Alan began, then clapped his trap shut, knowing that one exchange more, and there'd be no going back. I'll shoot off somethin' hot, and that's the end of me; he told himself; sure as Fate, he'd clap me in irons! "Sir," Lewrie assayed again, in a softer tone, "I assure you, you have the complete loyalty and obedience of every officer aboard."

"Then why don't I *see* it, Lewrie?" Braxton all but wailed with self-pity. "Get yourself out of my sight, sir. Attend to the steering tackle, as you should have an hour ago. And put Lisney and Spendlove up on charges."

"Aye aye, sir," he was forced to reply, looking Captain Braxton firmly in the eyes, and putting as much chirpy goodwill into his answer as he had left at that moment. He felt he was all but piping his eyes, racing off a chorus of "Rule, Brittania," and breaking into some loose-limbed hornpipe to please.

*   *   *

Do I sneer? he railed within himself, standing far aft by the taffrails. His hands squeezed the timbers so hard he felt he could rip up a section and shred it to kindling. Or strangle it. *Am* I insolent to him? Well, perhaps . . . and who wouldn't be, I ask you! But . . .

He knew how well he could toady and fawn, how well he could, as every English gentleman was expected to do, bottle up his emotions and his private thoughts, wrap them in sailcloth, and dare anyone to say whether 'twas hidden claret or horse piss.

Toady? Right, I'm good at it; dined out on it for years!

Alan didn't understand what Braxton feared, to wish to cow the crew so completely—not only the crew, but the petty officers, the warrants and the commission officers, too. What might have happened in his miserable past, he wondered, that required treating *everyone* like rebellious, riotous gutter sweepings? It went, whatever it was, far past a dread that an English crew might be infected with the fever of Republicanism and Thomas Paine. It was brutal, thoughtless of the consequences.

He's right about one thing: he doesn't get joy of it. I doubt he's ever had joy of *anything*.

Do I sneer at him behind his back, Alan asked himself? No, I know better; I've been in the Navy long enough to know how to put the "eager-but-earnest" phiz on. I stamp down any who dare to sneer, too! Has anybody caught me at it, even in private? No. *Certainly* not to his face! I've been careful to sound dutiful. Dull and flat, maybe . . . But then, I've never served under *his* like. And I very much doubt many others have, either.

Lewrie felt that he *had* earnestly tried to please, to obey and carry out his duties, even within the confining strictures the captain placed upon him. They did have a well-drilled, well-trained ship and crew by now, able to respond smartly to any command, perform any drill, or face action. He had been, as much as he was allowed, a buffer between captain and crew, presenting, as best he was able, a going concern ready for their master's use. All for nought, it seemed.

"It's not *me*," Lewrie assured himself in a bitter, guarded whisper, his stomach churning with gall over his most recent scathing. "He just wants dear Clement for first lieutenant, and I'm in the way. Raise Scott to second, promote little Anthony Braxton to acting-lieutenant . . . God, I sound so bloody *pathetic*!"

Wonder if Lieutenant Mylett felt the same way right before he chucked it? he gloomed in silence, watching their wake fan out behind them.

He could not ask—for fear of sounding as if he was criticising; the rest could not volunteer information—he was duty-bound to quash such talk as disrespectful. So he knew little more about the mystery than he had the day he'd come aboard to join.

He imagined, though, that, from what little he had learned of Mylett in casual reminiscences, he'd been an honourable, decent man—too decent, too used to a more benign, less brutal order where officers did not despise the ship's people as a regular policy. And did not feel the need for a regime of near-terror.

What *was* terrorising, though, was his realisation that a third of the crew and perhaps half the Marines were experienced men who had served kindlier captains before, even if they were strict. Nothing, though, as strict as *Cockerel*. And if it continued . . . Defiance of ordained authority was the spirit of the age; the Colonies, now France and all that Republicanism, Thom Paine talk . . . Bligh's latest . . .

Mutiny!

It could make even an officer like Lewrie queasy to think that word, much less pronounce it.

You'll not have me, Lewrie vowed grimly, promising to force himself to sound and act even chirpier and more agreeable as second-in-command. Even that would not please Captain Braxton, he knew, but it might defuse any schemes to dismiss him for lack of evidence at a possible court martial.

But I'll not knuckle under and become *his* sort of officer, Alan also vowed; I'll not be his whipped dog, his dumb lackey. And I will *not* be hounded out. Or ousted.

Hmm, though, he pondered; where's the middle ground? Stay and be-damned, sooner or later—go and be-damned a failure to the Fleet—stay and counter him, somehow . . . save the stupid bastard from himself, really. Oh, that's rich, that is!

"Christ, this is hopeless!" He all but wept in frustration.

CHAPTER 5

"There's going to be trouble," Lieutenant Scott intoned. They were inspecting the standing rigging along the larboard gangway. *Cockerel* had come about just after dawn, and was now standing nor'east toward Portugal. To their sou'west, far up to windward, the tops'ls of the line-of-battle ships could barely be seen, if one were high aloft.

"Yes, and you're not helping," Lewrie bitterly accused. "Cony has ears. Your man, too, I expect. Tongues, too, but . . ."

"But can't mollify 'em. They speak too much of obedience, it smacks of toadying cant, sir. And then they lose their 'ears' among the people. I did try, though, sir. Same as you," Scott rejoined, sounding sulky and heavy.

"I'm sorry, Mister Scott. It was unfair to you, what I just said, I know, but . . ." Alan muttered, pausing in their slow pacing to fix his eyes upon Scott's, as emphasis of his sincerity.

Captain Braxton had held his court, solicitously nodding with grim disapproval as the two midshipmen had presented their "evidence." Lisney and Spendlove were in Scott's watch, so he had spoken for them, as had Lewrie. As had Lisney and Spendlove themselves. So new at sea, Spendlove looked to Lisney, a man in his late thirties who'd spent his own boyhood in the Fleet, as a "sea-daddy" who knew all the knots, all the cautions. Lisney was a leader, looked up to by everyone, seaman or landsman alike, on the foremast. Oh, aye, there'd be trouble!

But Captain Braxton was intent upon punishment. And could that bitter man have awarded lashes for back-talking sea officers, Lewrie and Scott would have been due at the gratings themselves. Three dozen he'd foreordained, and three dozen it would be, this forenoon. Spendlove already had been caned with a stiffened rope "starter," bent over a quarterdeck six-pounder. Beating boys on the bottom was done much less formally than the gloomy, stylised ritual of a man's flogging.

There was only so much the officers could do. Obedience and loyalty in the Royal Navy were a captain's due, and the rigid Articles of War spelled out the consequences for those who didn't toe the line, even if they didn't agree, even if they felt a captain was a raving Bedlam 'bug-eater'—they had to support him totally, once he decided what was best. There was no recourse open to them that didn't smack of failure to support Captain Braxton, no one to whom they might complain. To inform a senior officer behind his back was disloyalty, and an officer's mutiny against him. Making matters worse, they could not even mention that dread word "mutiny" by way of warning yet. Braxton would become even harsher, perhaps spurring into occurence the very thing his punishments were intended to prevent. And their careers would be ruined in either case—for failure to support, and to inform him of their fears, until the situation had so festered that it was moments from eruption—or for failure to nip it in the bud in the first place. It might even appear at a court martial that they had encouraged it, or at least sympathised, and hidden a plot's existence.

"Like runnin' before a hurricane bare-poled, sir," Scott grunted, sounding almost amused. "One hears of it bein' done, but damme if one wants to try it firsthand. Damned if we do, damned if we . . ."

That made Lewrie grin for an instant, even so. Lt. Barnaby Scott was normally a loud, blustery jackanapes—exuberant and blisteringly profane, the sort who went through life windmilling his arms fit to wake the dead with an improbable curse, a side-splitting jest, and the sort of booming laugh that made one wish to place a bet or order one more bottle, even if one knew better. He was also exceedingly competent—more so, perhaps, Lewrie suspected, than he himself was.

"No leaders yet, though?" Lewrie asked softly as they gained the fo'c's'le ladders. "No *real* sign of trouble?"

"Not that organised yet, sir," Scott scoffed, looking at that moment anything but exuberant. "Leaders, well . . . none who stand out. For obvious reasons, too. Too new a crew, too many landsmen aboard, who've never known a fair . . ." He choked off his comments as a working party under bosun's mate Porter neared. It was dangerous to be heard criticising the captain by the hands, or be recalled later as one who mentioned mutiny. That would be *his* ruin.

"Yes," Lewrie agreed with a bleak nod. "After today, though, I'd expect that to change, don't you? Black as their mood is . . ."

"Count on it, sir."

"And then we'll be in the uneviable position of being *bound* to tell him of our suspicions, else . . ." Alan shrugged heavily.

"More suppression, even more floggings," Scott agreed gloomily, lifting his hat to swipe his unruly hair. "*Make* it happen."

"Duty-bound to uphold . . . *him*!" Lewrie fretted, " 'Cause when it does occur, there'll be a court, and we'll end up tainted black as—"

"*SAIL HO!*" came a wild cry from the mainmast crosstrees.

They froze in their tracks, sharing astonished looks.

"Where away?" Lieutenant Braxton on the quarterdeck demanded.

"*Two* points off t'*starb*'rd bow, sir!" came the singsong reply, like the wail of a passing soul. "T'*gall*-ants! Three . . . *FOUR*! Four, sir! Four *sets* o' t'*gall*-ants!"

"A French squadron out for prizes, I'll wager!" Lewrie yelped with sudden joy.

"Convoy, p'rhaps, sir!" Scott countered, whooping fit to bust with his own excitement. "Rice ships from New Orleans? East Indiamen, loaded gunn'l-down! Prize money, sir! Lashings of it! Action, at last!"

"Maybe salvation, at last!" Alan hooted, clapping Scott on the shoulder.

Cockerel had gone to Quarters, with a purpose for once. Drums rattled, fifes peeped, the ship rang to the slamming of doors as the temporary partitions were struck below to the orlop. The cabin furnishings were removed to a place of safety, and to lessen the danger of splinters. The gun deck and the mess deck became two long roadways, bare of any fittings or comforts. Sand was slung to give gunners and gun carriages a grip on the white-sanded planking. Fire buckets were topped up, slow match was lit and coiled in case the flintlock strikers of the artillery failed to work. In case they had to board a foe, the weapons chests were flung open, and pistols, muskets and cutlasses were distributed, piled 'round the bases of the masts below the wicked pikes in their beckets.

Twelve minutes it took to convert *Cockerel* into a vessel ready for battle, a little slower than the previous day's drill, Alan noted, but still a respectable time. Perhaps the hands were clumsier and more nervous than before, since it was a real foe they'd be spying out.

"Give us three points free, quartermaster. Steer east nor'east," Captain Braxton commanded, sounding grumpy and out-of-sorts. "Mister Braxton, signal to *Windsor Castle*: 'Enemy In Sight'."

"Aye aye, sir," the midshipman snapped, turning aft to the taffrails. A moment later, the proper signal flag soared aloft on a light halliard. With a jerk of the line, when it was "two-blocked" as high as it would go, the bunting bale burst open.

"Deck, there!" the lookout howled. *"Tops'ls*, now! *Tops'ls*'re *'bove* t' 'orizon, sir! *FIVE* chase, now, sir! Five chase!"

"We're overhauling 'em damn' fast," Lewrie exulted. He looked aloft. The signal flag was streaming at an odd angle, which made him frown. The westerlies which prevailed 'round Cape St. Vincent were at this latitude usually tending northerly, down where ships turned for the Caribbean. Today, though, they were perversely backing, blowing from west-nor'west, and it wasn't exactly the clearest day he'd ever seen, either. "Mister Braxton, any reply from the flag?" he inquired.

"Uhm, nossir," the midshipman replied, a digit up his nose.

"You can't tell from the deck, sir," Lewrie rasped. "Go aloft. They may not have seen it yet. Captain, sir?"

"What is it, Mister Lewrie?" Braxton grumbled impatiently.

"Signal flag's streaming, larboard quarter to starboard bows, sir. Might be unreadable yonder."

Captain Braxton rocked back on his heels, craning his neck to peer upward over his shoulder. "Has the flagship replied?" he bade of the midshipman, now in the mizzen-top.

"No return signal, sir! They're barely in sight!"

"Damn," Braxton growled, scratching his unshaven chin. *Cockerel* was almost t'gallants-down over the horizon from the squadron, with the wind fluttering her alert *towards* the unidentified ships.

"Mister Lewrie, we'll put about. Lay her closehauled on this larboard tack. We'll close the flagship, *then* spy out our visitors."

"Aye aye, sir. Bosun!" he roared through his brass speaking trumpet. "Hands to the braces! Man for full-and-by!"

Lewrie had little charity for the captain; even so, he thought it professionally slovenly not to have alerted the squadron first off, *before* going to Quarters and turning eastward, even further downwind out of visual, and signaling, range.

Cockerel came trundling about, bows chopping on the lively sea, shrouds and lines beginning to moan to the apparent wind. Abeam the wind as she'd been sailing, it had not seemed so boisterous; but now spray dashed high as the bulwarks, and she heeled, hobby-horsing over long-set wavetops, loping into the wind something champion.

It took a quarter-hour on that exhilarating beat before they fetched high enough above the hazy horizon, before *Windsor Castle* rose tops'l high, and finally caught her urgent signal. Bunting soared up the flagship's masts, and sails foreshortened, as the squadron of line-of-battle ships altered course eastward, to get in on whatever it was which the scouting frigate had found.

"Now, by God . . ." Braxton snapped. "Put about, Quartermaster. Make her course due east. Haul our wind, Mister Lewrie."

Back they flew toward the unidentified ships which were now well below the horizon, without the tiniest scrap of masthead trucks visible, guessing at where they might reappear.

"Buggered off to loo'rd once they spotted us," Lewrie opined with Mr. Dimmock. "If they had a lick o' sense, o' course."

"Bound for Toulon or Marseilles, perhaps, sir," the sailing master agreed. "But . . . be they French East Indiamen, they'd hope to get in-shore, finish at that L'Orient of theirs, on the Bay of Biscay and—"

"Silence, both of you," Braxton barked. "Speculate off duty, not on. We've work to do. Or hadn't you noticed, sirs?"

"Of course, sir," they almost chorused.

"*SAIL HO!*" the lookout shrieked. "*Four* points off t' *star*board bows! *Five* sail, same'z *afore*, there!"

"Running?" Braxton shouted back.

"Can't tell, sir!"

"Allow me to go aloft, sir," Lewrie bade, wriggling with curiosity. And to get away from Braxton for a few precious moments.

"Uhm . . . very well," the captain grudgingly allowed, giving him a grumpy once-over. Lewrie snatched his personal telescope from the bin-nacle-cabinet rack and dashed for the mizzen chains.

Up the ratlines on the windward side, where the ship's angle of heel made the ascent less steep, laying out on the futtock shrouds, then up and over the mizzen-top deadeyes onto the upper shrouds for the cross-trees, with *Cockerel* shrinking to a toothpick below him. A heaving, wal-lowing toothpick, and the mastheads swaying like treetops in a stiff wind.

They were almost hull-up to him, those unknown ships. Running downwind almost at *Cockerel*'s point-of-sail, with the wind large on their larboard quarters. Big, dark, bulky three-masters, as impressive as 1st Rates. There were winks of cloudy sunshine on their wide sterns, on transom windows, gilt galleries and an acre of glass. But they were not warships. They looked like *Compagnie des Indies* ships, stiff with price-less Asian cargoes, and loaded so heavily they wallowed in the sea like cattle on a boggy moor. *Cockerel* had fetched them hull-up, almost in the time it had taken Lewrie to scale the mast! They could not outrun her. Slow and logy as the squadron's line-of-battle ships were to the west, even they would overhaul them within the hour.

"Seen their like before, Gittons?" he asked the mizzen lookout, lend-ing him the heavy, shotgun-long telescope at full extension.

"Lor', sir! Indiamen, sure'z Fate. Too fancy t'be 1st Rates . . . e'en

Frog 1st Rates," he cackled. "Be some prize money comin' our way, by God, they'll be, Mister Lewrie. Whaww, though . . ."

"Where away?" Lewrie asked, knowing from Gitton's cautious tone there was trouble in gaining that fortune in prize money.

"Almos' dead on th' bows, sir . . .'at fifth sail? Abeam th' wind, almos' cocked up full-an'-by. 5th Rate, I say, sir. Big frigate."

Lewrie retrieved his telescope and swung it to the left. There was a large ship there, at right angles to their course, one of the big forty-four-gunned 5th Rates the French were building, with eighteen or twenty-four-pounders . . . the sort of frigate they might use to command a small overseas squadron. And she was already flying her national colours, the vertical stripes of blue-white-red of Republican France.

"Warship!" Lewrie bawled. "Deck, there! Frigate on our lee bow!"

He took hold of the standing backstay, slung the telescope on his shoulder, and half-slid, half-monkeyed his way back down, his legs clasped about the stay.

"A 5th Rate, sir?" Braxton demanded before his feet hit the deck. "A warship, sir? What about the others?"

"Indiamen, sir. With one warship for escort. They're running almost free on a landsman's breeze," Lewrie explained, panting with his exertion and his excitement. "She's bearing almost north, closehauled, to interpose. She'll cross our bows in a few minutes, sir."

Braxton tucked his hands behind his back and paced the windward side of the quarterdeck, a naval captain's inviolate sanctuary when he was on deck. Lewrie noted that Braxton's blunt fingers were twining and fretting.

"And the squadron, Mister Lewrie?" he grimaced, turning to look inboard to his officers.

"Uhm . . . coming up astern, sir. I didn't . . ." He flushed.

Petulance twisted Braxton's mouth; it looked like he had muttered *fool!* "Aloft, there! What of the squadron?"

"Courses 'bove t' horizon, sir!" the lookout shouted back. "Be line-abreast, starboard quarter, off t' wind, sir!"

God, one could espy their tops'ls from the deck, Lewrie thought! There they were, stretched out, bows-on to *Cockerel*, arrayed like beads on a string, a little sou'west of her stern. Were there to be a fight, they could bear off, or bear up to windward, and form line-of-battle. Or dash on, if Vice-Admiral Cosby ordered general chase, and run those Frog merchantmen to ground, one at a time.

"Mister Lewrie," Captain Braxton decided, snapping his fingers to summon him to the windward side. "We'll harden up, closehauled."

"Same course as yon forty-four, sir," Lewrie nodded in understanding. "Trading shots with her, though, sir . . . eighteen-pounders . . ."

"Are you a coward, as well as a fool, sir?" Braxton blustered.

"Sir, I am not!" Lewrie shot back. "I'm as ready as you, when it comes to fighting this ship. I wished to ask if you wanted to overhaul in her best gun range, sir, or lask down to her on a bow-and-quarter-line. Allow me to suggest we lask, sir, then haul our wind, cross her stern and rake her . . . sir."

Call me any kind of fool, or sham, he thought; but you *never* call me a coward, you bastard. Now you go too bloody far!

As if sensing that he *had* gone too far, Braxton stifled a belchlike flood of outrage which rose in his chest, and turned away.

"Closehauled, aye aye, sir," Lewrie parroted, going amidships. "Bosun, hands to the braces! Hard-sheets! Lay her full-and-by!"

He could see the French frigate from the deck by then, long and sleek, like a cut-down line-of-battle ship, a touch of poop, a bit of forecastle, with her courses well up over the horizon. She swung from dead on their bows to the starboard side, just forward of abeam as *Cockerel* turned nor'east. They would slowly overhaul, and head-reach her on this course, though a couple of miles out of gunnery range. Or their own. Alan expected her to haul her wind any moment. Surely the French lookouts could see the squadron's threatening tops'ls by then.

What a bloody wasted effort, Lewrie thought, his senses acute and calculating. He felt they should be hauling their wind, going for the Frog 5th Rate like a terrier, then nipping past her stern at close range. Give her a well-timed broadside, then dash on past to get at the merchantmen. Every ship in sight would share in the prize money if one or all of them were taken. But *Cockerel* was the only frigate present—the rest were too far to the south, or far to the north of the squadron. Their misfortune, he smirked! Out of sight, out of the running. And that was what frigates were for.

Cockerel barreled on, surging and slashing at the uncooperative sea, slowly head-reaching until the French warship was just a bit aft of abeam. They could turn now, go tearing down on her, and still pass within half a cable of her stern, if she held her course and did not shorten sail. Lewrie began to pat his foot in anxiety.

"Excuse me, sir," he asked, going back to windward to join his captain. "Should we not allow her four-points-free, so we may fall to loo'rd, onto her, sir?"

"It is my decision, sir. Now be still!" Braxton hissed, wheeling on him. "The squadron, sir, will daunt them. She'll haul wind, she can't trade fire with the liners. Attend to your duties, sir."

"Sir, should she haul her wind, there's still the Indiamen—"

"I gave you an order, *Mister* Lewrie!"

"Aye aye, sir."

"There, d'ye see, hah?" Braxton hooted with scorn suddenly. "She's falling off, at last. Turning to run! Now, Mister Lewrie . . . *now* you may haul our wind. Gybe, and steer sou'east."

"Aye aye, sir," he replied evenly.

Damme, another puzzle, he carped! Should be *due* east, by God; go right for 'em! This'll put us the same distance from the Indiamen, *or* the frigate. What's Braxton playing at?

"Bosun, prepare to wear to the starboard tack."

"*Wear*, sir?" Bosun Fairclough gaped from the waist below him.

"Aye, wear, Mister Fairclough," Lewrie repeated testily. "Stations for wearing ship! Main clew garnets . . . buntlines, there!" He called through the speaking trumpet. "Spanker brails, weather main and lee braces! Manned?"

Hands darted to the pin rails and fife rails to undo belays on the running rigging, to tail on and prepare to take a strain once the lines were free of all but the last over-under hitch on belaying pins.

"Come on, lads! Smartly, now!" he urged them. "*Manned*, damnyer eyes? Smartly, I said!"

"Drive 'em, bosun! Smartly!" Braxton interrupted. "Lay on yer starters!"

The hands *were* readying for a wear, but it was damn' slow work—handsome work—church work. Petty officers and midshipmen lathered the slow and the clumsy (and there were more than a few on the gangways who were suddenly struck clumsy, Lewrie noted!) with rope starters. The hands flinched, like flicked steers, as the starters cracked on their coats. But that didn't make them very much faster.

"Oh, Christ . . ." Lewrie whispered, seeing the game for what it was at once. "Come *on*, lads! There's a fortune in prize money downwind, so let's be *at* it! All manned? Haul taut! Ready about? Up mains'l and spanker! Clear away after bowlines! Brace in the after yards!" Lewrie turned to the senior quartermaster, and in a softer voice cautioned, "Handsomely does it. New heading, sou'east. Right! Up-helm, quartermaster!"

"Aye aye, sir."

"Overhaul weather lifts! Man the weather braces! Rise fore-tack and sheet!"

Cockerel fell off the wind, heeling harder to starboard, laying her shoulder to the sea, sloughing and snuffling foam as she lost way, and the sea gripped her more firmly. With the wind swinging rapidly onto her larboard quarter, growing finer and finer, Lewrie looked to the commissioning pendant aloft, then aft, judging the best moment to anticipate a stern wind. There!

"Clear away head bowlines, lay the head-yards square! Shift over jib fore-sheets! Come *on*, smartly, now! Move!" he fumed at the crew, whose efforts had turned so ox-slow, so hen-headed awkward.

"Jaysis, bloody . . . !" the senior helmsman yelped suddenly, and Lewrie turned his head to see the huge double wheel's spokes spinning like a Saint Catherine's wheel at a fair. The steering-tackle ropes bound 'round the wheel drum were sizzling and smoking as they unwound themselves! "No helm, sir, no helm!"

"Avast, there!" he called, trying to head off disaster. "Back the fore-sheets, flat 'em in! *Lee* braces, bosun, main and . . ."

Too late. *Cockerel* was across the eye of the wind, with her after and main yardarms angled to take a stern wind, the main and fore-courses smothered so far, but not for long. She carried a lot of weather-helm, and was going to round up. For a moment, her yards would luff ineffectually, then, as she swung her bows windward, they'd fill again— pressing *against* the masts and spars, snapping her upper masts like carrots, if they weren't quick about it!

This ought to be damned int'restin', Lewrie thought, with what felt like a stupefied calmness; we're going to *broach* this barge!

"Lee braces, damn you! Smartly! Let go weather braces!"

With a tremendous whooshing sound, much like a gargantuan bird, the spanker filled and flew across the quarterdeck overhead, dragging the men of the starboard after-guard, tailing on what was now a weather sheet, in a tug of war they could never win.

They let go, tumbling in a heap. They let *go*! The spanker was a slightly older design, a loose-footed trapezoidal sail suspended from a light wooden gaff, with the after-most, lower-most corner, the clew, the attachment point for the sheets. With a sharp crack, the gaff yard met the much heavier mizzenmast cro'jack yard, which directed the set of the mizzen tops'l and spread its foot. The spanker gaff shattered, of course, dangling half the upper length of the spanker like a duck with a broken wing, which let it swing further out-board to tangle in the larboard mizzen stays! Taken by surprise, the larboard sheetmen of the after-guard stood slack-jawed, and slack-fingered, and let the larboard sheet snake over the side, along with the weather sheet!

Both sheets, Lewrie goggled: *both* the bloody sheets?

"Heavy-haul on the braces, fore, main and cro'jack!" he howled as

Cockerel wallowed, now heeling to larboard. They *could* save their masts, if the bows could be got down. They *could* steer downwind without the rudder, for a time, if the hands were quick.

But the deck was already inclined over twenty degrees of heel, and the men were laid back almost parallel to the gangways. It wasn't clumsy, semi-mutinous theatrics now. They began to slip and fall, to go sprawling on their backs, to slide to leeward into the bulwarks as their bare feet lost purchase; or were dragged toward the pin rails as they tried to hold onto the braces, by the enormous pressure of wind on the sails which exerted tons of pull on the lines.

Cockerel groaned in outraged protest as she swung up a-weather, the wind rapidly clocking forward of abeam, laid over so far that water surged high as the gun ports on the lee side, and the breeching ropes of the starboard battery sang a taut torment. Masts, spars, rigging, hull . . . her wail was a chorus of danger, and the sea surged hungrily.

At least 'thout the spanker, Lewrie thought bitterly, we won't have weather-helm for long! Or masts, either, he concluded, hanging light-footed from the starboard mizzen stays by a death-grip.

The flatted-in jibs and fore stays'ls saved her, pushing down her bows, keeping *Cockerel* from broaching, though she lay hard over on her larboard side for what seemed like forever, her rudder quite ineffective, even if it *had* been attached to something. Alan whined with a brief terror as he looked *down* at the hungry ocean, at the image of course-sail yards dragging wakes in the sea! The ship creaked and moaned, with ominous sloshes and thuds echoing from below on the orlop deck. Round-shot tumbled from their nests along the hatch rims or the rope shot-garlands to bowl down alee and *thonk*! into bulwarks.

Then *Cockerel* rolled back upright, rebounding so quickly that he was flung hard up against the mizzen stays, even as she began to pay off the wind, at last. But she didn't come quite level after that; she was still alist to larboard. Cargo and ballast shifted, sure, Alan thought, as his feet at last found a place to stand, as he darted for the nettings overlooking the waist.

"Bosun!" he bawled, "Get below and set relieving tackle to the tiller head! All hands, secure from Quarters! Mister Scott, take the foc's'le and foremast, set the sprit-s'l, fore-tops'l and forecourse for a run. Main-mast, mizzenmast, there! Topmen aloft! Trice up and lay out! Brail up all sail! Clew up now, Mister Porter, Mister Thorne. Clew up the mizzen t'gallant, main course, main tops'l and t'gallant! Spanish-reef 'em, for now! After-guard, mizzen tops'l braces!"

They'd have to have the foresails for drive, and a lifting effect, making the stern heavier for a repaired helm. The mizzen tops'l could serve for steering, of a rough and clumsy sort. The rest of her square sail would be drawn up by the clew lines toward the yards which hung them, baggy and bat-winged, toward the tips of the yardarms, close and snug inward toward the masts . . . Spanish-reefed.

He dared allow himself at last a deep, shaky breath and a look aloft. Well, that didn't help his nerves much, he thought, blaring his eyes in wonder—there were t'gallant and top-mast shrouds flying free as the commissioning pendant up yonder, and the light upper masts were swaying a *lot* more than normal as *Cockerel* wallowed from side to side, her untended lift lines allowing the yards to droop a-cock-bill.

"What in the name o' God d'ye think yer playing at, sir!" the captain fumed as he made his way amidships of the quarterdeck. "Get the bloody hell outa my way, you brainless, cunny-thumbed . . . !" Captain Braxton screamed to all and sundry, shaking his fists as if he wished to bloody his knuckles on the quarterdeck gunners and after-guard.

"They're *firing* at us!" Midshipman Braxton shouted from aloft. "The French are firing at us, sir!"

The 5th Rate had rounded up abeam the wind, about four or five miles alee of *Cockerel*. The roar of her upper-deck guns could not be heard, of course, but they could see the puffs of gray-tan gunpowder erupt from her sides as the forty-four-gunned vessel delivered a slow, timed salute—a most mocking and derisory salute to their "seamanship"—before hauling her wind once more and loping away eastward to guard her convoy, which had used their entertaining diversion to sail away from harm, toward the Straits of Gibraltar.

Cackling their fool heads off, Alan thought miserably.

"Fowkner," he called to a senior hand of the after-guard. "Get aloft. Get a line on the spanker gaff—what's *left* of it— and haul it clear of the shrouds. Boat hooks, you men. Get the spanker sheets in-board, and ready to lower away. Mister Spendlove? Inform one of the bosun's mates to fetch out one of the stun'sl booms and 'fish' it to the broken spanker gaff."

"Aye aye, sir."

"You, sir!" Braxton snarled, hatless, his fists balled for a fight still, as he came to his first lieutenant. "Of all the stupid, inept—!"

"Steering tackle parted, sir," Lewrie tried to explain. "There wasn't much we could—"

"That you should have rerove completely before, you—!"

"Captain, sir," Lewrie replied, "you were there when we overhauled it. You said yourself you were satisfied—"

"You disputatious dog, sir!" Braxton shot back. "Think I can't see your game? Think I'm blind, do you? How convenient the hands, of a sudden, were struck—"

"Captain, sir," Mr. Dimmock interrupted from the other side, "I think a little calm is in order, sir. 'Least said, soonest mended' and all that? The hands, ye know . . . won't *do*, in their hearing, sir."

"I'll kindly thankee to keep out of this, *sir*," Braxton sneered. "I want your advice, I'll ask for it. Now, be silent."

"No, sir," Dimmock quailed, though determined to have his say, at last. "Not this time. You're saying Mr. Lewrie put the people up to it, is *that* your meaning, sir? And I say that is wrong, sir. Were it not for *his* quick wits, we'd have rolled the 'sticks' right out of her, sir. Frankly, Captain Braxton, *Cockerel*'s damn' lucky *somebody* kept their wits about 'em when perfectly sound steering-tackle ropes snapped, at the worst possible moment. Tackle you *did* inspect, sir."

Braxton seethed, turned red as turkey wattles, but realised he was in the wrong place to shout the dread word "mutiny." "How dare you, sir, *deign* to interfere!" he hissed, in a much more private, though much more threatening voice.

"There *may* be trouble 'mongst our people, sir," Dimmock told him in a mutter, "but I may swear to you on a stack o' Bibles, 'tis none of Mr. *Lewrie*'s doing."

Dimmock had such a way of canting his accents, of laying stress on innocuous words, that his meaning was quite clear at that moment; and quite accusatory, too. Though were his statements recalled at any court martial, verbatim, they could sound quite innocent. He'd as much as implied that the source of the crew's unrest lay solely with Captain Braxton. He'd further implied that when *Cockerel* had come nigh broaching, her captain had uttered no orders for her salvation.

"You, as well, sir?" Braxton sniffed, raring back with outrage.

"Sir, you *can't* believe that. We're all as—"

BOOM! From windward.

Windsor Castle had fired a forecastle chase gun to get *Cockerel*'s attention. She and the rest of the squadron were completely hull-up to them, and had been flying "Do You Require Assistance" for some minutes, until at last their admiral had become so exasperated at their lack of notice he'd ordered a gun touched off. The line-abreast warships were going to pass *Cockerel* close-aboard soon, as she staggered sou'east with the wind right up her stern, and they continued east-nor'east in chase of the French convoy. Some of them might have to alter course to avoid her, slowing that pursuit even more.

"From the flag, sir!" Midshipman Braxton screeched aloft. " 'Do You Require Assistance,' it reads, sir!"

"We can see *that* from the deck, damn you!" Lewrie hailed upward. "God help your slack arse, *Mister* Midshipman Braxton!" he vowed. He'd have the lad bent over a gun, should the Devil himself dare to cross him. "What reply do you wish to send, sir?" he asked the captain, in a more civil tone.

"No!" Braxton thundered. "We require no assistance!"

"Very well, sir. Mister Spendlove? You're free aft. Hoist a Negative."

"Aye aye, sir!"

"Might ease the starboard mizzen tops'l braces, Mister Lewrie," Dimmock advised, in his proper role of sailing master. "Haul taut on the larboard, and we may be able to pressure her 'round more east'rd."

"Thankee, Mister Dimmock. Should I attend to that, sir?" Alan asked the captain.

Braxton's mouth worked in anger. To fly up as lubberly as some first-time lake sailor in a dinghy . . . to completely ignore a signal of their flagship . . . ! His abiding wish that *Cockerel* distinguish herself as the best frigate in the Fleet was in shambles.

"I have the deck, sir," Braxton snarled at last. "Do you attend the purser below. We're alist, sir. Ballast has shifted, stores . . . I vow you've done quite enough for one day, sir."

"Aye aye, sir," Lewrie replied as chearly as he might.

"Whoo, neck-or-nothin' there, for a moment, hey, sir?" Banbrook the Marine crowed, fanning himself with his hat as he and O'Neal came up from the waist.

"On your way, see what's taking Mr. Fairclough so long to repair the steering tackle," Braxton continued.

"I shall, sir," Lewrie vowed, doffing his hat in salute.

"I say, Mister Lewrie, sir?" Banbrook nattered on, nearing their small gathering, completely unaware of any problems, now that the ship no longer appeared to be in danger of sinking.

"Might I suggest, Captain, sir, that the master-at-arms take a muster?" Lewrie dared to suggest. "Hard as we were slung about, it'd be a miracle were no topmen dashed over the side, sir."

"Umph!" the captain grunted, calling for his son to attend to it.

"Then I shall go below, sir," Lewrie said in parting.

"Uhm, Mister Lewrie, sir . . .'bout the whore-transport?" Lieutenant Banbrook inquired breezily. "All these repairs and wot-not . . . does this mean we miss our turn with her, sir?"

Good God, Lewrie thought, appalled; not *now*, you blitherin' . . . !

Captain O'Neal took Banbrook's arm to jerk him out of earshot, coughing fit to die—much too late, of course.

"The *what*?" Captain Braxton roared, wheeling to look at Banbrook with a mixture of utter loathing and complete incomprehension on his phiz. "The bloody *what*, sir?"

"The whore-transport, sir," Lieutenant Banbrook began gaily. "The one the wardroom told me about?"

A very tardy realisation struck the young Marine officer at last. "The one with the . . . uhm . . ." he stammered, blushing beet-red as he discovered himself the goat of their cruel jape. "Well, the . . . whores aboard? Who come alongside and . . . ?"

"Get off my deck! Get off my quarterdeck, you *useless* damn fool!" the captain screamed, again in full cry, and with a suitable target for his pent-up wrath. "I want this . . . tailor's dummy . . . under close arrest, Captain O'Neal! Under close arrest, sir!"

Time to bolt, Lewrie thought.

He made his way down a quarterdeck ladder, down the midships companionway hatch, safely out of screeching range, as the full fury of the captain's storm broke.

The first people he met as he attained the orlop deck were the ship's carpenter, Mister Dallimore, and his carpenter's crew, all of whom were hugging carline posts, and each other, sniggering and chortling.

" 'Hore-ship, megawd!" one of them wheezed.

"T'ain't funny, damn yer eyes," Lewrie snapped. "Look at this bloody mess, Mister Dallimore."

Huge water butts, salt-rations barrels, beer kegs, piled ship's stores . . . half the well-ordered stowage on the orlop was now lumbered loose to larboard. They'd be half the watch shifting it, the waisters and idlers, such as Dallimore's people, and probably require Marines to pitch in, too, to shift ballast in the bilges.

"Aye, sir. Sorry, sir," Dallimore tried to reply, though it was more like a strangling, sneezing sound.

"Get to work, there. Turn a hand, and stop that sniv'ling."

"Aye aye, sir."

Lewrie stomped stiff-legged aft to the tiller head in the midshipmen's cockpit. The bosun and a few senior able seamen were finishing up the first vital part of the repairs, stringing a block-and-tackle series to the tiller head so *Cockerel* could be steered from the cockpit, with helm orders relayed down from the quarterdeck. Reroving new rope and long-splicing old would take longer, before the wheel would serve.

"Whip-staff an' windlass, Mister Lewrie, sir," Fairclough told him, "but t'will do f'r now. We've our rudder back."

"Herdson, go on deck and inform the captain," Lewrie ordered.

"Aye aye, sir."

"Buggered, sir," Fairclough grunted, shifting his quid.

"When? How?" Lewrie demanded.

"Lookee 'ere, sir," Fairclough whispered, drawing his attention to a squarish hole in an overhead deck beam, hard by where one of the turning blocks for the tiller ropes would pass. "Looks t'me, sir, if a rat-trail rasp'z drove in 'ere, it'd chafe th' steerin' tackle sore, Mister Lewrie, ever'time a spoke'r two was put over. There's frayin' on the lines, aye, but . . . ye can see where some'un couldn't wait, an' cut it."

"Sometime after we went to Quarters, I suppose," Lewrie sighed.

"Aye, sir, else the 'younkers'da seed it bein' done, and . . ." Fairclough shrugged heavily, lifting thick brows in studied perplexity.

"And I didn't think they'd found leaders yet," Lewrie muttered softly. "Looks like they have, though."

"Aye, sir," Fairclough agreed, sounding shifty and truculent.

Damme, Alan recalled suddenly—Dallimore and his crew—they had a tool box with 'em! Rasps, punches, hammers, saws . . . and draw-knives! And I'd wager it wasn't just Banbrook's lunatick gaff set 'em to laughing! The newcomers, the lubbers, the waisters . . . they'd never think of such a stunt. It was the *experienced* crewmen who'd know how to disable the ship, who'd know how to make the landsmen slip, fall, or look clumsy. Who'd know just how far they could go without really disabling *Cockerel*, or endangering her or themselves.

"A word to the wise, Mister Fairclough," Lewrie said sternly, finding another conspirator in the way the bosun could not seem to meet his intent gaze. "And I believe you might just have a very good idea of who those . . . *wise* . . . are, hey? There will be no more. Once was the limit, and there . . . will . . . be . . . *no* . . . *more*! Because if there is another oc-curence, if things go farther, then it won't be floggings for the ones involved . . . it'll be courts-martial . . . and that means the noose for 'em. And if I'm forced to search out the man, or men, who hobbled our ship, I swear to God, I'll have their nutmegs off with a dull knife! Do you understand me plain, Mister Fairclough?"

"Aye, sir," Fairclough nodded sadly.

"Signal sent, read and understood, I believe, then," Alan said, "The crew's . . . and mine."

"Aye aye, sir."

"And a further word of warning, bosun. They'd best be the finest crew a captain could ask for from now on—else even he'll take notice and flay 'em to bloody rags, first, and 'scrag' 'em, second."

"Aye aye, sir," Fairclough huffed, looking as if he wished to be anyplace but there at the moment, getting flayed himself. "Best behaviour, sir."

Lewrie went back amidships to find the purser, his Jack in the Bread Room, a working party of gangway idlers, the sailmaker, carpenter and their crews, with Marine help, heaving nigh to ruptures to set the shambles right. He slithered and scaled the piles forward to the cable tiers for a better view.

There, somewhat separated from the hands, and in delayed but shuddery relief that *Cockerel* hadn't been dismasted, hadn't broached or rolled completely keel-up and killed him, he began to snicker to himself. He put a hand to his mouth, looking as if he was about to "cast his accounts" to Jonah, as an uncontrollable, lunatick fit of mirth quite took him. Lewrie was forced to duck deep into the cable tiers, amid the stinking mile of thigh-thick hawsers for privacy.

"Whore-transport!" he whispered to the darkness. And then he began to laugh himself sick, until his sides hurt.

CHAPTER 6

"That's a new'un," Capt. Sir Thomas Byard, captain of *Windsor Castle* and flag-captain of their squadron, remarked with a quirky look as he tugged his nose. "I must pass it on to our senior midshipmen to try out on the 'younkers.' *Much* droller than sending them on deck to hear the dogfish bark. And your Leftenant Banbrook is still confined to cabins?"

"Uhm, no, Sir Thomas," Lewrie replied, now that he had his wits back. "His close arrest ended after the second dogwatch."

"Hmm, good," Sir Thomas approved, then looked around the quarterdeck at *Cockerel's* frazzled professionals. "So!" he demanded, in a semijoshing tone. "Why could you not have done this well yesterday?"

To that, though, Lewrie could have no answer; nor could any of the officers or warrants.

A little after breakfast in the morning watch, HMS *Cockerel* had been ordered to close *Windsor Castle* and take station under the flag's lee, quickly followed by the dread summons, "Captain Repair on Board." Off Braxton had gone in his gig, with a thick canvas packet of ledgers and documents under his arm. But, most surprisingly, over had stroked Captain Byard's gig, and, once he had been received aboard with proper honours, and had been genteelly introduced, he had begun issuing most disconcerting orders.

"Strike topmasts, Mister Lewrie," he had snapped.

"Sir?"

"Strike topmasts, I said!"

For the rest of the morning watch, and through the entire forenoon, *Cockerel* had been exercised. They had stripped her down to the fighting tops and gantlines in a credible half-hour, then hoisted the topmasts, spars, sails and shrouds aloft once more. They had Beat To Quarters, heaved empty kegs over the side, and made passes at them with the great-guns booming. They'd gone through cutlass and musketry drill, officers and hands alike. Then it had been signalling practice, towing the ship with the boats, lowering the larboard bower into a cutter and pretending to anchor to it; they'd passed towing cables to the flagship then cast them free and winched them back aboard with the capstans. An hour had been spent making and reducing sail, reefing down for heavy weather, or setting "all to the royals," with stuns'ls on the fore and main course yards. Then they'd practiced fetching-to, wearing, tacking and weaving through the line of slow-plodding line-of-battle ships like a water-walker skittering 'round leaves in a fish pond. There had been fire drills, man-overboard drills, more going to Quarters and shooting at crates thrown over the side.

"Very good, Mister Lewrie, you may set your regular watch-bill."

"Aye aye, sir. Mister Scott, you have the watch. Bosun, pipe the change of watch. Larboard division on deck, starboard division to be relieved."

"Aye aye, sir!" Bosun Fairclough shouted back from the waist. He hauled out his silver bosun's pipe and began a shrill on the "Spithead Nightingale."

"Well done, Mister Fairclough!" Sir Thomas called down to him, after his pipe was done, and he'd bellowed his orders in a voice that could carry to windward in a full gale. "Still have it, I see."

"Aye, Sir Thomas, an' grand it be t'see ya once again, sir!"

"You were shipmates, Sir Thomas?" Lewrie asked, trying to find a polite way of mopping his streaming face with a handkerchief, after a long, trying morning of funk sweat.

"*Robust*, when 'Terrible Toby' had his first warrant, and I was fourth officer, sir," Sir Thomas chuckled. "I went shares to purchase his pipe. Damn' good man, is 'Terrible Toby'."

"And still is, Sir Thomas," Lewrie assured him.

"I am gratified to hear it, sir. What time do you make it?"

"Uhm . . . half-past noon, sir," Lewrie replied, after producing his watch from a fob pocket in his breeches.

"My apologies for delaying the hands' dinner, then. *And* 'Clear Decks and Up-Spirits.' Is your Captain Braxton one to 'Splice the Main-Brace,' Mister Lewrie?"

"No, Sir Thomas, he is not. So far, this passage, at least."

Alan imparted that with a straight face, biting his cheek.

"Pity. I should not wish to call for anything your captain may not allow. But . . . they did well, I thought. Did they not, sir?"

"Very well, Captain Byard," Lewrie agreed.

"Then it is my wish that you, this once at least, indulge me."

"Aye aye, sir. Mister Fairclough . . . Mister Husie? Capt. Sir Thomas Byard commands we 'Splice the Main-Brace'!"

That raised perhaps the first cheer ever heard aboard *Cockerel*. The daily rum issue would be full measure, with no deductions for men on punitive deprivement, no "sippers" or "gulpers" owed amongst them.

"Three cheer f'r th' flag-cap'm, lads!" Fairclough demanded of them, and it was lustily answered: "Hip hip . . . hooray!"

Toady, Lewrie thought cynically. Still . . . maybe he thinks Sir Thomas'll pluck him out of this damn ship. Hmm, might suit! *Toby*!

"You smile, Mister Lewrie?"

"Sorry, sir," Alan sobered at once. "It's just . . . hard to feature Mister Fairclough having a diminuitive of his Christian name."

"Called him 'Terrible,' 'cause he was a holy terror. Eyes in the back of his head, bad as a master-at-arms, was Toby. Taut hand. Firm but fair, though, once he'd seasoned," Sir Thomas reminisced with joy. "I seem to recall . . . one of our frigate captains told me of you, sir. I believe you have the good fortune to own an acquaintance with Keith Ashburn, of *Tempest*?"

"Keith, sir?" Lewrie grinned completely, his first of the day. "Aye, Sir Thomas, I do. Pray, sir, do you meet with him in future, I would be much obliged should you be able to give to him my warmest and most heartfelt regards. And my congratulations he's made 'post'."

"And his to you, sir, had it not slipped my mind until this instant," Sir Thomas nodded. "I believe, further, that he told me you had a so-briquet of your own, sir. 'Ram-cat' Lewrie, you're known as? How come you by that, sir?"

"Uhm . . . my choice of pet aboard ship, sir," Alan fumbled, feeling that was the safest explanation.

"Ah, I see. Lady Byard's fond of 'em. God knows why. Eat the dormice . . . heartbreak in the nursery, then! Give me a good hound any day," Sir Thomas grumped. "Odd. Mister Lewrie, other than fresh meat on the hoof, forrud in the manger, I can't recall any animals aboard. You do not, this commission, bring a pet with you?"

"Captain Braxton does not allow pets, Captain Byard."

"Devil you say," Sir Thomas snapped. "*Windsor Castle's* loaded with 'em. I've a pup of my own, from the last litter. Just the one, o' course, but . . . pets do wonders to improve the morale of the hands."

"I quite agree, Sir Thomas," Alan answered quickly.

"I also note . . ." the flag-captain said, pulling at his nose once more, "your crew labours in dead silence. E'en now . . . yonder. Now they're queued up for their grog, they're quiet as mice. Why?"

"Captain's orders, sir. He prefers it that way."

"Good practice, perhaps . . . no bawling aloft and back. A twitch of a halliard is good as a bellow. 'Specially in a raw-blowing gale, a tug on a brace is as good as a wink. Yet . . . any skylarking allowed, sir? 'Make and mend'? 'Rope-Yarn' Sundays? Hornpipes in the Dogs?'"

"Uhm . . . the captain is not completely satisfied with them yet, Sir Thomas," Lewrie squirmed, trying to find a safe answer, yet a way to impart *some* clue—and wishing, not for the first time, that a junior officer could just blurt out raw truth to a senior. "One may not presume to speak for one's commanding officer, sir, towards his motives, but . . . we're a new crew, with most of them landsmen and lubbers. And it may be that Captain Braxton is more used to a well-drilled 'John Company' crew. They have not yet met *his* high standards, Captain Byard."

"Raw men, that obtains in every ship in the Fleet, Mister Lewrie," Sir Thomas scoffed. "I cannot guess your captain's standards, either, but . . . were I a younger man, entrusted with such a smart frigate, I'd be over the moon that my crew had shaken down so nicely in such brief practice."

That did not require an answer, until Sir Thomas pressed him to give an opinion; all Alan could do was nod enthusiastically.

"Well, hard as I pressed, I can find no fault in *Cockerel*, sir. She's weathered my scrutiny smart as paint. All of you did."

"Thankee kindly for your good opinion, Sir Thomas."

"Keep it up, though," Byard warned in a softer, more intimate voice. "I don't need tell you my admiral's . . . wroth with you."

"Me, sir?" Oh, damme!

"With *Cockerel*, I should have said," Byard expanded. "A convoy . . . a deuced *rich* Frog convoy, and all that prize money, lost? And a French national ship allowed a laugh at the Royal Navy's expense. More to the point, sir, at Admiral *Cosby's* expense, d'ye see."

"I should imagine so, Sir Thomas," Alan nodded somberly.

"Deaf, dumb and blind, swanning about like a fart in a trance, and cunny-thumbed seamanship . . . dear Lord, sir!" Sir Thomas winced, as if recalling his vice-admiral's tirade of the day before.

It cheered Lewrie to imagine that tirade, though; surely Captain Braxton had spent the past six hours in a living Hell, and had gotten at least the afterglow of all that rancour heaped upon his head, soon as he'd gained Cosby's great-cabins.

"Had this ship not performed so well this morning, well, then . . . heads would have rolled, sir, indeed they would have."

Good God, I saved the bastard from dismissal, Alan wondered? Or did I save myself? No heads to roll, no brutal shaking up, then? What a bleak idea. More of the bloody same! With official sanction!

"Order your officer of the watch to close *Windsor Castle*, Mister Lewrie," Sir Thomas instructed. "Put us under her lee once more, and I shall take my leave of you."

"Aye aye, sir. Mister Scott! Stations for wearing ship. Close the flagship, in her lee."

"Very good, sir," Scott rejoined, then began bawling orders.

"That will give me a few minutes to speak with 'Terrible Toby.' Before I do, though . . ." Sir Thomas concluded with a searching glance.

"Aye, Sir Thomas?"

"Is there anything pertinent I might be remiss in asking, sir? Any matter you'd care to impart concerning *Cockerel*?"

Oh, Christ, Lewrie sagged in bewilderment; I can't! One simply can't; it's not on. That's insubordination, disloyalty. He *seems* as if he sees what's going on, but . . . ! It's not a direct order to tell him, it's only a request. God, make it order!

"I . . . there is nothing which strikes me at present, Sir Thomas," he was forced to intone, though keeping his eyes level and unblinking as he locked gazes with the flag-captain. And hoping the misery and the lack of enthusiasm in his voice might make the first shoe drop.

"I see," Byard harumphed softly. Neither disappointed nor disapproving, but with no hint of approbation for loyalty, either.

Leaving Lieutenant Lewrie to wonder just exactly what the Hell "I see" really meant.

Book IV

Quae classe dehinc effusa procorum bella!

Ah, what wars shalt thou see when the suitors pour forth from the Fleet!

—VALERIUS FLACCUS
Argonautica, Book I, 551–552

CHAPTER 1

It was surprisingly cool in the Mediterranean. So cool that charcoal braziers and a goodly supply of fuel had to be taken aboard once *Cockerel* had victualled at Gibraltar. Though the fires had to be extinguished at 9:00 P.M. each evening, along with all glims or lanthorns, their meek efforts did transform the wardroom to a fair measure of comfort, after a four-hour watch in a raw, chill wind.

Fluky, too, the Mediterranean was, compared to other oceans Lewrie had experienced. First of all, there were no tides to reckon with, which could be a blessing. Otherwise, though, he thought it a perverse bitch of a sea; there were perils enough in the irregular and unpredictable changes of currents that could put them miles out of any reliable "fix" of their position. And the winds were wickedly fickle, backing or veering as confusingly as the Bahamas in high summer. The frigate might beam-reach east with the wind steady to larboard in the forenoon watch, yet be taken aback by a capricious shift, and end the day beating closehauled on starboard tack to make the same easting.

The beaches they saw when close inshore on patrol were pebbly, rock strewn, with only a thin rime of sand beach, and many anchorages were treacherous, rocky-bottom holding grounds—or the worst sort of semi-liquid mud that swallowed anchors, but gave no secure purchase to the flukes.

And there were the dread Levanters—brisk easterlies arising off Turkey, that could roar down in a twinkling with no high-piled bit of storm-cloud warning. At least the Siroccos out of Moorish Africa down south, which could arise just as quickly, were prefaced by bluffs of hazy, sand-coloured cloud fronts, which appeared as substantial as an arid landfall's mountains.

*   *   *

Positively frigid, not cool, was the most apt word for the ship's mood, though. Following the crew's brief moment of rebellion, and Captain Braxton's return from the flagship with his face suffused as a strangled bullock, floggings had abated, though not ended. Some men still had to go to the gratings for real, not imagined, offences. When they did go, their alloted number of lashes still remained high. But Lieutenant Braxton walked smaller, and morosely bitter, about the other commission and warrant officers, no longer the raging pit bull. Neither did the younger Braxton midshipmen tear through the ship, cackling with glee in their hunt for victims, though victims they still discovered, among the foolhardy and the stupid.

What was most surprising to all was the sea change in Captain Braxton. He was rarely seen on deck, and kept to his great-cabins for the most part. Most mystifyingly, those abundant occasions which had summoned him forth in the past, fretful to supervise the least evolution, looming ominously over junior officers and hands alike until they were done to his satisfaction—those he now waved off, and left to his subordinates, unless it truly was serious enough to endanger the ship.

When Lewrie reported to him now, Captain Braxton seemed careworn and spent, as if command of a King's Ship was something with which he could no longer be bothered. Their relationship, never of the best, had degenerated to a stiff, icily formal and punctilious politeness. A rigid nicety between two men of the merest acquaintance, both with the manners of lords, an observer unfamiliar with the situation might have concluded. Yet Lewrie could sometimes espy the quick-darting resentment of old in his glare, hear the tiniest rasp of abhorrence in the man's tone—as if Captain Braxton were biding his time, waiting for some unguarded moment when he could drop his sham of formal politeness, and get his own back.

And the hands . . . well, they were as efficient as ever they had been, on their best days, that is. They still performed their labours in silence. Yet, in the second dogs before sunset, on the mess deck, some now dared to jape and raise their voices to a somewhat normal level. Lewrie was pleasantly surprised, now and then, to hear the scrape of a fiddle, the peeping of a flageolet, a chorus of rough male voices harmonising over an old song, or a single shaky tenor lilting rhapsodic. Below decks—never on the weather deck—*Cockerel* sometimes softly trembled to the stamp of bare, horny feet, as old hands taught new hands the way to do a true tar's hornpipe.

Each Sunday after divisions inspections and a perfunctory Divine Service, there was now—if only because the flagship decreed it—a "Make and Mend" in the day watches (weather and duties permitting) and once a month in the dreary three months which had followed, there had been ordained a "Rope-Yarn Sunday," a whole day in which the crew caulked or yarned, slept or chatted, repaired clothing and hammocks, carved snuff boxes and brooches out of dried chunks of salt meat (which took a high gloss and lasted long as most woods!), made ship models, or intricately woven twine articles—coin purses, belts and bracelets, brooches, rings and knife lanyards.

With such until-then unknown ease, they should have seemed a happier lot, now they were treated like an experienced and trusted ship's company. But they were not. Their grudge against the Navy, and the captain, was by then too deep. The damage done could not be undone in three months, and their resentment would continue to fester. They would serve the ship, yes . . . but nothing could make them glad about it.

As first lieutenant, Alan was alarmed by their continuing bad mood, almost as much as he had been by their earlier, bitter silence. A crew could be cowed into trembling obedience for only so long before an explosion occurred; they had proved that! Yet a crew allowed too much indiscipline by a slack captain was just as bad, and would result in much the same sort of explosion, if they thought they could get away with anything that entered their heads. Look at Bligh after his long idle months at anchor at Otaheiti, Lewrie thought!

Whatever had transpired aboard *Windsor Castle*, whatever reason for Captain Braxton's indifference, and the sudden abatement of his too-harsh taut-handedness, this particular stewpot, lidded too long, had been relieved much too quickly. It had not boiled over, thanks be to God . . . but it still could.

For Braxton's recent aloofness from the ship's company, and the seeming disdain he now had for how his juniors ran *Cockerel*, was sign to the crew that they had won some sort of victory over him. Let them think they had the upper hand, even for a moment, and they would lose respect for all authority.

Even a junior such as Lewrie knew that a man could not command a King's Ship inconsistently, blowing cool one day and hot the next, being harsh and tyrannical one moment and gentle and considerate as a mother with her babe another day. It sowed confusion and disrespect. At the moment, though, *Cockerel's* captain pretended to command, and the crew pretended to obey him.

Leaving Lewrie and the rest in a worse predicament as the only enforcers of authority, the ones who were forced to use the lash and restrictions to prevent the men from believing that their lot could be changed.

Sadly, Alan concluded that the tiny, too-clever "mutiny-ette" should have been the entire raucous show, complete with brass bands and fireworks, a real cutlass-waving rebellion. Or it should never have happened at all. At least, the first instance would have been put down from without, Braxton court-martialed and found responsible, and no matter the blight on one's career, it would have been over and done with, and he would be in another ship, the hands parcelled out—those not hung in tar and chains from Gibraltar gibbets until their bones fell apart—to other ships as well, where they would find new captains who weren't brutes, and would finally discover what pleasure it could be to serve under someone firm, but fair.

In the second instance, though, there had been no way to avoid it happening, not with—

"Oh, the Devil with it," Lewrie muttered sadly, taking stock of the world, far aft by the taffrails once again. "Thankee, Jesus! We need a little help here. 'Cause just when I think it can't get any darker, here we are . . . in the darkest!"

CHAPTER 2

"Penny postman," Captain Braxton sneered in disgust once he had clambered back aboard. He bore more packets than those he'd taken with him when he'd departed to the summons of "Captain Repair on Board" from HMS *Victory*. "Here, Mister Lewrie, these, I'm told, will come in handy for cooperation with our new . . . *allies*. See the officers of the watch and the midshipmen have 'em learned, quickly."

"Our new allies, sir?" Lewrie inquired.

"Signals books," Braxton harumphed sourly, "so we may talk with the Goddamned Dons!"

"We're allies with Spain . . . I see, sir," Lewrie replied levelly, though it was hellish hard to fathom how *that* had come about. After so many years of war, mistrust, condemning each other as either heretics to Catholicism or brisket-beating papist devils.

For all we hate 'em, since Drake and Raleigh's days? The Armada and all, Lewrie thought? Englishmen burned at the stake, tortured by the Inquisition, hung as pirates . . . well, some of 'em *were* pirates, o' course . . .

"Is the ship ready in all respects for sea, Mister Lewrie?"

"Aye, sir," he was relieved to be able to announce.

"Then we shall weigh at once," Braxton ordained. "We're bound to Naples. Dispatches for the British ambassador. Crack on all sail once round Europa Point, commensurate with the weather. Inform Mr. Dimmock he is to plot us the most direct course, twixt Corsica and Sardinia."

"Aye aye, sir! Bosun! Pipe 'All-Hands'! Stations for weighing anchor and getting underway!"

And, he thought sadly, so much for even finding out if we've any mail from home, or getting a chance to explore fabled Gibraltar!

*   *   *

It was a rough passage. Days of the Mediterranean's usual fluky winds, glowering skies, wind and rain, at least once or twice a day, between tantalising glimmers of sunlight. Butting into Levanters with green seas breaking over their frigate's beakhead and forecastle, and seething in foaming off-white sheets of water on the gangways and gun deck, soaking through the planking joins, soaking through the gaps in pounded oakum insulation and tarred seams, to drizzle clammy and cold on swaying hammocked off-watch sleepers, or the mess tables when men fed. Even the wardroom was not spared. Everyone was chilled and miserable, with no chance to dry out bedding or a change of clothing from one watch to the next. And this was only late June!

Occasionally, though, the winds veered more abeam, the skies cleared somewhat, and the dank below-decks and upper works steamed in sunshine, and *Cockerel* laid so thick a mist about her from drying timbers that she fumed as if on fire. Then she could crack on eastward, her shoulder to the sea, and lope like the lean ocean greyhound that she was across what the classic poets called "a wine-dark sea," power and wind humming in the rigging, her quick-work hissing and drumming as she ploughed impatiently over wavecrests, furrowing ocean to a wide frothing swath on either beam.

That was the kind of sailing that sometimes made it all worthwhile, that furious bustling, that paean to Neptune singing aloft and the dun sails stretched taut as drumheads, perfectly angled—for a time, only a time on any wind and sea—a ship making the best of her way, on her best point of sail, quick-stirring and alive.

Welcoming, warmer (well, to be frank, downright hottish) was the Bay of Naples, where they dropped anchor a week later, in the lee, so to speak, of that fuming ogre of ill repute, Vesuvius, a stone-toss away from the ruins of ancient Roman Pompeii.

As something of a classical scholar in his pre-Navy days, at a myriad of schools (and were one *exceeding* charitable about those scholastic attainments, mind), Lewrie was entranced. Who'd have thought, he asked himself, that he would ever have a chance to actually see the places mentioned in his dull, bone-dry Latin recitations? That Roman imperial translations would ever be anything more than garbled verbs, incorrect genders and tenses . . . and canings on his bottom? Yet here he was . . . here *it* was, before his eyes, a city so Roman . . . ! He half-expected it to be a phantasm, sort of like having an ancient statue in the entry hall become animate and begin carping about the temperature, it didn't seem real. All he had to do was wake, or blink . . .

Even before the best bower had been let go, and the kedge rowed out, even as they sailed into the Bay of Naples on a tops'l breeze, he thought the place magical, innately more inspiriting than any of the other places he'd seen so far in the Mediterranean. Anchored a bare quarter-mile offshore of the main harbour and the quays, Naples seemed to teem with an open, exuberantly cheerful, elbowing and dodging zest.

Fishing smacks, oddly rigged and exotic, looking as if they had not changed one iota since their like had been carved in Greco-Roman bas-reliefs, ghosted about *Cockerel*. At the quays, fantastic Arabic-looking merchantmen and coastal traders lay stern-to to the piers, almost ashore on the harbourfront roadways, sporting short masts and long lateener booms, garishly painted, with eyes below their bows to guide them home.

Music, hubble-bubble, the screaks and clangs of wheeled commerce, and soft, liquid foreign jabber drifted offshore from the many open-air wine bars and cook shops, from chandlers' stores and warehouses.

So, too, did enticingly alien aromas of cooking, of unknown but beguiling, savoury spices and dishes he'd never tasted. He felt his saliva froth, after six months of plain-commons ship's fare. He could almost hear eggs sizzling as they first struck a hot pan, the succulent juices dripping from fresh meat onto coals . . . the cheery gurgle of wine, aromatic and purply red, as it was poured. Fresh wines that hadn't been jogged about on the orlop deck; and were Neapolitan wines cheap, well . . . they probably were still fresher and more appetizing than the wardroom's cheap clarets and bumboat ports from Lisbon, or the purser's thin and sour by-the-keg issue wines they'd been forced to buy— Black Strap (a bilious, tannery-tasting red) and Miss Taylor (a hocklike white that could stun barnacles). And they would be clearer than ship's wine, all cloudy with wave-stirred lees.

Food! Fresh, hot food! An entire new cuisine that had nothing to do with bland English ordinaries, something beyond the regimen of over-boiled or overroasted salt meat, rank from a brine cask. Or the dessicated, reconstituted "portable" Navy soup!

"Boat, sir?" Mister Fairclough asked, breaking his gastronomic fantasies. "Row 'bout an' square th' yards, sir?"

"Aye, bosun. And keep the bumboats off us. Captain's gig?"

"Unner th' starboard mainmast chains, sir, ready t' go."

"Very well, carry on."

The local bumboats, aswarm already, hovering to either beam. The jobbers and pimps were shouting their wares, waving straw-covered jugs or long, thin stone bottles, bragging on their doxies, waiting for the "Easy" pendant to be hoisted.

And what fetchin' doxies, too, Lewrie thought, after a peek at his watch, and a frown at what might be keeping Captain Braxton below.

Bountiful, sloe-eyed, raven-tressed young girls in almost every boat . . . not an artificial blonde in sight! Smooth, dusky olive shoulders bared by low-cut peasant blouses, shapely (mostly) lower legs in view below the hems of bright-satin-shiny and elaborately embroidered skirts, clad in white cotton or silk hose. Some were tricked out with parasols, garish hats, tarted up in castoff sack gowns, but in hues never seen in staid old England. They waved, too, giggling and cooing at *Cockerel's* love-starved hands, hawking their own delights with all the open and amourous airs such as Lewrie imagined the ancient Romans might, at one of their pagan fertility festivals!

"Christ!" Lewrie moaned softly, in a half-strangled and heartfelt *cheep* of lust. And shuddering with how intense that sudden bout of lust felt! Six long months at sea, six long months apart from home and hearth, from bedding and . . .

No, I dasn't, he cautioned himself; I cannot! Seven years I'm wed, and damn' *well*, too. Father of three, for God's sake. Times are diff'rent now, besides . . . I'm first officer, there's an example to set for . . . I'm an example to . . .

To just bloody *whom*? his passions countered querulously.

No, I'm past thirty, I'm past all that. The others'd talk, and it'd get back to . . . well, maybe it *wouldn't*. Ah, but the captain, damn 'is eyes! Hates me worse than cold, boiled mutton. I doubt he'd give me leave to set a single *foot* ashore, this commission, just to be bastardly about it . . . Well, damme, where is the old turd, after all?

Captain Braxton had been on deck all during their foul weather, as spooky as Saint Elmo's ghost in his white tarpaulins, a grim, brooding spectre, far aft of the helm. Fair weather times, though, and most happily the last day or two, he'd all but abandoned the quarterdeck to his juniors, which had made their brisk passage even more joyous. Pop his head up over the coaming of his private, after companionway ladder now and again, between day-sleeps to snore off his silent foul-weather vigils, perhaps . . . like his son Hugh coyly playing "Peep-Eye."

Yet the ship was anchored bow and stern, her sails furled, and the quarterdeck awnings were strung for cooling shade, and his boat was waiting, with still no sign of him. The glazed panels of the skylight coach-top aft of the wheel were still closed snug. It would be stuffy in the great-cabins, Lewrie knew for certain; stuffy as Sunday dinner with the in-laws. What could be keeping him?

"I wish to see the captain, Corporal Scarrett."

"Aye, sir," the Marine sentry nodded, slamming his musket butt on the deck and barking out, "Fuhst awf'cer, SAH!"

No reply from within the gundeck entry. Lewrie and Corporal Scarrett exchanged puzzled frowns.

"Captain, sir?" Lewrie called again. Still no answer. Lewrie opened the doorway and stepped into the shuttered gloom of the narrow passage between the chartroom and the dining coach.

"Mister Lewrie, really, sir . . ." Mr. Boutwell, the captain's clerk, snapped fussily, as he came bustling forrud to confront him.

"Mister Boutwell, the ship is moored, and the captain's gig is in the water, ready to carry him ashore," Lewrie waved off impatiently. "He's dispatches for the British Ambassador, letters to—"

"Ahem," Boutwell coughed into a plump fist. "Sir, How . . . Captain Braxton is not well."

Thankee, Jesus, Alan delighted to himself!

"You've summoned Mister Pruden, the surgeon?" he asked, though, with seeming, and becoming, sudden concern. "Is it . . . serious?"

"Well, sir . . . 'tis hardly a matter for a ship's surgeon, Mister Lewrie," Boutwell countered, blocking his way as Alan tried to get past him, laying a civilian-soft writer's fist on his chest.

"Unhand me, sir!" Lewrie hissed. "Damn your blood, what ails him that's not serious enough for the surgeon, but keeps him from his duty? I have to see for myself. To ascertain how bad it is, and how long he may be incapacitated."

"Really, Mister Lewrie . . ." Boutwell whined, all but wringing his hands as Lewrie shouldered him aside. He, in desperation, seized Lewrie's arm to impede him.

"I warned you to keep your hands off me, sir!" Lewrie snapped, though stopped for another moment. "I'm an English gentleman, *and* a sea officer. People've been flogged for less. 'Specially aboard this ship! Now, what ails him, sir?"

"Uh . . ." Boutwell deflated, withering in stature, without the partition to the day cabin. "Sir, Captain Braxton served many years in the Far East. There, I fear, he once contracted malaria. It comes upon him now and again, as an ever-recurring fever. Once took, you know . . . of *course*, you do, Mister Lewrie! *You* were in the East, too. You've seen how it takes a man."

"I have to see him, Mister Boutwell," Lewrie insisted. "Fever or no."

"Very well," Boutwell surrendered, opening the partition door.

A fetid, sick-bed odour struck his senses at once. There lay Captain Braxton, swaddled in every blanket he possessed, tucked in as snug as a baby's swaddles in the thick coverlet, with his dark blue watchcloak and foul-weather tarpaulin atop. Shivering like a drowning victim fresh plucked from an icy shipwreck. His steward was setting out a fresh cedar bucket by the side of the hanging cot, and grimacing manfully as he lifted the used one at arm's length to dump its gruesome contents out the transom sash window, the only one that was left open, and that only for the length of his duty. A sea-coal fire was fuming in a brazier nearby, making the great-cabin's bed space a breath from Hell itself.

"M . . . more coals!" Braxton managed to say between chattering teeth. "Bloody Jesus, I'm so cold!"

"Sir?"

"W . . . what . . . Devil you want, s . . . sir! Ge . . . get out! This instant!" Braxton growled from wobbly jaws.

"Mister Boutwell, I must insist the surgeon see him," Lewrie sighed, though not without a measure of secret glee. If Braxton got sick enough, and if official notice of his condition was taken among higher authorities, surely he'd be relieved of his command! Another promising officer, a commander, say, or one of Hood's admiral's flag-captains, would suddenly be "on his own bottom," in a fine frigate!

"He's had the headaches, the sweats yet, Mister Boutwell?" Lieutenant Lewrie inquired.

"Last evening, sir," the clerk informed him.

"And you did not think to inform me *then*, sir?" Lewrie chid him sternly. "Damme, we're talking about a King's Ship, sir. Had we been brought to action by a French vessel, run into another gale . . . and us, unknowing . . . ! You carry personal, family loyalty too far, sir. You are *not* an officer who may make such a decision."

"Lieutenant . . . the second officer bade me—"

"And *he* has no right to conceal anything from me *either*, sir! An offence worthy of a court martial, I'm bound."

"Mister Lewrie, this mustn't . . . I mean, surely, you cannot think of . . ." Boutwell pleaded, though on very shaky ground, now that tables had turned on him. "You have your diff'rences, but for God's sake . . . !"

"T . . . toddy!" Braxton whinnied from deep within his covers, oblivious to their spat. "Hot!"

His steward ran to fetch a toddy, stirring in powdered quinine, "Jesuit's Bark," the rob of lemons, hot water . . . and a goodly dollop of brandy. Eager as Captain Braxton wished to seize it and drain it, his hands shivered so badly his steward had to prop him up and almost spoon it down him, ounce at a time.

Lewrie noted that there were several empty bottles loose atop the wine cabinet in the day cabin. The doors stood open, revealing a suspicious scantity. The captain had depleted his personal stores in private, thinking to ward off, or burn out, any onset of fever.

Barrel fever, more like it, Lewrie thought disgustedly. Hearty as he liked his spirits, good as any English gentleman, the sight of a fellow who should know better, gunn'l's awash, was repulsive.

"He'll not cure himself with spirits, Mister Boutwell," Lewrie told the cringing clerk. "You take that right away from him, now, and you *will* admit the surgeon, at once. Thank God we're in port, and if anybody knows malaria, it's Dons and Dagoes. We may have to send for a physician from shore, if he gets bad enough, and well you know it. Either that or he dies, if Mister Pruden's physick fails us. Quinine and hot water, only. Sugar it to make it palatable, if you must, but no more brandy, nor any other drink. Get out those dispatches. They have to go ashore, and they're late enough already."

"You will not . . . ?" Boutwell asked hopefully.

"Let him get back on his feet first, sir, if he will," Lewrie sighed, "but we must deal with your conniving and Lieutenant Braxton's lack of sense later. Now, fetch me those dispatches."

"Yes, sir," Boutwell cringed.

"That's 'Aye Aye, sir,' Mister Boutwell! Even the Marines say it. You've been aboard ship long enough to learn our ways, surely."

"Aye aye, sir," Boutwell parroted meekly, worriedly.

CHAPTER 3

"Sir William will see you now, Lieutenant Lewrie," the major-domo informed him with the lofty, nose-high air common to all clerks to important men. Lewrie rose from his comfortable chair, shot his cuffs, settled sword and waistcoat, and followed the mincing twit into the presence of his betters.

"Sir William, Your Excellency, allow me to announce Lieutenant Lewrie, Royal Navy . . . of the *Cockerel* frigate, sirs. Lieutenant Lewrie," the flunky said smoothly, with a grandiloquent gesture toward the two elegantly garbed gentlemen, chummily seated to either side of a massive marble-topped desk. "Sir William Hamilton, His Britannic Majesty, King George the Third's ambassador-plenipotentiary to the Court of the Kingdom of Naples and the Two Sicilies. Further allow me to present you to His Excellency Sir John Acton, Bt., Prime Minister of the Kingdom of Naples and the Two Sicilies and to His Majesty, King Ferdinand the Fourth."

"Sir William, Milord Acton . . . Your Excellencies," Lewrie began, making a deep bow and leg to them, hat over his heart. "It is my honour to convey to you, Sir William, most immediate dispatches from Admiral Lord Hood."

And thank God for malaria, he thought, smug over this opportunity to make the acquaintance of important people, thankful for a chance to "sport showy." And doubting if Braxton could have pulled it off with as much innate grace. He stepped forward and laid his canvas-wrapped, tape-and-riband-bound sealed packet on the vast expanse of pale gray marble. He was glad to be shot of them, frankly; they were weighted with grape-shot, and were the very Devil to carry for long.

"Ahum . . . hah," Sir William began, drawing the bundle to him and cutting the tapes with a desk knife, after assuring himself that seals had not been tampered with. "And where is our illustrious Admiral Hood at present, Leftenant Lewrie?"

"We departed Gibraltar a week ago, Sir William. The fleet was at that instant putting to sea. Twenty-two sail of the line. Our orders were that we might rejoin off Cape Cicie or Cape Sepet . . . somewhere off Marseilles or Toulon." He had had time to glean that much from the separate set of orders, also weighted and marked FOR CAPTAIN HMS COCKEREL'S EYES ONLY. Under the circumstances, he'd *had* to look at them!

"You are rather junior to command a frigate, I am thinking," Sir John Acton commented as Ambassador Hamilton read his dispatches, humming to himself, his ancient patrician face creased with flickerings of concern or satisfaction, by stages.

"I am merely first officer, Your Excellency. I regret to say that my captain, Captain Howard Braxton, was . . . uhm, detained aboard by ship's business. Else he should have—"

"Really," Sir John drawled, lifting one expressive brow. "Such would have been unthinkable when I was at sea. A captain, entrusted with matters of such import, and he fails to present himself, sends a junior in lieu of himself? Pardon, but I have never heard the like."

Sir John Acton sounded English, sort of; he was fluent, but his voice had a more Mediterranean lilt to it, a subtle shading, a lack of true English syntax and usage. Perhaps from long custom among Dagoes, Lewrie thought.

"You served in the Royal Navy, did you, milord?" Lewrie asked, to finesse the subject.

"Ah, no, I never had that honour, sir," Acton sighed wistfully. "I speak of my time as an officer in the French Navy."

Bloody Hell, Lewrie gawped! And this . . . Frog!—well, he's an English baronet—*half*-a-Frog is sittin' in, spying, hearing all, at the side of an English ambassador? What sort o' business they *do*, in Naples?

"Uhm, hah . . ." Lewrie flummoxed.

"I alarm you, sir?" Acton all but simpered. "I was born of English parentage, but in France. Naval matters . . . diplomatic duties . . . I am regretful to say, I have never been in England. I served also with the Tuscan and the Neapolitan navies as well, before rising to the office of prime minister here in Naples. Tell me, Lieutenant Lewrie, did your gallant Lord Hood also entrust you—your captain, pardon—with any messages to His Majesty, King Ferdinand the Fourth?"

"Uhm, no sir . . . Your Excellency . . . none I'm aware of, unless a letter is in that package, to be relayed to you through Sir William."

Lewrie felt a sudden urge to fan himself with his hat and tug at his too-tight neckstock. So much for "sportin' showy," he sighed.

"Ah, surely, though," Sir John sighed in concert, all but biting his thumbnail, and turning a hopeful eye on Sir William. "As events develop . . . but no? How distressing."

"Sir John, old fellow, Admiral Lord Hood would certainly not be guilty of presuming to speak beyond his brief," Sir William assured the younger man. Lewrie thought Acton was in his late thirties or early forties; Sir William Hamilton in a spry sort of sixties. "Events are, as you say, developing quite nicely, in point of fact. Our ambassador to His Most Catholic Majesty in Madrid, Lord St. Helens, encloses his latest success. The Spanish are in, at last."

"Aha!" Sir John smiled, gaining enthusiasm.

"We were given signal books, so we might speak any Spanish ship we met, Sir William," Lewrie offered.

"And did you meet any, Leftenant Lewrie?" Sir William smiled.

"Aye, sir . . . a whole fleet of them. Seventeen sail of the line, with frigates, on our passage here. On the second of July."

"Already at sea, aha!" Sir John exclaimed.

"Uhm, on their way back to Cartagena, Your Excellency. Their hoist said they had scurvy aboard, and were running short of rations. They'd been at sea a little less than two months."

"Aha," Sir William sighed, much less cheered by that news. In point of fact, quite deflated.

Lewrie shrugged his comment; what could one expect of Dons? A damn' fine-looking fleet of ships, but the men . . . ! The officers, and such. Scurvy? After less than two months at sea? Puhl-lease!

"Yet Admiral Lord Hood is by now, surely, off Toulon and Marseilles," Sir William continued. "To blockade the ports, bottle up the French Mediterranean fleet in Toulon . . . or bring it to battle, should they come out. He has succeeded in joining his scattered squadrons and uniting them as one. Twenty-two sail of the line. And, Sir John, we both know, as does Leftenant Lewrie, that when the Royal Navy gets to sea, there they stay. I am most confident the Spanish fleet will, after replenishing stores at Cartagena, be able to join him off Cape Cicie, creating an irresistible force. Or carry ashore, as . . . hmm."

"Une flotte respectable, Sir William, mon cher . . ." the prime minister blathered on for a moment, "as we tentatively agreed."

Oops, ah shit, Lewrie cringed; time for me to scamper. They want to talk something secret, and I shouldn't be privy to it. Aye, look at the scowl on Hamilton's phiz.

"Your Excellencies, I think I'd best take my leave now. Our ship will of course remain at Naples until you may have dispatches for us to carry to Lord Hood, Sir William. May one of your aides introduce me to your embassy's shore agent? I would like to arrange for wood and water, and for our purser to replenish stores."

"Leave for your crew here in Naples, as well, Leftenant?"

"Well, uhm . . ."

There came a knock on the door, and the flunky reappeared, most hideously humble, bowing and scraping. "Excuse me, Your Excellencies, but this note just came for the naval person? Quite urgent, I think."

The *naval person*, indeed, Lewrie fumed as he opened the note!

"Christ," he whispered, wiping his brow. Mr. Pruden had looked in on Captain Braxton, and his prognosis was grim. The captain needed a physician, instanter, else . . .

"Trouble aboard your ship, sir?" Sir William asked.

"The captain, Sir William," Lewrie had to confess. Damnit all, he would be the *very* last to miss Braxton, should he pass over . . . do a little hornpipe of grief, perhaps? . . . but he couldn't ignore this. That'd be as much as if he'd murdered the man, by neglect!

"He is ill, Sir William. Our surgeon urgently requests a physician, someone experienced with malaria. An old fever, come back—"

"Aha, so that is why you present yourself in his stead!" Acton exclaimed with sudden understanding, clapping his hands, foreignlike. "You wished to save his honour, not knowing how sick he was. Hoping he is better on the morrow, hein? You must be très . . . *very* loyal to him, I am thinking. How admirable. Does he not appear so, Sir William? And to inspire such loyalty . . . what a remarkable man his captain must be!"

Bloody Hell, are *you* dense as marble, Lewrie gawped to himself.

"Such loyalty towards one's superiour is a given, which goes in our Royal Navy without notice, Sir John," Ambassador Hamilton boasted gruffly, though with a soft twinkle in his eyes. "I do allow, though, that such a touching and fiercely protective loyalty as the leftenant manifests towards his captain may only be construed as the merest indication of Leftenant Lewrie's true qualities. Which I find, sir, are as commendable and admirable as ever I did see in an English gentleman."

"But, I merely . . ."

Shut *UP*, fool, he warned himself! Aye, give a dog a good name! They want to think well o' me, then who am I to complain?

"I merely . . . you are too kind, Sir William," he said instead, all but scuffing a toe in modesty, as he strove to evince a seemly and humble blush. The irony of the situation, and that too-tight neckstock, helped, as he ducked his head like a stableboy.

"I insist, Sir William, that you allow me to suggest the offices of signor dottore Spadolini to see to your captain," Acton offered.

"Your court physician?" Sir William posed dubiously. "Surely, with Her Majesty so near her time, ahem . . . still racked with grief over the death of her dear sister . . . perhaps it might be better were my own physician, dottore Granuzzo, to attend him. Else, we might lose an heir to the throne. We could have him moved here, to Palazzo Sessa."

"Perhaps it might be best, Sir William, to have your physician come out to the ship first," Lewrie countered, fighting a smile over the thought of Braxton being physically removed from his ship, of coming to his senses ashore, and wondering if *Cockerel* had mutinied once more, and sailed off and left him! "He may be too ill, for a time, to be moved."

"I will see to it, at once, Leftenant," Sir William announced, picking up a tiny china bell to ring for a servant. "In either case, your ship will remain in port, anent your captain's health . . . and how certain pending matters of state . . . uhm, develop. And what dispatches I may have, regarding those selfsame developments, for Lord Hood."

"I, and *Cockerel*, are at your disposal, Sir William," Alan said.

"And for your generosity of spirit, Lieutenant Lewrie," Sir John rejoined, "Naples is yours to command. What service may our kingdom do the Royal Navy? There was talk of shore leave, before we were interrupted."

"Well, milord, there's firewood and water, the usual plaint," Alan replied with a small grin. "Our purser, Mr. Husie, would always wish to go ashore, to replenish stores, purchase livestock for fresh meat and such. I had hoped, once we'd provisioned, to allow our crew out of discipline for a day or two. Not *shore* leave, though . . ."

"Send your purser to our shipyard, sir," Sir John offered with a grand, expansive spread of his arms. "Your ship purchases nothing. We will gladly offer you the bounty of Naples. Fresh meat and bread, vino . . ."

"God bless you, Your Excellency, I am overcome by your generosity," Lewrie declared happily. Sure, too, that Mr. Husie would also be turning St. Catherine's wheels over free victuals.

"And for yourself, sir?" Sir John went on, tapping himself on the side of his nose cagily. "I know what sailors most desire, having once served in deprivation, aha . . . you see?"

"To sample the cuisine of Naples, Your Excellency. To try some new dishes. *Eat* my way back aboard ship, I should think," Lewrie said, beaming now, happy as a pig in the corn-crib. "I've simple needs."

"Then you shall do so, as our honoured visitor," Acton promised, with another, cagier look. "Perhaps you should sample some fried fish, hein, Sir William?"

"Ah. Perhaps that may . . . uhm, advance matters," the ambassador agreed, almost tipping the prime minister a conspiratorial wink. "Yes, I daresay it might. After a certain period of, uhm . . . briefing?"

A briefing on how to eat fried fish? *Right*! And both of 'em as cozy as a pair of housebreakers, Lewrie wondered. At least it sounds like there's a free meal in it. But, dear as he wished it, that very instant . . .

"Your Excellencies will excuse me, I trust, but I must return to our ship. There are matters to arrange, and duties in my captain's stead which I must see to, first."

"You have a competent wardroom, sir?" Acton inquired.

"Aye, sir."

Well, damn his eyes, Lieutenant Braxton *was* good at his job. Can't be faulted professionally. Just personally. Scott to keep an eye on him, and Dimmock, Bosun Fairclough . . .

"An hour or so? I quite understand, Lieutenant Lewrie," Acton nodded, and gave him a shrug of nautical cameraderie. "We both know, and appreciate, how so akin are the demands of a beautiful ship, such as your frigate, and the demands of a beautiful woman, n'est-ce pas?"

"Quite, Your Excellency," Lewrie smiled in return.

"Uhm," Sir William frowned, peering at a distant clock of impressive dimensions and baroque gilding. "It is now half-past nine or so. Do you return to Palazzo Sessa by . . . half-past eleven? Will that be time enough, sir? Good. You are turned out reasonably well. Your current uniform and toilette will suffice. I do not believe there is need for anything more formal, not today at any rate. From here, we may all coach together. Do you concur, Your Excellency?"

"Absolutely, Sir William," Acton agreed.

"My physician will be along presently. You may coach together to the quays," Hamilton decided, getting to his feet, creaking in the effort; for all his urbane grace and patrician leanness, he was an old man. He put his hands in the small of his back and leaned backward.

"Aye, Sir William, and thankee again. I cannot express how much I am indebted to you. One thing before I go, however. Uhm . . . exactly where will we be coaching *to*?"

"Why, to introduce you to Neapolitan cuisine, Lieutenant," Sir John Acton smirked, sharing another of those maddening conspiratorial grins with the ambassador. "You may try some fried fish. And be presented to His Majesty, King Ferdinand the Fourth. The King of Naples.'

CHAPTER 4

"Now, he'll not stand on much ceremony or formality, beyond a natural courtesy, d'ye see, sir," Sir William Hamilton tutored on the short carriage ride from Palazzo Sessa. "The King of Naples is . . . uh . . . you've never been presented at Court back home, sir?"

"No, Sir William," Lewrie had to admit.

"He does carry himself well, though, Hamilton, does he not? And you told me not half an hour ago that his deportment towards you and Sir John lacked for nothing," Lady Emma Hamilton teased.

Informal or not, Lewrie had scrubbed himself as clean as could be expected aboard a ship, donned his best uniform, and was now perched on tenterhooks on a plush-velvet coach bench, facing rearward towards Sir William and his wife. His very much younger and hellish-fetching wife. At the moment he felt, diplomacy bedamned!

"Uhm . . ." Sir William allowed. "True. True, my dear."

"Neapolitans call him Il Re Lazzarone, sir," Lady Hamilton went on. "That means king of the commoners. He's adored by the common folk. By all, but . . . by all but the very rich and most pretentious. Those with titles who were born expecting more respect for their dignity."

She snorted like a short-changed shopkeeper's wife.

"You have no Italian, sir?" Sir William inquired hopefully.

"None, I fear, Sir William," Lewrie had to say. "Some doggerel Don. A smattering of French, o' course."

"That would *hardly* be the language to use around 'Old Nosey,' sir!" Lady Hamilton laughed again, a deeper-in-the-gut, full-voiced guffaw, her merry light blue eyes sparkling with mirth.

" 'Old Nosey,' Lady Hamilton?" Lewrie flummoxed, trying hard to retain all he'd so quickly been tutored on, in the short time allowed.

"Il Vecchio Nasone, his subjects also call him. Try it. Il Vecchio Nasone. Eel ve-keeoh nah-sohnee. Give me half a day, Hamilton, and we'll have him so fluent in Italian, he'll be waving his hands and slapping his forehead!" she boasted.

"I should not dare speak French to him, no matter it's called 'la langue diplomatique,' since his queen, Maria Carolina, was sister to Marie Antoinette. I see."

"Quite right, sir," Sir William gloomed, though he had bestowed upon his wife the beamish smile of a typical, love-stricken old colt's tooth. "And as for *don*, well . . . ! One cannot hope, I suppose, that a sea officer may be *master* of the art of diplomacy, or by the very . . . uhm, detached nature of his calling, have much use for it, in truth. But His Majesty King Ferdinand is of royal Spanish Bourbon blood. He has been King of Naples and the Two Sicilies since his boyhood, yet he is, at bottom, Spanish. It would be . . ."

"Oh, Hamilton, you know how suspicious 'Old Nosey' is about his relations!" Lady Hamilton interrupted. "All the years he's spent here, monarch in his own right, no matter *how* indebted he originally was, he has no love for Spain. For his family, perhaps, but not for Spain, or their ambitions. Any more than he felt for French Bourbons, and *their* ambitions. He's fiercely protective of his kingdom, Leftenant Lewrie."

Handsome or not, she talks too bloody much, and man's business, too, Lewrie thought; politics, so please you! Must have the old dolt wrapped round her least finger, to get away with such . . . boldness. It's desexing, that's what it is! Immoderate! Promising poonts, though . . .

"Even so, my dear, it would be a mistake for the leftenant to become, in the excitement of the moment, perhaps . . . *too* informal. And I would most strenuously conjure you, Leftenant Lewrie, to attempt to eschew such animadversions or colloquialisms—"

"Hamilton, dearest," Lady Hamilton interrupted again, touching her husband on his knee with her fan. "Not possessing a word of Italian, and dependent upon a translator, I'm sure he will not shame us."

"Indeed *not*, Lady Hamilton," Alan nodded to her with gratitude. He was sure that he'd have had a considerable strip torn off his hide, had it not been for her presence, which hampered Sir William from delivering a harsher reproof.

"He'll be good," she added, giving him a taunting smile behind her husband's view as she leaned back in the coach seat they shared.

"Cross my heart and hope to die, Lady Hamilton," Lewrie smiled.

"Emma, *do*!" she insisted suddenly, taking her husband's veined old hand for a squeeze. "May Leftenant Lewrie be familiar with us, my dear? After all, he will be doing us an immense service. Already has, hasn't he, coming from Admiral Hood with his news. And showing Ferdinand what real British sailors are like. Why, this may be the very act which firms Neapolitan resolve to join the coalition!"

"Uhm, Emma . . ." Sir William dithered in warning.

"Oh, pish!" Lady Hamilton snorted once again, this time in vexation. "What is needed by Lords Dundas and Grenville in London is the help of the Sardinians and the Neapolitans. Austria is in, Prussia is in, but they're off to the north and east. All royalist Europe must be in. Surely, Hamilton, he must be told enough, so that he will not make a mistake, out of ignorance?"

"Leftenant Lewrie . . . His Majesty's Government desires, and shall pay handsomely for, any military or naval assistance against Republican France. Matters are in hand . . ." Sir William said cautiously. "Sardinia, for example, will be recompensed upwards of £200,000 to raise an army of 50,000 men, and subordinate her fleet to Lord Hood's orders. I have been discussing a similar arrangement for a fiscal subsidy with Sir John Acton, anent Naples, pending certain steps which His Majesty's forces would take in the Mediterranean."

"What Sir John referred to as une flotte respectable?" Alan said with quick understanding and a sly look. "The presence of our fleet is the precondition towards Naples joining the coalition. And what would their contribution be, Sir William? And how good are they?"

"We, uhm . . ." Sir William stalled, loathe to reveal all his cards to a stranger, grown used to a life of secrecy in his king's service. "A force of 5,000 to 6,000 troops. Three or four ships of the line and the requisite numbers of transports. Perhaps six or eight lesser ships. It is no secret that King Ferdinand has always been suspicious of France's territorial ambitions. Now so, more than ever. No matter the government in power in Paris; their appetites are constant."

"And with France gaining Corsica rather recently, he fears their further expansion overseas. If they can threaten and gain Corsica, what else might they take from the weaker Italian states by force," Alan surmised. "Once they consolidate their political power, eliminate their last internal foes . . . and get their army and navy sorted out."

"Capital!" Lady Hamilton hooted in triumph. "Oh, Hamilton, did I not tell you he'd be good?"

"Yet Corsica's not quite in the bag, I understand," Lewrie went on, leaning forward over his sword hilt, which rested between his knees. "There's Italian resistance to their occupation. So I would assume we will be invading Corsica, once we've dealt with the French fleet? That is why Admiral Hood is blockading Toulon, their main naval base?"

It made imminent sense, Lewrie thought smugly, secretly glad he was showing so astute, and enjoying the alarmed expression on William

Hamilton's face. But any fool could read a map, any fool could follow events in the papers! What all these Foreign Office, Privy Council, or diplomatic types never seemed to realise was that an hour in a coffee-house or an idle afternoon in a workingman's tavern would reveal that what they treated as utterly covert, was general gossip!

Too, it made imminent sense that England would provide the navy to allow the lesser Italian kingdoms to invade Corsica, marshal armies on France's eastern frontier near Genoa and Leghorn, backed by Austria and her magnificent troops . . . best in Europe, Prussian pride notwith-standing! Liberation from revolutionary tyranny, a cheque to French dreams of expansion . . . can't do it without a fleet! . . . and provide the first measure in cooperation, and a victory, so the combined armies of the coalition would be inspirited when they marched into France herself!

"We . . . rather, our superiours in London, dream a tad bit larger than merely occupying Corsica, Leftenant Lewrie," Sir William grudgingly admitted, leaning forward himself to whisper more confidentially. "I grant you, all you say is true. Yet, there is also resistance to Paris and the revolutionaries in France, as well. The Midi . . . Var, Pro-vence . . . along the Biscay coast in Vendée, there are many adherents to the royal family. Regions openly in rebellion versus the Republicans. What you are told now is to be held in the *strictest* confidence, sir, but . . . Admiral Hood *may* be able to exploit Royalist sentiment in Southern France. He is charged by Henry Dundas to attack Marseilles, if at all possible, blockade Southern France, bottle up or destroy the French fleet, and in the last instance, exploiting Royalist sentiments, lay siege to, thence capture the naval port and fortifications of Toulon. So you see, Leftenant Lewrie, Corsica would be a poor second. A sideshow. *That* is the aim of the coalition in the Mediterranean. And *that* is why I have courted the Kingdom of Naples and the Two Sicilies so ardently."

"Good God!" Lewrie exclaimed in a covert mutter, leaning back in amazement. "Yes, I *see*, Sir William. So your hoped-for treaty is just about completed."

"Hamilton *has* it, Leftenant Lewrie," Emma Hamilton boasted, giving her old stick of a husband a supportive grin. "It's a pat hand already, really. Naples isn't powerful enough to resist France alone, in the long run, so they *must* side with us. He is *too* modest about his accomplish-ments."

"I'm not to know that, I presume, nor anything about the treaty," Alan spelled out aloud, partly for his own use. "But, asked my opinion, I should express the belief that France should be crushed quickly. And that the Royal Navy is more than able to defeat or blockade the French. I just have to avoid saying or doing anything stupid."

"Heavenly! Aptly put!" Lady Hamilton cheered, rewarding him with another encouraging smile. "One *might* allude to Toulon and Marseilles . . . as hotbeds of Royalist sentiment, though, sir. Without belabouring the subject."

Good *God*, Lewrie thought, a bit shocked; who exactly *is* the ambassador to Naples? She's the nutmegs of a Grenadier Guard—and when excited, as she was at that moment, could lapse into most unladylike speech; a trifle too loud, too. She was a forward piece, no error, Alan thought.

Emma Hamilton was not the typical batter-pudding most men of the age preferred, the sort who could snuggle under a fellow's chin on her tiptoes. Nor was she fubsy, either, though she was more of a pillowy kind than he usually liked. A dimpled chin, nicely dimpled cheeks when she smiled. Bright, pale blue eyes, huge 'uns! A good brow, and her eyebrows and hair were almost raven, dago-dark. A somewhat coarse complexion, though free of smallpox scars. Her teeth, as she displayed them in a pleased grin, were a little irregular. But then, what person *didn't* have a few missing by her age, or erose teeth to begin with, he realised! How old *was* she, he wondered?

There was an intriguing cast, a tiny brown mote, in her left eye, he noted, as she continued to lecture in a very vivacious, hurried way: damn' charmin', he thought suddenly; no, not a bit fubsy. Just the tad bit stout . . . or would be later in life, like a country girl. And, when excited, she *sounded* a bit country, too! Midlands, Alan decided; Nottinghamshire, Staffordshire or Cheshire, by her accent, which surfaced, in spite of obvious coaching, in a more genteel London style.

In her thirties, he asked himself? No, late twenties, at best. And with this old colt's tooth *how* long? Hmmm?

". . . Il Re Lazzarone," she was saying, lifting her hands to talk dago-fashion to stress her syllables, twiddling short, commonish fingers on hands a tad too rough for a woman born to the idle aristocracy. "Do try it, sir. Lots-ah-*roan*-ay!" she giggled.

"Eel Ray Lots-ah-*roan*-ay," Alan parroted, warming to her infectious vivacity. "And . . . uhm . . . Eel Vekee-oh Nah-*sohn*-ay."

"Oh, *very* good, sir!" she laughed. "Buon giorgno . . . that's good morning . . . buona notte is goodnight. Scusi, that's excuse me. And one *can't* go wrong with grazie. Thank you. Grazie, signore . . . grazie, signorina, or signora, if she's married, d'ye see. You are a . . . tenente, so if you hear someone say tenente, you may be sure it's you they're speaking to. King Ferdinand would *adore* a few choice Italian phrases. He speaks Italian better than *ever* he did his native Spanish. Though they are similar."

"You'll only confuse him, Emma. Or arm him too lightly, just enough to encourage him," Sir William grumped, though gently. Dotingly.

"Your first name, sir?" she demanded suddenly. "Isn't it so *very* stiff, calling you Leftenant Lewrie, and me Lady Hamilton? I am Emma."

"Were Sir William to allow me? Thank you, Sir William, I am honoured by your condescension. Lady Emma, then," he experimented, with a smile. "Uhm, you say His Majesty is not too formal . . . ?"

"The *most* unassumin' monarch ever you did see, Alan," she cried boldly. "Goes about the town afoot, on his own half the time, chatting up just *anyone* of his subjects he comes across. For a Spanish Bourbon . . . what you call a stiff-necked *don* . . . !"

"Emma, really," Sir William interjected, merely pretending to be scandalised.

"His people love him, and he truly loves *them!*" she prattled on, all but squirming on her coach seat. "He gives them festa, forza, et farina. Oh, see how much Italian you're learning, Alan? Festa, forza et farina . . . festivals, force and flour. For bread and pasta. There are *some* think it boorish, but he realises there's more commoners than rich, and if the commoners . . . the lazzarone . . . support him, then his crown is safe. And, of course, what he calls the *other* three pillars of his reign . . . church, crown and mob. Heavens! So *much* to relay, and so little time, Hamilton," she said, almost breathless in her haste. "Quite *another* reason King Ferdinand and Queen Maria Carolina are deadset against the revolutionaries . . . they're *Catholic* monarchs, in a Catholic country, and not only did the Republicans supplant royalty when the king and Queen Marie Antoinette were beheaded . . . the French are preaching atheism! All sorts of vague, humanist prattle . . . Deist at best! All the churches turned into Temples of Man . . . priests thrown out, called to the armies to get them out of the way . . . churches closed, and rich properties seized for the state . . . it *is* a pity, Hamilton, that Alan cannot be presented to Maria Carolina."

"I believe she is in the last weeks of her confinement, Lady Emma? And in grief over her royal sister's . . . murder."

"Exactly. God, you should *see* her. Big as a *house!*" Emma hooted with earthy good humour. "But, were you to meet her, and get to see her resolve, her *mind*, Alan . . . you'd meet one of the most formidable women in Europe, she's so . . ."

"Ah, we're here," Sir William announced as their coach jangled to a halt. And with the slightest sound of relief from his wife's enthusiasm in his voice. "I will, of course, alight first, sir. Would you be so good, once you have done likewise, as to hand Lady Hamilton down?"

"Like the Navy, Sir William? Seniors last in, first out?" Alan snickered. "It will be my pleasure to assist Lady Hamilton."

Dear God, I hope *so*, he thought, giving her what he also hoped was the sort of significant grin that had worked in his past. Coarse and too damn' forward she might be, but she was, by that very nature, damned intriguing and exotically exciting. Like Naples itself.

He slid near the door, waiting for the tall Sir William to set foot on the iron coach step, to plant his shoes on the ground and move far enough away to give him room to alight. He was taking his own, old sweet, arthritic time about it. Lewrie glanced meaningfully to her once more as she gathered her skirts.

She lowered her gaze slowly, in what looked to be a most covert nod of agreement. Slowly she glanced out the windows of the coach, to Sir William, who was huffing, grimacing and accepting the arm of a liveried postillion boy. She looked back to Lewrie just as slowly, smiling a bashful smile over her husband's infirmities, as if to say, "What may one do?" Then inclined her head to one side, ever so slightly, presenting a strong yet graceful neck. Her gaze became less bashful, turned forward and bold. She appraised him, cocked hat to well-blacked shoes. And gave him another brow-lifted nod of acceptance.

Thankee, Jesus, we're *aboard*, Lewrie thought triumphantly!

He alit at last, once there was space enough, and reached in to hand her down safely, in front of what appeared to be a most plebeian fried-fish shop. Her silk-hosed ankles winked for a dizzying moment as she emerged. She took his offered hand, and as she departed their coach (with only moderate grace) she gave his fingers a firm and intimate squeeze, and both their grasps lingered far longer than his gentlemanly task demanded.

"Old Nosey's a caution, Alan," she whispered, leaning close to his head in final warning; using that final warning as an excuse for a public intimacy. "A bit on the loud side. A touch . . . vulgar . . . for what most deem acceptable behaviour for royalty. More exuberant than British visitors are wont. I'd tell you more, but time does not admit it."

"Perhaps later, Lady Emma?" Alan suggested, almost leering now. "I'm asea, with need of tutoring. And you the most capable. And the most handsome."

"I expect you have very little need of tutoring, Alan," she said with a light laugh, which quickly became a full-throated guffaw. "Come. Be presented."

And she brushed past him to join her husband, leaving him wondering if she'd been teasing after all, and had just laughed all his lustful pretensions to scorn.

CHAPTER 5

King Ferdinand the Fourth was a touch more than crude. Il Re Lazzarone was as vulgar as a horse-coper. For a moment Lewrie was not sure which of the low figures in the cook shop he was, until a tall, beaky fellow came from behind the counter, dressed in a flambouyantly figured black-and-silver waistcoat, silk shirt and laced stock, in fawn breeches and gleaming top boots. He wore a white publican's apron, which he cast aside as he approached.

Sir John Acton presented him, then stood in as translator. A moment later, after the latest news had been digested, Lewrie ended up in a bearhug, being bussed on both cheeks over and over, lifted off his feet, and danced round the cook shop, as a pack of wastrels and idlers cheered lustily.

"His Majesty cannot express his joy upon learning..." Sir John condensed for him.

"He's doin' main-*well*, consid'rin', Sir John..." Lewrie muttered as he tried to maintain an innocent, unabashed fool's face as the ruddy-featured monarch jounced him around.

"...this vow made by His Britannic Majesty, now fulfilled...the prowess of British arms..."

"Uhm, speakin' of *arms*, Your Excellency...?"

King Ferdinand the Fourth set him down at last, clapped him hard on both shoulders, and rattled off a positive flood of Italian.

"He offers to feed you now," Acton concluded.

And then, in a run-of-the-mill cook shop, not much grander than a coffeehouse, chophouse or tavern back home, he was sat at a red-and-white chequered table, with a prime minister, an ambassador and his lady, had a glass of wine shoved into his hands, and was presently presented with soft breadsticks and an assorted plate of sliced cheeses and meats by the very hands of a king. A remarkably florid and ugly king,

151

he thought; but a king, nonetheless. The experience was nearly as heady as the wine, a rough but full-bodied local vintage, fruity yet dry. It went devilish-well with the strips of ham and sausage rounds and the cheeses.

The place was festooned with hunting trophies; boars' heads and stags, shaggy horned mountain goats, bears, lynx, stuffed geese or ducks.

"His Majesty adores the hunt, do you see, sir," Acton explained.

"Ah, si," King Ferdinand agreed, followed by another linguistic avalanche, to which Lewrie could but nod and smile, a breadstick near his middle chest, wondering if one could partake as long as a king was talking. And the smell of frying fish, broiling fish, the tang of oil and garlic, onion and God knew what else, the smoke from the grill like a thin mist overhead, the very rafters redolent with rapturous . . . !

"Mangia, His Majesty says. Do not stand on ceremony. Eat!" Acton encouraged. "Marvelous big hunts, His Majesty stages, sir. Whole villages for beaters . . . with the gun . . . with the lance . . . with the sword he takes his prey," Acton relayed, cocking his head towards his monarch to catch it all. "Thousands of beasts, thousands of birds has he taken, signore tenente. His Majesty believes, the bigger the slaughter, bigger the 'bag,' the better, ha ha!"

"Ah, like the maharajah do in India, Your Excellency," Alan said, appalled. Wasn't *his* idea o' huntin'!

"Ah, India!" Acton said with much the same delight as his king had. "His Majesty bids me tell you, he would give anything to be invited by His Majesty, King George's East India Company, of course, to go to India and hunt in the Grand Moghul style. His Majesty would like to kill *many* elephants and tigers."

"Convey to His Majesty, King Ferdinand that *I've* been to India," Lewrie smiled, with a crafty look. "My father is a colonel in the East India Company army. He hunts Bengal, from the back of an elephant, he wrote me last year. He's a little busy now, though . . . hunting Frenchmen, I'd imagine."

Though Sir William Hamilton winced, King Ferdinand laughed so hard he shook the table, then pounded it with a fist.

"His Majesty inquires if you also hunted game in the East Indies, tenente Lewrie?" Acton translated, though his own polite smile was forced, and his laugh sounded edgy.

"I was too busy myself, Your Excellency," Lewrie replied. "We chased French pirates, in the Great South Seas. They were not only giving arms and encouragement to the most bloodthirsty native pirates, to raid the China trade . . . they were taking ships themselves, selling good Christians in Malay or Mindanao slave markets. Or leaving no witnesses. Breaking their treaty agreements after the last war. Getting ready for the next. Sponsored, unofficially, of course, by their Ministry of Marine. French warships . . . in disguise."

"And . . . His Majesty inquires . . ." Acton posed nervously, after a sober palaver in Italian which shut every mouth, cocked every ear in the shop—and left Lady Emma Hamilton gape-jawed and flushed—"what did you do with them, tenente?"

"We brought them to battle sou'east of Macao . . . at Spratly Island, and hunted 'em down to the island of Balabac," Lewrie said proudly, rolling the unfamiliar names off like an ancient and honoured regiment's list of glorious victories. "And when we were done, they were utterly defeated and destroyed, their leader in chains. Royal Navy fashion."

"Magnifico!" King Ferdinand bellowed gruffly, his face even redder, pounding on the table again. "Magnifico! Ecco, la regio marina de la Brittania . . . !" He rose to his feet, swinging his arms and giving every customer—and Lewrie realised that some of those customers were courtiers and advisors, or Privy Council—a long rant.

"His Majesty says, tenente . . ." Sir John Acton muttered with a very cat-ate-the-canary look at last, "that with such an ally, what is there to fear from the French? Uhm . . . a bit sacrilegious, I fear, but 'with Almighty God on our side . . . buttressed by the fabled wooden walls of the ever-courageous and implacable British Royal Navy . . . who can be against us'? Bellissimo, signore tenente, bellissimo! That is to say, beautiful. Handsomely done."

"Thankee, Your Excellency. But I no more than spoke the truth."

A gnarled old hand touched his lightly for an instant from his right; Sir William Hamilton drawing his attention from the cheering to nod his approval and give him a warm smile.

Marvelous, Lewrie thought; I just started a *war*! Damme, what's next I can get myself into?

The king calmed at last, sat back down, and shouted instructions to the kitchen. Out came aproned flunkies, beamish young boys with olive complexions and dark hair, excited and trembling. Would they be at some regimental recruiting office by next sunrise, Alan wondered? They seemed bloody cheerful about the prospect!

Out came a thatch-covered bottle, a red wine fruity and dusky, so dry it made him pucker. *Lacrima Christi*, he was told it was; the Tears of Christ, which he thought fitting. There was a heaping platter of a stringy glop . . . pasta, he was also told: *spaghetti al dente*, shimmering with olive oil, flecked with oregano, sun-dried tomato bits and garlic, with a thin sera of tomato sauce. Also arriving was a selection of hot fish. Fried shrimp—*gamberetti*—done to a tawny crispness, but pink and succulent inside. More shrimp, filleted and skewered and grilled.

"Eat, eat, tenente!" Sir John insisted, once the uproar had at last died down. Something momentous seemed to have been settled, but Lewrie wasn't sure exactly what, since it wasn't formal yet, and no one was going out of their way to explain such diplomatic intricacies to a lowly such as he. "His Majesty operates the cook shop himself, and he is delighted to see a man with a hearty appetite. He catches many of these fish himself, off Fusaro and Posillipo, he bids me tell you. He is a great fisherman, as well as hunter. He sails his own boat, too."

"As far as the Isle of Capri? I've heard how beautiful . . . how bellissimo . . . !" Lewrie said between heavenly mouthfuls.

That set the king off on another paroxysm of rapture, over Capri's magnificent coves and beaches, its vistas, its ancient structures.

"I would delight to see it, do we stay long enough in Naples," Alan said to the prime minister. "Just as I adore tasting new foods, I delight in seeing new and exciting places."

"You like common Neapolitan foods, His Majesty wonders?"

"Ambrosia of Heaven, Your Excellency. I may never lay knife to English foods again," Lewrie declared, not anywhere near toadying.

"His Majesty demands you stay ashore this evening. Dine with us at the reggia, the royal palace. All common Neapolitan menu, he promises. He will stuff you, His Majesty assures me. And give you a good night of rest in a real bed, not a seaman's cot, for once."

"Should I, Sir William?" he asked. "What if I . . . slip up, or . . ."

"We shall be with you, Leftenant. Never fear."

"Please, Your Excellency, convey to His Majesty my undying and heart-felt gratitude for his most generous invitation. One to which I look forward with unbounded gustatory anticipation!"

He looked at Emma Hamilton, who was fanning herself, still rapt upon him, after his brusque description of his East Indies' service.

And that's not all I'm looking forward to, he thought, giving her a grin and a brief nod.

CHAPTER 6

Had a hole in me, I think; hollow leg, or something. But, Lord! It was all so bloody good! So grand!

Minestrone, the plebeian vegetable and pasta soup—even that was head and shoulders above Navy fare. Meat-stuffed pastas, layered with a tomato sauce, dripping with melted cheeses! Veal *marinara*, game fowl jugged in a wine sauce, domestic chicken breasts done in a cream sauce with wide egg noodles. More fried fish, more grilled goodies. God knew how they'd done it, but there'd been ices with the fruit for a last course, tart and sweet sorbets, and creamy—what'd they call 'ems?—*gelati*? And for the levee preceding the actual promised stuffing—*antipasti*. Lovely cheeses, thin-shaved prosciutto; and, of course, the sybaritic pleasures of fresh-baked bread, piping hot, crusty and white milled flour, with dollops of churned butter!

Wines, too. Sweet Marsalas and sweetish, sparkling spumantes. Then butter-smooth, aged reds that rivalled the best Cabernets France could boast. Thank God for the food, he thought; I've taken a barrel aboard, feels like. I'm well and truly foxed!

A minor kingdom, in the greater scheme of things, Naples might be, but King Ferdinand's palazzo was a bejeweled, begilt faeryland of high, ornate baroque ceilings, well-figured marble walls awash with statuary and gigantic tapestries, overscale paintings (dead relations, mostly—or hunting scenes), shiny with Chinee wallpapers, glittering with crystal sconces, chandeliers, glowing amber with a shipload worth of real bee's-wax candles, festooned with silver and gold, niello or cloisonné, strewn with furniture too precious to sit upon. It was so grand, so showy, after half a year of those wooden walls of his, so different from his bleak daily vistas of rolling sea. And the music!

A chamber orchestra still sawed away in an upper gallery, just as they had through the levee and the supper. Light, airy, delightful stuff—

155

sonatas by Giovanni Gabrieli, Giovanni Battista Fontana, and Marco Buccolina. Or so he'd been informed.

If Naples was not indeed Heaven, it was very close to it, Alan determined. With a traitorous snifter of French Armagnac in his hand, he let go a more than gentle burp of contentment.

The supper was over, the *écarté* and music was winding down, and it was too late for the last guests to stay and dance. Sir William and the prime minister were gone somewhere. King Ferdinand had spoken some brief last words to him and had plodded off, too.

Have their three heads together over the treaty, I expect, Alan thought; thankee, my boy, but we'll take it from here. Oh, well.

"Scusi, signore tenente Lor . . . L . . . Liri," a white-wigged footman announced by his side. He was holding a six-armed candelabra.

"Lewrie," he muttered, barely glancing at him, searching for Emma Hamilton, who had also scampered off somewhere.

"Si, signore tenente Liri," the servitor persisted, "you pleaseah toa follah me, signore tenente? I lighta you . . . up . . . toa bed, signore."

Well, shit, he sighed to himself. Right, then . . . I should have known better.

His chambers were magnificent. The night was warm and fragrant; the two pairs of doors which led to a wide, fret-stoned balcony were open. The suite was as large as an admiral's great-cabins. There were side tables bearing cloisonné, gilt and silver gewgaws, a writing desk of tortoise-shell mottled wood, heavily inlaid with ivory, urns filled with fresh-cut flowers everywhere he looked, an expansive wine cabinet big as a duke's sideboard, an intricately carved armoire big enough to hold a corporal's guard, and a bedstead as wide as a quarterdeck, with silk sheets and satin coverlet already turned down, the two pair of pillows plumped up invitingly.

"Willa they bea anythin' elsea youa wan', signore tenente?" the footman intoned, sounding both hesitant and grim. Lewrie glanced at him and noted his lips moving after his statement; probably in rote rehearsal of his little English over the most probable statement he might next make.

"Anything else?" Lewrie grinned.

"Si, signore tenente Liri," the man answered, then repeated with effort: "Willa-they-bea-anythin'-elsea-youa-wan', signore?"

"Dancing girls," Lewrie bade, tongue in cheek, just to see how the poor fellow might handle the unexpected. "A string quartet. Some courtesans. And magic. I insist on magic."

"Uh, scusi, signore tenente . . ." Sweat popped on his upper lip as he flummoxed. "Willa-they-bea-anythin'-elsea, signore tenente?" He reiterated, sounding a bit desperate.

"No, nothing else," Lewrie relented. "Thank you. Goodnight. Or how you say . . . ? Uhm. No, grazie. Buona notte."

"Ah, si, tenente!" the man bobbed with relief, bowing himself out quickly. "Si, grazie. Buona notte, signore. Buona notte!"

"Call me at first light," Lewrie insisted. "Sunrise. Giorgno? First sparrow fart? Bloody . . ." He pointed at an ormolu clock, stuck his hands in his armpits, and crowed like a rooster. The footman came back, pointed to the Roman numeral V and shrugged quizzically. Alan pointed to the VI, mimed shaving and washing.

"Ah, si, signore. Awakea you . . .'ota wat'r. Buona notte!"

"Damme, *another* bloody foreign language I have to learn," he groused softly as he stripped off his own coat and waistcoat, ripped his laced stock from his throat and unbuttoned his shirt collar. A peek into the various chambers of the suite revealed that his kit was already stored in the armoire. He hung his things up, found the necessary closet and, much eased, padded in bare feet to the wine cabinet. It may have been French, but there was Armagnac, sweeter and mellower than any brandy or cognac. With his snifter topped up he went out onto the balcony, not feeling treasonous at all to drink it.

Heaven, Naples might seem, but it reeked, as did any city with a large population. Night soil dumped out chamber windows, animal ordure, rotting garbage, and too many people who bathed too infrequently crammed into too small an area. But the palace's flower gardens atoned for all.

There was something else, too, as if antiquity had a scent, dusty and sere, as if a thousand years of living, breathing history, and aeons of Mediterranean sunshine could have a mellow, dry-old-wine aroma. Alan could identify woodsmoke, sour, water-staunched charcoal cooking fires. Wine and laundry, tanneries and hot iron, the aftertaste of succulent spices. The wind off the sea . . .

Naples lay spread at his feet, beyond the palace grounds and the protective walls. Vesuvius was over his left shoulder, gently fuming a thin, indistinct pipesmoker's pall. Dark slopes tumbled to the fields where Pompeii and Herculaneum once stood, and from Torre del Greco, all ephemeral with dusky blue moonlight. Umber walls and terracotta roof tiles shone icy with moonlight, rendered snowy blue white or black now. Tiny amber sparks on the hills, on the flatlands far away, in the town, marked country crofts, villages, or late-night taverns. To the west, the Bay of Naples shimmered on the moonglade, in silver and black, and ships lay still as discarded playthings on a nursery room floor below him, bare-poled and silent, with only faint glims by belfries and taffrails. HMS *Cockerel* lay off to his right, silhouetted ebony on flickering argent waters which reflected pale yellow cat's-paws on a quicksilver moon trough, brushed by the light night breeze. Squinting, he almost thought he could espy a pattern to it, a chimera about to rise, like an ever-pirouetting dancer. To the sou'west, there was a darker hump on the sea's horizon, the steady, measured flick of a lighthouse. Capri. Tucked like an apostrophe near the tip of a finger of distance-grayed land, at his angle of view.

"Punta Campanella," Lewrie murmured with pleasure in the novel and alien, savouring the taste of its strange wonder on his tongue as he recalled the peninsula's name. Along with the heady fumes and bite of the Armagnac. And that tiny smear of light, that sleeping village on the peninsula's north shore which faced his balcony?

"Damme, I had a squint at the chart. So what's the bloody place called? Sam . . . Ser . . . S, something."

"Sorrento," a soft voice said behind him.

He started with alarm, spun about to spy out who his tutor was.

"Sorrento," Lady Emma Hamilton whispered as she emerged from the darkness of the far end of his balcony. Came near enough to take the snifter from his nerveless fingers and drink deep. "A lovely town, is Sorrento. There are some who like the Bay of Salerno, beyond the Punta Campanella. But I *much* prefer the Bay of Naples. Don't you?"

"Immensely," he assured her, getting his poise back.

"When Goethe was here, not long ago, he told me . . ."

"You *met* Goethe?" Lewrie marveled.

"But of course, Alan." she laughed low in her throat. "Everyone comes to Naples, sooner or later. Goethe said, 'Naples is a Paradise. Everyone lives, after his manner, intoxicated in self-forgetfulness.' Languid . . . romantic beyond words . . . tolerant and accepting. I've been here for years. I cannot imagine living anywhere else."

"In self-forgetfulness," he prompted and smiled.

She lifted the snifter, drained it to heel-taps, and set it on a marble-topped wrought-iron wine table beside her. Then slipped into his embrace boldly. She turned her face up to his, pressing her lips first warm and inviting, then fierce, turning her head and groaning as their mouths parted, as eager breaths mingled.

"How did you manage . . . ?" he murmured against her throat, as he lifted her dark, curling hair to kiss her below her ear, to devour her neck and soft bared shoulder.

"Palazzi . . ." she chuckled, with more than amusement, writhing against him. "Passages, vacant adjoining suites . . . unseeing servants. Hurry!"

He frog-marched her backwards into the suite, across the room and onto the edge of the high bedstead, all the while fumbling with the buttons and hooks of her sack gown, with her strong, capable hands on his breeches flap and belt in a fury. They tumbled onto the piles of goose-down mattresses, his feet still just touching the floor. Up went his hands, searching and hungry, lifting skirts and petticoats, sliding needful and possessive along her silken knee hose, up along the outside of her thighs, bare and soft, so milky white and malleable.

"Caution," she insisted, lifting his head from his delightful work, whimpering and panting with want of her own, taking his face in both hands and raining wide-mouthed, writhing, dewy-wet kisses on him. "Caution. A moment. Have you . . . ?"

Bloody Hell, what if I don't, he groaned silently. Kissing her one last time, he shucked his breeches and strode in his shirttails to the armoire, digging into his shore kit.

God, thankee, Cony, you still know how to pack for me! Shaking out one of Mother Jones's very best (guinea the dozen) lambskin cundums from the Old Green Lantern in Half Moon Street, he went back to her.

She'd snuffed candles, all but the last on the nightstand, and shed her gown and petticoats and chemise. Almost demure, tucked into bed beneath the silk sheets, her mass of ebon curls spilling stark on the shining pillows.

He slid into bed with her, sinking into the mattresses, sliding together as the center gave and the edges rose to enfold them in sleek luxury. She raised a thigh, hugged him fierce again and let him roll atop, between . . . enfolding him with her own soft, yielding flesh. He went back to her shoulders, her breasts, sliding down to render total worship, but she almost dragged him to a stop, reached down, dandled his manhood, and chuckled deep in her throat as her hands surveyed his size and strength. Helped him with their "caution," then guided him . . . guided him . . .

"Ah, God!" she muttered huskily, straining with him, lifting her legs high about him, pressing her ankles and heels into his buttocks, rocking her hips to exact his last, full measure, to the very depths of her. "Lord, yes, I . . . !"

"Emma!" he panted, against her mouth, cupping his hands over her shoulders, sinking into her, losing himself in her.

"Gawd," she cooed, bemused by her own responses as she clasped him snug and rocked him, thrusting upward to meet him, "I'll never in my life know . . . what it is . . .'bout me and sailors!"

✻ ✻ ✻

He felt insatiable. Lucky for him, Emma Hamilton was a perfect match. Though she did tend to babble more than he liked, between bouts.

He learned, whether he cared to or not, that she'd been born a village girl, one Emma Hart, daughter of a smith in Neston, Cheshire. Close enough to Liverpool, so her first lover had been a sea officer, when she was in her mid-teens. Then had come London, and the stage . . .

Or at least something *close* to theatrical, Lewrie smirked, in fond remembrance of the "actresses" who plied their wares about his old haunts of Covent Garden and Drury Lane.

Blithering away, chirpy as a magpie, she boldly confessed she'd taken up—"under the protection," she put it—with the wealthy Sir Harry Fetherstonehaugh, and had lived at his fabulous estate, Up Park, in Sussex, for a time, grooming her stage presentations, whatever that signified. But then something cross had occured between them, and he shipped her back to Neston. Yet soon after, she'd lived under the protection, again, of Charles Greville. Through him, she'd met Sir William Hamilton when he'd come home from Naples for a visit, had come away with *him*, had lived in his palazzo as his paramour for five years, and had then become his wife for the last two.

"Separate bedchambers, I take it," Lewrie murmured, rolling to embrace her and nuzzle suggestively. Out of her rags, he found her to be a touch more fubsy than he'd thought; but it was such a welcoming and biddable fubsiness! "An old man, with his infirmities?"

"Hamilton was a soldier, a sportsman. He's climbed Vesuvius, Lord, I don't know, twenty times since he's been here. Poor dear isn't as infirm as you think, Alan. No," she frowned, sloughing off his attentions to stretch for the Armagnac and plump up the pillows to sit against the headboard. "It's more . . . you come to our palazzo, you'll see. Hamilton is a collector. Roman, Etruscan, Greek antiquities . . . books and maps, rare old things. Palazzo Sessa's more museum than house, all on *loving* display," she sneered into her snifter.

"So, are you on display, too, I take it?" he pressed, sliding up to join her and take a sip from her glass.

"Yes, in a way, I am," she chuckled, a bit moodily. "Everyone tells him what a delightful and wondrous *adornment* I am to his house. Like his vases and kraters. As if I should be in a niche somewhere, in one of the galleries, where the light's best. One man even dared to say—in my hearin', mind!—that I was a credit to the station to which I'd been raised!"

"Yet you're not on display. You put a foot forward, bold as I ever did see," he cooed to her, blowing her a kiss, which she turned and intercepted, leaning over him to bestow the real thing. "An ear for languages . . . on familial terms with royalty . . ."

"God, sometimes I wish to God I was a man!" she huffed, and he tried to jolly her out of her pet, in his own, inimitable fashion. But she was having none of it, at that moment.

"How far may a woman go in this world? Aye, I've sense, more'n most. An ear for languages, music . . . books and learning. Not just the frightful novels. What you described this morning, about fighting the pirates and all. I'd *love* to be able to do something meaningful . . . be a voice people heeded. Wield as much influence as you did. Hamilton . . . well, he *is* happy with me. He tolerates my . . . enthusiasms, yet . . ."

And you know which side your toast is buttered, Lewrie thought.

"*His* passion, though . . . I think he saves his passion for diplomacy, for antiquities . . . studying volcanoes. We're comfortable together as old shoes. Because I ornament him so well, like his marbles." She sighed and took a deep sip of brandy. "He bought me, you know. Same as his ancient urns," she confessed with a shrug and pout-lip sigh.

"He bloody what?"

"Charlie Greville is Sir William's nephew, Alan," she told him, snuggling close, confidentially, her head on his shoulder. "I lived quite happily with him, but . . . he wanted to improve his estate. He'd more than enough, I thought. Though his condition was not of the *very* best, it was more than comfortable. He had a chance to make a rich marriage, and . . . I'd have been quite content to stay with him, but for that. Anyway, Hamilton came home on leave, to palaver with the Foreign Office or something, and . . . blink of an eye, I sailed away, here to Naples."

"The cads. Both of 'em," Lewrie groused, slipping a protective arm about her shoulders.

"Oh, no! Never say that about 'em, Alan," she dissented, sitting up and away. "Charlie Greville was wonderful to me! He's still a dear friend. Before Charlie, I hadn't two letters in my head, and as for my cyphers . . . ! He saw I was tutored. Speech, singing, music, and cultural attainments. He brought my mother down from Neston, to be my companion. Bought both of us the best of everything, paid for . . . well, paid for what Sir Harry would not, settled . . . well. And as for Hamilton! He's such a dear, a true gentleman. Mentor, companion, loving friend to me! He's opened my eyes to so much, introduced me to so many wonderful people. Goethe? Where'd a chit from Neston *ever* have the chance to meet Goethe, sit at table with him and chat him up? Haydn . . . kings and queens?"

"I see your point. Like being royalty yourself? Ennobled?"

"Exactly!" she giggled, "Why, tonight, after supper, I went up to Maria Carolina's chambers, swept in like family, and had a chat at her bed-side . . . all sorts of womanly matters, frank and first-name as a sister. Think of it, Alan! *That's* why I love Naples so, it's so accepting. Here, I can be who I was truly born to be. Not like sneering London. Cold and hateful, stay in your place . . . well, when Hamilton and I go back to England, authors of a treaty that won the war and put every royal house in Europe in against France . . . and France is done to a turn. You *will* do France to a turn for me, won't you, Alan? Do just think how people will have to take to me, no matter what!" Emma boasted, brazen, yet wistful for what-was-to-be. "Heavens! Is that the *time*?"

She sprang from the bed, bouncing prettily, though without much grace, and bent for her discarded chemise.

"Hamilton and Acton said they'd be up late. Gave me a chamber, in case I wished to stay and coach home with him later. Two down, not to worry. Do me up, dear man," she ordered, stepping into her petticoats, hoops and pads.

Lewrie went to the armoire and retrieved a silk Chinee dressing gown for himself before obeying. It was fiery red, lambent with moiré dragons in green and blue, with ivory eyes and teeth.

"Hamilton won't take much notice, but Sir John might. And Lord, mother! She has eyes in the back of her head, I swear!"

"Your mother's still with you?" Lewrie asked, ready to hand her her gown as she carefully aligned her underdresses and hair in a tall oval-framed gilt mirror.

"Companion, advisor, cook," she chuckled throatily. "She goes by Mistress Cadogan now. Though, you're *not* to know that, when you come . . . Great God! What a *horror!*" She stopped primping suddenly, on espying his dressing robe in the mirror. "Wherever did you get *that*?"

"Canton, China, if you must know," Alan said, a trifle sulkily. Nobody seemed to care for it, it seemed. It had been relegated to his sea chest—out of sight, out of mind—lest he embarass others back home. "I rather like it," he continued, self-mocking yet defensive. "Though my wife . . . uhm . . ." *OH, DAMME!*

"Your wife," she replied evenly, cocking a brow. After a moment she grinned ironically. "Yes, well . . . were I your wife, Alan, I would object to it, too. Let me hazard a guess. You've been wed . . . at *least* seven years?"

"Uh, as a matter of fact, just barely seven . . . and a bit," Alan blushed.

"Dear Lord, seven years, the two of us," she sighed, surprising him by stepping to him and hugging him close. "Each to our own fashion, mind. Dear Alan, it does seem *such* a milepost in life, don't it?"

"Amen," he sighed with an afterglow of pleasure, kindled by her scent and the warmth of her flesh. They kissed again, soft, lingering—almost a fare-thee-well, instead of a goodnight.

"Come to Palazzo Sessa," she ordered, taking her gown from him. "It would help if you express a keen interest in antiquities. Hamilton will be delighted to tour you round. In the afternoon, he has his 'grampus-puff.' His nap, silly goose! A most sensible Neapolitan custom, is siesta. Especially for a gentleman his age. Do me up whilst I preen, will you? Then . . . the view from my chambers are just as good. And there *are* so many galleries, full of art . . . full of nude statuary. Quite inspiring, some of 'em," she taunted, leaning her bottom back to his groin as he coped with getting the right hook or button in the correct slot or eye.

"Sounds delightful," he murmured against her neck as she lifted her hair and began to pin it properly.

"Perhaps we may even dine you in," she went on matter-of-factly, a pin in her mouth. "And after supper, I will pose for you. I will do my 'Attitudes.' Hamilton loves them. I was known for them, when I was still in the theatre. He helps me with the lights, the drapes . . ."

"A ménage à . . . something?" Lewrie gawped. "Mean he takes part?"

"Not like that, silly man," she laughed, turning to view his work in the mirror. "I *do* poses. *Tableaux!* Dressed, mind." Emma said with a fetching moue. "Classical figures, famous people, the ancient gods . . . with a tambourine and shawl, very few props. *Ecco!*"

She stepped to the sideboard, picked up a silver salver, struck a pose with her profile to him. "For you. 'Brittania, Mistress of The Seas.' " Quickly she changed, moving to another, announcing what allegory she represented. "A poor girl of the streets . . . an Amazonian warrior queen . . . Pallas Athena . . . d'ye see? Oh, pish! I've spoiled it for you! You'll know them, and they won't be a surprise!"

"I swear I'll show all gape-jawed wonder, Emma," he promised.

"I must go. But we're not done yet, Alan. We cannot be!" She sighed, bitter at their parting, clinging to him and kissing him, dewy and full of promise of delights to come. "Dear as my life's become, I sometimes have to dare, to feel alive again. Swear you'll dare all as well. God save me, but I cannot thrive on esteem and companionship, I *must* have passion. Rare as it is in this world . . . rare as it's been in my life. But, when the right man appears and I feel so half-seas-over, like a girl again . . . then *hang* the risk!"

"Uhmhmm," Alan commented (sort of), nodding against her hair, and wondering just what half-cocked idiocy he'd gotten himself into *this* time. And what sort of swoony lunatick he was dealing with.

She broke free of his embrace at last, strode to the balcony doors, and turned . . . to *pose*, one hand high on the door sill. "For all the time you remain in Naples, dear Alan. All the time we have, be my bold captain. Fortune *favours* the bold. Buona notte, caro mio. Until tomorrow, and tomorrow . . . and tomorrow!"

And then she swept away dramatically, making a grand exit, back for her secret passage to her borrowed chamber. Back to an air of respectability.

"Whew!" he exclaimed at her departure. Speaking softly to himself, in case she had lingered to count the house. "Buona notte, me dear. Grazie, o' course. *Damn'* grazie! Lord, though . . . wonder what Italian is for 'daft as bats'!"

CHAPTER 7

"Aye, sir, their mountebank was here," Mr. Pruden told Lewrie on the quarterdeck. He didn't sound impressed by a high-flown Italian physician. "Same nostrums as I had aboard, Jesuit's Bark and such, in a tea. He went from cold to hot, 'bout the end of the second dog last evening. Sweated it out, I should think. Mercury and laudanum, that raises a sweat."

"I have to see him," Lewrie commanded.

"His 'top-lights' are still out, sir. Dead to the world."

"Still, Mister Pruden, as first officer . . ."

"Very well, sir,"

Captain Braxton was still unconscious, and the fever hadn't done his appearance much good. He lolled on the pillows, face slack as some dead man, his mean little mouth canted to leeward, his skin as sickly a buff yellow as old parchment, his shortish hair tousled and glued to his scalp by perspiration. Mister Pruden lifted the captain's wrist to feel for a pulse.

"Thumpin' away like a band, still, Mister Lewrie," Pruden smiled. "No more shivering ague, no more hot flushes and sweats. Feels cooler, too. I think this bout's over."

"How much longer will he be unable to command, sir?" Lewrie asked.

"Mmm, Lord . . . no tellin', Mister Lewrie, sir." Pruden shrugged in puzzlement. "Man his age, fit as he is . . . well as he *appeared* before the fever took him? It may be several days before he regains strength enough to hobble about. Then again, it may be a week or better."

"Should he be sent ashore to convalesce, sir?" Lewrie hoped aloud.

"No need for that, sir, not since the fever burned itself out. A spell of bed rest, of a certainty. Depending on how the fever debilitated him,"

Pruden countered, a bit sadly. "God has a wicked sense of humour, Mister Lewrie. Here He strikes our tyrant down, raising our hopes. And then restores him to health, just when we believe we're liberated."

"Well, at least we're spared his rod, long as he's horizontal," Alan sighed, shaking his head. "Had he informed you of his infirmity before, sir? Any cause for wariness over his health?"

"None, sir. Though I *did* make it my duty to inquire, to assemble a roster of past injuries and illnesses among the crew. You recall, I asked of the wardroom as well, so, should some condition, my ignorance of which might do harm—"

"You asked the captain directly, sir?" Lewrie pressed, getting a germ of an idea which restored his hopes.

"I did, sir, in the pursuit of my bounden duties as ship's surgeon." Pruden nodded somberly, as sober as if testifying at a court.

"And his reply, sir?"

"To, uhm . . .'bugger off,' sir, and not to meddle," Pruden smirked.

"So you think he intended to hide the possibility of a recurrence from you, sir? In your opinion, as a qualified and warranted surgeon?"

"I thought he was being his usual 'tetchy' self, Mister Lewrie. But, aye . . . there's a possibility. Of course, it may be that malaria had not recurred on him in several years. He may have put it 'out of sight, out of mind,' sir. Like a bad tooth which really should come out, but a man'll ignore 'til it festers his gums, Mister Lewrie."

"Very well," Lewrie sighed, putting his hands in the small of his back and pacing, ducking the overhead beams. His eyes fell on the thick log-book on the desk in the day cabin. There was still a way!

"Mister Pruden, you keep a journal of treatment, do you not?"

"Aye, sir."

"I will require a notice from you, in the ship's log, that Captain Braxton fell ill of fever, and that in his stead I had to assume command temporarily. To explain why I was forced to," Lewrie demanded.

"I would be most happy to comply, sir," Pruden beamed, getting his drift. "And should anyone care to take notice, I will write up an entry in my own journal, including what nostrums I prescribed, and their cost, of course."

"How fortunate we were, to be in port at the time," Alan hinted. "And to obtain the services of our ambassador's physician. For free?"

"Certainly, sir," Pruden agreed, jiggling with wry good humour. "I'll go and do it now, whilst my memory's fresh, shall I, sir?"

"I would be deeply obliged if you would, Mister Pruden," Lewrie said with a grateful bow. After the surgeon had departed, he sat down behind the captain's desk, opened the logbook and thumbed through to the last entry in Braxton's own hand. There had been no entry for the day before their arrival in port, Lewrie noted, most happily. Captain Braxton was more than likely already ailing and unable to write.

"Sentry!" Lewrie bawled, sure that a thunderclap under his cot could not rouse the captain in the sleeping cabin.

"Sah!" the Marine bawled back, stamping into his presence.

"Send down to the wardroom, Private Cargill. I need my lieutenant's journal. My compliments to them, and I'll want the sailing master's . . . and Lieutenant Braxton's, as well."

All Commission Sea Officers were required to keep a daily journal; practice for log entries later in their careers. From their observations and inscriptions, battles were sometimes reconstructed, careers made or broken, discipline meted out after-the-fact at courts-martial, or meritorious deeds recalled and rewarded, sea conditions agreed upon.

Somewhere in the leaky, waterlogged basements of Admiralty, on high chairs when the Thames backed up on them, a host of molelike writers gleaned those journals for any new information, any pattern to be deduced in wind and sea conditions for given areas of the world, for a change in headlands, a new seamark erected since the last time a Royal Navy ship had chanced there. Depths especially, dangers, new entries in sailing instructions or coastal pilots . . . to those myopic scribblers nothing was inconsequential, and once stored, nothing was ever tossed.

From his lieutenant's journal, and from Braxton's, Lewrie reconstructed the observations proper to a ship's log, stating that the log had not been kept up . . . and most importantly, why.

11 July 1793, by Alan Lewrie, First Officer, HM Frigate *Cockerel*; log entries for the preceding day, 9 July, our Captain indisposed on 9, 10, and 11 July, and unable. Dawn, 9 July: winds SSW, ½ S, and blowing a quarter-gale. Sea state mildly disturbed, cat's paws and horses, visibility clear, 10 Miles. Straits of Bonifacio astern 10 leagues, Isle of Caprera stbd quarter. By sextant, distance 10 Sea Miles . . . Course ESE, ½ S, spd 7¼ knots. Exercised the . . .

It took an hour to transcribe everything, to recreate the voyage, from the straits to fetching Naples at first light on the 10th; anchoring, discovering the captain's illness, meeting the ambassador and delivering the secret papers . . . being presented to the king, and being forced to dine and sleep out of the ship. Pruden's note came to him, and he transcribed that, then took the fateful step of declaring in writing that he had assumed temporary command, until such time as the surgeon deemed Captain Braxton hale enough to resume his duties.

Then Alan entered the damning statement that the second lieutenant had not informed him of the captain's condition, though he noted in his journal that he'd been dined-in on the 8th and 9th, and had made no mention of the captain being sick after being at table with that worthy.

"Sentry!" he called again, after he'd sanded his last words.

"Sah!"

"Send for the second officer, Mister Braxton. Present to him my compliments, and I require Mister Braxton to kindly attend me, in Captain Braxton's quarters," Lewrie related, with an expectant smile.

"You sent for me, sir?" Clement Braxton asked, a little fearful. Whether he dreaded what was coming, now that Lewrie was temporary Lord and Master, or whether he more feared dire news of his father's condition, it would be hard to decide, Lieutenant Braxton glanced hangdog towards the door to his father's sleeping coach, and at the novel sight of Lewrie at ease behind his father's desk, with equal trepidation.

"Mister Braxton, you've been a *very* bad boy," Lewrie sneered.

"Sir, I—"

"Your father, it seems . . . our captain, is going to recover."

"So Mister Pruden and the civilian doctor were kind enough to inform me, sir, aye," Clement gulped, bobbing with that good news. He assayed a sheepish grin—more a rictus than anything else. Alan was having none of it, however.

"You almost *killed* him, you damn' fool!" Lewrie barked suddenly, crashing a fist on the ornate desk. "You and Boutwell *knew* he was sick as a dog, since we cleared the Straits of Bonifacio. You *knew* he needed the surgeon, but you hid that! Kept him from medication!"

"Dear God, sir, I . . ." Braxton swayed, like to faint.

Lewrie shot to his feet, temper aboil.

Thank God for all my lessons, he thought; I've been browbeat or tonguelashed by the *best*! All those officers who'd shouted at me, superlative howling sessions . . . and now it's *my* turn!

"By God, sir, you saw fit to hide his illness from *me*, not only endangering your father, but the *ship*, Mister Braxton!" Lewrie shouted. "You take filial loyalty too far, sir; too far by half! You are either a Sea Officer, charged upon your sacred honour to put the needs of the ship first, last, and always . . . or you're a bloody fraud! Derelict in your duties . . . who'd put personal, family concerns *above* duty!"

Clement Braxton blanched, reeled backwards half a step as he saw how deep was the pit he was about to shoved into.

Damme, I'm good at this, Lewrie exulted, inward! Though all his talk of honour and duty did make him cringe a little, at his own hypocrisy. It sounded like the worst sort of cant, coming from *his* sort!

"Sir, there was no intent to be derelict . . ." Braxton babbled.

"Sir, I tell you that you were. By omission. Your journal. Two nights you dined with the captain, alone. Seeing how ill he'd become. Yet, there is no mention of it. You did not tell Mister Pruden about a recurrence of malaria. You did not tell me, to prepare me, should I have to take over. The *ship's* log, sir . . . no entries past dawn of the 9th," Lewrie pointed out, hefting the bedraggled, salt-stained journal like God's book of the Saved at Heaven's gates. "Good God, are you so witless, you couldn't have cobbled *something* together from your daily journal? Or were you so afraid of him being dismissed the Sea Service that you thought to hide the truth from there as well, Mister Braxton?" Lewrie thundered. "False log entries . . . *no* log entries, is an offence against the Admiralty, sir! Under Article the Thirty-Third, sir. Fraudulent Behaviour!"

"I could not, sir, not in the log, I . . ." Braxton moaned, twisting slowly in the wind. "He urged me, but I could not! He ordered me direct, sir . . . but that *would* have been lying, sir. I could not."

"Ordered you direct to hide the truth from me, sir?" Lewrie said derisively. "Ordered you to falsify the log? Which?"

"Both, sir," Braxton sighed, red-faced. "He hasn't suffered any fever since '91, sir. Thought, back in cooler climes, he wouldn't. A tropical thing, left behind, we prayed."

"And you thought he could hide out until he'd dealt with it and gotten better, did you?" Lewrie snapped.

"The last few times, sir . . . more like a bad cold, sir, nothing worse. Fa . . . the captain hasn't had a *really* bad spell since '89, so we thought . . . *he* thought, that is . . ." Lieutenant Braxton snuffled.

"Well, it wasn't. He almost died of it, and he's going to be flat on his back for some time. That leaves me in charge. It makes *you* first officer. But I tell you, sir, I will dismiss you from all duties if you even *think* of deceiving me, or hiding something from me again."

"I give you my solemn oath, sir, I will not!" Braxton cringed.

"Come here, Mister Braxton," Lewrie commanded. "Do you look at the log. Note I've made it current, from our journals. Look it over, and determine if there's anything omitted or amiss." Lewrie paced the day cabin, hands behind his back again. "You will also note, sir, that I have made a formal statement of your father's illness, and my taking temporary command whilst our ship operates independent of the fleet."

"I see it, sir," Braxton flinched after a quick peek, as if sight of the log was like espying Medusa and her head full of snakes, which would turn him to stone at the very sight.

"Is there anything untrue in my account, sir? Any matter which you dispute? Including your failure to inform me?" Lewrie growled.

"Uhm, no, sir," Braxton sighed, rubbing his brow.

"Then please be so good as to affix your signature to it, sir, as witness. Leave room on the page for Mister Scott, Mister Dimmock, and our surgeon's names. I'll have them in in a moment."

"Aye, sir," Braxton sighed again, sounding like he was deflating. He slumped deeper, slacker, into his chair like a sack of laundry. In black-and-white, he had been found remiss. He reached across the desk for a quill pen, dipped it in the inkwell, and scratched his name.

Know what you're thinkin', Lewrie told himself smugly; daddy'll get better, he'll fix it for you. Soon as he's back on his pins, I'll be back under his thumb. But, you damned fool, it's in the log now, for all back in London to read! They all get read, sooner or later. Then a note goes to Jackson or Stephens, and questions get asked, and that goes in your permanent records! Maybe not this commission, with daddy to protect you both, he *can't* rip those pages out! They'll ask what action daddy took. Or didn't take. Might even convene a court. Braxtons may've ruined *this* ship, but you'll never ruin another!

"Will that be all, sir?" Braxton asked, dumbfounded in his doom.

"No sir, it will not be. As captain *pro-tem* I can go a step further. I can enter a formal reprimand against you and Mister Boutwell. 'Our ship then engaged upon the urgent delivery of secret dispatches of the highest import, standing through enemy-controlled waters' . . . well, you know the tune, sir. I can order you to sign that, too, or be relieved of duties immediately."

"Sir," Braxton gasped. That was much worse than simple dereliction of duty. It was a career-ender, a reason for a court martial. "Sir, I know father . . . the captain and you have differed. Believe me when I say that I agree with *you*. But he's my father. More than any captain, I owe him support. Dear God, I wish to the Almighty that I'd never set foot aboard this bloody ship!"

Well, that makes two of us, don't it, Lewrie sneered to himself.

"I didn't wish to serve under him, sir, but he plucked strings," Braxton muttered. "We're a Navy family, sir. That's our problem. My grandfather was a post-captain, his before him. Go aboard a gentleman volunteer when you're eight, to your father's ship, your uncle's ship. *You* know how

it works, sir, surely! Grandfather makes rear-admiral . . . half-pay, that.
Ashore." Braxton was nigh to snuffling in his grief. "But I've made my *own*
way in the Fleet, sir! After the leg-up. Rose on my own merits. No one can
grease those wheels for you, once you're a commission officer, away from
direct family. I didn't want to take this commission, I wanted to wait for
something else, but mother . . . she made me swear, just before I came
away. Father'd arranged it all, told me about it, and expected me to be
glad about it. She knew he'd need all the help he could get."

"His recurring malaria?" Lewrie asked, more gently.

"That, sir, and . . ." Braxton heaved a deep sigh, like a drowning man
will suck precious air the first time he surfaces. "He's changed, sir. Off
in the Far East, home for a month or so, between the round voyage.
Mother's health is too frail for the East Indies. She removed to Lyme
Regis, years ago. Rest of us off at sea, never quite connecting . . . never
quite connecting when we *were* together, either, sir. No, it was his temper. His moodiness. She knew how much command of a warship meant
to him, after all . . . Christ!"

Damme, don't do this to me, Braxton, Alan squirmed, his rarely used
conscience plaguing him; here I hate you more than cold boiled mutton . . . and now I'm beginning to feel *sorry* for you!

"Father's had only a moderately successful career, midshipman to
commission in seven years, even *with* family patronage, sir," Lieutenant
Braxton explained. "Nothing distinguished. Two commands, both during
the American War. But they were in the Far East. None since '83. God,
he wrote and wrote, damned near got down on his knees, to any old
friend or patron with ha'pence influence!"

"He *had* command. His Indiamen," Lewrie coolly pointed out.

"Just for the money, sir," Braxton shrugged. "We may be an old Navy
family, but never wealthy, and times were tight. Aye, sir, he had a
ship . . . but t'wasn't *Navy*, d'ye see. Command, respect . . . and the pay
was hellish good."

Braxton waved an inclusive hand about the cabins, at the luxuries
"John Company" service had earned. Yet with a flip of dismissal.

"Away from home so far, a year from a favourable reply from the
Admiralty, sir . . . if there *were* an offer of a commission," Lieutenant
Braxton sniffed. "Pining away, year after year, with never an offer, going
up in seniority on the living captain's list. But no matter how high he
climbed, never an offer. And seeing old shipmates junior to him being
made post, captains below him on the list making admiral. Then at last
we have a war, and they *have* to call him up, sir. He finally gets the
chance to serve again, to *shine*, Mister Lewrie! He was so elated, and
determined!"

"Perhaps a touch *too* determined, sir?" Lewrie suggested wryly.

"We could not know . . . well, Mother did. She knew how desperate he'd been, how sad. And how important this was to him. I expect she also knew his limitations best. She was afraid for him, sir. Not just his health," Braxton confessed. "She told me he'd need the finest sort of loyalty and support. I couldn't refuse him. I couldn't turn my back on him. Apart so long, sir . . . I hardly knew him. Or what he had become, and when I saw . . . it was too late."

"Weeding out Lieutenant Mylett?"

"Not *family*, sir," Braxton smiled shyly. "A stranger. Father hounded him out. Like he tried with you. Made life a living hell for the man. I should have seen the signs . . . I don't know what happened, 'tween the wars, sir. Something in the Far East, I think."

"So that's why there's no mention of our little . . . near-mutiny in the log, either," Lewrie surmised. "Though he *was* informed of our suspicions."

"Oh, he knew, sir. But, it's his last chance, sir, d'ye see? He *has* to succeed. There cannot be a single flaw, this time."

"Well, there is," Lewrie summed up. "For now, Mister Braxton, there will be no formal reprimand."

"Thankee, sir," Braxton perked up. "I won't let family matters hurt my performance again, sir. My word on't!"

"Your *career* on't," Lewrie gloomed. "Our good repute, too. I expect my tenure won't last more'n a week or two, Mister Braxton, and then your father'll be well enough to restore him to his due authority. We can't change his ways too much, lest the crew run riot. And I tell you true, sir . . . his ways aren't my ways. And I despise him for *making* me do things his way. You can make a difference, though. Take those relations of yours and rattle 'em 'til their teeth fly, if that's what it takes, but we cannot have any more terror below decks. They might listen to you."

"Aye, sir, consider it done," Braxton vowed.

"Do you have any influence over him?" Lewrie asked, flicking a hand toward the sleeping coach.

"Not much there, sir. Sorry. Believe me, I have tried to warn him before." Braxton shook his head sorrowfully. "I've tried as son. I've tried as a commission sea officer, a fellow professional. There are some things he simply cannot abide to hear."

"Then God help us, when he's back in charge, Mister Braxton." Do what you can, there. We'll have the other officers in now. And once we've made formal declaration of the change in command, we'll hoist the 'Easy.' From noon today 'til end of the second dog tomorrow, say. I think our crew's earned it, don't you?"

"They have, indeed, sir," Braxton almost smiled.

Lewrie swiveled the log book about so he could read it. He took up the pen and dipped it. "There is, I believe, Mister Braxton, space enough for me to amend my statement about you, after all."

"Sir?" Braxton frowned warily.

"To note the fact that you were most unfairly placed in an impossible position, between direct orders from a captain, and from a father. And were forced to choose whether to obey, disobey, or to take no action at all. I think that may best explain your actions. And soften Our Lords Commissioners back home."

"Thankee, sir," Braxton shuddered with gratitude. "Thankee!"

"Assuming, of course, you perform as first lieutenant to *my* satisfaction," Lewrie both tempted and put on notice, "I do believe that when I've relinquished authority to our rightful captain, I can insert something more praiseworthy in the log."

"I will give you no cause for dissatisfaction, sir. None!"

There was a rap at the door, the bang of a musket butt on the deck outside. "Sah! Mister Midshipman Spendlove, *SAH!*"

"Enter," Lewrie replied coolly, with the tone of a captain.

"Sir, this note came off shore for you just now," the grinning imp reported, hat under his arm, and glancing about to see if rumours were true. "It smells *very* nice, Mister Lewrie, sir."

"Wonder how Naples looks from the masthead, Mister Spendlove?" Lewrie pretended to frown at him. "Horrid place to spend a whole *day* . . . even for a japing monkey such as your wee self, hmm?" he asked as he opened the scented note paper, sealed with a florid daub of wax and addressed in an ornate, high-flown hand.

"Sorry, sir," Spendlove swore, ducking his head properly, though he looked anything but contrite as Lewrie quickly perused his note.

"I will be going ashore for dinner, Mister Braxton," Lewrie told him, stuffing the note in a pocket quickly. "Some . . . ah, further palaver with the local authorities," he lied.

"You will wish the captain's gig, sir?" Braxton asked.

"Not mine to borrow, really," Lewrie decided. "The jolly-boat'll suit. I should return, hmm . . . sundown, I should think."

He didn't really expect to get another "all-night-in" with Emma Hamilton; nor was he sure he could stand another whole night of prattle. No, an afternoon'd suffice. Watch her do her "Attitudes," of course. And then beg off, pleading too much ship's business.

And Lord knows, he sighed, there's more'n enough o' that!

CHAPTER 8

Their idyll in Naples ended soon afterwards. A formal treaty with the Kingdom of Naples and the Two Sicilies was signed, with Lewrie proudly witnessing the ceremony. But then on 14 July, he was hustled off to sea with more urgent dispatches. Captain Braxton was making a miraculously speedy recovery, so there was no need to send him ashore, nor would a sea voyage threaten that recovery, the Italian physicians assured him after a final call on their patient.

And that voyage back to the Fleet went quickly, in good weather and brisk, invigourating winds. *Cockerel* scudded along like a migrating goose, winds on her larboard quarter, sails set "all to the royals," slicing the seas with the elegance of a rapier.

"How dare you!" Captain Braxton spat at him. "How dare you put such nonsense in the log, Mister Lewrie!"

"I wrote no more than the truth, sir," he replied resignedly.

"Truth?" Braxton hooted. "The truth is not *in* you! You're out to destroy me, sir. My entire family, all our careers! It's all mendacious tripe. For two pence, I'd . . . !"

He made as if to seize the offending pages and rip them out, but stopped. There was no expunging the brutal facts, none that would not represent a greater crime in the Admiralty's eyes. Captain Braxton had no recourse. Furiously, he realised that Lewrie knew that.

"Now that you are well again, sir," Lewrie offered as a sop, "I doubt the matter will come up."

"Oh, not this commission, damn you!" the bitter old man snarled.

"Signal from the flag, sir!" Lieutenant Scott shouted down the skylight from the quarterdeck. "They acknowledge our 'Have Dispatches' and send us 'Captain Repair on Board.'"

"Very *well*, Mister Scott!" Braxton bellowed in exasperation.

"Sir, are you that hale?" Lewrie asked. "To scale a 1st Rate's sides? It's only been a day since you resumed—"

"Your consideration for me is *touching*," Braxton snorted. "By God, sir, Admiral Lord Hood demands *Cockerel*'s captain, not you! And her true captain he shall have." Braxton lifted the weighted packet and reached for his hat.

"Would you at least let me brief you on what 'you' did ashore, sir?" Lewrie offered, trying to make some amends, at least. "Were he to question you about the dispatches—"

"I met our ambassador, delivered dispatches and got more from him, then sailed instanter," Braxton sneered, bustling for the doors. "Naples is in. What more is there to say? Now we have *two* weak allies 'stead of one. Thank you, but *no*, Mister Lewrie . . . I require no more assistance from you! You've my gig ready? Good. Get out of my way."

"Very good, sir," Lewrie replied, crisply.

'Least I tried, damn yer eyes; and if Admiral Hood catches you in a lie, God alone help you. It's no skin off my backside.

But Captain Braxton evidently did not put a foot wrong. He was aboard *Victory* for about fifteen minutes, then came sculling back with even more bundles. He didn't drop like a leaf from her side and drown himself, didn't dodder. By sheer willpower, he scaled *Cockerel*'s side and took his salute, though he looked white-faced and pinched once he attained the gangway, swaying more than did the deck.

"Mister Lewrie, there's mail for us. Distribute it," he said, weakening fast. "I'll be in my cabins." And he staggered away.

"Aye aye, sir!" Lewrie cried, all but pouncing on the discarded mail sack.

Mail—word from home! How rare it was to get it. Ships went down in storms, taken by privateers, and precious letters with them. Months, a year behind, they were, even under the best of circumstances. All too often they arrived at the wrong place, chasing the erratic and unknown movements of a squadron. Or might reach the squadron, but moulder in the mail sacks for months, held for independent ships. And that capriciousness worked both ways, for both senders.

Lewrie had letters from India, from his father, and from Burgess Chiswick, his brother-in-law, a captain in his father's regiment. They were over a year in transit, round Good Hope to the Admiralty, then to

Anglesgreen, then . . . There was information from his bank, his solicitor, from creditors. Those he set aside for later.

And a bundle from Caroline and the children.

In the privacy of his narrow cabin he opened the earliest dated letter, hoping the salt, rain, tar smudges and mildew hadn't ruined what she had written:

My dearest Husband,
We are all so immensely proud of you, far off in our King's Service. Your spring letters came at last, delighting us. Yet how immensely Hard is my continuing burden of Loneliness, how oft . . .

Bloody Hell, he groaned, tearing up a little as she described her own tears. He gazed at a miniature portrait, a rather good copy of the one hanging in their entry hall.

God help me, I'm *such* a bastard, he thought. A hound! Rakehelling about, back to my old ways. Putting the leg over just any new piece that crosses my hawse, no matter my . . . well, she was a rather *good* bit o' batter, wasn't she, that Emma? Oh, I'm such a *low hound*, though, to . . . I feel so guilty! I mean, I *should* feel guilty . . .

Hold on, though . . .

Hmmmm!

He recalled the free black woman, the widow he'd met in Clarence Town, in the Bahamas, after six months of exile in the Out Islands. A single afternoon of rutting, because he'd been so *very* lonely, too long separated from Caroline . . . didn't recall her name, but she had been so bloody good at lovemaking, and at restoring his spirits.

Mean t'say . . . ! Shouldn't I feel . . . abject? Or something?

He felt the urge to measure his pulse, to see if he was human. Oh, well . . .

The children missed him sorely, he read on; Sewallis has a new tutor and is learning his letters. There was scrawled proof of that in the margins—but it was early days as to what they spelled. Hugh left a thumbprint and an even shakier *X*, his mark. Charlotte was now on solid foods, toddling about, taking her first steps and out of her swaddles at last. Mrs. Cadogan, Caroline had dismissed; she'd simply gotten too dictatorial about running the entire household. There was a scandal about Maggie Fletcher, the vicar's daughter's maidservant, Maudie Beakman jilted by the same man who'd . . .

The planting season had gone well, and the weather bid fare for a bountiful harvest. And old William Pitt had passed over.

"Oh, damme . . ." Lewrie sighed bitterly.

I do not know how to tell you this, beloved, but Pitt is gone. Once you went to sea, the poor old dear began to fade. Lord, how sad he also seemed, prowling the house and grounds, as if in search of you, ever-napping in your chair alone, upon items of your clothing were they left out, and crying piteously for attention, demanding explanation of your absence. He climbed into my lap his last afternoon, as I sat and knitted by the garden. He played with some wool, then curled up and went to sleep, and I sensed, somehow, that I should not disturb him, no matter the distraction. He woke, looked up, put one paw to my breast, and then he lay back down, uttering one last trill . . .

"Oh, Pitt!" Lewrie cried, dropping the letter to his lap, tears in his eyes for certain now. "Poor old beast. Poor old puss! Least your last years were peaceful. Chickens to chase . . . Catnip and cream, good scraps . . ."

God, you inhuman *bastard*, he scathed himself. No remorse for cheatin' on your wife . . . yet you cry over the death of a stupid *cat*!

"Maybe it's all of a piece," he muttered throatily, covering his face with a dirt-stiffened towel so no one else would hear as he wept. Very possibly, for all.

BOOK V

Ne tibi tunc horrenda rapax ad litora puppem ventus agat, ludo volitans cum turma superbo pulvereis exultat equis ululataque tellus intremit et pugnas mota pater incitat hasta.

Let not then the driving blast carry your ship to those dreadful shores, what time the troop in arrogant sport fly here and there exultant on dusty steeds, and the ground trembles to their halloing, and their sire incites them to battle with the brandished spear.

—VALERIUS FLACCUS
Argonautica, Book IV, 606–09

CHAPTER 1

"All secure!" Midshipman Anthony Braxton read off the bunting hoisted on *Victory*. "Fleet . . . Will enter Harbour! . . . In Columns of Divisions!"

"They're just *giving* us the place, then?" Lieutenant Scott marveled.

"So it would appear, sir," Captain Braxton grunted, lowering his telescope, lips snug with aspersion—perhaps at French timidity. "Captain Elphinstone's landing at the fort yonder has cowed 'em, at last. They're streaming out of their forts, inland . . . nor'west for those farther hills."

"Well, it beats fighting our way in all hollow, sir," the Marine captain O'Neal opined darkly as he beheld the towering heights, rough headlands, and the many forts and batteries of Toulon.

"Granted, sir," Braxton grumbled, sounding disappointed, though.

"We've what, barely 1,000 Marines with the entire fleet?" O'Neal said in a softer voice to Lewrie, standing nearer the wheel. "Had this fleet tried to force a landing against opposition, we'd have lost half on the first fortifications alone."

"With the city for us, though sir?" Lewrie scoffed gently. "I doubt they'd have put up much resistance, even if it had come to that. The Republican diehards were in the minority, thank God. And they were not to know how much we had at our disposal. Twenty-one sail with us, and God knows what over the horizon."

After rejoining Hood's fleet, it had looked to be the very worst sort of naval service—blockade duty; slowly plodding in neat ordered lines of battle from Marseilles, round Cape Cicie to Toulon and back, parading the might of the Royal Navy, jogging off-and-on that forbidding coast, in hopes that the French might sally forth for battle. Rumours, and a "spying out," under cover of a truce mission by Lt. Edward Cooke of *Victory*, had determined that the French had at least twenty-one sail of the line in port, seventeen of them more or less ready for sea, and frigates and sloops of war, two-a-penny. But for a few fast frigates, ordered to trail their coats into the Bay of Toulon between Cape Sepet and Cape de la Garonne to tempt a response, Hood hadn't tried to enter in force, and the French had remained strangely somnolent.

Those Royalists in Toulon, though, the ones Sir William Hamilton had spoken of . . . they'd sent a two-man committee to *Victory* under a flag of truce on 23 August. Lt. Edward Cooke had gone ashore on the 24th, then one more time, to carry Hood's reply. Cooke had been shot at by a frigate with Republican sentiments, hailed as a hero and damn near chaired in triumph to a meeting of a Royalist committee intent on surrender, arrested by Republicans on the way back, then freed by a Royalist mob.

Again, on the 26th, he went ashore, returning with a French Navy officer, Captain d'Imbert of the seventy-four-gun *Apollon*, and the agreement was ratified. Toulon was theirs!

So now *Cockerel* was inside the Bay of Toulon, slowly heaving her way under a tops'l breeze from the south, beam-reaching towards the inner roads, just north of the peninsula which formed Cape Sepet, the southern guard of the great port, where before they would not have dared.

It helped that the revolutionary government in Paris had just proscribed Var and Provence, warning that troops and guillotines were coming if they did not immediately submit to the Republic.

The situation was what some might call interesting, to say the least. While a fair majority of Toulon was Royalist, declared for some prince now called Louis XVII, there was a moderately sized minority of Republicans, mostly the poor or the bitter, dead set against the aristocracy, the large landowners, and the merchant class. With opportunists on either hand, it went without saying. Yet the French Mediterranean Fleet held only a minority of Royalists, and a majority of Republicans. Rear-Admiral St. Julien, second-in-command, had seized forts facing the inner, Little Road of Toulon, with the crews of seven line-of-battle ships, about 5,000 men, disobeying orders of the staunchly royalist Rear-Admiral, Comte de Trogoff, who actually commanded the port.

Early on the 27th, a force of 1,500 men, the greatest portion of two regiments embarked with Hood's fleet, reinforced by about 200 Marines and seamen, under the overall command of Capt. George Keith Elphinstone of HMS *Robust*, had landed at Fort La Malgue, on the right side of the spit of land that divided the Little and the Great Roads, high enough to overlook and dominate St. Julien's much lower-set forts.

Elphinstone had sent a demand for St. Julien to surrender, and had warned that any vessel which did not enter Toulon's inner basin, land its powder and send its crew ashore, would be taken under fire.

That was enough for St. Julien. His honor had been satisfied, by token resistance, so he had decamped. And now, Admiral Hood could sail in.

Without a shot being fired, without a single casualty, they were in total possession of a French city, an entire French fleet, and a naval base with all its arsenals, powder mills and stocks, foundries for cannon and anchors, and immense quantities of naval stores.

"Hard to think of us taking all this, even were we fifty sail," Mister Dimmock spoke up, nodding to the Marine captain. "First, weather Cape Sepet, as we've done. And it's simply stiff with guns. There, young sirs—" he pointed out to the midshipmen with a ferrule in his hand, as they gathered about for a lesson—"near the end of the peninsula, on the highest hill of Cape Sepet, that's . . . what, Mr. Spendlove?"

"C . . . Croix des Signaux, sir."

"Aye, the signals cross. That's fairly new. Semaphore tower." Dimmock beamed his approval. "The old one, the Great Tower, is further inside the harbour, near Fort La Malgue. Now, below Croix des Signeaux, there's Batterie la Croix, north shore of the peninsula. Then west of that, there's Batterie des Frères . . . 'The Brothers' . . . go farther west and you come in range of Fort Mandrier, which commands the south side of the Great Road, next to the Infirmarie . . . sort o' like our Greenwich Naval Hospital back home, 'cross an inlet from Fort Mandrier, just at the thinnest shank of the peninsula, facin' the Golfe de la Veche. Mr. Dulwer, would you anchor in the Bay of Toulon, sir?"

"Uhm . . . perhaps not, sir? Not all the time?"

"Don't sound *too* definite, will ye now, Mr. Dulwer?" the sailing master sighed. "No, ye'd not. Too deep for the proper scope on cables, e'en do you weight 'em with gun barrels, and a rocky bottom. Levanter comes up, it throws a heavy sea from the east'rd, crost all that open water from Plage de la Garonne. Plage means beach, right, lads? Right. Now, between Batteries Croix and Frères, it's no more'n one sea mile to Cape Brun, on the north shore of the mainland. Batteries there, too . . . with forty-two-pounders. North tip o' Cape Sepet and Cape Brun squeeze in to mark the entrance to the Great Road. You have a little more shelter in the Great Road. It's still foul holding ground, but shallower'n the bay. West of Cape Brun, there're batteries on a high cliff, on this spit of land . . . here," he said, indicating the chart. "Can't rightly see it from the quarterdeck . . . all our fleet in the way, ha ha!"

The midshipmen made sure to sound appreciative of Dimmock's jape.

"Then to the west of those batteries is Fort La Malgue, which we took this morning, on another steep headland. Little water-fort guards the foot of it, Fort Saint Louis. West o' La Malgue, there's this peninsula . . . long, narrow, and steep, almost vertical cliffs. Great Tower on its tip, where it juts southerly, and pinches off the Great Road from the Little Road. Guns a'plenty there, too, mind. This narrow pass, not *half* a sea mile, from the Great Road to the Little. Le Goulet, Frogs call it . . . that's the Gullet, in real language. Across the Gullet is where the Frogs tried to make a stand this morning, northern side of the Golfe de la Veche, on Hauteur De Grasse. Big, round hilly thing, just on our bows if ye care to look. Two little spurs on its tip. Southern has Fort de Balaguer . . . the northern Fort L'Eguillettes. Lower than La Malgue, so we could've shot howitzers or mortars into them. So that's why the Frogs took French leave, ha ha!"

Another wave of laughter swept the quarterdeck, more sincere this time over Mr. Dimmock's pun, including the officers and seamen.

"The Little Road. Would you anchor *there*, Mister Dulwer?"

"Aye, sir," Dulwer shot back quickly.

"Aye, ye would," Dimmock agreed. "Very sheltered, fairly shallow. On the small side, though. Get out of the shallows along the shore and you don't have much room to swing. Maybe three or four ships may lie in the Little Road. Sou'west end, that's La Seyne . . . civilian harbour, so they take most of the available space. More batteries, unfortunately. Coverin' La Seyne is Fort Cruyon. A very low shore battery in an inlet north of there is Dubrun. Then another, on the north side of the Little Road, that's Le Millaud. Powder mills there, too, I recall. Atop them all, west of town, above these marshes, is Fort Malbousquet, then Fort Missicy, at the foot of this other hill, below Malbousquet."

"So . . . where do they *really* keep their ships, Mister Dimmock?" Spendlove asked, squirming with either boredom or confusion.

"Do you get past all this, into the Little Road, sir, you come about, hard t'starb'd and sail north. Through the pass in the channel booms . . . log and chain, stout as anything . . . and there's the Basin of Toulon. They can cram up to thirty sail of the line in there t'gether, bows or stern-to the quays, as most do in the Mediterranean. Fenders betwixt, so they won't chafe their gunn'ls off. Walk all day in shade along the quay, below their bowsprits . . . Not a stone's throw from warehouses and such. But . . ." Dimmock warned with a theatrical pause. ". . . to get into the basin, there's one damn-all tough nut still to crack, young sirs. There's the jetties, the breakwaters that make the basin. They're built so low to the water, it'd be like hitting a piece of driftwood. Laid out in a fleur d'eau . . . the very worst sort of coastal fort. They're hollow and bombproof, and stiff with guns. Entrance channel isn't a musket-shot wide, with forty-two-pounders to either beam. And the town's like an old king's castle. City walls are like a fort, with moats and drawbridges and gates . . . part of it they call Fort de France. And above it all . . . look up yonder, behind the town, sirs? Eighteen-hundred feet high, that chain of hills are. A ravine on the nor'-west . . . Gorge St. Antoine, and another narrow valley north. Steep,

crumbly stuff. There's forts all over up yonder . . . with ovens for heating
shot, high 'nough for accurate plungin' fire."

"What an effort they put into this place," Lt. Clement Braxton commented, with a whispery whistle of awe. "Marshes . . . seepy springs, I've
read, everywhere one looks. And no low tides to give them time to dig
or lay foundations. It's an engineering masterpiece."

"Aye, Mister Braxton, yer correct, sir," Dimmock agreed heartily.
"Can't wait to get ashore an' look it over, myself. East side of the basin,
they keep the lesser ships o' war, frigates and such. Shipyard and launch-
ways, graving docks. And there's a drydock that'd rock you back on your
heels, too. Brute of a thing. Think of how they managed to build *that,* sir!
Seal it, and pump out with convict labour, I think. Aye, sir . . . Toulon
mayn't be the world's best harbour t'lie in, but . . . it's the world's most
fortified, and most impressive built! Well, end of yer geography lesson,
lads. Back to your stations. We're sure to come to anchor before the hour's
out."

"From the sea *and* the land," Lewrie commented, coming to join
them as the midshipman scattered. "Hellish fortified."

"Better for us, when it comes to holding it, sir," Captain O'Neal
agreed.

"*Nine* fath'm! *Nine* fath'm t'this line!" a leadsman called from the
larboard foremast chains. *Cockerel* drew three fathoms, when deepladen.

"Steady as she goes, quartermaster."

"Aye aye, sir, steady'z she goes."

A weak sun shone that day, for a wonder, as if in celebration of their
bloodless victory. Quite unlike the weather of their short blockade,
which had shipped green seas, and gale-force winds at times, scattering
the squadrons and straining their masts nigh to snapping. Watery, wan
sunlight reflected from the charcoal-blue sea of the Great Road, wave-
motes of light dancing on the sides of the massive warships, and dun
sails and dull colours were stage-lit to an artist's whiteness or sheening
brilliance, as if posed for a commemorative oil.

During those rare moments of clear weather, Southern France had
appeared rather attractive, Lewrie'd thought; much like Naples, though,
in rockiness and semisere harshness. Whenever they'd gone close in-
shore, he'd espied hamlets and fishing villages that seemed cheerful
enough. And, on the slopes of Southern France, there was a softer and
lusher palette of greens than Naples could ever boast, more verdantly
bright, less dusty and muted. From high summer, thatchy tan to spring-
shoot green, the grasslands, vineyards and forests, olive groves and pas-
tures seemed to roll and tumble as they were brushed by some bright
scudding clouds' shadows.

Apart from Toulon, where sunlight dappled and sparkled, and the clouds scudded, the headlands and hills appeared to glow gold and umber, the tiled terra-cotta roofs were lit flamine red, and the very least cottages of Var and Provence were exotically lambent.

But not Toulon.

Around Toulon there seemed a pall, an ominous trick of lighting, as if the capes, the headlands, the bays and massive hills—mountains really, Lewrie decided—were shrouded by a funereal gloom, as if some storm clouds *must* hang perpetual. As if, for some malevolent reason, her harsh grayness of stark granite forts was forever deprived of any warmth, or hope, of Mediterranean sunshine. Pent from the lushness of her hinterland by grimly looming, bare and lifeless mountain masses, and begirt with the sinews and engines of warfare.

With the ship well in hand in a deep-water fairway, Lewrie took time to peer at the chart Mr. Dimmock had left tacked to the traverse board, looking past his usual sailor's concerns of depths, bearings and seamarks, to the hills beyond.

Toulon was girded by a host of lofty fortresses and redoubts: St. Antoine, St. Catherine, Artigues, Pharon, La Garde and La Vallette, and a myriad of lesser forts, redans, batteries and strongpoints which guarded the forbidding mountains, the narrow valleys between, and the passes and gorges. The terrain was fairly open to the east, sprinkled with villages and châteaux, gently rolling and benign along the Plaine de la Garde divided by a narrow ridge that ran west-to-nor'east above the road to Hieres, before the mountains shouldered into the coast, above Forts St. Catherine and La Malgue.

On the western approaches, from the pass at Ollioules through which the Marseilles road debouched, was a harsher coastal plain, this one puckered, pimpled and stippled with many mountain spurs, crablike hills and rugged prominences, and the roads wound snakelike to conform to them.

Fifteen miles, he marched off with a pair of brass dividers on the chart; fifteen miles of perimeter and approaches which had to be garrisoned and guarded, manned with troops and guns, if the coalition was to hold Toulon.

Say Naples sends their promised 6,000, like the treaty said, he speculated—though what little he'd seen of Neapolitan troops, and that with an untrained sailor's eye, hadn't impressed him that much. And were their Military Commissariat anything like what Mr. Husie had reported after visiting their naval supply establishment, then it was perhaps a cut above a barking shambles. *But not by much.*

Sardinia, they're down for 50,000 men—say we get a tenth of that army we're paying good golden guineas for. Spain, of course . . . ?

Why *of course*? he snickered to himself, still amazed that they were now firm allies. Correction—just "allies." Just this morning, the Spanish fleet had come up over the horizon at last, like a Jack-in-the-Box, rushing in untidy order to enter harbour at the same time as the Royal Navy. Troops aboard, he wondered? Sure to be. *Have* to be!

Spain had a huge army, but a narrow, rugged border with France along the daunting Pyrenees. Poor and downtrodden as their peasants were, as arrogant and stiff-necked—as benighted!—as their top-lofty aristocracy was, it was in Spain's best interests to send a big contingent quickly, to stamp the French Revolutionaries into the floor like cockroaches, before any of that "Rights of Man," egalitarian bumf caught on in Spain itself. He thought 10,000 men would be a safe wager.

And English regiments, that went without saying. There were men at Gibraltar, and with Spain allied, there'd be no reason to keep them there, no worry about a siege such as the one his father'd gone through when he'd won his knighthood, in the last war but one. Troops out from home, too, if Lords Dundas and Grenville had been scheming this one up as long as Sir William Hamilton had alluded. Bags of 'em!

Austria? Well, maybe too busy on France's eastern borders, Alan decided; they and the Prussians would mass to walk into France along the traditional routes, but part of the Austrian Empire was in northern Italy, so surely . . . another 6,000 or so, cutting west from Genoa or Leghorn? Or get us to escort transports from there, and bring 'em direct. And quick, he decided. It'll have to be quick, or . . . soon as they get word from us!

That brightened his prospects for a moment. Dispatches would go home, to all the allies. To Naples, for certain. *Cockerel* might sail on the next morning. He could go ashore again, visit Emma Hamilton one more time. Emulate some of those erotic Etruscan fragments they'd seen in their gallery of choice, the ones with the cavorting . . .

Well, maybe that's not a good idea, he sighed, leaving the chart: wondering again where his conscience was hiding, or if he, in truth, *had* one. Once was enough . . . took the edge off. Every six months'r so . . . ?

His brief enthusiasm left him, and he shivered inexplicably to a brisk African wind on his left shoulder that gave no warmth.

Hellish gloomy damn' place, he concluded.

"Abandon all hope, ye who enter here," he muttered.

"Sir?" the senior helmsman inquired, shifting his quid to another cheek.

"Nothing," Lewrie grunted. "Steady as she goes."

CHAPTER 2

Perhaps it was just as well that Capt. Horatio Nelson's sixty-four-gunned *Agamemnon* bore the word to Naples, Lewrie thought. With the French Mediterranean fleet captured in one fell swoop, all her proud, large line-of-battle ships in the bag, the more impressive British liners were freed to make the diplomatic calls about the region—those ships captained by men of greater stature and diplomatic experience.

Cockerel idled about in the Golfe du Lion for a few days to keep an eye on Marseilles, round Cape Cicie to the west, before that pointless task was undertaken by a small squadron of British 74's, and she returned to Toulon. There was nothing much to guard against, since only a scattered handful of French frigates and corvettes were still free to operate, and those few were alone, uncoordinated and fearful

"You really *can* walk in their shade," Lt. Barnaby Scott commented as they toured the basin a few days later.

Everywhere there was bustle. Proud French ships were being stripped of their guns and powder, rowing boats worked like a plague of water-beetles to carry captured supplies out to the Spanish and British ships. And a horde of curiosity seekers such as Lewrie and Scott had come ashore to gawp over all they'd won so easily, and crow with elation.

And from the moment their cutter had touched a quay, they'd been gawped at in turn, cheered by Royalist Toulonese, gushed over by women and men with white Bourbon cockades on their coats or their hats. Any restaurant would kick Frogs out to seat them and fête them, any desire they had was fulfilled (mostly), and they couldn't seem to buy a drink in the town—it was given with bubbly expressions of gratitude.

"Damn' friendly lot," Barnaby Scott opined. "For Frogs."

There was martial music, clattering hooves on cobblestones and the heavy drumming of field-artillery carriages and caissons as a Spanish half-regiment paraded by above the basin, on the main water street.

"S'pose we should be about our shopping," Lewrie shrugged, still uneasy with the concept of friendly Frenchmen. Besides, ambling about by themselves, surrounded by convict labourers in their filthy slops and irons, surrounded by milling packs of truculent and beetle-browed French sailors who were most pointedly *not* wearing Royalist cockades, and who hawked and spat behind their backs, or muttered sneering words behind their hands as they passed . . . well, they *might* be disarmed and supposedly harmless, but Lewrie didn't want to take the chance of risking the drunkest or the surliest of them. No matter how near help, in the form of Royal Navy working parties or Marine sentries, might be.

On the northern shore of the basin's quays, it all spread out before them as they stopped and stood, gazing down upon the pool of water between the jetties and the warehouses, dry dock and arsenals: A host of docked warships, frigates, corvettes, gunboats, floating batteries (that looked more like ancient oared war galleys), 74's and 80's of the line, and two monstrous 120-gun ships of the 1st Rate, so huge they dwarfed all others, even British 1st Rates.

"Comfortin' to know we'll have use of all these," Lewrie said on. "Frogs build damn' good ships. Finer entries, leaner quick-work . . . sail faster than ours, and that's a fact. Always have."

"Ah, 'tisn't the ship makes the difference, sir," Scott scoffed, a trifle bleary from all the "gratitude" he'd taken aboard. "'Tis *men* who decide a battle. Frogs've *never* had the stomach for fighting, not at musket or pistol-shot, broadsides to broadsides. Lay off, so please you, and fire at your rigging! Pack o' spineless, snail-eating' Mollies, they are. *Frog*-eatin' butt-fuckers. All they know how to do is mince!'"

"A little less of it, Mr. Scott," Lewrie cautioned. "Those near us aren't mincing, exactly. Why don't you smile and nod?"

"Shit on 'em, sir," Scott sneered. "Shit *on* 'em! I was raised t'hate a Frenchman worse'n 'Old Scratch' himself. Hate 'em worse than Dons, when you get right down to it. Damme if I'll pander to any Frog, no matter he's licking mine arse to save his. Let 'em bring on their guillotines, I say! Cut the odds down for us first, and we'll sort out the survivors later. And spare the world any more of 'em."

"I truly *do* despair of you, Mister Scott," Lewrie replied sternly, not for the first time. Bluff, humourous and "me-hearty" as Scott could be, he had a surly side when he'd been tippling. Which he did about as often as the unfortunate "Little Leftenant Do-Little," Banbrook, in the past month or so, Lewrie had begun to notice.

As that other unfortunate, Lt. Clement Braxton, had tried anew to ingratiate himself with his own messmates after his father's illness, it had been Scott who'd still have no truck with him. Which made it harder for the others to relent, to realise that the son was nothing like the sire, and accept his shy and clumsy offerings.

"I despair of the whole shitten mess, sir," Scott gloomed, taken by a Blue-Devil mood of a sudden. "Braxtons and Braxtons, then even more Braxtons, generation unto generation, pestiferous as Frogs in—"

"Shut up," Lewrie snapped.

"Sir?" Scott looked at him owlishly, like Falstaff called down by a drinking partner. But he did shut up, at least.

"If you cannot control yourself, sir, go back aboard."

"You'd deny me a few hours of peace, of freedom from our tyrants, sir?" Scott wheedled, sounding genuinely hurt. "Send me back to more—"

"Shut *up*, Mister Scott!" Lewrie snarled. "I mean it. Aboard or ashore, there'll be no more of that talk. Sets yourself a bad habit. Carp all you like two years from now, when the commission's over, but manage yourself now, sir."

"Mister Lewrie, you hate 'em as much as I do, as much as we both hate Frogs and Dons, I know it, so—"

"Sir, will you obey me?" Lewrie demanded, suddenly fed up with it; with Scott, with his impossible task. And begrudging his own few hours of freedom, interrupted by a maundering, half-drunken pest. Scott was, he'd imagined—til now, at least—a kindred spirit. Cynical, sarcastic, wryly funny to talk to, a rakehell and a rogue. But no, Scott had a deeper, darker streak that he didn't much care for.

"Very well, sir," Scott replied stiffly, drawing himself up to a full height, doffing his hat in salute. "I'll say no more. I trust you may excuse me, then, sir? Since you find my company distasteful, I will spare you any further . . . I will take my leave, sir."

"Very well, Mister Scott," Lewrie sighed, wondering if he had not lost the man's respect, and his authority over him, as well as what had passed for a tentative beginning to a career-long friendship. He suspected that he had; Lt. Barnaby Scott was the sort who'd hold a grudge over a trifle such as this, drunk or sober. "Keep yourself out of any trouble, Mister Scott. Your opinions anent Frogs, *that'd* spare you no end of grief. And be back aboard by sundown."

"Sir!" Scott said stiffly, almost clicking his shoe heels like a Prussian grenadier, and departing, a trifle unsteadily, parting a path through French citizens, subjects and sailors by his brusque mood and his daunting, damme-boy bulk and height.

"Shit, I give up!" Lewrie sighed in a bitter whisper. He'd just lost an ally in the wardroom, perhaps made a sullen enemy. It was as if Scott felt betrayed that Lewrie, who should have been on *his* side, had aided Clement Braxton's tentative essays at camaraderie, much as a jilted lover might turn on the suitor who'd scorned her. "What next, I ask You?" Alan queried, turning his face up to the sky.

"Pardon, m'sieur? Votre ami, 'e eez beaucoup trink, hein?"

"What?" Lewrie snapped, turning to find his accuser. "Wait a bit." He brightened, trying to remember where and how he'd met a French naval officer, "Damme, I *know* you, don't I?"

"Saint Kitts? Votre frégate . . . mon frégate, ve battaille?" The other fellow beamed: "*La Capricieuse?* Et votre . . . corvette, I am s'inking . . . ? Charles Auguste de Crillart, a votre service! Et vouz . . ."

"Of course!" Lewrie exclaimed. "Alan Lewrie . . . a votre service, aussi, m'sieur. God, it's been years! Wasn't I your gaoler?"

"Ah, mais oui, Alain Lewrie," Crillart grinned, doffing his gold-laced hat and making a formal leg before shaking hands. "You vere ze meed-shipman, zen. An' maintenant, ze lieutenant, hein? Con-grat-shu-lay-shins," he pronounced carefully, still capable of only fragmentary English. "Et votre ship?"

"*Cockerel,*" Lewrie laughed, then crowed like a rooster. "À la chan-ticlier? First officer, now. Premier officeur? Et vous, m'sieur?"

"Ah, moi aussi! Premièr lieutenant de frégate *Alceste*. She is 'ave ze trente-six canon . . . ze s'irty-six? Mais . . . las' mont' Admiral St. Julien, 'e dismiss me, say I am Royalist, zo . . ."

"You don't go by Baron de Crillart, either, I take it?"

"Ah trés dangereuse, mon ami," Crillart sighed heavily. "Avant ze Terror, trés early? I go to Paris to 'ow you say, un delegate in ze Etats-Général. To sit? Oui, to sit as delegate. I am fill avec beaucoup élan, n'est-ce pas? I serve in America, I meet américains . . . read ze Bill of Rights, ze Declaration of Independence. Ze Paine, ze Jefferson an' Adams. An' I meet ze grande Lafayette, zo I s'ink wan I come 'ome . . . je suis ze nobleman, ze jeune homme, vis duty to aid ze country . . . 'elp amend eet. France is ze bankrupt, ze people starving, out of work. Ve vere not wealthy, powerful . . . old famille viz titles only, an' people in Normandie respect us."

"Yet they ended up turning on you, after all?" Lewrie asked with sad foreknowledge, having read several accounts of the Revolution's early days, when it had looked to be a gentlemanly, civilised reform, not a peasants' revolt and a bloodbath.

"Ah, oui. D'abord, ve dare un peu, a leetle?" Crillart said as he gazed out with sadness on the proud but idle ships. "Beet by beet zey dare more, an' ze radicals take over, zeyr decrees more revolution-airre . . . incroyable! Zen, zey purge L'États-Général. À bas aristos, hein? Down viz all aristocrats? I am dismiss. Revenir au Normandie . . . mais non, ze madness come zere, aussi. Neighbours, amis, peasants we know all zeyr lives turn agains' us. Mon père, maman et moi, ve renouncons ze titles. Declare as citizens. Even zat buy us leetle safety."

"So how did you get to Toulon, and stay in the Navy?" Alan asked.

"Ah, avant ze Terreur, we sell ev'rys'in'. Bribes? I declare for Repub-lique, zey need trained officeurs Jacobiste . . . I arrange post here an' bring maman, mon frère Louis. Mon père, il est mort, of ze malade de coeur. Zo many Royalists in Toulon an' Provence, ve s'ink ve be safety. Ma cousin Sophie de Maubeuge, elle flee Paris, join us. More bribes, hein? Ev'rys'in' ve lose, mais notre vie . . . our lives. Maintenant . . . ?"

"You're safe as houses, maintenant, mon ami," Lewrie insisted to perk him up. "The coalition is sending troops. We'll hold the place until we raise the whole of Southern France, and Austria and Prussia kick the doors to Paris down."

"Zo do ze Republicains, ami Lewrie," Crillart disagreed. "On ze west, Général Carteau an' Citizen Mouret, zey conquer Marseilles a day be-fore votre fleet enters. On ze east, Général Lapoype an' ze Armée du Italie. Nord, Général Kellerman eez in Lyons, an' marchin' sud viz ze trente mille . . . ze s'irty s'ousand men."

"Bloody hell, that many?" Lewrie frowned.

"Mais, your soldiers, zey fight Carteau an' Mouret las' week," Crillart went on, cheering up slightly. "You' capitaine El . . . Elf . . ."

"Elphinstone?"

"Oui, Elphinstone. 'E comman' Brittanique an' Espagnole soldiers. 'E beat ze Republicains badly, take all zeyr artillerie, 'orse, an' baggage. Make great casualtie, with 'ardly any loss. West of 'ere, at ze village de Senary, an' ze pass at Ollioules."

"Good on him, then," Lewrie crowed. "And there're Sardinian troops coming. Neapolitan, British, Austrian, more Spanish. Then, there's the garrison here at Toulon. Sure to be men loyal to Louis the Seventeenth."

"Oui," Crillart allowed with another heavy shrug. "Ze Espagnole zey lan' un mille . . . one s'ousand men. Royaliste Toulonese, peut-être two s'ousand men, only. Many, zey desert. 'Ave très fear? *Votre* armée, viz matrossez et Garde du Corps . . .'ow you say . . . ?"

"Our sailors and marines, and two regiments of infantry?"

"Oui, per'ap' ze . . . uhm, one an' a 'alf s'ousand?"

"Hell, is that all, so far? I'd have thought sure . . ." Lewrie exclaimed, thinking again of that fifteen-mile perimeter. Though the troops present—so far—were better drilled and more experienced than Republican peasant levies, that still sounded like they were more than a *bit* thin on the ground.

"Pardon, avez-vous manger? 'Ave you eaten, mon ami?'" Crillart asked.

"Well, not exactly . . ."

"Zen you mus' come 'ome viz me, ami Alain!" Lieutenant Crillart cried. "Maman, Louis et Sophie, zey will be fill viz delight! An' ze cuisine à la Toulonnaise . . . le vin! Magnifique!"

"It was wine I was after," Lewrie explained, waffling. "I came to do some shopping for the wardroom, and . . ." The others had entrusted him and Lieutenant Scott with a cache of coin so they could purchase fresh livestock, eggs, cheeses, breads, and most especially, wine to replenish stores. Between Royalist "gratitude" and stark fear for the morrow among their hosts, they'd anticipated some truly outrageous knock-down bargains.

"Ve do zat, maintenant. I aid you viz ze storekeepers, hein? An' zen, you dine viz us, as our 'onoured guest. I insist!"

"Well, in that case . . . I'd be delighted," Lewrie replied, never one to turn down a free meal. "Lead me. I'm yours."

CHAPTER 3

They were, the de Crillarts, a rather nice family . . . for Frogs. After an hour of shopping and, with Charles's help, the discovery of a well-stocked chandlery, and a chandler who wasn't trying to pay off the national debt, they'd sent the cutter back to *Cockerel* gunn'l-deep with everything they'd hoped for.

Lt. Charles Auguste de Crillart and his relations lodged in what they termed an *appartement*, very West Indies in character, with wrought-iron balconies and tall windows overlooking the basin, high up on the sloping town's heights. The late afternoon vista was pleasant and fairly cool, the apartment airy and well lit, but a bit on the tattered side. Shabbily respectable, but certainly not one of the better neighbour-hoods. Not what Lewrie would have thought suitable for aristocracy, even genteelly straitened aristocracy; as if Charles was forced to live on his naval pay—and that, given the times, uncertain in amount and reg-ularity of payment.

Maman was one of those long, horse-faced, stout-jawed ladies of the old school, who clung to pale face powders and white-floured wigs. Hortense de Crillart was in her middle fifties, and might have been a handsome woman in her day. She had not been as enthralled as Charles had said to have another maw at her table, though Lewrie had mollified her misgiv-ings with a basket of victuals and wine from the chandlery as a house gift.

Louis, the younger brother—Chevalier Louis de Crillart, he went by—was a sulky, pimply sort, dark-haired and dark-eyed, initially stiff with grave hauteur, though he'd thawed a little as the evening pro-gressed. He was twenty, and had been a junior officer in a famous cavalry regiment, much like a British coronet in a unit which could boast "The King's Own . . ." in its designation. The regiment had been disbanded, its aristocratic officers dismissed or beheaded, and it was now run by corporals and sergeants, to Chevalier Louis's great, and voluble, disgust.

Lewrie sensed that there was some rancour among the brothers, Louis and Charles, as if the dead father and Charles—the current baron—had made a Devil's bargain in relinquishing their titles, in selling off their estates, and fleeing instead of fighting.

Though they tried to be affable and gracious to their guest, Alan caught a few flurries of rapid French tossed between them like grenades now and then, not meant for his ears. Poor his French might be, but he did catch enough of their gist to realise that Charles's declaration for the Republic, which had saved their lives from the guillotine, and his first enthusiastic support of the Assembly, was a black betrayal to Louis, the intensest sort of Royalist firebrand. Looking at him as he spoke, his eyes glaring, darting under his dark brows, the quick, impatient way he tossed his loose-gathered hair away from his face, Lewrie could imagine him the same sort of fanatic as the ones who'd launched the Terror—a fanatic equally dedicated to his bright, shining cause—on the opposing side.

Charles, without his uniform coat and hat, at ease at the table with a glass of wine in his hand and a fund of stories about shipboard life in the French Navy, seemed much the same charming fellow he had in the Caribbean after Lewrie's ship *Desperate* had taken *Capricieuse*, and they'd dined together so often on the sail back to Antigua, with Lewrie rated midshipman and master's mate, in charge of the prize, and Charles on his parole. Not like a baron at all, then or now, Lewrie thought.

Charles appeared more like a member of the petit-bourgeoisie, a chap more comfortable in furry slippers after a long day at a clerking desk. He was distinguished-looking, about Lewrie's age; nothing to write home about, though. Regular features, average height and all the usual forgettable bumf.

The intriguing member of the family was the younger female cousin, Sophie de Maubeuge. Her story was more tragic. Whilst Charles's presence in the Estates-General had saved his family, her father and all her relations had been too well-to-do, too resistant to change—too well known and powerful. She'd fled her convent school to hide in Normandy with the de Crillarts, whilst the tumbrils and the mobs had claimed most of her kin, including her immediate family. She was now the sole survivor, the last Vicomtesse de Maubeuge.

It was a heady title for such a sylphlike, shy, soft-spoken girl. Sophie was only fifteen, slim and petite, the sort who softly whispered when she spoke, and that, rarely. Though graced with the innate, bred-in-the-bone polish of aristocracy, the tutoring in social arts and such, she was as meek as a scullerymaid, and smiled or laughed seldom; though Lewrie considered her recent horrible history a damned good reason for her gravity. That, and a proper convent, sergeant-major nun upbringing.

She was of middling height, a bit less than five and a half feet tall, between seven and eight stone in weight. Sophie's features were bewitchingly gamine. High cheekbones, a pertly tapering face, full and wide lips, and crowned by overly large, slightly almond-shaped eyes of a startling green hue, brilliant as cat's eyes, and set like glittering gems in a flawless, "peaches-an'-cream" complexion. Her hair, which she still wore long and simple in girlish fashion, was a fascinating reddish auburn hue, more russet or red chestnut than anything else Alan could think to compare it to. And the very idea that some bloody-eyed peasants, gutter sweepings and mobocracy could even begin to think of chopping the head off such an entrancing and harmless young thing set his blood boiling. Quite apart from being covertly besotted, he found his heart going out to her in sympathy.

There was trouble there, too, he'd noted, when he tried to be his most charming and amusing self, to cosset her into a better mood with songs or japes. Chevalier Louis had left off berating Republicans to glare at him for being amusing, for monopolising her attention. And, Lewrie also noted, when tender young Sophie de Maubeuge had sheep's eyes, or laughed at last, she directed her gaze and encouragement towards Charles, her saviour, as if to share with him!

It had been his family fortune, what little of it was left after selling their estates and most-prized possessions to gimlet-eyed agents or hateful neighbours, that had supported her, had brought her down to Toulon and safety. And, Alan learned, it had taken more than Charles's declaration of support and allegiance to the Republic—it had taken hefty bribes to keep her off the local committee's lists of those who deserved their necks stretched below the blade of a guillotine.

Supper with the family—a hearty and creamy soup, laced with onions and a few dubious shreds of chicken. Scads of crusty bread and butter, a runny omelet served with well-seasoned sliced and fried potatoes, and a small veal cutlet nestled at the side of his plate, aswim in a thin wine gravy, with an abundance of mushrooms, disguising what a tiny cutlet it was, ladled atop. And a marvelous St. Emilion Bordeaux, several bottles in fact, to wash it all down. Enough wine to at last mellow even the sulkiest to a semblance of good cheer, and put a dimple in Sophie's cheek.

"I must be going, Charles," Lewrie said at last, after mangling a tune on a borrowed recorder and returning it to Sophie's care.

"Back to your ship," Crillart shrugged. "I walk viz you to ze quays, Alain."

"Permettez-moi, maman?" Sophie said quickly, sounding more like a regular girl, eager to go out, at last, as she fetched Lewrie's hat; like the daughter of a middling-common family might, instead of waiting for some servant to do it.

"Oui," Maman allowed grudgingly, with a stern expression. Her lips flattened over her long teeth and gums, making her look even more horse-faced, and Lewrie caught another subtle undertone, as Madame de Crillart darted her glances to both Sophie and Charles, then at Louis.

Alan made his most courtly goodbye, bowed low in *congé*, expressed how much he'd enjoyed himself, and promised to repay their generous hospitality. Maman replied in kind, though she sounded doubtful.

It was a lovely time for a stroll. Close to sundown, with cool breezes ruffling the waters of the basin and the farther Little Road, the street lamps being lit, and the apartments and shops aglow with a candle or lantern in every window. The sun was quite low, and it was a gold and orange sunset, dusky rose-reddish gray to the south and east. Louis, thankfully, did not accompany them, so Charles and Alan strode to either side of the shorter Sophie. But it was upon Charles's genteelly extended arm that she rested her fine, white hand.

"Such a lovely evening," Lewrie commented as they strolled downhill. "All the ships, outlined against the setting sun."

"Ze *Dauphin-Royal*," Charles pointed out, indicating the massive 120-gunned ship on the east side of the basin. "Ze Republicans, zey vill change 'er name. Ze ozzer, *Commerce-de-Marseille*. An' ze quatre-vingts canon . . . ze eighty guns; *Tonnant, Triomphant, Couronne.*"

He reeled off the majestic names of the seventy-four gunned ships, those the Royal navy would term 3rd Rates: *Apollon, Centaure, Lys* (now named *Tricolor*), *Scipion, Destin, Dictateur, Duquesne, Héros, Heureux, Pompee, Commerce-de-Bordeaux, Censeur, Mercure, Alcide, Conquér-ant, Guerrier* and *Puissant, Suffisant* and *Souverain*, now called with levelling, Egalitarian logic, *Souverain-Peuple; Généreux, Orion, Entre-prenant, Patriote, Duguay-Trouin, Languedoc* and *Trajan.*

All as harmless now as a pack of dead otters, their powder away in warehouses ashore, small arms taken off and locked up, though seamen still thronged their decks, for lack of a better place to house them. Strangely silent ships, too, with none of the usual dogwatch music or humumm to be heard, their yards still properly squared and crossed and rigging taut, spider-mazed black against the sunset. Few lights showed, even through lower-deck gun ports opened for ventilation. Glims at the belfries and wheels, from wardroom or great-cabin windows, perhaps, but little else; their taffrail lanterns for night-running dark. And flying no flags of any kind.

"An' *Alceste*," Charles muttered gravely, gazing with a spurned lover's sadness at his ship, his beloved frigate, squeezed in so snug between others on the eastern quay that she looked as forlorn as some barge abandoned in a weeded ship-breaker's yard. "Peut-être . . ."

"Soon, Charles," Lewrie assured him. "With enough loyal seamen, surely it's in the coalition's interests to raise a Royalist squadron, to show the world. And encourage the other maritime provinces, such'z the Vendée, Corsica . . . perhaps . . . peut-être, hey? . . . they'd promote a loyal lieutenant to, how do you say? . . . capitaine de frégate?"

"Capitaine," Charles mused with a slight smile. "Zat soun' trés bon. Oui . . . peut-être, mon ami."

"Capitaine de frégate, Charles Auguste, Baron de Crillart," the girl tasted, in a slightly bolder voice than her meek, kittenish tone, and beamed a hopeful smile at both of them. "Oui, zat soun' magnifique! An' 'e vin beaucoup fame, as 'e conquer."

Poor little mort's head over heels in love with the man, Lewrie laughed to himself. And all he looks is . . . modest? What a twit! Take what you may, fool! And the best of luck to you. Oh, give her three'r so more years, o' course, but then . . . make sure I dance at yer weddin'.

"Why not admiral, mademoiselle Sophie?" Lewrie teased slyly, to see what her response might be. "Once the revolutionaries've been beat, and France is herself again, well . . . sky's the limit."

"Sky . . . eez ze leemeet?" she frowned. "Oh! Le ciel! Ah, oui, m'sieur Lewrie! Zen 'e 'ave . . . recover eez estate . . . all ze estates . . ."

"He settles down as a duke. A most eligible duke," Lewrie coaxed. "Charles, I'm amazed, all this time, you haven't married?"

"Ah, you see, mon ami," Charles stammered, turning as mottled as the sunset clouds, and Lewrie was rewarded by a sly, and thankful, look of near adoration from the girl, a gratitude which warmed him right down to his toes. "Ze marine royale, uhm . . . ze marry officeur, 'e eez . . . zey s'ink 'e eez lack le dedication . . . ?"

"Lieutenant Lewrie, *tu* es marié . . . *you* are married, n'est-ce pas? Encore, marine royale de la 'bif-tecs' . . . oh, pardon!" She cried, using an insulting (for the French, anyway) colloquialism. Blushing to the roots of her hair under her stylish little hat, she struggled with her most important point. "Votre . . . Royal Navy, yet *zey* do not . . ."

"Oui, mademoiselle, je suis marié," Lewrie replied, with a wink to her, though it cut a bit rough to declare such to a girl as desirable as she, no matter her age. Damme, but that makes me feel ancient, he cringed! "With three children," he went on, feeling even more ancient. "I wed in '86. And Caroline sailed with me to the Bahamas. Where we had our eldest son." Cruel it might be, but he delighted in encouraging her fantasies; and perhaps in opening Charles's eyes. "And the Royal Navy doesn't think any the less of me," he lied, and that most arrantly, too.

Merci, m'sieur! She mouthed at him in silence, with her back to her intended (whether he knew it or not yet), almost bouncing in her glee.

"Well, I must leave you now, Charles . . . mademoiselle. Pardon, Vicomtesse de Maubeuge . . . Baron de Crillart. My undying thanks for . . ."

They bowed their last departure, and Lewrie watched them with a wry eye as they began another long stroll home.

Cousin or not—and he still wasn't sure how close their consanguinity was—she'd be a fine catch, no error. He'd be a fine catch, too.

Lewrie whistled for a passing boat, and the coxswain lifted his arm and put his tiller over in reply.

It struck Lewrie that he'd thoroughly enjoyed his brief stint of domesticity, of being, even for a few precious hours, more intent upon civilian, familial concerns, instead of *Cockerel's* sea of troubles.

He'd quite enjoyed being avuncular with the young girl, even if he had turned out to be a mischievious, meddlesome sort of uncle. "Better Charles than Louis, that's for certain," Alan muttered to himself as his boat approached the landing steps. And he was sure Maman Hortense would agree with him. Louis . . . there was a lad needed shunning, fast! He might be closer to Sophie's age, might be half-seas-over about her, whilst Charles was blind as a bat, but . . . there was too much anger to him, too much sulkiness. Too much of the fanatical young fireeater about him. Alan didn't think that portended a long life for the young chevalier, not in these times.

With another of his sudden chills, Alan recalled another time in another revolution when he'd encountered such dedicated hatred, and such fanaticism for a cause. Just after they'd escaped Yorktown and the surrender, down on Guinea Neck with Governour and Burgess Chiswick and their remaining handful of North Carolina Loyalist riflemen. That meaningless last skirmish before their escape cross the Chesapeake that'd slain so many people. And that despicable young lad who'd led the French to them, the one Governour'd gut-shot after, and left to die in writhing agony.

And after Yorktown, where'd I go, he asked himself? To Wilmington to help evacuate the Cape Fear Loyalists. Where I first met Caroline and the rest of the Chiswicks. Loyalists. And the Crillarts . . . Royalists.

"Same bloody thing," he growled. "Nice people caught up in the worst of circumstances, and everyone out for their blood, same as . . . damme!"

He shivered at the appalling coincidences. And hoped that this time things might turn out different.

CHAPTER 4

"Ship's comp'ny, off hats, and . . . salute!" Lewrie ordained as Captain Braxton scaled *Cockerel's* side, to appear in the entry port to take his due honours, and doff his own hat briefly. Lewrie hoped that he was in a good mood for a change. They'd swung idle to a best bower and kedge anchor for a whole dispiriting week with nothing to do, and the crew's behaviour, never of the best, had gotten surlier, no matter how much make-work they'd laid on.

"Mister Lewrie," Braxton appeared to smile for an instant.

"Sir," Lewrie replied with a hopeful nod, and thinking that his captain must have gotten a glass or two of something welcoming ashore, during his interview with Rear-Admiral Charles Goodall, the appointed military governor of Toulon. He seemed positively mellowed, for once.

"Dismiss the hands, Mister Lewrie," Braxton drawled, then bestowed upon his first lieutenant another mystifying smile.

"Aye aye, sir."

Two in a week, that's damn near . . . *fright'nin'*! Alan thought.

"Then join me in my cabins, sir," Braxton prosed on. And then smiled one *more* time before descending to the gun deck.

Three? Lewrie noted. *Three*? Dear Lord, what's he know that I don't? Alan shuddered.

"Just had a long chat with Goodall," Braxton began to explain. He left Lewrie standing before his desk without offer of a seat, as he took his own ease in his chair. He did not offer Alan a drink, though he was sipping a coolish glass of Rhenish. "Quite a conundrum we have here, Mister Lewrie."

"Sir?" Alan said warily.

"Half our line-of-battle ships off at sea, doin' God knows what Lord

Hood wishes 'em to do," Braxton speculated as he undid his stock. "We've stripped the larger vessels of hands and Marines, to flesh out the garrison and man the artillery before our reinforcements arrive. And *still* have need of men ashore. Beginning to get my drift, are you, Mister Lewrie?"

"I believe so, sir," Alan said with a sick nod.

"Hirin' Maltese seamen, would you believe it?" Braxton cackled, somewhere between real mirth and sour surprise. "The Grand Master of Malta will sell us the services of 1,500 of the bastards, for a hefty fee, I'd wager. Then *we* have to pay 'em able seamen's wages, to boot!"

They'll starve to death on *that*, Lewrie thought.

"That way, Mister Lewrie, more experienced British tars . . . *and* their officers may be spared for land service."

"Aha, sir."

"Quite the protégé of Lord Hood, aren't you, now, sir?" Braxton all but simpered. "Yorktown and all that, I'm told? Some work ashore in the Far East before, with troops and guns? Oh, Admiral Goodall was all ears, perky as anything, when I told him your sterlin' qualities. 'Have to have a stout fellow like him,' he told me, Lewrie! And so he will. I volunteered you. Told him you were eager as anything to get at the Frogs. I don't misrepresent you, do I, sir? You wouldn't get cold feet, would you, now? No, that wouldn't look good in your record. Nor to Lord Hood, either. Bein' called a coward, who'd . . ."

"I will pack my sea chest, sir," Lewrie sighed.

"Thought you might," Braxton relished.

"Will *Cockerel* be giving up any hands to assist me, sir?"

"I'll give you Mister Scott and Mister Midshipman Spendlove. Your man Cony off the foremast. And twenty more hands. Only half of 'em able seamen, mind. Can't spare much beyond them. Idlers and waisters off the gangways."

"Any of the Marine complement, sir?"

"Can't spare a one, Mister Lewrie," Braxton sighed, almost making himself sound sad. "With Maltese newcomes aboard, I'll have need of Marines more'n ever. That's where *Cockerel*'s bound, don't ye know, sir. Malta." Braxton rose from his chair to shuffle round his desk. "Where I'll get myself a crew, at last, with all dross weeded out, with willing Dago riffraff to take their place. Men who'll work chearly for me, and toe my line to the very inch, Mister Lewrie! To the very inch!"

"It would seem so, sir," Alan sulked. And you'll get your son as first, your nephew as acting lieutenant. And then you can do as you damned well please! Or so you think.

"And, I'm shot of you at last, Mister Lewrie," Braxton muttered. "Believe me when I tell you, once you're gone from us, I can find an hundred ways to make sure you *never* return. I don't care if you make 'post' overnight, I don't care if you earn yourself a bloody knighthood ashore! I'm shot of you, and I'll sing your praises to Heaven itself, if that'll *keep* you gone. Enjoy your duties *ashore*, Mister Lewrie. Take joy of 'em. Whilst I'm at *sea*, beyond the reach of your obstructions! You are free to leave now, *Mister* Lewrie. Dismiss!"

"Aye aye, sir," Lewrie huffed, though secretly happy to be free, no matter how outmaneuvered he felt at that moment, how stupid he'd been, to have not seen the chance of this coming. "Uhm, sir . . . about the men."

"What about 'em?"

"*You* will pick the . . . uhm, our 'volunteers,' sir?"

"Picked 'em already, sir," Braxton grinned malevolently. "Weeks ago. Months ago, I made my list. *Ev'ry* bad apple we have is yours."

What Captain Braxton termed "bad apples" turned out to be a fair pack of men: Bosun's Mate Porter for the senior hand, though Braxton thought him too young and soft-handed. Able Seamen Lisney and Gracey, Landsman Preston, Able Seaman Sadler, Ordinary Seamen Gittons and Gold . . . his least-favourite men, those who'd scowled too darkly after their floggings, or had shown too much independence of spirit. His least-favourite midshipman, Spendlove, most importantly not "family" . . . a gunner's mate who hadn't licked his boots, a quarter-gunner and four gun captains, along with enough landsmen to pulley-hauley, serve as rammers and loaders for captured French guns. And a few of the truly criminal and bootless, a few of the weaker, spindlier types who'd never had any business going aboard a ship of war, a few of the tom-noddies with which every military or naval establishment was cursed—those too dense to come in from out of a driving rain, but whose backs and sinews were stout.

"Don' know whether t'laugh'r cry, sir," Cony muttered as a cutter bore them shoreward. He was well turned out in a dark blue, round shell jacket, blue-and-white chequered gingham shirt, reasonably clean white slop trousers and a stout pair of shoes, well blacked; as was his wide and flat-brimmed tarred sennet hat. A small sea chest and a loose kit bag rested by his toes.

"Amen to that, Cony," Lewrie sighed, looking back at *Cockerel* as she receded in the distance of the outer Road.

"Weep, that's certain," Lt. Barnaby Scott gloomed beside him near the tillerman. "Christ, 'least she was a *ship*!"

" 'Ell-ship, she were," someone up forward whispered, and Lewrie turned, but could not discover whether it had been one of his Cockerels who'd spoken out, or one of the anonymous oarsmen.

As much as his own feelings on the matter of his expulsion were still unsettled, he could see the same mirrored on the faces of the men. Relief, a jeering, taunting joy, now they were free of their oppressors . . . or a darkly glum glower. Hell-ship or not, she'd been home, anchor to the familiar, and now these sailors were cast adrift, cut off from fellow sufferers with whom they'd come to enjoy sharing their suffering.

"Feel I've just been sent down from Harrow," Lewrie smirked, trying to buoy his emotions, turning again to study his ship.

"Hmmph!" from Lieutenant Scott, hulking over him. *Hmmph!* to good public schools, to class and advantage, perhaps. Or to being "sent down" with Lewrie, through no fault of his own, and brooding on the injustice done him. Scott abhorred *Cockerel* and his Braxtons, one and all, yet . . . now he was just as adrift as one of the snuffling powder monkeys, torn from the comforts of the wardroom, the certainty of a limited world, and his rightful station in it. His duties and his honour, which were simple and understandable. Ashore, God knew what he'd be asked to do, how far out of his proper depth he'd be tossed. And from his black glower and his *Hmmph!*, Lewrie knew he highly resented his loss. And the poor sort of company with which he'd been marooned.

Lewrie got his party ashore at the north quay of the basin, drew their attention back to him from their rubbernecking and gawping about at the massive ships, the immensity of all they'd captured.

There was a post-captain to receive them, with a harried midshipman who bore a sheaf of pages. And there was nothing more dangerous in the entire Royal Navy than a midshipman with temporary authority and a sheaf of orders he thought he understood.

"Mister Lewrie, Mister Scott, sirs," the teen said crisply. "I've orders your party will berth in yon guardhouse, sirs. Hard by the gate to the dockyard, just cross there, sirs? Temporary, I believe, but . . . if you would be so good as to follow me, sirs?"

Off they went, with Lewrie, Scott and the bosun's mate whipping-in the stragglers like exasperated sheepdogs.

"Bloody 'ell, ye can't go adrift in a furlong, can ye, Newton?" Porter snapped. "*Keep* yer mind on it! An' who's the fool wot lef' 'is sea bag b'hind? Bloody . . . !"

The guardhouse had been a barracks for the dockyard sentries, and the hands oohed and ahhed as they quickly explored it, hooting with pleasure as they discovered its luxuries.

" 'S got the real beds, it 'as!" Sadler boomed from the back. "No more 'ammocks!"

"Bloody hell, they's good mattresses, too, lads, lookit!"

"They's a well inna back, an' wash- 'and stands. Pumpwater, an' coal grates. Us kin make 'ot!" a younger voice piped in wonder.

"There are officer's quarters above, sirs," the midshipman said in a softer voice. "Rather nice, I'm told. Conveniently placed, so you may keep an eye on them after dark. These . . ."

He indicated a locked rack of muskets, St. Etienne Arsenal, .69 cal., a case of bayonets, a wall hung with powder horns and cartridge boxes, crossbelts and infantry hangers.

"I'm afraid your men will have to use these, for lack of British arms, sirs," he told them with a faint moue of disgust. "Anything else you need, sirs, simply go cross to the warehouses on the west side and indent for. The Frogs have mountains of supplies."

"Temporary, you said? Any idea what we're to do, now we're here?" Lewrie asked.

"Not the faintest, sir, sorry. Once you've settled your people, you may inquire at the Governor's offices, uphill yonder, sir, in that house with the flagpole. Can't miss it. King's Colours and a Spanish flag flying. Military commandant is a Don, Rear-Admiral Gravina. Will that be all for now, sir?"

"Aye, I suppose," Lewrie sighed.

He did a quick inspection of their quarters. The guardhouse was fairly dirty, littered with discarded trash, castoff uniforms and such, the blankets piled in a stinking heap, and half the cooking equipment missing. There was dust, lint, some roachlike scuttling . . .

"Right, lads, muster in the guardroom!" he shouted, hauling his charges from their delighted play. Some of the younger hands were dotted with feathers from overly exuberant pillow fighting.

"First off, we're going to clean this pigsty from truck to keel," he announced, to a faint chorus of groans. "Working parties. Mops and buckets, brooms and all. Get the French stink out of this place. It's to be our mess deck, and *you* know proper British seamen'll never abide filth. A total scrub-down, fore and aft, up the walls and down. Hose it out, if that's what it takes. Those blankets reek. Chuck 'em over. I expect our hosts pissed on 'em 'fore they left, just to be Froggish. You've your own, and we may draw an extra blanket for each man from the warehouses. Lisney, you know your way around a galley?"

"Aye, sir, some," Lisney confessed, wincing at what he feared to hear, at what onerous duties he might be ordered to perform.

"Take two hands and set the galley right, see what's needful for cooking. I'll want to eat off the deck, I want it that clean. Any pots and such we may draw from the warehouses, later. And we'll decide who does the cooking later, too. Cony, there're officers' quarters above. See to setting them right. Take two hands to help you. Bosun Porter? A sentry at the door, now. Draw equipment from these racks. Count 'em first, then keep 'em under lock and key. And appoint two men masters-at-arms to help you. You men in the duck feathers. Just 'cause things don't belong to you is no reason to destroy them."

"Thought that was what wars were all about," Lieutenant Scott muttered, just loud enough to be heard, and to elicit a laugh.

"Silence!" Lewrie snapped, his neck burning with anger. "Listen to me carefully. Just because we're ashore doesn't mean you're any less out of the Navy's eye. We're not here to gambol, we're not here for a 'Rope-Yarn Sunday.' I, or *any* officer, will read the Articles of War the same as if we were on *Cockerel's* decks," he said, turning to glare a warning to Scott. "We may guard the harbour and basin, or we might end up in those bloody great hills behind us, manning guns, eye to eye with French soldiers, living rough as any Redcoat. And the man who forgets that, the man who acts like this is a lark, the one who doesn't believe I'm a taut hand, well . . . God help his soul. *And* his back."

He made an effort to lock eyes with every hand, even those back in the rear of the guardroom who were shying sheepish and hangdog at his sternness.

"Right," he concluded. "Let's be about it. Mister Scott? A word with you, sir."

"Aye, sir," Scott nodded, clenching his massive jaws.

"Outside, sir," Lewrie ordered, walking out on him. He paced a good ten yards, well out of earshot, before rounding on him. "Damn you, sir. Don't you ever make mock of me in front of the hands. Don't you ever dare make light of why we've come ashore. Heard of Yorktown, have you, Mister Scott?"

"Aye, sir, and I know you made a name—"

"Damn you, that is *not* what I mean, sir!" Lewrie thundered. "Take a good look about, Mister Scott. Fifteen bloody miles of border, and we mean to hold it with less than four thousand men? With three armies on the way to crush us? Aye, they're *Frog* armies, peasants in rags to you, not worth the powder to blow their tag-rag-and-bobtail arses away, hey? And we're here, you and I, with charge of twenty hands. And if one of them dies because you didn't take this bloody serious . . . damn it! They are our men, sir! We own the grave responsibility to care for them, to feed 'em, tuck 'em in, fight 'em . . . and maybe die with 'em, if it comes to that."

"I see, sir," Scott sobered, a little of his rancour receding.

"Nothing *like* a lark, is it, Mister Scott?" Alan demanded, though more softly. "You may resent me to the Gates of Hell if you wish. Feel sorry for yourself gettin' slung ashore all you want. I mean to keep as many of these men alive as I can, sir, do we win or lose. But I can't do that with you sulking behind my back, and giving them the impression we're off to 'Fiddler's Green.' They're as much your responsibility as a sea officer as they are mine, you know. I *will* have your support and your loyalty, sir, no matter your grudges. Or else. As my father'd say, 'shut up and soldier.'"

"Aye aye, sir," Scott grunted, nodding vigorously, his face red. Whether with more resentment or shame, Lewrie didn't much care at that moment. Just as long as Scott did his job.

CHAPTER 5

The first use of their services, though, was nothing even close to belli-
cose. Toulon was still plagued by the presence of nearly 5,000 truculent
French sailors, most of whom either openly or secretly supported the
Revolution, with a fair minority who might not have adored the Republic, exactly, but were mortal certain they could not abide British or Spanish troops on the sacred soil of La Belle France. The town rang to their
disobedience, their drunkenness, daily. And, seeing how many they
were, even disarmed, and how few Coalition troops were present, it
would only be a matter of time before they arose, weaponless or not, or
began to engage in sabotage.

Lewrie's party, with others, readied five ships from the basin to take
them away. Five of the least serviceable—an eighteen-gunned brig of
war named *Pluvier*, the 3rd Rate 74's *Orion, Entreprenant, Patriote* and
the *Trajan*—were taken out of ordinary, stripped of all their guns but
two eight-pounders, stripped of all their powder but for twenty light,
saluting or signalling charges, and stocked with food and water. Then
they were warped or towed to the Great Road, and the French seamen,
and those officers who wished to depart, were put aboard. Under flags
of truce, they departed for Bordeaux, for Rochefort, L'Orient and Brest,
on the Biscay coast, on 14 September.

"And that," Lewrie told himself over a glass of wine that evening at
Lieutenant de Crillart's favourite open-air *bistro*, "will make Toulon a
much quieter place, all round."

Fumm! Umumm. Crack-whish!

"What the devil?" Alan cried, leaping from his bed. He flung the
shutters to his room open to peer out, to look down at the seaman sentry
at the door of the guardhouse below him in the small courtyard.

Fumm, fumm! And echoes. Followed by two more crack-whishes.

"Some'un's firin' cannons, I reckon, sir," the sentry called up to him in reply to the perplexity on his face. "Soun' like h'it's ah comin' fum yonner, sir." The sentry pointed vaguely sou'west.

Clad in only his shirttails, Lewrie fetched his telescope and leaned out the window. Bang went the shutters on a neighbouring room and Scott peered out blearily, rubbing sleep from his face with rough hands. He'd made a rare night of it in the city, a proper, caterwauling "high ramble." A moment later, a pert female face, capped with a mass of dark brown curls, appeared next to his. She was clad only in a sheet. Wide-eyed and excited, she seemed equally curious as to the source of the noise and what her neighbour looked like.

"Morning, Mister Scott," Lewrie took time to smile.

"Argh," Scott muttered, wiggling his tongue and grimacing with the taste of cognac still in his mouth. "Morning, Mister Lewrie, sir," he managed, thick-headed. "What the Devil's goin' on?"

"Bonjour, m'sieur Luray," the girl called cheerfully.

"Bonjour, mademoiselle," Lewrie replied with an approximate bow.

"Phoebe," Scott supplied gruffly, dry-swabbing his face some more and knuckling his eyes, childlike. "I think she said. Scrawny little chit, but . . ." He shrugged and gave her a pinch, making her yelp.

But damned fetching, Lewrie took more time to note.

"Sounds like it's coming from beyond Fort Malbousquet," Alan said, returning to professional matters. "Maybe that Général Carteau finally marched from Marseilles, got his guns up during the night. I . . ."

There was a slowly rising tumulus of powder beyond Malbousquet, and the hills to the sou'west, sour-looking, grayish tan. *Fummfumm-fumm*! this time in rapid succession, and another belch of smoke rose into the sky, a twining, twisting ball to join the rest. *Umummum* they echoed on the hills. Yet there were no strikes on Fort Malbousquet, the most important redoubt which guarded the western approaches. Lewrie swung his telescope right and left, to see what they were shooting for. There!

Crack-crack-crack!

Explosive shells burst when their fuses burned down. But burst in the Little Road, around the anchored prize-frigate *Aurore* and two floating batteries. Two went off very close to the water, roiling the road waters with spreading trout splashes of ripples; the third burst too high, due to a shorter fuse, scattering iron slivers that created a miniature hail storm across the waters beneath an unfolding rose of powder smoke.

Fumm-fumm! Came a double report, from a second set of guns this time, a little farther off to the south. These were improperly fused, too.

They fell into the roadstead, erecting tall twin candlesticks of spray as they struck and sank. Followed a moment later, as the fuses reached their powder charges, by dirty humps of smoke-gray foam, which hoisted aloft in gigantic featherlike plumes as tall as mast trucks.

"Masked batteries," Lewrie said to one and all. "Heavy guns, by God."

"Siege guns," Scott opined, awake now. "Twenty-four-pounders?"

"Firing masked, though . . ." Lewrie countered, shaking his head.

Fumm-fumm-fumm! He began counting the seconds to himself. Now that he was listening for it, Alan could hear the faint shrieking moan of shells lofted through the early morning air. Three new pillars rose in the Little Road, hopelessly wide of the ships. So far.

"Mile and a half, I think, Mister Scott," he called out. "Don't think they're siege guns. Firin' masked, they'd have to elevate high, and anything over what? eight degrees or so'd—burst the barrels."

"Howitzers," Scott guessed.

"What's an army lug about," Lewrie shouted back, getting excited there might be some action at last. "Six, eight, or twelve-pounder howitzers? Little too far, even for them. I think they must be mortars."

He'd experienced mortars; all those weeks under the drumfire of a French artillery train at Yorktown, aiding the Rebels. Twelve-or thirteen-inch they'd been, some as big as sixteen-inch. Massive shells they'd fired, solid shot, bursting shell, their fuses glowing in the night like fiery banshees—and carcases; flaming wads soaked in anything that'd burn . . . and keep on burning once they buried themselves in a house . . . or a ship.

"Les Republicains?" Little Phoebe asked fearfully, pulling her sheet up higher about her. "Mon dieu!"

"Well, they ain't the Royal Horse Artillery," Scott sneered.

"Oui, mademoiselle, ils sont les Republicains," Lewrie told her. "Mister Scott, get the hands mustered. I'll dress and run up to headquarters to see what's what."

"Ve 'ave brea'fas', Barnaby?" Phoebe asked. "Le petit déjeuner?"

"Run along, squirrel, there's work to do," Scott said.

That shelling had started on 18 September. Next day, more batteries had opened fire upon the tightly packed ships in the Little Road— batteries masked by the sheltering heights of La Petite Garenne and another middling hill a little sou'west of the first. Twenty-four-pounder siege guns joined in, too, firing direct, though at maximum elevation on their trunnions, from high ground near La Seyne, the civilian harbour.

This forced some of the shipping to move, out through the Gullet to new anchorages in the Great Road to the east, or closer in towards the jetties of the basin. A brace of gunboats, floating batteries, were got out of the yards, manned and sent to the nor'west arm of the Little Road near Fort Millaud and the Poudrière, the powder-magazine. And they were reinforced by a full crew of gunners on the *Aurore*, and the presence of Rear-Admiral John Gell's flagship, the mighty ninety-eight-gunned, three-decker *St. George*.

The French had the advantage, though, of being masked, their exact position unknown, and were able to fire with more or less scientific accuracy from stable, fixed positions, with observers to correct the fall-of-shot. Sooner or later, trigonometry, ballistics, and the right guesstimate on powder measure to be ignited, and the right length of fuse to be fitted, would score a hit, and that a devastating one.

The British gunners could only roughly guess where behind the masking hills the batteries were, firing from ships which, even at anchor, shifted and recoiled with each massive discharge. They had to probe with their shells, much like a blind man must feel for the kerb with his cane, hoping for the best.

French fire was so gallingly accurate, towards the afternoon of the 19th, that the gunboats had to slip their cables and retire. They returned to the duel on the morning of 20 September. And by midday, one of the floating batteries was hit and damaged, and the second was sunk outright.

This they watched from a post on the basin's western jetty, engaged in trundling powder and shot out to the thirty-two- and forty-two-pounders, just in case . . . Between trips, during a dinner break, or a rest stop with mugs of appallingly piss-poor French beer, Lewrie and his men had ringside seats, right up to the ropes, as it were, where they could best see the opponents toe up and square off.

"Hmm, I wonder . . ." Lieutenant Scott grimaced, turning to peer towards the west beyond Fort Malbousquet, then to the heights to the north.

"Wonder what, Mister Scott?"

"Your pet . . . did that Crillart fellow say how many men they have yonder, in Carteau's army?" Scott inquired.

"Two divisions . . . maybe six thousand or so, if they're up to the old establishments yet, I think I heard."

"And we've barely five thousand so far, guarding . . ."

"Guarding bloody everything," Lewrie snorted. "Lapoype from the east might be about the same size." He sat uneasily, trying to at least appear calm for his men, on a massive granite block of the jetty's breastworks, swinging his heels over the waterside. "Least this bugger's not done much else but shell, so far. No infantry probes to speak of."

"Maybe Carteau's leadin' us by the nose, waiting for all the men coming down from Lyons. Keep our attention fixed here, whilst . . ."

"Oh, there you are, Mister Lewrie, sir!" the teenaged midshipman cried, the same little pest they'd met their first day ashore. "Been searching all over Creation for you," he panted. "Rear-Admiral Goodall's finest compliments to you, Lieutenant Lewrie, and he begs me to direct you to his presence, as soon as is practicable, sir."

"Something useful for us to do, at last?" Lewrie wondered aloud.

"One may not presume to, uhm . . . presume, sir, but . . ." the midshipman shrugged.

"Mister Scott, take charge of the hands. Keep 'em busy, whilst I toddle off," Lewrie said, swinging his legs back over the bulwark.

"Aye, sir," Scott replied. "And whatever business they wish of us, sir . . . ?"

"Aye, Mister Scott?"

"Well, damme, we're sailors . . . keep us out of those hills, could you, at least?" Scott implored.

"I'll do my best, sir," Lewrie smiled.

CHAPTER 6

Lewrie *had* kept them out of those forbidding hills, though he wasn't exactly sure he'd done them any favours. Rear-Admiral Goodall had only the briefest sketch of Lewrie's career, and had been intent upon a large map of the area, in the middle of a conference with his opposite number, Rear-Admiral Gravina of the Spanish Navy, and a host of subordinates, all of whom had a loud opinion of what should be done, and at that very instant before . . .

"Commanded two bomb ketches, I see, sir," Goodall had commented.

"Yes, sir, but—"

"Batt'ry at Yorktown, by God. Land service."

"Yes, sir, although—"

"That folderol in the Far East, shellin' pirates an' such?"

"Well, in fact . . ."

They'd been *converted* bombs, reduced to tiny but stoutly built ketch-rigged gunships; his two-gun batteries at Yorktown hadn't fired a single shot, much less had a target; the folderol in the Far East was not *exactly* mortar work now, was it, but . . .

"Cheesy-lookin' raft," Lewrie muttered. "Ain't it."

They'd given him a floating battery. They'd also given him an "all-nations" to sort out. Lieutenant de Crillart showed up, full of ginger and good cheer, eager to be doing something at last, out of the water once more. He brought with him about forty men—all Royalists, thank God—former members of the Royal Corps of Marine Gunners, once a body of 10,000, the most expert and perfectly trained naval artillery known. With cunning, the latest scientific artifice, lavish support from the greatest minds and mathematicians, the most modern gun foundries, they had developed a complete *"la jeune école,"* a New School for gunnery.

The Revolutionaries, though, had broken them up, parcelled them out in tiny leavenings to land units, unable to abide *any* elite superiour to the Common Man, nor any organisation left over from royal days.

There was a further complication, an equal draft of artillerists more experienced with mortars, for which Lewrie might have backhandedly thanked God. Unfortunately, they were *Spanish* bombardiers under a lean, haughty coach-whip of an officer; one Comandante (Major) Don Luis Emiliano de Esquevarre y Saltado y Perez. To make matters even worse, he was not a naval officer but a *military* artillerist, and had about as much English as Lewrie had Spanish. Which wasn't saying much, beyond *"dos vinos"* and *"sucar tus putas."* El Comandante would be in charge of the pair of massive thirteen-inch brass mortars sunk in the middle of the waist, where the mainmast used to be, whilst Lieutenant de Crillart and his grizzled veterans would service the six heavy thirty-two-pounders, three to either beam.

Zélé, the battery had been named once, a proud two-decker 74 of about 160 feet on the range of her gun deck and over forty feet in beam. Now, she was a "rasé," a ship shaved down. Gone were her tall foc's'le and poop deck. Gone, indeed, was her quarterdeck as well, along with an upper gun deck and the original sail-tending gangways.

She'd been reduced to a hulking, squat water beetle, wide and low to the water, with the only shelter for her crew the foremost wedge of the bows on the remaining gun deck, and what went unused on that deck aft, under what was left of the upper gun deck. Her mainmast had been drawn out like a rotten tooth, and her fore and mizzen had been reduced to the fighting-tops—"to a gantline," they would say in the Royal Navy. There was still a forecourse yard on which a sail was set, an inner and an outer jib forward set on stays which ran to a shortened jib boom without a sprit yard doubled atop it. Aft, the mizzen could set a course on the usually bare cro'jack yard, and an ancient lateen spanker awaited.

Lewrie didn't think he'd be winning any regattas with her, though. Her sails were tattered and mildewed, mere afterthoughts. Had she half-a-gale abeam, he reckoned, she *might* log a quim-hair above two knots. No, to get this beamish, overbuilt and deep-draughted beast about the bay, it would be necessary to use the long, thick sweep oars which lay piled atop the centerline of the gun deck, and extend them out the many ports where artillery no longer nested. Sure enough, he could see thole-pins the size of pier bollards at several empty gun ports.

"Christ, what a bloody . . ." he began to carp. "Ow! Goddamn an' blast it . . ." He'd stubbed his toe on a knot. The ship was so old, so pared down by holystoning during her half century of service, that hard pine knots had arisen from the softer planking material, and now stood as high as flattopped islands all over the gun deck, making an archipelago of dark burls against the pale gray of her weathered decking.

"So what do *we* do, sir?" Scott asked, looking about as dubious as Lewrie did about their prospects.

"We're the coachees, Mister Scott," Lewrie told him, rubbing his foot through his shoe. "The Frogs and the Dons shall make the loudish banging noises whilst we steer them round, wherever they wish to go."

"Hack-work," Scott opined. "We'll need more men, a power more, just to row her, or . . ." He pointed at the size of the capstans fore and aft. They'd *have* to row her, then anchor with both bowers, the stream *and* the kedge, put springs on the cables, and use the secondary capstans, which were about as massive as *Cockerel*'s, to nudge her bearing, so the guns and mortars could aim.

"About forty more hands, I should think," Lewrie scowled. "Landsmen, mostly. Be wonderful, were we to get 'em. But . . . we're not. This is it. All the Fleet or the garrison may spare right now. Charles?"

"Oui, mon capitaine?"

"We'll need your men to share the sweepwork, when it's needful. La . . . oars? Les capstans?" Alan flustered, trying for the life of him to recall what the French called things. "Until we're in position and ready to open fire, of course."

"Ah, ze rames et ze cabestan, je comprend. D'accord. I . . . un'erstan'. Oui, I agree, Alain," Crillart beamed most agreeably.

"Still, there're the Spanish. We could use their help, too," Alan said. "If we really have quick need of 'em. Uhm, perhaps *you* should be the one to broach the subject with Don 'whatsit,' Charles. You have so much more Spanish than I."

"Moi?" de Crillart sighed, taking a long look at the nose-high, and immensely bored, expression of their bombardier. "Merde."

CHAPTER 7

Falconer's *Marine Dictionary* had quite a lot to say on Mortars and Range, and the precautions the prudent officer might undertake to keep from being blown to flinders. So, too, did de Crillart's tattered copy of Le Blond's *Elements of War,* and Lewrie's copy of the standard Muller's *Treatise on the Artillery.*

Zélé should have had munitions-tenders astern, where the shells were filled with powder, and rowing boats to fetch shot as needed, and where, during transit, the fuses were inserted, the fused shells being termed "fixed"; then hoisted aboard and stored in a hide or hair-cloth covered rack on the safest space of the deck—called "kiting." Well, they didn't have tenders, and too few men to spare to row shells about, so they extemporised.

The rudimentary captain's cabin aft under the thick remains of the upper gun deck was to be the filling room, its doors and windows covered with tanned hides, equipped with water tubs, and the passages to it constantly watered with a wash-deck pump. The filled shells to be carried most carefully to the waist, where two senior bombardiers would "fix" them with fuses, as needed for each shot, and no shell was to be "fixed" and "kited," then left untended, no matter how secure a storage area they had.

There were more tubs of water round the depression in the waist where the mortars sat, two more bombardiers or gunner's mates on duty to oversee port-fires and slow matches the mortarmen would apply to the fuse and the mortars' touch holes. Propellant gunpowder charges were loaded below, in the old orlop hanging-magazine, also well watered and guarded, with the door shut except to pass out premeasured cartridges through a secondary felt screen inside the actual door, slitted to let the charges be passed out in fireproof leather cylinders.

The fuses would come from a "laboratory chest" in the captain's cabin, too. These were conical tubes made of beech or willow wood and filled with a composition of sulphur, saltpetre and mealed powder. A mixture of tallow, pitch and beeswax sealed both ends. The tapering end of the cone would go inside the shell, stripped of its protective coating, but the great end must keep its tallow until just before firing. And they all agreed that, whilst the mortars were in service, it would be impossible to employ the thirty-two-pounder great-guns simultaneously, for they would require other lit port-fires and slow matches, and that was a risk too great to contemplate.

It helped immensely, Lewrie learned from observation, that their mortars were mounted on central pintles which passed completely through the bed of the mortar carriages, through the supporting timbers and deck beams of the mortar wells, through the overhead beams on the orlop, and terminated in large baulks of timber which held the whole affair up; so the mortars could be "laid" or "pointed" left and right. All they had to do was anchor with the best-bower and a single kedge (with springs, of course, on their cables), roughly abeam of the target or the coast, and the bombardiers could heave their massive charges about for aiming.

Thirteen-inch mortar; weight, eighty-one hundredweight, two quarters, one pound, according to Falconer. Powder charge when the chamber at its base was full, thirty pounds. Weight of a "fixed" shell, 198 pounds; and filled with seven pounds of the very best powder. The shells were cast-iron balls, hollow, with their greatest thickness on the bottom, the better to resist the awful force of discharge from the bore, and to keep that heaviest part away from the fuse, flying first through the air, and landing on that thick portion, with the thinner, and lighter, filling and fusing end uppermost. There were two carrying handles cast or hammer-welded to either side of the fuse hole. Perhaps to avoid confusion for slower minds.

Beyond that, Lewrie's theory got a little vague; he'd never had the greatest head for numbers. Falconer's, under Range, listed a table of practice for sea mortars, giving the specific weights of propelling charges, and the proper fuses to use. For instance, he could discover that at forty-five degrees of elevation, a thirteen-inch mortar took an eighteen pound charge to hurl the shot, which resulted in a flight of twenty-six seconds, and range of roughly 2,873 yards. And for the fuse to explode at the right moment, burning at the rate of four seconds and forty-eight parts to the inch, would require a premade fuse of the exact length of five inches, seventy-two parts, to be selected from the "laboratory chest." Then, of course, there was the niggling matter of the gunners who would light the fuse, and the mortar's touch hole with slow match, doing both at the same instant. But Alan assumed that the Spanish bombardiers, and the insufferably laconic Don Luis, might know what they were doing, and if they made a hash of it, then it was their own damned fault.

Lavishly reequipped from those mountains of French supplies in the basin's arsenals and warehouses, they sailed *Zélé*, her new sails almost virgin-white, from the docks, through the opening between the bomb-proof jetties, and out to join *St. George* and *Aurore*, just after first light on the 24th.

"Springs on the cables, sir," Lieutenant Scott informed him.

"Wash-deck pumps going? Filling room *and* magazine passageway?"

"Aye, sir."

"Let's be at it, then," Lewrie grimaced, his stomach chilly with trepidation at the unknown nature of their work. And over the danger, which was *very* known, of any clumsiness or inattentiveness.

"Might as well be, sir," Scott dared to assay a tiny, wry grin. "It appears the Frogs already are."

They walked amidships, to peer down into the mortar wells, then tip their hats to Crillart and Esquevarre, who stood close together by the rearward lip, evidently engaged in some heated discussion.

"Non non, Comandante, Le Blond . . ." Charles de Crillart objected gently. "Alain . . . mon capitaine, I attemp' to tell zis . . . monsieur Le Blond say ze s'irty pound' charge eez beaucoup, mais zis . . . ze Comandante insist . . ."

Don Luis de Esquevarre rattled off an expostulation in rapid Spanish, out of which Lewrie caught perhaps the odd word in ten, most of those mildly insulting.

"Señor," he said, whipping out his copy of Falconer. "Allow me to quote, and do you translate, Lieutenant Crillart . . . aha, here it is.

Mr. Muller in his Treatife of Artillery, very juftly obferves, that the breech of our 13-inch fea-mortars is loaded with an unneceffary weight of metal. The chamber thereof contains 32 Lbs. of powder, and at the fame time they are never charged with more than 12 or 15 pounds by the moft expert officers, becaufe the bomb-vessel is unable to bear the violent fhock of their full charge."

" 'E say eez Inglese bull-sheet, mon capitaine," Crillart translated back. "Zat eez on'y pour ze cylinder chambre, et we 'ave een zis bombard, ze conical. 'E also say 'e eez trés esperience viz artillery, an' 'e 'ave no need to be tol' . . .'ow to soock eggs? Comment?" Crillart shrugged in bewilderment.

To Crillart's even further confusion, Lewrie laughed out loud, prompting a tiny upturn of one corner of Don Luis's mouth in return.

"Señor Comandante, I have implicit trust in your experience," Lewrie cajoled, phrase by phrase as Crillart transposed for him, "but this is a ship, not a firm battlement or well-prepared battery . . . do you see here, under Range . . . practice table? Weights of charge?"

"Ah, sí, capitán!" Don Luis brightened, pulling from a voluminous pocket of his ornate uniform coat a much-tattered, oft-rolled and thumbed table of practice, expostulating eagerly.

Fumm-fumm! Umumm. Scrreee-BLAM! BLAM! All this time, Republican shot had been falling into the Little Road, *St. George* belching displeasure, and *Aurore's* six-and twelve-pounders, breeches resting flat on their carriages for greatest "range at random-shot," had been barking away. And once in a while, other floating batteries had erupted in fog banks of powder smoke.

"Ze trés peu malheureusement . . . ze lettle mis-un'erstan'ment?" Charles said with relief, at last. " 'E eez 'ave een min' ze less of ze powder. 'E ees s'inking ze, uhm . . . nine poun', at firs'?"

"Whew!" Scott breathed out.

"I defer to his greater knowledge, tell him, Charles," Alan said, doffing his hat, making sure he was grinning when he said it.

Up from the orlop came a powder charge, sacked by the called-for weight. Spanish bombardiers used paper cartridges. From the filling room came a shell, two burly Spaniards grunting with effort to carry it by its small, slippery handles. Don Luis and his *aspirante*, or ensign-in-training, and a hirsute, cursing bear of a man, a sergeant-gunner, Diego Huelva, directed the work of heaving the after mortar, the left hand of the pair as they faced the coast, into line. Then began to elevate it to forty-five degrees. They fussed and hopped, peered and tinkered at screws, until satisfied, then waved for the shell to be brought forward.

Down it went into the well, as the powder charge was rammed deep into the chamber, and the priming iron was thrust into the touch hole to both clear the vent and puncture the bag. Slowly the fixed shell was lowered into the stubby bore, handles and fuse hole up.

Don Luis took a deep breath, almost made to cross himself, as he waved the excess hands away and ordered the tallow seal on the fuse to be opened. "Fósforo, preparado . . . !" He cried. "Fuego!"

The smouldering port fires touched both fuse and touch hole, and there was a split second of sizzle, then a tremendous blast! Down went the deck, as if shoved by the hand of God, and *Zélé*'s timbers groaned.

Not so much a sudden detonation as it was a physical force, Alan felt his lungs rattle, his groin shrink, and his heart flutter when the mortar touched off, felt an invisible wave of pressure shove him back, rattle his coat-tails and hat, and fill his ears with a sound beyond a sound, almost too loud to register, except to set them ringing. Spent powder smoke spurted aloft in a sickly yellow-white column, reeking with sulphur and rotten eggs, smelling singed as lit kindling.

"Bloody Hell, that was . . ." he coughed, fanning the air for some fresh as the gush of gunsmoke dissipated. "That was *magnificent!*"

He'd loved the great-guns best of all the things he'd learned in the Navy; the power, the stink of them, their recoil and shudderings. From little two-pounder boat guns and swivels to long-twelves, from far-firing twenty-four-pounders to the stubby, ship-breaking "Smashers," the carronades, Lewrie delighted in things that went *Boom!*—and exulted in seeing the damage they caused aboard a foe. It was irrational, brutish and savage, this joy he found in gunnery, so viscerally *beneath* a reasonable man's ken, so insensible a passion, yet . . .

"Damme!" Lewrie called, feeling a boyish glee rise in him. "Don Luis! Volver a hacer? Let's do that *again!*"

That afternoon, *St. George* retired from the artillery duel, due to depart for Genoa, and her place was taken in the Little Road by the *Princess Royal*, another 98, Rear-Admiral Goodall's flagship. In lieu of his presence, her captain, John Childs Purvis, commanded. A Spanish 74 joined the bombardment.

French bursting-shell drummed around *Zélé* all day, fortunately never discovering the right solution in propellant charge and length of fuse, though it did get interesting at times when a shell would splash somewhat nearby, raise a feather of spray by its impact, then explode underwater a second or so later to produce an even more prodigious spout of brine which would fall like a cascade on the decks and gangways.

Don Luis Esquevarre concentrated their fire upon the lesser battery to the sou'west, the one with two guns. Patiently, firing perhaps a round every two minutes, he probed the hills, first with the left mortar, then with the right hand. A dram less powder in the charge cartridge, three drams more the next shot; a tiny tinkering with elevation, half a turn on the great screw by the bracing block; heaving to turn about a single degree on the pintle.

"Fósforo . . . preparado . . ." he called, coatless and hatless by then, his voice hoarse from inhaling spent gunpowder and shouting for half a day. "Fuego!"

Another monumental clashing roar, and the floating battery shuddering to her very bones, timbers crying in torment. Lewrie stood aft away from the noise, on what passed for a quarterdeck, a telescope to his eye, rested steady on the larboard mizzen-stay ratlines.

"Nineteen . . . twenty . . . twenty-one . . ." Midshipman Spendlove tolled off, counting on his fingers, for his watch only had a minute hand.

Brum! Umumm. Came from the hills.

"Struck, sir. Twenty-two seconds," he announced, and looked up to see a darker gout of smoke rise, almost mingling with the forest-fire pall that hovered continually over the Republican mortar battery. "Oh, well. Closer, I *think*, though, sir," he sighed disappointedly.

Suddenly, there was a massive eruption of smoke yonder, rising as silent as a squall cloud might on the sea's horizon, as if the French had reinforced the masked battery, and had just let fly half a dozen shells.

Brummmbrummmm-Bummm! spoke the masking hill, later than the gunpowder pall. And the pall swelled upward, outward, turned darker, shot through with dark flecks, with black writhing licorice sticks of smoke—tinged at the bottom, just atop the hill, with dying embers, with a ruddy orange loomlike flickering, like a lighthouse's loom just over the horizon's knife edge.

"Hola!" Don Luis shouted, raspily enthused, and his bombardiers began to cheer and dance, to caper round the deck and in the wells in triumph.

"We did it!" Lewrie cried, ready to dance himself. "We hit 'em! Blew 'em to hell, by Jesus!"

Bumm-bumm-brubrumbumm, more secondary explosions thundered, and the hills quaked to the destruction, and they could feel it in their bones and on their faces, a tremendous distant blast that rattled the earth, the shoals, and transmitted itself through the waters. They'd holed out, not on the mortars themselves, but in their magazine, where fixed and kited shells had been stored. Too many of them, fixed ready to fire, kited too close together, and even being sunk into the earth, protected by wet hides and haircloth, hadn't saved them.

Lewrie dashed down to the gun deck where Spanish, French and English sailors cavorted and clapped, tossing their caps or hats into the air and huzzah-ing.

"Marvelous!" Lewrie told Esquevarre when he reached him. "Magnífico! Marveloso! Genius!"

Esquevarre was thumping Crillart on the back, Crillart was bestowing Gallic kisses on those lean aristocratic cheeks, and Don Luis tweaked Charles's nose playfully as he stepped back to clasp Lewrie to him and dance him around the deck in a stumbling bear hug.

Must be something in the water, Lewrie thought, not exactly that pleased to be bussed and hugged by a man; bloody foreigners!

"Charles, tell him we'll celebrate," Lewrie called over Comandante Esquevarre's shoulder as they tripped past him in a shuffling circle. "Vino! Plus vin? My treat! We'll splice the main-brace . . . uh, splice-o las main-brace-o? Sí, amigo, sí, Don Luis? Bueno!"

By sundown, they heaved to short stays on the kedge and broke it free of the rocky bottom, heaved then to short stays forrud on the bower and sailed back to the fortified jetties. The larger three-gun masked-battery's fire had sputtered out by then, daunted perhaps by the sudden destruction of its fellow, and the Little Road became peaceful. Sweeps had to be used as the wind faded to puzzling little zephyrs across the lake-smooth waters. Once tied up, instead of boiling salt rations in steep tubs, appropriated charcoal braziers were lit atop the jetty and fresh meat was roasted. Wine and beer were doled out, the rum ration was issued, and fresh bread and butter appeared from the town for all hands.

Crillart, Scott, Esquevarre and Lewrie left the ship, repaired to a restaurant and celebrated—rather heavily, in point of fact, in all respects—wine, cuisine, music—and ended up being run out after they called for dancing girls. Esquevarre couldn't quite understand a restaurant that didn't have people who could play the guitar or do the flamenco—nor "do" the appreciative patrons who flung coins to them.

"France," Crillart translated haltingly on their way back aboard. " 'E say, mon ami . . . ve are la nation du . . . 'tight-arses'? Comment?"

The next morning, with a monumental head, Lewrie arose to the soft *fumphing* of thunder. He flung off his blanket and staggered to a water butt, his mouth as sour and dry as dessicated ordure. There was a knock on the door to his tiny cabin.

"What?" he croaked.

"Sir? Midshipman Spendlove, sir."

"Enter."

Spendlove came inside, dry as a bone; Lewrie expected rain, with that far-off thunder. He was too bleary to puzzle it out.

"Excuse me, sir, but . . . the Frogs are at it again. There's a midshipman aboard from Admiral Goodall, sir. He says we're to stand out into the Little Road, with all dispatch."

"Uhuh," Lewrie nodded heavily. "Very well, Mister Spendlove. Do you wake the others, and I'll be on deck directly. Warn Porter to have the hands roused and at stations for shoving off."

"Aye aye, sir."

Already at it again, he wondered as Spendlove departed; don't the Frogs ever learn their lessons? Wondering, too, if, after the celebrations of the past evening, they could hit a bull in the arse with a bass viol this day.

CHAPTER 8

The *Colossus* 74 came in from Cagliani with 350 Sardinian soldiers. On the 28th, *Bedford* and a Sardinian ship fetched 800 more. A convoy arrived from Spain with 4,000 foot, horse and artillery, and on the same day, two Neapolitan liners brought in 2,000 reinforcements, and a Marshal Forteguerri to command them. There was some problem with Forteguerri—he would not subordinate his men to the Spanish military commander, Rear-Admiral Gravina, insisting that Naples's treaty was with Great Britain only, and he would only take orders from British officers.

Fortunately, Brigadier General Lord Mulgrave had come to Toulon with a detatchment of British troops, a single battalion of one regiment, which raised British troop strength to about 1,500. Forteguerri considered himself under Mulgrave's command. There was talk that one more British general was coming, Major General O'Hara, with another regiment. There was also talk that a Spanish general had been appointed, and would be arriving soon; someone senior to O'Hara.

There was a tremendous scare on the night of 30 September. It was a night of thick fog and swirling mist. So far, the only action had been skirmishes between cavalry vedettes to east and west, some desultory artillery duels between light field guns outside the perimeters of Toulon. The skirmishes had become a little fiercer, as more Republican troops from Marseille and the Army of Italy arrived; and troops in the heights behind Toulon had reported the presence of French units at Jourris near Fort Valette, patrols probing in the valley of the Faviere River, down toward the nor'east pass at Argeliers towards open ground. Yet the artillery duels in the Little Road were the constant, the only serious action so far.

Suddenly, though, there were French regiments in the hills the night of the 30th, popping up from God knew where, scaling goat tracks thought unscalable, carrying light field guns up the steep, crumbling mountain paths. They erupted, without a shred of warning, upon Spanish troops on the Heights of Pharon, the eastern half of the northern massif above Toulon! In the confusion, the Spanish were routed from their positions, run pell-mell down from the Heights of Pharon in the dark and the fog, abandoning all but their personal weapons, leaving the Republicans with fortifications and heavy guns, which looked down upon the very heart of the enclave and the Great Road.

It looked very much like a disaster that night to Lewrie and his men, taking a much-needed rest from bombarding hidden batteries by dint of a fog so thick they could not spot the fall of shot. Spatters of gunfire could be heard far off above the basin where *Zélé* was tied to the jetty. Spatters turned to ripping volleys of musketry, punctuated with tiny flat bangs of "grasshopper" guns and lightweight mountain howitzers, and dread rumours passed up and down the jetty were two-a-penny.

Yet in the morning, Brigadier General Mulgrave, Spanish Rear-Admiral Gravina and the game Captain Elphinstone led a hastily mustered force back up to the Heights of Pharon—Spanish troops eager for the restoration of their honour, grim British veterans experienced in the bayonet and drilled to professional perfection, the newly arrived Sardinians and Neapolitans, and sailors and Marines from the fleet with boarding pikes, pistols and their fearsome cutlasses.

They scaled the heights on tracks no less steep than the French had managed, slipped and slid on the dry, gravelly, crumbling soil and suffered miniature avalanches. And after forming quickly upon narrow level places, rushed the trenches and redoubts. Nearly 2,000 Frenchmen had taken the Heights of Pharon, but only 500 were in any condition to flee after they were overwhelmed and broken. The Coalition lost eight killed, seventy-two wounded (one of them Rear-Admiral Gravina, shot in the knee) and two missing, with forty-eight Spanish hauled off as prisoners earlier.

A little scare after all, the matter was quickly handled, and any dread of Republican rabble was blown to the four winds, if they were *that* easy to rout! The enclave breathed easier for a time, chuckling over their silly foreboding—yet looking more to the hills, and wondering . . .

And through all those weeks, Lewrie was busy with *Zélé*. Daily they sailed out to do battle, carefully selecting a new anchorage each dawning, which would take the French gunners hours to pinpoint. But the French shifted their batteries each night, returning the favour to make themselves equally elusive.

Down to the far south, behind La Seyne, there were several new batteries to deal with, on the Heights des Moulins and Reinier, above the civilian port, the next hill back from the Hauteur de Grasse, upon which stood Forts de Balaguer and L'Eguillette. The forts were manned by Coalition troops, as was Fort Mandrier and the lesser batteries on Cape Sepet's peninsula. The French had no hope of rushing across the narrow tongue of land which connected Sepet to the mainland. That thin land bridge, called Les Sablettes, which formed the bottom of the Golfe de la Veche, was bare as a baby's bottom, and two field guns could do terrible slaughter to troops attempting to rush across it, packed into a killing ground along the road, which bridged a salt marsh.

Yet the batteries atop the heights, twenty-four-pounder siege guns and howitzers, could scald the Little Road, deny any use of the Golfe de la Veche, and torment the defenders of Fort Balaguer. From anchorages at the south end of the Little Road, using Crillart's thirty-two-pounders and his experienced gunners, Lewrie engaged those guns on the heights. Or hid in the shallows near the north shore of Hauteur de Grasse, and let Don Luis de Esquevarre pound them with his mortars. Some nights, they did not return to port, but hid in the Little Road under cover of darkness, all lights extinguished and under oars, to sneak out through the Gullet and anchor round Fort Balaguer. There they mortared French gun batteries from shorter range, letting the Army at the fort report their fall-of-shot with wigwag signals. Or dared the shoals of the Golfe de la Veche, off the Infirmarie, to hammer the batteries on the heights at an oblique angle with thirty-two-pounders, somewhat safely out of French arcs of fire through narrow openings in their breastworks.

It became quite a game, an exciting though rather noisy sport, to match wits with the Republican gunners. But no matter how many times a breastwork was pounded into gravel, no matter how many earth-and-wicker gabions were burst, or guns dismounted, and no matter how many French artillerists they slew, the French guns were always back in action in a day or two, in a new position, and no amount of mortaring or cannonading seemed to deter them.

On 8 October, Lieutenant Colonel Nugent led a night storming raid on the southern batteries: Spaniards, Piedmontese, British troops, with sailors and Marines under Lt. Walter Serecold. Once more, pluck and daring paid for all. There'd been 300 French in the batteries, with another 1,200–1,300 infantry in their rear for support. The Heights des Moulins and Reinier were no less steep or treacherous than those of

Pharon. Yet they annihilated the French gunners and routed the rest. Under field-artillery fire, they could not haul away their prizes, so they spiked or destroyed the guns, burning the carriages and mounts, blowing off the trunnions, effectually making scrap metal of a four-pounder, a six-pounder, two sixteens, three twenty-four pounder siege guns, and two huge thirteen-inch brass mortars. Then returned to their quarters in the forts without harm!

But the French came back, hauled new pieces uphill to replace the old, rebuilt their breastworks and gabions, dug a little deeper in the hills, like soldier ants rebuilding their hive after children had kicked it over. Like the tide, they came back. And got just a touch closer to Toulon.

Lieutenant General Valdez had come into port on 18 October to replace Rear-Admiral Gravina. And the senior Spanish navy officer, Adm. Don Juan de Langara, went with Valdez to Admiral Lord Hood to insist that Valdez be given complete command of all troops in the enclave (His Most Catholic Majesty had given him that grandiloquent appointment). Hood demurred, pointing out that Toulon had surrendered to Britain alone, that allied troops supplied men on the stipulation that the British command. And that Major General O'Hara already had been given that command by His Brittanic Majesty, King George III.

Hood had sent so many ships away on various missions that there were scarcely ten sail of the line in harbour, while Langara still had his original seventeen. Langara put his three-decker flagship alongside *Victory*, placed two other 1st Rates at bow and stern, hinting more than strongly that he'd open fire if Valdez wasn't proclaimed as supreme commander of the allied forces at Toulon. To his credit, Admiral Hood would not be bullied, and *Victory* beat to Quarters. Valdez and Langara backed down, and returned their ships to their berths.

And Major General O'Hara did arrive a few days later, as did a Major General Dundas, with a commission to replace Admiral Goodall as military governor of Toulon. Unfortunately, O'Hara did not bring the troops expected; a mere 750 men from the garrison of Gibraltar came to Toulon with him, half of the number ordered to be transferred.

More Sardinians dribbled in, the last promised draft of Neapolitans came, a few Piedmontese, a few more trickles of able-bodied French royalists—civilians for the most part—driven in by the advancing Republican columns, with their guns and their guillotines.

By the beginning of November, 1793, they had on hand:

French Royalists 1,542

Piedmontese 1,584

Neapolitans...4,832

Spaniards 6,840

British 2,114

Of the 16,912 men total, no more than 12,000 were fit for duty, the rest off in hospital sick or wounded, and of those fit, 9,000 were tied to the perimeter, scattered all across the many posts, with only a meagre 3,000 available to respond to a French thrust.

CHAPTER 9

"How did it go ashore, sir?" Lieutenant Scott asked when Lewrie came back aboard *Zélé* from headquarters.

"Routed 'em, thank God," Alan replied sleepily, too sleepy to be enthused. "O'Hara's aide-de-camp was crowing merry. Six hundred frogs dead or wounded, he said. We lost sixty-one or so."

"Bloody good odds, then," Scott crowed in his turn. "And damned good return on investment."

"They think the frogs threw an entire corps against us," Lewrie yawned. It was barely first light, and a chill mist hung over Toulon. He'd been roused long before his usual hour—nothing new in the Navy—but with a bit more urgency than usual, too urgent to allow him his morning tea or chocolate or a morsel of bread. "Think of it, a whole corps! That's what . . . three divisions? Nine or ten thousand? If we'd lost Fort Mulgrave, we'd have lost the whole of the Heights of de Grasse and both the forts by the Gullet. *Then* where'd we be, I ask you? If they have that many to throw at us on a whim, then . . ."

"Aye, and we'll keep on killing 'em, sir," Lieutenant Scott boasted with his usual scorn for French courage and skill, "at ten or twenty to one. They'll go bankrupt, wagerin' at those odds. On a whim."

"It's too early to argue the toss," Lewrie sighed. "Have we anything hot yet?"

"Frog coffee, sir," Scott scoffed. He was a tea-and-beer man. When forced to drink coffee prepared in French fashion, he found it a too-hot, too-stout and bitter brew.

"Gittons?" Lewrie called. "Send down to the galley for a mug of coffee for me. I'll be in the chart space."

"Aye, sir."

"Mister Scott, round up Lieutenant de Crillart and the Comandante, if you'd be so kind. We've something new planned for today."

* * *

"Here, sirs," Lewrie said, with a jab at the chart with a ruler. "On the east, for a change . . . in the Plaine de la Garde. We hold Forts Malgue and Saint Catherine on the east side of town, the batteries at Cape Brun, the Post of Brun, and little Fort Saint Margaret, about at the midpoint of the coast . . . here, to protect the Bay of Toulon. A few days ago, the Frogs . . . pardonnez moi, Charles . . . the Republicans, under General Lapoype, moved into Fort La Garde and occupied it. And the ridge here, in the middle of the plain behind it. I'm told we had La Garde long enough to ruin it . . . blew its powder vaults, toppled the parapets, disabled the guns there . . ."

"No way to 'old eet, so far from ze ozzer posts, wizout cavalry for ze resupply, hein?" de Crillart surmised.

"Exactly, Charles," Lewrie agreed, much more agreeable with his second steaming mug of coffee in his other hand. "We have to resupply all our coastline posts by water, as it is. Well, General Lapoype has guns and mortars in the ruins of La Garde again, and he's opened on any supply boat he sees. Malgue's guns don't have the range to reach that far, and the ridge blocks Saint Catherine's. The coastal strong points have guns, yes, but they're sited to fire to seaward, and the garrisons have only field guns . . . regimental six-pounders and such . . . facing inland. Saint Margaret is taking a pounding, too. So, were we to work our way to . . . here, east of Saint Margaret . . . There's a low spot along the coast road, near this beach. And about a quarter-mile offshore there's six fathom depth. Stripped as this raft is, we only draw two. More muddy sand that close ashore, and the rocks are smaller, so we'll have better holding ground."

"An', ve observe s'rough zis gap, from ze fighting-tops, oui?" de Crillart smiled, then translated for Comandante Esquevarre.

"Ze Comandante, 'e say alzo, mes amis . . ." de Crillart supplied after a long palaver, "zat ze enemy 'ave trés difficulté to attack zose coastal posts, vere ve to destroy zese string of ponts. Deux roads de La Garde, sud of ze ridge. One eez good groun', direct at ze Sainte Margaret, 'ere. Go pas' Les Savaux, Plan Redon, to ze coast road. Mais ze ozzer, east of ze Plan de Galle, eet go sud, to Notre Dame de Bon Salut an' ze Château des Pradets, zen down to ze Plage de la Garonne."

"Ahah?" Lewrie inquired.

More palaver back and forth.

"Ah, ze Comandante, 'e say, vous-êtes sailors, mais 'e eez soldat. 'E see what vous do not. Zey place batteries on ze heights near ze Notre

Dame des Bon Salut, an' to ze west . . . zey comman' ze Bay of Toulon. Non sheep enter or leave ze bay. Zey shoot into ze Great Road."

"Ah," Lewrie said with slow comprehension. "That *does* put a different light on things."

"But, 'e say," Lieutenant de Crillart continued with a sly grin, "zere are le Petit Pont, 'ere. Groun' eez . . . mmm, 'ow you say . . . ?"

"Marshy," Scott offered with an impatient grunt.

"Ah, oui, marshy! Merci, m'sieur Scott. Deux bridges, zen road cross zis stream on a s'ird . . . anozzer bridge cross marshy . . . marsh, zen a fift', ware ze sud road cross ze la Reguana Reever. Comandante Don Luis, 'e weesh to use ze mortars on zese bridges, aussi. After ve bombard ze Fort La Garde."

"So if they mean to move their army against Toulon, they'd have to come direct west, right into the teeth of our fire, or try to skirt past the end of the ridge and face the guns of Fort Saint Margaret, on their flank, while they're all strung out?"

"Ze Comandant do not believe zey do zis, mon capitaine. 'Ere are ze reever, an' ze stream, zey mus' still cross, on ze good road to Plan Redon, zen turn west across Pont de la Clue. But zat ees covered by Fort Malgue, Post de Brun, Saint Margaret . . ." Charles shrugged in heavy, Gallic fashion, with a snort of amusement to show how hopeless an endeavour that might be.

"Comandant, just to do a complete bit of work, why don't we blow this Pont de la Clue whilst we're at it, today? Last of all?" Alan suggested. To which, after a translation, Don Luis was quick to express his agreement.

"Cony?" Lewrie called out the door to the gun deck.

"Aye, sir?"

"How's the fog?"

"Thicker'n London, sir," Cony answered, after a weather-wary eye at the sky. "But, 'ere's a wind comin' up, sir. Not much o' one, but a breeze. Might blow off, in'n 'our'r two, sir. I c'n see 'bout two musket shot'z all."

"That'd be just enough visibility for us to warp out and row," Lewrie speculated, tossing away his ruler and dividers. "Sound our way down to the entrance in the log boom, then set course through the Gullet. Hug the coast all the way, so they won't even know we're in place until the first shell. Let's be at it, then. Cony, my respects to the Bosun, and he's to sound 'All Hands'. Stations for leaving harbour."

"I think I can see now," Lewrie enthused, aloft in the foretop. It had been hours before they could make anything out farther off than a quarter-mile, and had more felt their way east, than anything else. But they had *Zélé* anchored now in four fathoms of water, east of Saint Margaret in a little cove where the Hieres Road ran close along cliffs which were much lower than the rest of that daunting coast, where that road dipped between two hills into a depression. "That's it, I think."

"*Has* to be La Garde, sir," Lieutenant Scott muttered, spying the place out with his own telescope. "Now the fog's burned off enough . . . sure to be. The only hill west of the ridge. Circular central keep, with four arms and circular ends. Just clear enough . . ."

Scott traded his telescope for a sextant and slate.

"I make it a mile and three-quarters, sir," he concluded. "And it appears we're anchored broadside-to."

Lewrie looked at his watch: quarter 'til ten in the morning and nothing stirring yonder, due to the fogs. The French had been blinded as effectively as everyone else on such a gloomy morning. There was a wind up now, from the sou'west, blowing into the cove quite briskly, and rattling a chop against the base of the cliffs, ruffling wavelets over the wide, shingly beach to their right. A wind which would blow their powder smoke away quickly, making it difficult for the French to discover their position. It might even take them awhile to find that it wasn't a new mortar battery installed at Fort Saint Margaret itself!

"Let's give it another quarter-hour, Mister Scott. Let Don Luis have a peek at it, and then we'll open fire," Lewrie decided.

"Aye, sir. I'll fetch him."

By the time Don Luis de Esquevarre, his *aspirante*, and sergeant-gunner Huelva had ascended the mast, though, the fog had been blown clearer. Fort La Garde was no longer nebulous, but sharp-edged in the telescopes, and Don Luis was eager to open upon them at once, pleading that it would take hours to further reduce the place. It *was* a masonry fort, after all!

"Bueno," Lewrie grinned, clapping Esquevarre on the shoulder. "We begin, Don Luis. Sí. Fuego."

Lewrie went back to the deck by a standing backstay while Comandante Esquevarre and his aides had to use the lubber's hole in the top and clamber down the ratlines and shrouds with landsmen's clumsiness. A full ten minutes was spent inspecting safety precautions, just to be sure no one had omitted a step in the drill due to overfamiliarity or boredom. The gun deck was running with water from the pumps, the companionway to the orlop was trickling sea water, the magazine passage was wetted down from overhead to decking, the felt screen was soaked, the hides were up in the laboratory aft . . . Only four kegs of powder were aft to fill shells at any one time, the excess covered with wet haircloth, the fuse chest covered except for extraction of the called-for timing. Thirty-two pounder great-guns empty and tompioned, bowsed up to the port sills, and only two sets of slow match burning in the mortar well, properly guarded.

"Gargeun los morteros," Esquevarre ordered. "Garguen a bombardear."

The left-hand mortar was prepared, the touch hole reamed out and primed with fine-mealed powder. The tallow seal was scraped off the top end of the fuse. "Fósforo . . . preparado . . . fuego!"

Another day of noise and smoke had begun.

"Over . . . and left, sir!" Mister Midshipman Spendlove shouted down from the fore-top. "At the foot of the hill!"

"Close, for a first try," Lewrie beamed, as the *aspirante* told his commander what that meant in Spanish. Esquevarre fiddled with the traverse a touch, cranked in a tiny change in elevation for the right-hand mortar whilst the left hand was being thoroughly swabbed out. Up came a powder charge. Out came a fixed shell.

"Fósforo . . . preparado . . . fuego!"

Blam went the world, loud as thunder at one's elbow, rocking the floating battery so hard it felt like she'd been hit with a substantial slab of cliff.

"On target! Right in the center, sir!" Spendlove screamed with delight. "Spot-on! Yayy, give 'em another!"

"Carry on, sir," Lewrie laughed. Damme, but we've gotten main-good at this service, he thought smugly, going to the ratlines to go aloft to enjoy the morning's work.

With French and British help to do the carrying, they got into a rhythm of one shell a minute. It took the French at least ten to even begin to respond, and their first shots in reply were directed at the closest coastal fort, Sainte Margaret, just as Lewrie had thought. And he didn't think the small garrison there enjoyed being taken for the goat.

Within an hour of hot practice, the fire from La Garde began to slack off. It had been furious for a while, shells dropping all over on the cliffs, on either side of the saddle between the hills, probing far afield, into the cove and upon the beach as they shot over initially.

Then the first shell came singing overhead with a whistling moan. It landed far out to sea, perhaps half a mile away, to splash a feather of spray, then burst. A minute later there came a second, also an over, more off the bows, to their right, but closer in.

"They're correcting to our smoke," Lewrie sneered to Spendlove as yet a third shell followed the same path, and blew up close to shore but far to the right, almost dead on their bows. The wind was veering, more from the west now, ragging their stupendous powder pall eastward, lower to the water before it collided with the back eddies off the bluffs, so it might appear to the French that a gunboat was hidden in a cove even farther east, where it at last arose beyond the lip of the cliffs.

"Just as long as they can't see our fore-top, sir?" Spendlove inquired, full of good cheer. Nothing tremulous to *that* young man's tone!

"It's barely over the saddle, e'en so, Mister Spendlove," Lewrie chuckled. "And with no topmast standing?"

"Preparado . . . fuego!" BLAM!

They turned to the next fall-of-shot. 3,080 yards they were firing: twenty-seven seconds of flight time for a shell, with a quim-hair less than a six-inch fuse, and four drams shy of twenty pounds of powder down the chamber-of the mortar. Zélé was shuddering like a kicked hound to each shot. In the fore-top that resulted in a shock, then a sway, judders so short and sharp it felt like the mast was going to be kicked out of its step far below on the keel.

"Twenty-five . . . twenty-six . . . twenty-sev . . . hit!" Spendlove said with glee, as he had every shot of the morning, hit *or* miss.

Brumm! La Garde groaned, as a section of tumbled wall was blown out, massive blocks of masonry sent flying like so many rooks, scared from one gleaning to the next by a farmer's fowling piece. Dirty rags of smoke gushed out behind them, gunpowder-tan at first, then darkening as other things began to burn in the aftermath of a magazine strike to grow to a spreading, wind-flattened pillar of smoke worthy of a burning city.

And a shell splashed down behind Zélé, out to sea on her starboard side. But close enough to rock her when the fuse burned down underwater and made it explode as it sank to the rocky bottom.

"Found us," Lewrie frowned. "Well, it only took the clowns over an hour, this time. That may have been their parting shot, though."

Esquevarre kept on throwing a shell a minute at La Garde. Once more, though, there was a shell thrown back—two, in fact. One burst on the beach, scooping up a hail of gravel to add to its shattered iron cloud of shrapnel. Rocks and metal slivers pattered in a rain into the sea between the beach and the larboard bows. The second shell struck in the middle of the cove, equally between their floating battery and shore. And even on the fore-top, Lewrie and Spendlove were doused by spray.

" 'Bout time to shift anchorage, Mister Spendlove. Lay below to the deck. Inform Mister Scott he is to ready the ship to hoist anchors, and for the comandante to secure his guns."

"Aye, sir," Spendlove replied crisply, then, agile as a monkey, took a stay in a hopeful, but sure, leap and slithered down, half sliding to the deck, hand-over-hand.

There were sharp noises, more bangs. For a moment, Lewrie thought that Fort Saint Margaret had opened fire with her six- and twelve-pounders, to delude the French; though with the harsh pounding they'd taken earlier, he rather doubted they'd be that charitable. There was a splash, about the bows.

The bows? he frowned. And no explosion? Solid-shot!

He looked east, towards Notre Dame de Bon Salut.

There! A wisp of powder smoke. It hadn't come from the arrow-tipped bluff above the beach, the Lord be praised, but farther east on the coast road, just where it began to crest the eastern hill, firing from defilade. Sure enough, another shot erupted from what he took to be at least an eight-pounder. And Fort Saint Margaret's shot moaned overhead in reply, to strike flinty, gravelly soil and leap and bound in deadly ricochet around it, puffing up clumps of dust at every touching.

"Damned right, we're shifting anchorage!" he groaned to himself. "We're getting out of here!" A second eight-pounder now opened alongside the first.

There was a moaning in the sky, the *skree* of a heavy shell on its way into the cove from La Garde. Lewrie stopped, with one hand on the standing-backstay, to see a second slow in its upward flight, to stand still in the air as a tiny black mote for a split second, then dash to invisibility again. Hadn't he heard, if you could *see* it, it was dead on, and . . . ?

With a sick premonition, he looked down to the deck, where Comandante Esquevarre was looking up as well, his face blanched, even under the grime of gun soot. Then the gun deck disappeared.

They struck *Zélé*, right in the mortar well. A shell must have been in the well, fixed and ready to be loaded. A powder charge, too, nearly twenty-pounds worth, free of its leathern cylinder, wrapped only in an easily ignited paper cartridge. There were two sharp explosions in one, almost atop each other, and a hail of splinters howled around him, blown upwards to spatter into the bottom timbers of the fighting-top!

Lewrie leaned back quickly, throwing himself flat, feeling wood jump beneath his belly, as smoke gushed up the lubber's hole, and the foremast shuddered and groaned. He started to rise, but fell flat at the second skree. That was the one he'd seen stopping, he hadn't even seen the first that took the well, he . . .

Another crash aft. No explosion. He turned his head to look and saw a star-shaped hole in the rear of the quarterdeck, right through the tough planking and beaming of what had been an upper gun deck . . . into the filling room! If it . . .

BLAM!

Timbers flew, heavy beams shattered, and wood splinters mixed with jagged iron splinters. More groanings and wood shrieks. And men crying out in pain and fear. The mizzenmast toppled forward, shorn off at its base, furled and gasketed sails smouldering, and rigging lines burning like slow match. Toppled forward by the force of the blast aft, draping itself over the larboard gangways, crushing them with its weight, that amputated trunk thrown forward of its stump!

Lewrie rose, saw that the standing-backstay was still firm, and slithered down to the deck through a fog of gunsmoke. And the smell of burning wood. Somewhere, they had a fire. Old and baked as their floating battery was, she'd go up like kindling, and soon.

"Where away?" he called to the first person he met, grabbing at the fellow's arm. The man howled with pain. That arm was cooked raw and black, still sizzling with embedded powder embers.

"Mon dieu, mon dieu!" The man staggered away, half his clothes blown off, screaming with terror and the agony of his burns.

"Scott? Crillart?" Lewrie shouted above the din. "Spendlove?"

"Ici, mon capitain," Crillart shouted back, emerging from the smoke. "Ze chambre de fille . . . zere is trés feu! Ze shells stored . . ."

They both ducked as another tremendous blast erupted aft, this time with ragged, hungry flames licking upwards from the second great rent torn in the quarterdeck.

"Scott?" Lewrie demanded, taking de Crillart by both arms.

"I do not know," de Crillart replied, shaky but determined.

"Get the men over the side, Charles. She'll blow sky-high, soon as the fire reaches the main magazine. I don't think we can save her."

"Oui, Alain, elle est morte, pauvre Zélé. Alors, mes amis! Nous abandonnons! Anglais! Ve abandon ship! Espagnole, el barco abandonar!"

There were not many Spanish gunners left alive to obey that command. Lewrie coughed on the smoke, looking down into the ruin of the mortar well. Sergeant Huelva, the *aspirante*, Esquevarre and the matchmen, the loaders . . . there was a ragged hole where the well had been, blown to the base of the orlop, and both mortars had crashed through it. Ruddy sparks glowed down there on the orlop, and greasy smoke coiled upwards. Of the men serving the mortars at the moment of immolation, there was little sign.

"Sir!" Bosun Porter shouted. He and Spendlove skidded to a stop near him. "We goin' over, sir?"

"Aye, we are," Lewrie agreed quickly, trying to take a breath to steady himself. What he wanted most of all to do was jump howling over the side that very instant, anything counter to that wish could just be damned, and God help the trampled!

But he was the captain. If they went over the side in a panic, it would be even worse. And there was the fact that he couldn't swim a stroke! With more courage than he felt he'd ever deserved, he caught that smoky breath, and told his jibbering terror to wait a bit.

"Bosun, gather up oars, spare spars, hatch gratings, whatever is loose. Get it over the larboard side, in the lee, and lash it together. Mats of hammocks, between baulks of timber as floats. Hurry, we don't have much time. Mister Spendlove, gather some hands to help. Cony!" He bawled.

" 'Ere, sir! I'm a comin'!" came a gladsome shout from somewhere forward. He looked singed as he came through the smoke, but Lewrie had never seen a cheerier sight.

"We have to leave her, Cony. We'll search for survivors first and get them over the larboard side."

"Got Gracey an' Sadler, sir, an' a coupla t'others. Hoy, here be Lisney!"

"How's it below, Lisney?" Lewrie asked.

"Fires is burnin', sir. Aft, mostly," Lisney coughed, hacking and spitting, blowing his nose on his fingers to clear soot from his nostrils and throat. "Transom's blowd clean out, sir. Ye kin see th' daylight through 'er. Floodin' bad."

"So we sink before the orlop magazine catches fire?"

"They's fires on th' orlop 'neath us, now, sir," Lisney cried between retches. "Nothin' big yet, but . . . after half, I reckon. Me'n th' gunner, an' 'is powder yeomen? Jus' come back. Too smoky t'see wot y'r doin'. 'Ey soaked th' made-up charges an' kegs good, long'z we 'ad water runnin' in th' 'ose, sir."

"We have to go below," Lewrie announced, chilling himself at his words, seeing the shiver of fear and awe reflected in his men, at what he was asking them to do. "There's gear below that'll float, lads. We need it. And, we have to check the magazine. Mr. Spendlove, inform Lieutenant Crillart where we're going, and have him round up as many as he can to assist the bosun. Then, see if you can find Lieutenant Scott. Right, men . . . after me. Let's go." Bloody daft, I am, he told himself; daft as bats!

But they followed him below, that clutch of shuddering men; went staggering down the companionway ladders into smoky darkness to gather up stools and armfuls of tightly rolled hammocks, which might make temporary life buoys before they soaked through. They ripped down partitions and doors from warrant and mates' cabins, cut down the mess tables hung from the overheads, and handed them up, looted the unused carpenter's stores for baulks and planks of dry timber.

Lewrie forced himself to enter the magazine, crouched low under the coiling smoke, coughing his lungs out, even so. The felt screen in the doorway was still wet and cool, the door slimy with water. Farther aft, the wooden bulkheads were only slightly warm yet. He felt over a pile of paper cartridges, sickly slick and tacky with water. He worked in the dark—Bittfield, their senior gunner's mate, had extinguished all the lanterns in the glassed-in light room which usually illuminated the magazine. Lewrie's feet slipped and slid in a slurry of wet gunpowder, gritty but soaked. He almost wet himself when he realised it. Normally, only felt or list slippers could be worn in the magazine to avoid sparks; no matter how careful the yeomen of the powder were, a small amount always spilled, and one scrape of shoe leather could set it off like a bomb! He heard trickling water.

God, yes! Forward there was a tin-lined water tank, used by the galley to fill the steep-tubs to simmer rations, and as a fire reserve. Bittfield had axed his way through the overhead planking and punctured it, hang the risk of a spark when his steel axehead had bitten into it. The tank was slowly emptying itself into the magazine, gurgling in shoe-heel deep. He felt the massive kegs in the dark. They were wet to the touch. Though Lewrie felt his "nutmegs" had shriveled up to the size of capers, he decided that the magazine would be safe just long enough for them to get away before it blew. There was double-banked timber on all sides, top and bottom, which would only smoulder and char . . . for awhile.

His hideous duty done, he quite happily fled.

"All clear, sir," Lisney coughed and wheezed at him when he came forward to the companionway, where there was at least the hope of air and a little light. Lisney was fuming that he'd taken so long, that he could not flee himself until Lewrie did.

Can't say that I blame him, Alan thought.

"Hatchets," Lewrie barked, between coughs. "Take the ladders, too. Break 'em loose, then we'll haul 'em up after us."

"Aye, sir," Lisney whined, impatient to be away. "Hoy, lads!"

It was a matter of seconds to break the ladders free, to scamper to the gun deck, then sling them upward and to the side. Lewrie followed them to the larboard side, the lee, and looked over. There was no more he could do. It was time to go.

"Half of 'em sir," Spendlove wailed, standing on the fore-chain plat-form, clinging to taut stays. "They just lit out for the beach, and I couldn't stop them! Didn't wait to help, or . . ."

"It's alright, Mister Spendlove," Lewrie said, peeling off his uniform coat. "They can't help it."

He swung a leg over the bulwarks and stepped down beside Spendlove, on the chain platform. It was only eight or so feet more to the water, but it looked one hellish-far drop. Terrified as he'd been down in the magazine, well . . . it didn't hold a candle to this!

No wonder they lit out, he shuddered, taking a look aft along the floating battery's side. She was slightly down by the stern, and fires raged unchecked aft, snarling like famished dogs over the forward edge of the quarterdeck, beginning to eat at the gangways on either beam, and the after-half of the gun deck was sizzling with low sheets of flamelets.

And shells were still falling from Fort La Garde, bursting above her, splashing down all about the cove, close aboard. One came down in a knot of swimmers and paddlers, clinging to any old sort of flotsam by the beach. Up rose a pillar of water, mud, gravel . . . men, or pieces of men; broken coop crates and bits of timber. When the feather collapsed, there weren't four heads to be seen still afloat!

"Mister Scott, sir," Spendlove cried, tears running on his face.

"Yes?" Lewrie asked, staring at the sea below him with foreboding.

Dear God, if I can't find something solid to cling to . . . ! Alan shuddered.

"*Dead*, sir!" Spendlove shouted, as if in accusation. "Blown to . . . dear *God*, sir, there were bits of him, scattered . . ." He pointed aft to the raging furnace of the quarterdeck, where Scott would have taken himself, to ready *Zélé* to up-anchor. Spendlove's shirtfront was wet with breakfast, his terrified reaction to his first dead men.

Lewrie could but nod at that sad news, more concerned with surviving himself at that moment, gazing like a hypnotised rabbit under a snake's steely glare, at the sea. Hungry waters lapped and gurgled with what sounded like glee against the side, as if they'd been waiting for him for a very long time.

"See to the men, Mister Spendlove. Get as many ashore as you can," he ordered. "Be calm. They'll need that."

"Aye, sir," Spendlove gulped, fighting back his own fears.

Waistcoat too, I s'pose, Lewrie surmised; good broadcloth, it'll soak up water like a sponge. He peeled it off and cast it away. Lewrie undid the buckle of his neckstock and lace front to toss them away, too. This day, he wore old cotton stockings, his worst-stained pair of cotton breeches, the working pair he'd had run up out of sailcloth.

It struck him that they were French, and he giggled.

Serge de Nîmes, they called the fabric . . . sailcloth. Bloody Frogs invented it, didn't they? But he could not recall what the French called "sails." *Vela*? No, that was Latin.

Weak and shuddering, feeling a bit faint at his prospect of drowning, chilling all over, feeling his knees buckling, and his death grip on the stay slipping, he imagined he was already a spirit, a shade, freed of his body's mortal husk, outside of himself and distanced from the world. His ears were ringing, not from an excess of noise but from an almost total lack of sound. A shell burst, its fuse wrongly selected, right over the bluffs, and he could barely hear its barking *Crack*!

"Sir, sir!" from far away. "Mister Lewrie, sir! 'Old on, Mister Lewrie, I'm acomin'!"

And there was Cony, paddling and treading water at his feet. So *far* below, though!

"Got ya somethin' t' 'ang onta, sir," Cony promised. There was a small, rectangular hatch grating from a limber hole off the orlop deck, a bar to intruders who had no business secreting themselves in the dark recesses of the bilges or the carpenter's walks; crosshatched of wood two-by-four, with ventilation squares. "It'll float like anythin', sir! Ya gotta jump on *down*, Mister Lewrie. I'll be right 'ere, no worries."

"Ah . . ." Lewrie said, grimacing with fear that looked like a grin.

"She's burnin' damn' fierce, Mister Lewrie, she'll blow sky-high any minute now," Cony insisted, swiping water and soaked flaxen hair out of his eyes. "Ever'body else'z off 'er, sir, ain't no reason t'stay no longer. Come *on*, sir!"

Lewrie sat down on the fore-chain platform, easing his buttocks to the edge, his toes dangling, terror-breaths whooshing in and out, as if the next would be the last.

"God love ya, Mister Lewrie, sir," Cony coaxed, his face crimped with worry. "All these years t'gether, I don't mean t'lose ya now. Wot I tell y'r good lady an' y'r kiddies, if I went an' lost ya? Come *on*, sir! 'Old y'r nose an' slide off! I'll be right by y'r side, swear it by Jesus, I do, sir!"

Well . . . he sighed. He clapped his cocked hat firmly on his head, took a deep breath, held his nose, compressed his lips, took one last fond look at the bluffs—and let go of the stay.

He fell, he splashed like a cannon ball, arrowing down . . . *down*, and *down*, wanting to scream, blinded by brine, forever lost, lungs aching, wishing he'd taken a deeper breath, deep enough to last forever . . .

"Shit!" he yelped as he broke surface, felt light and air on his face, felt Cony's hand on his shirt collar. Retching and coughing from smoke, from water in his mouth, his eyes, weeping with salt-water sting and pure, semi-hysterical relief.

"Grab ahold o' this, sir, there ya be, safe'z 'ouses," Cony cooed, and Lewrie flailed about until his hands seized the hatch grating, took it to his bosom trying to get his whole chest over the two-by-three foot grating. Feeling it wobble under him, threatening to tip him over.

"Shit!" he reiterated.

" 'Ang on, sir, jus' th' edge, t'keep y'r 'ead 'bove water, an' . . ." Cony instructed. "That's better, sir. You jus' 'ang on, an' I'll tow."

"Lost my hat," Lewrie carped, prying one stinging eye open.

"Hat's no matter, Mister Lewrie," Cony laughed. "Gotta get shed o' y'r sword, sir."

"No!" Lewrie insisted, almost petulantly.

"Drag ya down, do ya slip an' let go, sir," Cony explained.

"No!" Lewrie growled, groping fearfully for the scabbard which dangled between his legs. He dragged it around to lie athwart the grating before his eyes, then resumed his death grip.

" 'Ere we go then, sir," Cony fretted, beginning to side-stroke and tow. "Do ya kick y'r legs, sir? Push like ya wuz aclimbin' real steep stairs, that'd help. Y'll get the 'ang of it."

Once away from *Zélé*'s side, out of her lee, they met the wind, which helped propel them into the cove, towards the beach. Grunting as he gyrated his legs in an unfamiliar motion, he could begin to feel each tiny thrust as he clung to his raft, gagging and spitting with the water just under his chin, and wavelets slopping over his shoulders, to his ears at times, from behind. Halfway there, he lost his right shoe, no matter how he'd crimped his toes to keep it.

There were dead in the water, men floating face-down with their long hair come undone from tarry queues, fanned out like tentacles from flattened jellyfish. And bits and pieces of men who'd been torn apart by one of those underwater shell-bursts. Cony thrust their way through a bobbing assortment of broken barricoes, stubs of lumber, jagged, still smoking planks and ship's beams. Here an abandoned hammock, inches under but still afloat, there a man who'd drowned even with two rolled hammocks about his chest. Coils of loose rope, swaying upwards for the sun like sea snakes he'd seen in the China Seas.

Sharks! he quailed, to himself, grimly pushing and kicking, finding a rhythm at last with Cony's towing strokes. Bloody hell, I've seen 'em, every shipwreck, every battle, looking for survivors . . . Some bit of half-submerged flotsam touched his bare foot and he all but screamed, biting his sword belt to keep from unmanning himself.

Rumblings, distant earthquake quivers in the water, pressure he could feel squeezing on his stomach and lungs. Groans and cries astern. He dared turn his head to look, and saw Zélé with two-thirds heartily burning, the foremast toppling slowly, great gouts of bubbles foaming around her as she settled lower and lower. Her stern was probably already on the rocky bottom, he thought, with waves burbling around her great-cabin windows. She at least would not have far to go, not in four fathoms, and she drew two; she'd lay awash, until everything above that new waterline had charred to crumbly coals.

"Right, sir," Cony said cheerfully, "we're here. Hit me knee on a rock." He left off side-stroking and stood up, waist-deep. Alan was not that brave—he thrust with his legs until he was past Cony before he groped for the bottom with his feet. When he at last stood up, he'd reached thigh-deep water. And he was cold.

"Christ," he sighed, beginning to shiver, his teeth to chatter as that brisk November wind found every water-logged inch of him. Immersed, it hadn't felt quite so bad. His legs below the surface were warmer.

"Lucky we wuz so near th' beach, sir, else we'da froze up solid an' gone under," Cony said, hugging himself to still his own shiverings.

"Cony, I . . ." Lewrie blushed. "Thankee, Will Cony. Thankee."

"Aw, sir," Cony shrugged modestly as they splashed through tiny surf-rushes onto the gravel of the beach. "Weren't . . . well, sir. After all this time, I'd not care t'be servin' another officer. So I 'spect it'd be better t'save th' one I'm usedta."

"Whatever reason, Cony . . . my hand on't," Lewrie offered, shaking Cony's paw vigorously. "I'm in your debt. Damme, if I ain't."

"All these years, sir . . . well, I swore I wouldn't lose ya. An' so I didn't. Thankee, sir. Thankee kindly."

"Now, let's see what we have left," Lewrie said, breaking free, feeling a tad uncomfortable over such a close and affectionate display of emotion towards another man. Even one who'd just saved his life.

There wasn't much. Crillart and his gunners were grouped off to one side, only about half the number Lewrie had recalled, trying to put names to half-known faces, trying to dredge up the identity of missing men. Of Spaniards, there were only four still alive. Spendlove, Porter and Lisney were huddled together in a group. He still had Preston and Sadler, Gracey, Gittons . . . there was gunner's mate Bittfield . . .

"Bosun?" he called. "Taken a muster?"

"Aye, sir," Porter nodded, in a daze still. "Nothin' to write on, sir, I . . ."

"Later," Lewrie agreed, clapping him on the shoulder. "We'll sort it out later. Stout fellow, Porter. To get as many as you did ashore."

"Oh, aye, sir . . . thankee," Porter straightened, bucking up.

Lewrie undid the knee buckles of his breeches, letting a minor flood of sea water escape down his shins. He pulled up his stockings from his ankles, where they'd settled. And winced as he plodded across the rough shingle of the beach. Lock-Jaw Fever was so easy to die of, he couldn't recall a time he'd ever gone barefoot, even as a child.

There was a muffled *boom* from *Zélé* as part of her soggy powder at last took light in the magazine, a dull *whoomph*, accompanied by a spurt of smoke from her gun ports. She'd settled now, with only her upper bulwarks and gangways, her jib boom and quarterdeck above the surface. The fires had abated, with too little dry timber to feed on. She fumed now like a slag heap in Birmingham, the smoke thin and bluish like burning autumn leaves.

It struck Lewrie suddenly that he had just lost everything. His sea chest had gone down with her. All his clothes, books, a career-span of official documents and letters, orders and . . .

His two pairs of pistols, shoes, stockings, homemade preserves he had packed, that Caroline had put up. His dressing gown no one liked.

Christ, her letters! he groaned. And the miniature portrait, and Sewallis's crude first drawings, Hugh's messy handprints from the latest post . . . that *juju* bag, too. Lucy Beauman had had one of her family slaves make it . . . a "witch" to keep him safe from the sea, long ago when he was ashore on Antigua, recovering from Yellow Jack. He hadn't really worn it in ages, but to lose it. Yet . . .

"Fat lot of good it did me, after all," he whispered. "I got ashore without it."

Hurtful as his losses were, the one that really stung was that, for all his vows to keep his sailors alive, come what may, he'd lost some of them—he'd failed. And, for the first time in his career, he had lost a ship.

CHAPTER 10

"Charles," Lewrie muttered, standing over the despondent Lieutenant Crillart. "We have to get moving. We stay on this beach, we'll freeze to death. It looks as if we could climb up to the Hieres road and march to Saint Margaret. That's what, 'bout half a mile?"

"Oui, Alain," de Crillart nodded slowly, getting to his feet as creakily as a doddering ancient. Lewrie offered him a hand up. "All zose hommes splendide. Moi . . . my men!"

"I know. Mine, too, Charles. Mister Scott . . ." Lewrie replied.

"Sir!" Bosun Porter shouted in alarm suddenly. "Riders comin'!"

Spilling down from the gentlest slope above the beach, just west of where the French field guns had fired, were a knot of horsemen, men in oversized shakos, bearing lances. Blue uniforms, green uniforms all sprigged in red braiding. And the lances bore small, burgee-cut pennons of blue-white-red, the Tricolour. They were French. About twenty cavalrymen, followed by officers in cocked hats.

"Well, shit," Lewrie sighed as the leading horsemen curvetted all about them, brandishing lance points or sabres. "Stand fast, lads! Stay calm. Stand fast!"

It was all they *could* do. To run . . . well, there'd be no running, not shoeless on shingle, no escape from a lance tip in the back. They were already disarmed, except for Admiralty-pattern sheath knives, and Captain Braxton had made sure the points had been blunted long before.

"Silly-lookin' bashtids," Landsman Preston grumbled. Some of the cavalrymen wore braids in their hair, pigtails on either side of their faces, with the rest long and loose-flowing as women, or shorn peasant-short in Republican, revolutionary style. Tall dragoon boots above the knee, Republican trousers instead of breeches, gaudy new and unfamiliar uniforms. Not a queue, not a powdered head in sight. And they were a scruffy-looking lot, too, as if their new rags had been sewn up from a set of old rags. And they stank. Lord, how they stank, bad as rotting meat, their horses galled raw by hard service!

" 'Oo eez een charge?" a cavalry officer asked, one of the riders in green and red, with the ridiculous pigtails beside his cheeks.

"I am," Lewrie spat, disgusted at being captured, and so easily.

The cavalry officer extended his heavy sabre, blade inverted and point down, inches from Alan's nose, with a triumphant smirk on his face. "Parlez-vous français, m'sieur?" he sneered.

"Ah, foutre, non," Lewrie said with a sad shrug. "Je ne parle pas."

"Espèce de salaud!" the officer barked, making his horse rear and slash with its hooves, baring yellow teeth. "Je demande qu' est-ce que votre nom, vous fumier!"

"Lt. Alan Lewrie, Royal Navy," he replied proudly, refusing to give horse *or* rider an inch, prickly with pride—the only item he had left in any abundance. "Captain of the *Zélé*, floating battery." He pointed over his shoulder to the wreck. "Parlez-vous anglais?"

"Oui," the officer barked, not sounding very happy about speaking the language of an ancient foe. "You *'ear* me speak eet. Lieutenant, or capitaine . . . w'eech are you?"

"Both," Lewrie grinned, happy to have confused him.

"Et *Zélé*? Zat eez français."

"Captured. French ship, British crew, m'sieur. Why she sank so quick. French," Alan said with another expressive shrug.

"You mak' ze leetle joke, m'sieur, hein?" the cavalryman grinned without mirth.

"Oui, I make the little joke, m'sieur."

The rider clucked and kneed his mount to take a step forward, and Alan had to give ground at last. The sword point touched his chest and began to dig into his breastbone.

"Mais, ve *sink* you, an' votre ship . . . so 'oo is laugh, now, hein, un petit merdeux!" The rider laughed, and swung his arm back for a cut.

"Arrêtez!" a voice shouted from up the hill, leaving Alan with a hair's-breadth between life and death as he beheld the weak November sun twinkling on the sabre's fresh-honed edge. He *knew* he was being a fool, *knew* his truculence could get him hacked to bits. But he could not help himself.

But the officer balked, looked over his shoulder, and loosed the tension in his sword arm. The sabre came down harmlessly to the rider's side, and he jerked his reins to ride away, to speak with the clutch of officers who had called to him.

"Good God, sir, shouldn't you . . . ?" Spendlove shivered. "If we get 'em mad enough . . ."

"Aye, Mister Spendlove, I'll be good, from now on."

With the officer apart from them, the cavalrymen, the lancers and dragoons dismounted, hemming in the survivors to a tight knot, musketoons or long pistols out and half-cocked, to pat them down for weapons. For anything that struck their fancy, too, it seemed. A sergeant came up to Lewrie's side, turned out his pockets and got a few shillings, began to touch the sword. Alan glared at him and pushed the scabbard behind his thigh. Republican or not, an officer's glare was still useful on a Revolutionary. The sergeant moved his hand and tore his watch away, snarling a garlicky breath through dingy, discoloured teeth. He held up the watch, admiring the blue riband, fouled anchor and crossed cannon fob, done in damascene silver and gold, opened the case and held it to his ear to see if it still ticked. And made off with it, chortling and jeering.

Alan looked to the staff officers up the beach. The cavalry officer was catching pluperfect Hell from the fellow on the dapple-gray gelding. He sheathed his sabre, bowed his head and turned red as the froggings on his jacket. Then they were coming down the beach toward Lewrie, the one on the fine dapple-gray in the lead, the horse stepping and prancing as head-high as his master. He drew to a halt, tossed the reins without even looking to a lancer on the off side, and swung a leg over the horse's neck to spring lithely down.

Another bloody minikin, Lewrie thought sourly as he studied him; just like that Captain Nelson. And young, too. Christ, he don't look a day over twenty-one!

The officer wore glossy top boots, snug buff trousers and a dark blue, single-breasted uniform coat, cut horizontal across the waist, with vine and leaf pattern embroidery up the front, buttoned up against chilly winds almost to the throat. The stand-and-fall collar was also ornately embroidered with gold lace, very wide and spread halfway to his shoulders. A long burgundy wool sash about his slim waist, a silver-laced black belt over it with a damascened buckle supported the frog for a light-cavalry sabre. Long shirt collar turned up against his neck, wrapped in a silk stock. Plain black beaver cocked hat, big as a watermelon, dressed only with the Tricolour cockade, shadowed his eyes. Eyes, Lewrie noted, that were not young at all; very large, penetrating, studious and sober, and so reserved. Yet darting lazily, taking everything in. Lewrie reassessed his age upwards—maybe mid-twenties, he thought. The cavalry captain was, like all cavalry (English especially), hoorawing brutes, dangers to all, including themselves. But this fellow . . .

"M'sieur, permettez-moi . . ." the cavalryman said in a gentler and much more polite tone of voice as he did the introductions. ". . . ze lieutenant colonel, Napoléone Buonaparte, chef du artillerie, a' Général

Dugommier, commandeur de l'Armée. 'Is aides-de-camp, ze capitaines Marmot et Junot . . . m'sieurs, ici capitain Luray, marine royal, de roi brittanique, Georges troisiéme."

"Colonel," Lewrie nodded, laying a hand on his breast to salute with a slight bow.

"Capitain Luray, enchanté," the little fellow smiled of a sudden, and offered his hand, reeling off a rapid, very fluid French.

"Ze colonel say please to forgive, 'e 'ave no anglais, m'sieur," the cavalryman translated. "But 'e eez delight to mak' you' ac . . . acquaintance. 'E offer 'is congratulation . . . votre gunnerie . . . votre courage magnifique. You no strike votre flag, sink viz les canons blaze? Magnifique, treés magnifique!"

He had no choice but to take the offered hand and shake it, face to face at last with enemy Frogs, not the tame Royalists in Toulon. It was a wrench, though, to be forced by gentlemanly convention to have to be pleasant to the fellow who'd just sunk his ship. That was a tad more than he thought should be expected of anybody.

The cavalryman rattled on, laying on meaningless gilt-and-be-shit compliments. Colonel Buonaparte dropped his hand at last and took two steps away, removing his hat and finding a space of open ground where he could be seen better by everyone on the beach. Possibly to make a better spectacle of himself, Lewrie thought, listening with half an ear. Lewrie knew preening when he saw it.

And he was a pretty picture. Without his hat, he could show off his long hair, so fine and straight. It hung Republican fashion down to his coat collars, ungathered in any queue, fell straight down along each side of his face, and was combed forward over what appeared to be a good, squarish brow, like oils Lewrie'd seen of princes and pages in ancient times. Almost girlish, he grinned slightly. His nose was long and acquiline, but narrow, with wide-ish nostrils over a short upper lip, a pouty, thin-lipped mouth. But a most determined chin. Narrow, high-jawed face, lean as a scholar . . .

"Hmm? Please convey to the Colonel Buonaparte that I cannot in good conscience take credit for the accuracy of our gunnery, capitaine," Lewrie said, once he had a word in edgewise. "Our sea mortars were in the charge of a most experienced and talented Spanish officer, Comandante Don Luis de Esquevarre y Saltado y Perez, and his bombardiers. A most gallant man. He went down with the ship, unfortunately."

Least I can do for the arrogant shit, Alan thought; let *someone* remember his deeds, now he's dead and gone.

"Ah, m'sieur le colonel is sadden to 'ear zis, Capitaine Luray. 'E 'ad wish 'e may 'ave meet ze artilleriste avec ze grand courage. Ze colonel, 'e alzo say, 'e 'eez 'ave ze 'ighes' respect pour votre generosity a' votre late ami. Encore, 'e e'spress 'is amazement de votre brave deeds."

"I thank him kindly," Lewrie smiled.

"Colonel Buonaparte, 'e say 'e eez know les batteries de Général Carteau sink ze bateau, ze batterie le flotte, las' mont', in ze Petit-Rade, avant 'e arrive. An' now 'e 'ave ze grand distinction to do same. An' not only sink une batterie le flotte . . . but tak' 'er officeurs an' crew prisoner. Weech ze ozzer chef du artillerie do not," the captain said, with a smirk again.

Damme, there it is, Lewrie sighed; knew they'd get around to a surrender, sooner or later. To this vauntin' little coxcomb? Then we'll be months in gaol, maybe a whole *year* before France gets beaten silly. Christ! Damned if I think I'm going to like *that*!

"The colonel has been in charge of the batteries of La Seyne?" Lewrie asked, stalling for time, staving off the inevitable. And trying to think of something, anything, for a plan of escape. "Tell the colonel . . . the gracious Colonel Buonaparte, that my ship was the one that gave his gunners so much grief. By Balaguer? Oui, us."

That saved them another precious minute, as the young Bonaparte looked almost wolfish that he'd at last sunk his greatest thorn in his side; his *bête-noire*, as he put it. He smiled a bit wider, sure he had done something praiseworthy. And Lewrie could surmise by then that he was a man who lived for praise and honours. All the short ones did.

"Forgive me asking, capitain, but . . ." Lewrie said, almost chummily by then. "I thought it was the mortars at Fort La Garde that sank us. The colonel only had the two light field pieces, and never hit us."

After a long babble in frog, and some chuckles among Marmot and Junot, and a look on young Colonel Buonaparte's face like the cat that ate the canary, the cavalryman began to translate. The colonel crossed his arms over his chest, pouting chin-high in triumph. Posing!

Right, give 'em a chance to boast; works every time, Alan thought.

"Ah, oui, m'sieur Capitain Luray," the captain beamed slyly, "ze fort, mais oui, but . . ." he all but waved an impish finger at him. "Colonel Buonaparte, 'e eez in La Garde, ze inspection, n'est-ce pas? An' 'e say 'e realise, at once!"

The dragoon captain snapped his fingers for emphasis, as if he were tweaking Lewrie's nose.

"Le batterie jeune . . . new batterie, eez not Saint Margaret, but you' supplies arrive from la mer, ze sea, hein? Eef eez not Fort Saint Margaret, zen mus' be le batterie le flotte. Colonel Buonaparte realise . . . at once! . . . mus' be *near* ze fort, so . . .'ave to be *'ere*, m'sieur, no ozzer. Near La Garde, ze range? *See* La Garde, et ozzer hills trop haut. Too high? Ve ride out, vite, vis deux canon. An' ze flags des signeaux, you see. 'E direc' ze feu. Ze firing. Et, voila! Le colonel sink you!"

"He has my congratulations for his quick wits, sir," Lewrie said with another slight bow, feeling sick at heart at how easy it had been. "Though, of course, he does not exactly have my thanks."

"Ze colonel 'e eez delight to 'ear eet, m'sieur. Maintenant . . . ze wind eez cold, votre hommes, ils sont froid. Suffer? Ve mus' demand of you votre surrender, Capitaine Luray, vite. Colonel Buonaparte offer all officeurs la parole, you keep votre swords. Receive ze treatment beaux."

"I . . ." Lewrie began to say, fingers twitching on his scabbard. There was no more shilly-shally, no more delays he could think of, and most especially, not even the slightest hope of an escape attempt could he devise that wouldn't get a lot more of his men killed.

"And what will happen to my men, m'sieur?" he posed instead. "To my . . . matrosen, my sailors?"

"Zey be tak' away," the dragoon captain shrugged, as if concern about the fate of enemy sailors didn't signify. He looked them over with scorn, like a remount officer deciding to herd off a pack of old nags to the knacker's yard. "Zey go to un fort, under guard. Or ze prisoner 'ulks . . . w'en we take Toulon."

"And should I give you my parole, I'd be forced to swear, upon mine honour, that I would no longer engage in combat with France, long as the war lasts? Even if I was exchanged?" Lewrie pressed, hem-hawing for time, just a minute of freedom more.

"Zat is le convention, m'sieur," the fellow said, growing testy and impatient once more. "Vite, your response?"

Lewrie turned to look around at the hang-dog faces of his men, faces still creased in pain and shock, some mildly perplexed by the conversation their captain was holding with a foemen. Saw the vacant and weary, defeated gapings of men without another ounce to give. Men he'd vowed to defend, to cosset, to husband . . . or to die with, if needs must.

Should he give his parole, he'd be almost free, in some inland French garrison town, sleeping in clean linen, bathing and shaving regularly, eating and swilling as well as any French civilian. Receive a packet of half-pay through the cartels, letters from Caroline, arrange for extra funds to be sent him. Sleep late, dawdle, ride (under guard) with a sword on his hip, the gentleman still. Hire whores, if he felt the itch.

And all the while, these men would be in chains, fettered in a loathsome fortress cellar, chained like a coffle of slaves aboard some fetid, reeking condemned ship of the line like felons awaiting transportation for life, eating slops and mushes, and thinking themselves lucky if they only slept two to a blanket, flea-ridden, lice-crusted . . .

"Je regrette . . ." he sighed, dreading those prisoner-of-war gaols just as much as his men would. But he could not do that to them, could not abandon them without a backward glance. Dear as he wished he might toddle off and call it the fortunes of war, he could not. Nor end his naval career, miss out on the blazing finale to a short-lived war, as a mildly inconvenienced . . . idler!

He lifted his hanger from the belt frog, held the sparkling hilt up to the wan sunshine, in front of his face. Saw the seashells wink as it turned in his grasp. He kissed the handguard and held it out.

"Je regrette, messieurs, I cannot give you my parole."

The dragoon captain made to take it from him, but Colonel Buonaparte shouldered him aside and reached out for it. Somberly, he seized the scabbard at the midpoint, his arm level. With a sad gravity, the young French officer brought it to his own face, cradling it like one might a child, to bestow his own kiss upon the bright silver chase, and nod at Lewrie with those large, penetrating eyes of his, glowing watery.

"Sir," Spendlove said, stepping to Lewrie's side and offering up his midshipman's dirk. "I cannot give you my parole, either."

"Mon braves," Buonaparte smiled. "Vous avez du poil au culs."

"Et vous, m'sieur?" the dragoon captain asked de Crillart.

Oh, shit, Alan shuddered! They learn he's Royalist, they'll be havin' his head off 'fore dinner! And all his gunners, by sundown!

"He has no sword to surrender, sir, he lost it. M . . . Mister Scott, he lost his sword when the ship went down," Lewrie extemporised quickly, speaking loud enough for all his men to hear. "Permit me to introduce Mister Barnaby Scott, our . . ."

Bloody Hell, what is he, he flummoxed?

"Our purser. Le commissaire de marine? Vin, brandy, clothing? Le vêtements? La cuisine, the pay . . . le rente? Purser. Bursar?"

Buonaparte raised one eyebrow and spoke to the dragoon.

"M'sieur, ze colonel say votre . . . *purser*, 'e wear le culottes rouge . . . ze breeches red? Marine de France, aussi, culottes rouge." The captain posed suspiciously. "Officeur de la marine de France. 'E s'ink votre . . . Scott? . . . eez peut-être ze traitre . . . traitor, un officeur royaliste de Toulon!"

"Mister Scott? French?" Lewrie gawped, hands on his hips and forcing himself to laugh. "Lord, that's a good'un, that is. Lads, do ya hear that? This *soldier* thinks our purser, Mister Scott here, is a French officer!" He clapped a hand on Crillart's shoulder as if to lay claim to him.

"Haw, that's is a good'un, Mister Lewrie, sir," Cony barked with his own feigned amusement, catching his drift, and nudging the others to play along. " 'Oy, lads . . . 'Old Nip-Cheese' a Froggie?" They began to titter.

"We *do* have men among us whom you might consider French, sir," Lewrie confessed, ignoring Spendlove's startled gasp at his elbow. "We recruited in the Channel Islands. Guernsey, Alderney. Some of our best sailors come from there. The *British* Channel Islands, mind. Aye, they parlez-vous, some. But they're British tars. Well, we've four Spanish survivors with us. But the Royalists at Toulon are all soldiers. All the seamen left, weeks ago."

"Je ne sais pas . . . votre bursars wear rouge?"

"Any damn' thing they want, they're not really Navy officers," Lewrie lied, striking a breezy air. "Aye, red's their colour. Waistcoat's red, too. Plain blue coat, with cloth-covered buttons . . ."

"Say somezing . . . M'sieur Bursar Scott," the dragoon demanded. "Parlez-vous français?"

Crillart shook his head in the negative, shrugging, with a hopeless grin at the dragoon officer.

"Somezing in English, m'sieur?"

"Yes, Mister Scott," Lewrie prompted as well, turning to him in desperation. "Say something in *Royal Navy*, Mister Scott."

Crillart frowned, cocking his head to one side. It was his life he held in his hands, and the lives of his gunners, as well. And Alan's . . . once they found he'd been lying like a rug, and resented it.

"Arrh, matey," Charles pronounced carefully. "Aye-aye, cap'm."

Alan stifled such a monumental snort of stupefaction, he felt his sinuses were about to burst. Where the hell'd he learn *that*, he wondered? And why'd he dredge it up *now*? God, what a horrid choice!

"You may have a bit of bother understanding him, you see," Alan sped to explain, trying to keep a straight face, no matter how hellish dangerous it was. "Mr. Scott is a real *Scot*. A *Highland* Scot. Can't understand him meself, half the time, all his 'arrrhhin' and 'burrin.' "

"God-Damn-r'right, cap'm," Crillart added. "Blud-dy."

Oh, God, *don't* glid the lily, not when . . . ! Alan winced.

He was interrupted by the most wondrous sound he'd ever heard in his entire life—the sudden spatter of musketry! Everyone jerked their heads to the source, to espy a rank of shakoed heads on the tall bluff above the beach, on the coast road. Lance tips winked beyond on the hill, bared sabres flashed, and a trumpet sounded. They wore goldish yellow jackets with white facings. Spanish cavalry, by God!

Bullets spanged off the shingle, sparks erupted crisp as struck gunflints, horses reared and neighed, and men cried out in alarm, to arm themselves or to mount quickly.

Buonaparte and his aides mounted. Lewrie looked longingly for his sword; the bastard still had it. The dragoon captain reached for the hilt of his sabre. Lewrie shoved him, punching him in the face.

"Runnforritt!" he screamed, bolting away, dragging Spendlove by the elbow. *"This wayy!"* as he headed for shelter under the bluffs up the cove, under the guns of the cavalrymen. His unshod right foot took terrible punishment on sharp-edged stones and gravel, every lumpy rock he stubbed on made him wince. But it was better than a bullet in the back, or a sword cut. "Run, damn yer eyes! Run!" he panted.

There were shrieks, as a lancer got his tip into the back of a fleeing sailor, another piteous cry of "Madre de Dios, noo, *ahhh!* . . ." that ended in a rabbity screech as a Spanish bombardier was hewn down by a dragoon's sword, cut open from belly to breastbone. And French cries, music to Lewrie's ears, as men were spilled from their saddles by ball, or stirrup-dragged by panicked chargers over the rough beach.

They reached the cliffs, gasping with effort. Lewrie turned to see the French cantering south, in fairly good order, heading for the far side of the arrow-shaped bluff below the beach, where there was a way up and off; steeper than the one they'd descended. He spotted Lieutenant Colonel Buonaparte on his dapple-gray, patiently waiting as his lancers thundered up the draw past him, braving long-range musket fire as his dragoons formed an open-order vedette to screen the retreat.

Buonaparte made his gray rear, stuck his arm in the air to wave the captured sword. He was smiling, damn his eyes!

"I'll get it back, you bastard!" Lewrie howled in his loudest quarter-deck voice, jabbing a finger at the sword. "Je prendre mon . . . ! One day, I'll find you! Je trouvez-vous! Je prendre de vous, mon . . ."

Damme, what's Frog for 'sword'?

"Espèce de salaud!" he roared instead, his voice echoing off rocks and hills. "Va te faire foutre!"

Scabbarded, Buonaparte flipped the sword so the hilt was in his fist— raised it to his face in mock salute, laughed as his horse did another impressive rear. He may have had no English, and Lewrie might not have had anything close to fluent French—but he thought he understood well enough. With a saw at the reins, the colonel was gone in a moment, up the draw and out of sight.

"Señores, pronto!" a Spanish cavalry officer directed, skidding his mount to a sand-strewing halt near them. "Inglés? We go! Muy pronto! Darse! Hurry up!"

Not *another* language lesson, not two in one day, Lewrie sighed. The officer kicked an elegantly booted foot out of the near-side stirrup, reached down to offer him a hand as his men trotted up to aid the rest with spare French mounts, whose owners lay crumpled on the sands, or the mounts of Spanish soldiers who'd been spilled trying to rescue them. Alan hoisted his foot, reached for the saddlehorn, and hung on as the officer spurred his charger back up the draw to the Hieres road.

"A minute sooner," he muttered ungraciously beside his saviour. "Just a bloody minute sooner, thankee very much!"

Nothing could have spared him the shame of losing his ship, of course. But to see that swaggerin' little bastard ride off with his sword in his hands . . .

His very honour!

BOOK VI

Hic portus inquit mihi territat hostis has acies sub nocte refert, haec versa Pelasgum terga vides, meus hic ratibus qui pascitur ignis.

Lo! Here the enemy is affrighting our harbour, and here beneath the cover of night he renews the battle, and here, see! the backs of the Pelasgians in rout; this fire that devours the rafts is mine.

—VALERIUS FLACCUS
Argonautica, Book II, 656–59

CHAPTER 1

He dined alone, dispiritedly, picking at his supper and pushing it about his plate more than he ate. As thoroughly blockaded by land as Toulon now was, there wasn't that much food any longer, and prices had gone through the roof. At least the wine was still good, and cheap.

There were few other diners in the restaurant, half of them officers in strange uniforms, proud with gold or silver lace, sprigged in ornate, gewgawy appurtenances which, no matter their martial gaudiness, still made their wearers look like scared shopkeepers. Sardinians, Neapolitans, Piedmontese, Spanish . . . Lewrie was one of the rare British officers not out on the outposts. Bleak as his mood was, the others seemed even more morose. Large liquid Don and Dago eyes, aswim with fear or self-pity, hesitant gestures, where before they chopped at the air or waved their arms in braggadocio. Soft, sibilant mutterings of defeated conversation, much shrugging and sighing . . . stopping occasionally, as the drumfire of the artillery barrages increased in tempo or volume. Or a shell crashed into the town itself.

They'd been doing that a lot lately, the Frogs; lofting mortars into their own city, five or six rounds a day. Now they had the range. Kettledrums pounded, the candle flames wavered on his table, and glassware softly tinkled as siege guns tore loose upon Fort Malbousquet, and Fort Malbousquet responded. Worried looks were shared among the foreign officers, bleak little giggles in attempts at gallows humour.

And the French . . . pausing for a moment, stoic faces frozen in what they called *sang-froid*. Dammit, but the French *always* had *le mot juste*, the perfect word or phrase, he sneered. Alan chewed on a slice of goose and swirled the cabernet sauvignon in his large wine glass, studying his wine through the stuck-in-a-bottle candle flame. Studying the frogs, the other diners. Pére et maman, with their children. Old aristocrats still clinging to silks and satins, successful merchants in well-cut wool coats and waistcoats, the very image of moderate wealth and the latest styles. And so few of them still wearing their Bourbon-white cockades. The last few weeks they'd slowly shed them, like oak trees giving up their final leaves to the winter winds. On the outskirts of Toulon, it was said, the new style was red-white-and-blue Republican colours. And in the middle of town, there were hastily chalked or painted threats on walls, fresh each morning, no matter the patrols. Long, red-wool stocking caps were seen now in public, sported by sour-faced, hard-eyed commoner "patriots" . . . the *sans culottes*. Swaggering bullies who dared show the Tricolour, and glared at those who didn't, as if memorising faces and names. Later, they seemed to forebode. We'll know who you are . . . later.

"M'sieur weesh?" his waiter asked, pointing to his half-eaten and bedraggled supper. A ubiquitous omelet, only two eggs per customer now, a last gamy, oily slice of overcooked goose, and a heel of bread aswim in the fats of half-burnt, half-cooked pommes de terre escallopes.

"Non, merci," he replied sarcastically.

"Plus de vin?"

"Non. L'addition," Lewrie sighed. Nearly a shilling it cost, for what he'd have paid no more than four pence back home. *And* kicked the cook's arse for ruining it. He got to his feet, gathered up his hat and cloak, and departed.

The others watched him leave in silence, daunted by the grim look on the naval officer's face, the unspoken sneer of disgust he bore when he deigned to glance in their direction. Who is he to sneer at us, they seemed to say . . . a "pinch-beck" Anglais in a ragged, too-large coat, in slop trousers instead of a gentleman's knee breeches? Worn old Hessian boots, a plain blue civilian cloak, a hat that had seen a previous war . . . and that pitiful excuse for a sword!

It was cold that night, cold and icily clammy, with a light wind off the sea. Street lanterns wore haloes of mist, and it smelled like it might rain before morning. Lewrie wrapped himself in the too-large and tatty coat purchased off another officer, grateful its lapels buttoned over each other. Until he received his quarterly draft from Coutts's, he was forced to live on Navy pay, and a borrowed forty pounds—half of that gone already for the hat, cloak and a mediocre smallsword of dubious temper, the best of a table piled with second-hand blades of even more uncertain character at a civilian shopkeeper's bargain sale.

He walked downhill towards the harbour and the basin, listening to the drumming of the guns. The batteries on des Moulins and Reinier were blazing away, round the clock now. The Little Road had all but been abandoned. So fierce was their fire that no line-of-battle ship or floating battery could dare it for very long.

The streets were suspiciously empty of strollers or late shoppers, even of whores and Corinthians. And where almost every shop window or *appartement* above had been open and ablaze with light, they were now dark and shuttered, or out of business "temporarily." A waggon creaked down the street, drawn by four heavy dray horses. Moans of wounded could be heard within—a hospital wagon bearing the day's detritus to Hôpital de la Charité north of town, outside the walls. A half mile from the site of the latest disaster of two weeks before.

The Republicans had massed a battery on the Heights of d'Arènes west of Fort Malbousquet, twenty guns or better, and had begun a deluge of shellfire against that most important strong point, the key to the western side. Dundas and O'Hara had marched out next day on 30 November with 2,200 men: Spanish, Neapolitan, Sardinian, 400 of the few French royalist troops, along with 300 of their precious British; a majority of the mobile reserves who weren't tied to fixed positions, the best of their mediocre, ill-matched lot.

A brisk attack uphill had driven the French from their guns again. But instead of stopping there and consolidating, the troops had rushed on, down into a valley behind the Heights of d'Arenes to attack the next-west eminence. But upon that hill, all behind it, was hidden the bulk of Général Dugommier's main body, over 20,000; Carteau's men, Mouret's, thousands of soldiers Kellerman and Dugommier had brought in from Lyons and the north.

It had been a sharp slaughter, then a rout, and the French drove the remnants scurrying into Fort Malbousquet. General O'Hara had been wounded and taken prisoner, attempting to rally the troops by the guns. Twenty British had died, ninety wounded, ninety-eight had gone missing, and the allied casualties had been just as severe. The French got their guns back intact. And were now putting them to good use.

And the Austrians . . . *damn* their eyes, Lewrie silently fumed! God, how they'd sworn they were on their way, yet . . . Suddenly, the 5,000 men they'd promised from Italy couldn't be spared, and Rear-Admiral Gell and his squadron, waiting for weeks at Genoa and Vado Bay, had at last sailed back to Toulon, empty.

Sardinians and Neapolitans . . . liars, too, Alan cursed. Their commisariats too incompetent, disorganised or lazy to arm, equip or train the men promised; no matter how much money'd been thrown at them, they weren't up to the task. In the *spring* . . . perhaps, for *more* money?

"Fat lot of good they'll do us in the spring," Lewrie snarled in a harsh mutter. "Place doesn't have a *month* left in it."

And British regiments. That was the worst disappointment. With their so-called allies so suspicious and jealous of England and each other, hedging bets for after the war, arguing points of pride and honour, not cooperating . . . what looked at times as nigh to treachery . . . they had need of stalwart British regulars more than ever.

Yet where were they? Dundas and Grenville, the new prime minister William Pitt, the Younger . . . they'd settled for "war on the cheap." They planned long before the war started to fritter the Army away overseas in the West Indies, to destroy the economy of the French, to take the rich Sugar Isles they'd always lusted after. March up the Hooghly to Chandernagore above Calcutta, destroy the French Indian and Indian Ocean colonies. Destroy their trade and choke them to submission.

That's where the bulk of the British Army had gone, there or into Holland with the Duke of York. And for the enterprise at Toulon, they could not spare one regiment more. And the Army was now doing what all white troops did in the tropics . . . dying by the battalion of Yellow Jack and malaria without firing a shot, of no use to anyone, gaining nothing, barely able to muster enough strength to take what they'd been sent for!

Drumfire to the south. The Frogs had erected five new batteries in front of Fort Mulgrave on the Hauteur de Grasse, digging and trenching forward, moving nearer each day. If Mulgrave fell, there went Balaguer and L'Eguillette. And with them, any approach to Toulon's basin, or any hope of sheltering ships in the Great Road, too.

That little coxcomb Buonaparte's work, Alan suspected with a sour groan; aye, take joy of it, ya arrogant little bastard!

They were quartered once again in the guard house by the dockyard gate. De Crillart spent his nights at home with his family, high up in the town, but his twenty or so surviving Royal Corps of Gunners bunked with Alan's fourteen. Not enough to make crews for two cutters or barges. He'd been assigned a dozen more, men cut adrift from ships off on God knew what missions, more survivors of brave but doomed adventures, those plucked from the sunken ruins of other gunboats that the French had wrecked. No more gunboats for them, though. Floating batteries were a tad thin on the ground these days, as were the huge sea mortars. As were hollow explosive shells from the arsenals. And fuses and powder. The Poudrière and Fort Millaud had shut down their production after they'd run out of charcoal, saltpetre and sulphur . . . and Republican bursting-shell had begun to drum around them, threatening a tremendous explosion which would shave the hills level. They'd also run out of Royalist workmen who dared set foot in the places.

No, Lewrie and his men were boatmen now, ferrymen equipped with cutters which shuffled supplies and such about under lugsail or oars to keep the coastline posts fed and armed, to bear wounded from Hauteur de Grasse to hospital, or scuttle between the line-of-battle ships and shore with replacements, rum, biscuit and salt rations for their hands detatched ashore.

The wind was picking up, ruffling his cloak and hat, but Alan stood his ground near the guardhouse gate, unwilling to go inside to another night of frowsty air and lonelieness, cooped up alone in his miserable little room, with the stink of all those men below wafting up to him. There wasn't coal enough or wood enough to keep a warm fire going long enough to take off the chill, nor enough candles or oil to read by, what was the point; he'd lost all his books when *Zélé* had gone down, and didn't have the patience to ruin his eyes trying to puzzle his way through something written in French anyway. No, he would spend another night, mittened and cloaked, abed with his eyes wide open, staring at the low ceiling 'til sleep came. Or pace the wharves along the basin until he was too tired to care.

Something was moving on the esplanade besides himself. A woman, also cloaked and mittened, hobbling under the burden of a hard-leather portmanteau and a large cloth sack. Her face was concealed by her hood, and the sad straw brims of her bonnet, which the hood forced down either side of her face like horse blinkers, hunched against the cold winds.

"Bonsoir, m'sieur," she drawled. "Êtes-vous seul, ce soir?"

Oh, a whore, he sighed to himself. For a moment he'd thought it might be a refugee, looking for shelter, or some girl moving to cheaper lodgings.

"Seul, oui, mais . . ." he replied sourly, already dismissing her. "Alone, yes."

"Ah, m'sieur Luray!" she cried suddenly, dropping her luggage to come to his side. "M'sieur lieutenant? C'est moi, Phoebe!" She exclaimed, folding back the hood of her cloak. "Vous . . . remember? Bonsoir!"

Oh, poor Mister *Scott's* whore, he corrected himself.

"Bonsoir, Phoebe," he grinned. "Haven't seen you around, not . . . not since Mister Scott passed over." He shrugged in sympathy. She and Scott had become regulars with each other. He might have become all of her trade, the few weeks before his death.

"C'est tragique, pauvre Barnaby," she pouted. " 'E waz ze bon . . . good man. Trés gentil avec moi, beaucoup bonté, ver' kin'. Et généreux. Generous? C'est dommage." She shrugged. She did not say that Barnaby Scott had been gentle, just . . . kindly. In fact, Lewrie thought he'd dealt rather brusquely with her; too dead-set against all French people, even the one he'd been topping, to be civil or gentlemanly.

"Now?" Alan inquired. "Comment allez-vous, maintenant, mademoiselle Phoebe?"

"Ah, je suis trés seule, m'sieur," she replied, snuffling from the cold, though with a game little smile. "Am ver' 'lone. Avant Barnaby nous a quittez . . .'e lef' us, j'arrêtez m'affaires . . . ze beeznees I stop? Encore, je suis la pauvre jeune fille de joie mais . . . m'affaires ver' . . . bad. Pour *toute* les courtesans, all. Gentilhommes 'ave non time, non monnaie, phfft! Too beezy . . . too pauvre. Too effrayant. Frighten?"

That was another ominous portent to Lewrie's mind—that men in the enclave no longer had coin or time enough to waste on the whores of Toulon—too wrapped up in fears for their safety, too concerned about plotting their escapes with their whole skins to rattle? He'd expected the opposite would be true, that they'd be kicking her door down. Rantipoling always seemed to increase in the face of impending disaster, took men's minds off doom for awhile. Like that old adage, "Eat, drink and be merry, for tomorrow we die?"

"I waz 'ope you be 'ere, encore, m'sieur Luray," Phoebe told him quickly, taking his arm and sounding insistent.

"Me? Whatever for?" he scoffed, albeit gently, though he thought he knew already. Phoebe needed money, and a new gentleman-protector.

"Après votre navire a coulée . . . you' ship sink?" she explained. "An' you tell me, si chrétien . . . so gently, concernant Barnaby, zen j'sai . . . I know vous est le homme, si prévenant et bienviellant. You 'ave ze kin' . . . considerate 'eart? D'avance, you waz toujours bonté avec moi, m'sieur Luray, ver' gentle an' kin'. Non speak sévère to me, as putain. Toujours as la jeune dame, ze young lady! Si charmant et amusant!" She brightened, sounding almost wisftul, but sobered quickly as she sped on with what Alan was certain was a tale of woe.

"Now I am . . . in ze trouble?" the girl coaxed. "Oh, merde alors, ze trouble *terrible*, m'sieur! D'abord, I s'ink of *you*, seulement . . . on'y? I come 'ere, 'ope you are 'ere, you le plus, of all ze Anglais Navy? You, mos' of all." Phoebe fought a flood of tears, snuffling again, wiping her nose on her mitten. "Eef you do non help me, m'sieur, I am los'! Mais . . . I *know*, you 'ave pity vers moi! I know you 'elp me!"

"Phoebe, uhm . . ." Lewrie sighed. "Look, it's so cold out here. Si froid? Let's go over there, through the dockyard gate, out of the wind." He picked up her traps, already beginning to regret it. Once in the lee of a stout stone wall, in more privacy, he turned to her. "Now, what sort of trouble are you in, petite Phoebe?"

"I am so effrayant, m'sieur Luray," she began, shivering with more than cold, stepping closer to him. "I mus' 'ave votre protection! Plais, mon Dieu, you weel protec' moi, plais?" the tiny mort entreated, her soft brown eyes huge in a pinched little gamine face. "Les Republicains, les sans culottes . . ." she sneered for a moment, almost spit upon the pavement despite her fear, "les paysans *connardes*, wan zey reprendront . . . zey tak' Toulon, I die. Mais oui, I *know* zis! Merde alors, zey *keel* me! On ma mures et ma porte . . . walls an' door? Les sales *patriotes*, zey write: 'ere reside une peau de vache degueulasse, la sale putain des les ennemies Brittaniques cracra'! Zat I am ze traitresse?" She weakened and began to wail helplessly, though still with an undercurrent of anger and resentment. "La sale putain de l'aristos, hein?"

"Whoa, slowly," Alan said, trying to translate her rushed words. Cow's hide? Bitch of a hide, disgusting . . . *with* puke, or merely filthy?

She reached for his hands and took them in hers, drawing him near for safety, imploring, jerking at them as a petulant child might in punctuation. "Zey regardant, zey watch me? Leave me lettres, oh, les lettres ça pue la fauve! Avec tableaux . . . peekt'r of ze *guillotine*, m'sieur! Oh, plais! Je ne comprend pas . . . I 'urt no one, I am pauvre petite fille de joie seulement, I geeve no offence. Concierge, she t'row me out, ce soir she fin' 'er . . . patriotisme! I 'ave nulle autre part . . . now'ere else to be safe. An' I am si effrayant, m'sieur! J'suis dans la merde!"

"You need a place to stay," he replied, "to hide? Cacher?"

"Ah, oui!" Phoebe insisted, brightening at once, almost bouncing on her toes. "Et aussi . . ." she posed, taking on a shy but coy mien, all but biting her lip as she continued to gaze upward trustfully.

Here it comes, he sighed to himself, the hand on my purse.

"Wan you partez, you leave Toulon . . . ?" she dared to whisper up at him, head cocked most fetchingly. "You weel take pauvre Phoebe?"

That wasn't *quite* the request he'd expected from her.

She stepped closer, insinuating her arms inside his cloak round his waist, claiming shelter and warmth, with her thin young face turned up to his. "You tak' me aller de Toulon? Away? Aides-moi to . . . flee? You are in Navy, you 'ave les ships! Wan ze time come, ze royalistes, . . . zey run? But zey will 'ave no room for me. 'Elle est la putain cracra seulement,' zey will say." She began to weep at the injustice of it all. "On'y ze dirty little whore? An' ze Republicains . . . zey accusants, aussi, an' chop off ma tête! I beg you, m'sieur, let me stay viz you? You protec' me? An' tu mettes-moi . . . put me on ship?"

"Uhm," he softened, slipping his arms around her instinctively, though dubious of "adopting" her. "Keep you, and all?"

"Ah, oui, s'il vous plaît, m'sieur Alain!" she pleaded, looking up at him, her chin resting on his breastbone, her waif's eyes pleading as beguilingly as an orphaned kitten's.

"Je regrette, ma petite Phoebe . . ." he muttered, thinking of his few coins, and how far yet they might have to stretch. "Je suis pauvre, aussi. Un peu monnai? Après our ship . . . sank? Went down? I have so little money, now."

"Je m'en fiche," she declared, her little face solemn. "Do not..care? You 'ave la salle chaud, ze warr-um room? Un peu vin, et pain? A little monnai, c'est beau. Non monnai, c'est beau, aussi. You are ze homme seul, et moi, I am ze jeune fille, 'lone, aussi. Be kin' an' généreux to me, on'y un peu, et moi . . . I am générous à vous, hein? Quand, je serai *votre* jeune fille. Zan, I am *your* . . ."

Damme, the price sounds right, he thought; and she *is* a pretty little thing. Cundums! Well, my new'uns ain't Mother Green's Finest— they're frog. But I s'pose they know what they're about when it comes to amour. The others, though, Cony and all . . . they'll see her go up with me, and what'll they think . . . and just who *gives* a bloody damn any longer?

He looked down into her face searchingly. Though her belly was pressed against his in promise, her gaze was so forlorn, yet hopeful, her eyes aswim with tears. For fear of his rejection, and her Fate if he did turn her away. He felt his resolves slipping. Again.

"God save me," he whispered in surrender. "Know what your name means, Pheobe?"

"Je ne sais pas, m'sieur," she replied softly, putting all her kitteny fondness into her voice, sensing his agreement at last.

"It means 'sunshine' in Latin," he chuckled, giving in to her neediness. And his own. "Like a happy sun? Comme le soleil heureux."

She tittered, smiled at last, and took a moment to wipe her nose and eyes on her mittens, then threw her arms around his neck. "D'accord, m'sieur Alain? You protec' me? Vous demeuront . . . reside, ensemble?"

"Oui," he nodded, with a sheepish grin. "We demeuront, ensemble."

"Ooh!" she cried suddenly, bouncing on her toes to hug him and giggle with relief. "You are le homme trés sympathetique, so good, so gentil, si magnifique! Je suis si heureux . . . so 'appy! An' I mak' *you* so 'appy, aussi, quand . . . wan ve . . . coucherons, ensemble," Phoebe vowed suggestively. "Aimes-tu la coucher, Alain?"

"Oui," he chuckled. "Mais oui, beaucoup!"

"An' wan you leave Toulon," she paused, inquiring of him more closely for an instant, leaning back warily to see if all particulars of their bargain were sure, like any level-headed woman of business. "Et . . . ve sail way, ensemble, aussi, Alain?"

"Oui, I swear. I'll get you on a ship, when the time comes, ma petite jolie Phoebe. Swear? Promise? Uh, croyez-vous. Believe me."

He gathered up her bags, those two items bearing all her worldly goods. He led her into the courtyard of the guardhouse, past a sentry who first gaped, then averted his eyes. Up the stairs past the few men idling and yarning in the guardroom, daring them to gawp at him. Into his room, where he shut the door on all outside distraction and curiosity.

He lit a candle as she doffed her cloak and mittens and thawed herself at the small fireplace's grate. There was a bottle of cognac on the scarred, rickety night stand by the bed. Only one glass, which he filled for her, which she accepted eagerly. He drank from the neck, listening to the rising winds as they rattled the shutters. Someone—Cony perhaps—had been thoughtful enough to obtain a warming pan for the bed, and had set out a covered dish; a quarter-loaf of bread with a hank of sausage. She devoured it ravenously, child-cheerful, as he put the warming pan back on the grate and removed coat and waistcoat.

They hung their clothing on wall pegs, suddenly sombre and shy with each other, after she was done eating. She smiled at him as she pinched out the candle, and shooed him to turn around so she could undress completely.

"M . . . maintenant, mon cheri," she said at last, faint and shaky.

"Bloody . . ." he gasped as he turned about to look at her.

She stood nude on her knees in the middle of the bed, whore-bold. Yet as shy, as nervous and giggly as a virgin might on her first night of marriage, totally feckless and artless at that moment, without a jot of a whore's weariness, pouting boredom or experience.

Her light olive skin was dark against the pale sheets, caressed by flickers of firelight, her hair a long, curling, dark-brown cascade down her back to her waist, over her shoulders, half-concealing breasts small but well formed, almost perky. So slim and neat, so girlish and tiny she looked, almost thin . . .

"Je suis si *froid*, mon cheri," she shuddered in a wee voice as she hugged herself for a moment, her eyes huge with want. "Tu vas à moi . . . come to me? Dépêches, vite?" she implored, stretching out her arms for him.

He rushed to the bed to embrace her, to kneel close to her, run his hands hungrily over her velvety firm young flesh, feeling her goosepimple at his touch. "Si belle, tu es si belle, si petite, si . . . !" he praised. "Such a beautiful little pretty!"

"You mak' me warr-um, Alain?" she shivered, somewhere between a nervous laugh and a helpless plea. "You keep me safe an' warr-um, mon gentilhomme fantastique?" She leaned back from his kisses to take his

face in her little hands to regard him, to force him to regard her, for a
serious instant. "Alors, a' tu, je donne ma tout, mon coeur. Zen my
all . . . I give to you? Mon corps . . . mon coeur, moi-même!" she whispered in touching tears that scalded as they splashed on his cheeks as
they kissed again.

They fell into the warmed bed, hurling the covers up to their chins,
burrowing eagerly into the welcome warmth of press-hot sheets, grasp-
ing to clasp their warming flesh together, beginning to chuckle and sigh,
to simper and giggle like goosegirl and stableboy.

When did she learn my given name, he idly wondered, too busy for
much real thought as they rolled and interlaced, limbs twining as sinuous
as snakes, mouths pressed together, stroking and exploring . . . Scott?
Must have told her. She was always friendly enough . . . amusing and
anxious to please. To fit in. Hang everything, he decided. Just all of it—
hands, the war, the siege, all of it! Just a few nights, for the love of
Heaven.

"Ma belle," he sighed in her ear, lost once more, humours ablaze as
he nuzzled and savoured, afire for her and nothing else but a few precious moments of sweet, tumbling oblivion. "Ma petite. Oui, I'll keep
you warm. Je fais tu chaud . . . *and* safe."

"Oh, mon cheri," she swore, going breathless. "Mon coeur . . . mon
amour! Aime moi!"

To seal her bargain, to coax him or cajole him, to winnow her way
into his sympathy and affection to hold him to it, she repaid him in
the only coin she had left, or perhaps understood. But with passion so
intense, so open and eager, so far beyond a coquette's artful practice,
that he could not believe her giving of herself so completely was totally
feigned, towards the end especially. Panting on his shoulder, tears in
her eyes, kisses deep and searing, softly lingering and full of gentleness
and seeming affection. As if, for a time at least, the girl could shut the
door on her own very real fears for her future. Phoebe had as much
need as anyone to abandon herself, deny the terrifying world outside,
and sink mindlessly and carefree into a sweet oblivion of her own, surrender time and time again to pleasures so imperative that life beyond
her body's sensations had no terrors which could even compare.

And sleep, at last, draped half over him, her head resting on his chest,
clinging in her sleep as doggedly as he had to his raft, so light and sweet,
so soft and toasty warm, with her hair spilled like a quilt over them.
Sleeping peacefully, purring gentle and slow, twined about him. Completely spent yet happy.

Dreaming perhaps? he wondered as he drowzed alongside, his arms
cocooning her. What did whores dream about, anyway? Her world was

so narrow, so limited, and she such a willow branch to any wind that blew . . . did she dream of safety, new gowns, a little place to call her own? Of surviving long enough to continue her same narrow life?

He glanced at his new watch on the night stand by the firelight. Another cheap piece o' work. Just gone eleven, he yawned, completely, utterly spent himself. Yet happy as well, in his own way.

Whatever it'd been—a young whore's practiced arts to earn her passage, or a frightened girl's exquisite gratitude, some small measure of true affection and desire at last awakened—who knew, he asked the ceiling. It had been bestial, magnificent . . . tender. And grand.

He slept himself, then. As the skies opened and a cold sullen rain began to fall, slashing at the besieged port, driven by a half-gale of wind. Pattering and rattling on the shutters, drumming on the roof slates, making him glad he wasn't at sea on such a fearsome night.

He slept at last as real, natural thunder growled and rumbled, forcing him to nestle closer to Phoebe, to clasp her tighter and feel her reply with a snugger hug of her own as he rolled nearer. As a far-off storm voice marched closer and mingled itself with the dolorous drumming of the guns.

CHAPTER 2

Very far off, someone was shouting something incomprehensible, which sort of sounded like "Allez, allez, vite . . ." mumble-mumble "le blah-blah-blah . . . perdu." Dull thuds somewhere. Something Froggish, Lewrie half-decided, and snuggled closer to the warmth of his girl.

". . . les Republicains sont arrivant!"

Bad dream; bugger it. Sweet, soft, warm, smooth shoulder . . .

More thunderings; up the stairs this time? Or the storm still rumbling . . . guns still rumbling? What else was new?

"Merde alors," Phoebe muttered crossly in his ear, waking first, leaning across him to listen. Her long tresses tickled his nose, half smothering him, but drew him most unwillingly nearer the surface of his pleasant stupor. He opened one eye, beheld a perky young breast, dark aureola and pinkish nipple staring back, an inch from his lips. Alan gave it a little flick with his tongue, thinking that a marvelous way to be awakened.

"Oohn," she groaned, in spite of herself, with a chuckle deep in her throat.

More bloody bangings on the door, hard and insistent.

"Alain, someone eez . . ." Phoebe prompted sleepily.

"Hmmphff?" he grumbled, rolling on his back. "*What?*"

"Alain!" a voice shouted as the door burst open with a bang.

At the sight of a man in uniform, a *French* naval uniform, with a brace of pistols in his belt, Phoebe gave out with a loud scream of pure royalist terror as she sat bolt upright!

Lewrie felt his hair go on end for a second, until the dim light filtering through the shutters revealed the man to be Charles de Crillart.

"Sacre . . ." Charles gawped, his face suffusing.

"Christ, Charles, can't you *knock*, or something?" Alan carped.

"Alain, I . . . uhh . . ." Lieutenant de Crillart stuttered, his eyes swiv-

266

eling from Lewrie's puffy face to Phoebe's bare charms, then back. "Mon Dieu, pardonnez moi, mon ami . . ."

Lewrie sat up, claiming the top sheet to shroud his groin as he put his torso between Phoebe and de Crillart. She dragged the coverlet to her chin, huddling tiny in a corner of the bed by the headboard.

"Alain, ze Republicains," Charles explained, stepping out onto the small landing and half-closing the door. "Fort Mulgrave . . . c'est perdu. Lost!"

"What?" he barked, leaping from the bed for stockings and slop trousers. "Lost! How?"

"Ze storm? Early zis morn, zey avant vis ze bayonet, wan most of notre powder waz wet, hein? Zey rout ze Espagnoles, an' ze British could not 'old out. Une heure ago, zey at las' retreat, into Balaguer. Ze Republicains now 'ave Mulgrave, all ze canon . . . ze heights overlook L'Eguillette an' Balaguer."

"Christ, *that's* the end, isn't it?" he fumed, stomping into his boots, tearing his shirt from a wall peg to slip over his head.

"Zat ees non all ze worse, mon ami," Lieutenant de Crillart said in a funereal tone. "Ze sam' time zey . . . coordinate? Général Lapoype, 'is soldiers . . . zey march up s'rough Argeliers, an' zey tak' all ze posts on ze mountain of Pharon. Zey 'ave ze canon zere, too."

"Bloody hell." Lewrie paused, rubbing his face. He turned to share a look with Phoebe, who was white and blanched with fear. "Ah . . . any orders for us yet, Charles?" He hurried to button up his waistcoat and don his stock.

"Non," de Crillart sighed. "Eet eez still rain hard, an' ver' foggy. No one know anys'ing. Or see anys'ing."

Lewrie stepped out to join Charles now he was decent, and shut the door so Phoebe could spring from the bed and dress herself.

"Damme, Pharon gone," Alan fretted, chewing on a thumbnail for a moment. "Heated shot, and the whole place in range, far as Fort Mandrier, so we aren't safe even in the Great Road any longer. And Balaguer and L'Eguillettes under their guns, too . . ."

"Oui," Charles replied sadly. "Wan ze powder is dry, an' zey 'ave good view? Phfft. Tous c'est perdu. All eez los'."

"Your gunners, Charles . . . they've families in Toulon?"

"Oui, some of zem."

"Best tell them to fetch 'em. Here to the guardhouse, for the nonce," Alan decided. "Your family, too. And warn them . . . don't try to carry away *too* much of their belongings . . . do you get my meaning?"

"D'accord," de Crillart nodded firmly.

"I'll go up to headquarters; you take care of your own, for now,"

Lewrie offered. "We may not have long before the weather breaks, then not much time to arrange shipping. Surely, though, we'll try to get the troops away. And as many Royalists as want to go. I'll try for a ship."

"I will go now," Charles agreed, turning to descend the stairs.

"Charles, the girl . . ." Lewrie called softly to hold him. "While I'm at headquarters . . . do you return first? She was Mr. Scott's, uhm . . . girl? Do you keep her safe with the other families. I promised her I would get her on a ship, when the time came. Just didn't know it'd be *this* bloody soon."

"Oui, I remember 'er, Alain. She eez putain, but . . ."

"Aye, she is," Lewrie stiffened.

"Alain, mon ami . . . even les putains 'ave right to live. I keep her safe, until you return."

"Thankee, mate. Merci bien."

Admiral Lord Hood, Major General Dundas, Admiral de Langara and Lieutenant General Valdez, Forteguerri the Neapolitan, Rear Admiral Gravina, Sir Hyde Parker, Prince Pignatelli, Chevalier de Revel and Sir Gilbert Elliot held a quick counsel of war, as the sounds of battle and barrage faded away to nothing. For the moment, the Republicans were as spent as anyone else. Except for a few spatters of musketry as patrols in Toulon discouraged looting or *sans culottes* acts of patriotism, there was little to indicate a crisis had come.

Except for the people in the streets, the handcarts laden with household goods and valuables. Waggons streamed downhill from the outlying districts to the quays, piled up in confusion. Rain continued to fall, a chilly, drizzling misty rain that shrouded the Heights of Pharon and the surrounding mountains, almost cut off any view of de Grasse peninsula. Frightened as they were, the Royalists endured with a stoic calm, waiting for news, waiting for evacuation. Waiting for a ship to board.

It was the foreign troops who were the most unruly, those routed from the heights, the peninsula, those who should have still garrisoned the remaining posts, but who drifted back into town, looking for ships of their own. Neapolitan soldiers were already filtering aboard their line-of-battle ships, *Tancredi* and *Guiscardo*. British troops remained disciplined, as did the Spanish. It was they who maintained order in the ranks. Even if they had to threaten the Neapolitans with cannon to make them march out of their positions, turning their own guns on them. There had already been some shooting in Neapolitan lines, where terrified men had panicked and fired off their muskets at any affright, killing or wounding dozens of innocent civilians who'd streamed past on their way to the harbour, thinking them a French advance out of the fog.

Headquarters was not very informative. It was a beehive of men dashing about, of stacks of papers being sorted, of piles of rejects on pyres, and chests and campaign trunks being packed and slammed closed. The sight almost made Lewrie glad he had so little by way of possessions to worry about. He felt more mobile—and quicker when it came time to flee. It made him faintly sour, too, to see the many valuables being carted off. Silver plate, gold ornaments, clocks, an entire crystal chandelier, crates and barrels of rare-vintage wine, cognac . . . Toulon had been a very rich city, and it now appeared that it was being looted by the defeated, to deny the victors their proper spoils.

"Anything for me and my men to do?" he asked once more of a junior officer.

"For God's sake, sir, no!" the man shouted back, over his shoulder in passing. "How many times do I have to tell you, I have no orders for anyone in the Navy at this time!"

They *had* had orders, all contradictory. First, he'd been warned to ready his boats to aid in the evacuation of Balaguer, but before he could get that in writing, they were cancelled. Then it had been word to prepare to evacuate the batteries at Cape Brun and Fort Saint Margaret . . . but others thought that a bad idea, for it would expose every ship in the Great Road to enemy fire, were they not held to the end.

"Does *anyone* have a clue what's happening?" a frustrated post-captain shouted after the Army aide-de-camp in exasperation. There'd been a constant stream of officers from the ships in harbour, captains and commanders, first lieutenants coming and going—mostly with word to shift their anchorages to the Great Road or the Bay of Toulon, wait for further orders, to prepare all their boats. But mostly, to wait.

"Christ, not in *this* raree show, there ain't," Lewrie muttered.

"Anything but indecision," a post-captain near Lewrie agreed in some heat. "Anything but delay. High as I esteem Admiral Lord Hood . . . but perhaps the situation requires deliberate action. Careful thought and planning, else the evacuation will be a disaster."

"Can't imagine why they'd start thinking now!" Lewrie sneered softly, his face bearing a sardonic grin. "A bit late, that."

"They are still our superior officers, sir," the little fellow stiffened. Christ, it was Captain Nelson! "In our hour of travail they deserve our unstinting support, sir. I know you, do I, sir?"

"Alan Lewrie, Captain Nelson," he replied, stiffening himself in sudden wariness. "Of the *Cockerel* frigate. Currently . . ."

"Naples!" Nelson smiled of a sudden. "I heard of you from the Hamiltons. My predecessor to that delightful port."

You get stuck into Lady Emma too, did you? Lewrie thought.

"Before that, sir, during the Revolution."

"God, yes. Off Cape François?" Nelson enthused, recalling.

"Turk's Island, Captain Nelson, just a few weeks before the end of hostilities."

"Uhm, yess, Turk's Island . . ." Nelson frowned. He'd come a rare cropper over that one, trying to retake the island from the Frogs, who'd garrisoned it with more men than Nelson had in his entire ad-hoc squadron. A squadron he had no right to assemble or lead. "Brig 'o war . . . *Shrike*, was it not, sir? And your captain was grievously wounded."

"Aye, sir, still in the Navy, though. All thanks to your speaking to Lord Hood on his behalf. Captain Lilycrop? Lost the leg, but he's in the Impress Service, made 'post.' I never did get the opportunity to express my undying thanks for your kind deed, sir. I do so now, sir." He threw in a bow, leg extended, his hat upon his breast.

And maybe he'll forget the strip he was about to tear off mine arse for mouthing off, Alan hoped to himself.

"And mine to you, Lieutenant Lewrie; for preparing the ground, so to speak, in Naples, with His Majesty King Ferdinand," Nelson replied with an equal bow. He stepped closer and took Lewrie's hand. "Sir William, Lady Emma, Acton, His Majesty—all spoke highly of you."

"They are all well, sir, and thriving? Including Queen Maria Carolina? I did not have the opportunity to meet her, but . . ."

"Delivered of a healthy heir, sir, I am quite happy to relate, soon after your departure. Aye, well and thriving. Personally, that is. Though our impending defeat here will be no cause for delight with the Neapolitans. Enthusiastic allies . . . perhaps too enthusiastic to be firm, or *steady*, allies," Nelson gloomed. "Like many Mediterraneans, possessed of the ability to elate or despair, in equal measure."

"Do we get their troops away with no further losses, sir, then I am certain Sir William Hamilton and Lady Emma may buck their enthusiasms up again," Lewrie grinned.

"Aye, I dare say!" Nelson chuckled, lifting on the balls of his feet with an enthusiasm of his own. "An amazing woman, Lady Emma. So many-faceted, like a precious gem."

He *did* get the leg over, Lewrie speculated.

"Such perspicacity in a female, such wit and charm, and how well she wields her influence, so subtly," Nelson raved on.

Aye, nailed her!

"So talented. Were you a guest at Palazzo Sessa, sir? And view her

'Attitudes'? Oh, you had to sleep aboard your ship . . . too bad. The Hamiltons were most gracious to me. The Duke of Sussex was to visit in Naples, his guest suite was prepared, yet they lodged *me* in it. And Sir William informed me . . . I was quite thunderstruck by this . . . that in all the years he'd been plenipotentiary to the Kingdom of Naples, I was the *very* first naval or military officer ever granted such of his hospitality, can you imagine?" Nelson blathered on, seeming to preen.

The short ones always do, Lewrie thought, keeping a straight face: Nelson, that Frog Buonaparte. God, I'd love to get those two together— it'd be a cat fight, no error!

"And I avow, sir," Nelson said with a determined, wistful air, "as I wrote to my dear wife Fanny . . . that Lady Emma is a credit, sir, to the station in life to which she has been raised."

Ah, no . . . he didn't, after all, Lewrie smirked in secret.

"Captain Nelson, do you have any notion where the *Cockerel* frigate may be? We've been detached ashore since mid-September, with no communications with her. Under the circumstances, we should be . . ."

"Standing-off and-on, without Cape Sepet, the last I saw of her, Lieutenant Lewrie," Nelson informed him. "But that was days ago. You mean to tell me, your captain, in all that time, has not communicated with you? But I've seen her lying at anchor in the Great Road, quite nearby! Oh, she was off with Admiral Gell to Vado Bay, with the Royalist French Squadron, but she returned days ago, after the Austrians . . . well. The Austrians." Nelson sighed petulantly, pulling at his long, fair nose.

"Dear as I'd wish to return to her, sir, well, there're the Royalists I have with me," Lewrie explained, summarising his recent duties with de Crillart and his gunners, the families now assembling, dependent upon him, their crying need for evacuation.

"Ah, word at last, perhaps," Nelson broke off as the doors to a large salon opened, and the senior officers were summoned inside. "Do come with me, Lieutenant. It is sure to be informative."

"Gentlemen, it is unanimously resolved," Admiral Lord Hood began to speak—tall, beaky, hunched and weary-looking, wearing a floured periwig with elaborate horizontal side curls tumbling past his ears, a famous nose, riper and fuller than even Il Vecchio Nasone—"by all the allied representatives, and by the Committee for War which represents the native Toulonese, that our enterprise here is doomed to failure."

He went on to encapsulate the present situation, the command the Republicans now held over the forts, the harbour and the roadsteads.

"A few months ago I wrote London that, had I but five or six thousand

men, Toulon could not only be held, but could serve as base of opera-
tions for an invasion of the entire Midi, the south of France. The Republicans, however, have . . . according to the intelligence which we have
gleaned from various deserters or prisoners . . . over 45,000 men opposing us. And sadly, even should we, through force of arms, claim back
those redoubts which were lost last evening, well . . . the situation in
which we find ourselves would be no less parlous, anent another assault
upon us from the French of even greater strength. So . . . we must evacuate Toulon. Orders are being drafted now for military units. Pray, allow
me to refer to the map . . . the redoubt and lunette of Pharon, below
the French positions, will be abandoned. Troops there are to retire to
the forts of Artigues and Saint Catherine, and will hold them as long as
is humanly possible, to deny the Republicans entry to the town. The
major redoubts of both the Great and Little Antoines on the nor'west
mountain shall also evacuate. As will the Saint André, the Pomet . . . Fort
Millaud and the powder mills. And once the guns are toppled or spiked,
all troops at Forts L'Eguillette and Balaguer will cross the Gullet to Fort
La Malgue and Saint Louis, at its foot.

"At present, Fort Malbousquet and Fort Missicy still daunt Republican
troops from entering the city from the west. They shall be held," Admiral
Hood insisted with a stern glower at the clutch of senior Army officers to his
right. "All outlying posts to the east will be abandoned. We intend to begin
evacuating the wounded from the Infirmarie and the Hôpital de la Charité
at once. First to Fort La Malgue, thence down to the water fort, Saint
Louis, and embark in cutters and barges to such vessels of the Fleet as have
space for them and the means to care for them. We *may* have a day or two
as a grace period." Hood spoke with faint hope, even so. "The Republican
assaults resulted in many wounded among their troops. The weather is
abominable, and the trails and goat tracks are slick and wet, everywhere
they met with success. It may be some time before they are able to shift
heavy guns in numbers sufficient to threaten our ships. Or mount another
assault, so soon after the first, upon the city itself."

Whistlin' in the wind, Lewrie thought: if they're smart, they'll be at
us tonight! And I doubt we cost 'em tuppence.

"This should give us at least one full day and night . . . to prepare the
basin, the arsenals and the magazines for destruction. Accordingly, every
French ship which is in any forward condition, armed or able to go to
sea, shall be taken from the basin at once, and anchored in the Great
Road, there to receive troops as they come off shore. And those French
Royalists who may wish transportation away from Toulon."

Right, Lewrie sneered; as if *any* of 'em'd stay!

"Adm. Don Juan de Langara will be in overall command of firing the Inner Basin and the French fleet," Hood announced. "All the powder remaining will be concentrated in two prize vessels and sunk, at the last. The destruction of the fleet will not be undertaken until we have safely extricated troops and innocent civilians under cover of darkness."

Nelson's hand shot up at once, and Lewrie could see him quivering with eagerness to participate. Instinctively, he slid a half-step away from him. He'd seen Capt. Horatio Nelson at work before, at Turk's Island, and didn't wish to take part in another of his harum-scarums, neck-or-nothing damn-all adventures. He'd had quite enough lately, thank you very much.

"Ahum," Hood frowned, pulling at his florid nose as he gazed in Nelson's direction, shaking his head sorrowfully. "To command the British party from the Royal Navy, which will assist Admiral Langara in his endeavour . . . I have selected Capt. Sir William Sidney Smith."

"Dear Lord," Nelson whispered *sotto voce*, absolutely crushed he could not take part. He sounded truly, deeply disappointed. "How did he come by that? That . . . swashbuckler."

"Who's this Captain Smith when he's up and dressed, sir?" Alan whispered.

"The showy one," Nelson sighed, tilting his head toward a man in almost a parody of naval uniform. He was big, bluff me-hearty, Smith was, the sort who wore a perpetual "piss-me-in-the-eye" bellgirence, an exuberant sort who positively swaggered, bold as a dog-in-a-doublet. The sort with abounding self-confidence, who knew no fear whatsoever.

"Came in a fortnight ago from Smyrna, on the Turkish Levant," Nelson muttered from the side of his mouth. "Purchased a little lateen rigged boat, called it *Swallow*. Hired on a crew of Englishmen who had been languishing, out of work, there. Hoisted his own commission pennant, wrote his own Admiralty orders, in essence. And has been perfectly *thrusting* himself forward since, sir."

Ahead of *you*, has he? Lewrie deigned to think, with a dart at his putative "host," to see the envy burning in Captain Nelson' eyes. Sir William Sidney Smith wasn't the only enterprising and aspiring captain in the salon.

Hood made some dismissing statements; to gird their loins, stick fast, stout hearts and stalwart will . . . that sort of thing, just before they went their separate ways. Lewrie tagged along as Nelson approached the admiral.

"I'm sorry, Nelson," Admiral Lord Hood said, giving him a faint grin and taking his elbow protectively. "But I so prize your sterling qualities that I cannot find it in my heart to wager your future contributions upon a rather weak hand. And you have accomplished so much for me already. Tunis, Naples . . . though I would desire to reward you with a larger ship, a more important command. A 74, perhaps . . ."

"Milord, I am so completely in your debt, for all your many kindnesses, your espousal of my cause, with the finest, most gracious . . . and most indulgent patronage," Nelson sighed. "I *would* have liked to command the party, if only to, in the slightest wise, be able to reward all your goodness towards me with measure for measure, no matter the risk. I am, as always, at your instant command, of course."

"I know you're disappointed, but, after all . . ." Hood beamed.

"As for a larger ship, milord, I am so very happy with *Agamemnon*. For a 64, she's the fastest two-decker in the Fleet," Nelson rejoined proudly. "And as I have stated before, milord . . . no officer has ever been so blessed with such a talented, chearly wardroom as I. Offered *Victory* herself, milord . . . I would be forced to demur. I cannot give up my officers!"

"And you, Lieutenant Lewrie," Hood smiled pleasantly, turning to regard him. "My condolences upon the loss of your gunboat, *Zélé*, No need to even muster a court, once I read the accounts. How do you keep, young sir?"

"Most excellently well, milord; your servant, as always," Lewrie toadied to his patron, taking a page from Nelson's book on how to sound obsequious.

"Not that excellently, from what he told me, milord," Nelson interceded for him, quickly outlining Lewrie's plight regarding *Cockerel*, at Naples and the time since. And the refugees now gathering under his wing. "But I suspect Lieutenant Lewrie deemed his own problems too tiny to be of much concern, given the circumstances which obtain."

"You are too modest, young sir," Hood grumbled. "I mind, when your captain came aboard *Victory* . . . I gathered the impression *he'd* been the one who had visited with King Ferdinand, and had spoken so eloquently for an alliance. Now I discover, from Captain Nelson, that such is not the case? Hmmm. And for him to strand you, bereft of any ex change of communications. I once rewarded Lieutenant Lewrie . . . well, twice I have given him a command. In '83, as you recall, Nelson . . . at your behest. And in '86. After actions in the Far East so perilous, yet done to a perfect turn . . . I believe, young sir, that you may serve me best . . ."

"Excuse me for intruding, milord, but I shall be going now," Sir William Sidney Smith butted in. "I simply wished to thank you again for the faith you place in me. Which shall be amply rewarded with a conflagration so intense, they'll see it in Paris, milord. My word on't!"

Must not have a jot of brains in his head to rattle, Alan thought: he's actually lookin' forward to it! How'd our British cavalry miss recruitin' *this'un?*

Introductions were exchanged, Sir William given the briefest thumbnail sketch of Lewrie's qualities, and source of his patronage.

"Gad, just the sort I need with me, milord," Captain Smith said with a tooth-baring bray. "Neck-or-nothin', *stick* at nothin' fellow! 'Cry havoc, and let slip the dogs o' war,' hey, Mister Lewrie?"

Oh, bloody Jesus, meek an' mild, save me from this I'll be good swear it never rattle another mort me entire bloody . . . ! He prayed most earnestly.

"I am heartily sorry I cannot oblige you in this, Sir William," Admiral Lord Hood said, glancing at Lewrie for an instant, thankfully *not* seeing the shivers he fought. "I concur that Lieutenant Lewrie's courage would be of inestimable assistance to your endeavour, but . . . there are other duties I have in mind for him, in this fell instance."

Thankee God, thankee milord, bloody damned *right* there are!

After Smith had bowed himself away, Hood turned to Lewrie again. "There are ships in the Inner Basin, Lieutenant, nigh-enough ready for sea. This Lieutenant de Crillart of yours . . . he'd know them best. With his men and yours, you will ready one of them for departure. Warp her to the Great Road, soon as you are able. Provision her, and be ready to take aboard troops, refugees, or both. I recall your own worth, Lewrie. And I'll no more toss you away than I would my invaluable Captain Nelson. I fear this war will be much longer than any of us, at the onset, could have ever suspected. England will have desperate need of you both, in future. Orders will be forthcoming, empowering you to provision and arm to your personal satisfaction, Mr. Lewrie. You have but to present those orders, which shall bear my personal signature, and be assured that any reasonable request will be granted you, instanter. Should I not see you again in the days to come before we quit Toulon," Admiral Hood said a bit sadly, "do present to me your compliments, once you have attained Gibraltar."

He offered his hand for Lewrie to shake.

"And I wish the very best of good fortune go with you, sir. God speed, and fair winds."

"Thankee, milord, for your goodness to me," Alan said firmly, as he shook that offered hand. "And for your trust. I will safely bring away all you send me, milord."

"My dear Lieutenant Lewrie, I rely on that steadfast promise just as surely as I expect tomorrow's sunrise."

CHAPTER 3

"Zey are merde," de Crillart griped, picking at the faded bulwarks of their ship. "Ze discipline, phfft . . . an' no one care to keep zem in proper fashion. 'Cep' for mon *Alceste* . . ." he sighed wistfully as his precious frigate began to make sail, out past the log boom, in the fairway for the Gullet. Ragged her scratch crew was, sloppy and uncoordinated as a pack of complete landsmen. That was understandable, for *Alceste* had been requisitioned by one of the allies and now flew the Sardinian flag at her taffrail gaff.

After conferring with Charles, Bosun Porter and a senior hand from the French sailors' party, hurriedly inspecting several ships in the basin, they'd settled on a forty-gun frigate, an impressive ship to all outward appearances. Certainly not in cosmetics, but in lines.

Radical, she'd been renamed after the Revolution. But she had been commanded by a procession of jumped-up quartermasters and bosuns promoted to officers from the lower deck. Then she'd been run almost by committee and the Rights of Man, with but the easiest maintenance neglected by a vote of her crew! She'd rarely gone to sea, and then only in fair weather. And after the arrival of the Royal Navy back in August, and the departure of Rear-Admiral St. Julien's men, *Radical* had lain idle, stern-to at the eastern quays, sandwiched in between other frigates, and had slowly disintegrated, as all ships will, without reverent and daily care.

Her bottom, they could see, was weeded, but she'd been careened and breamed in May, and her coppering had supposedly been redone. The upper works were filthy and shabby, her bold paint faded and peeling so badly that she looked more like a merchant ship than a frigate, browned and seared, stained and gray. Her standing rigging was still sound, in need of slush and fresh tar, some hauling at the deadeye blocks to set her taut once more. Running rigging had stretched or shrunk, rope gone stiff and brittle, but a quick reroving with fresh from the warehouses could renew that. Once they set to, British sailors made half a day's labour of what might have taken her French owners a week.

The important thing was that, once swept fore and aft, swabbed out, and vinegared, all the accumulated rat droppings, spider webs and dust, piles of trash and detritus overboard, she would be roomy. She would have bags of space on that long, beamy mess deck to accomodate hundreds of refugees or soldiers for the short voyage to Gibraltar. Should the winds turn perverse, she had the waterline to make a goodly way closehauled, the beam to survive rough seas, especially as short-handed as they'd be forced to man her. And there was depth enough on the orlop to store salt meats, water casks, wine and biscuit to feed a multitude for an entire month, if need be. And those salt rations already aboard were still fairly fresh, so provisioning took less time on her than it would have aboard another ship.

Guns? Lewrie was a bit worried about that aspect, though being in a convoy with warships near at hand shouldn't present too much danger. *Radical's* former owners had been in the process of rearming, with eighteen-pounders to replace the twelve-pounders frigates usually bore. Some guns had come aboard before work had ceased in August, and she'd been robbed of artillery since, to augment the firepower of Coalition strong points ashore. As a consequence, she had only four eight-pounders on her quarterdeck and two long eight-pounders on her forecastle as chase guns. Her main deck carried only a dozen pieces of artillery, a pair of her original twelve-pounders forward, one to either beam, and a matching pair aft, beneath the quarterdeck—and eight eighteen-pounders, four per beam, fore and aft of the main mast, all spaced out so far apart they appeared as afterthoughts. She was technically *en flute*, a warship stripped of artillery to make room for the transfer of troops. Were her gun ports to be opened, the empty ones would resemble the finger holes in a piccolo. But that was Alan's intent in the first place; another reason she was more suitable.

They could have taken others. There were even larger forty-four-gunned frigates, 3rd Rate 74's with even more space aboard—but they'd demand a much larger crew to work them properly. And some of those others had been in even poorer material state, so emptied of guns and rations that it would have taken a week to prepare them for sea, or were so weeded to the bottom of the basin, so neglected, it was a wonder they hadn't sunk at their moorings.

They chose her by midday on 17 December. And by dawn of the 18th, had her ready to warp out of her berth, set scraps of sail and work her out past the bombproof jetties, carefully keeping east'rd of the shoal which ran from the west jetty to the narrow channel through the log boom. By dinner, they were anchored close to the water-fort of Saint Louis, beneath the protective shelter of Fort La Malgue. They'd simmered up supper for their refugees the night before, and had served a cold breakfast and dinner by then. Though nothing they could do by way of hospitality could really cheer those refugees.

Chevalier Louis de Crillart had come aboard, a lieutenant in command of a remnant of his Royalist light-cavalry troop, about a dozen men all told, and their families. There was a Major de Mariel, whose vineyards and estate lay just a little east of Fort Saint Catherine, an infantryman with wife and three children, servants and their families, and perhaps twenty of his remaining soldiers and their families. Charles de Crillart's gunners—half of them had wives, girlfriends or kids. Some of Lewrie's own British Jacks had made the acquaintances of girls of their own, and had snuck out to fetch them to the guardhouse, onto *Radical* before she even left the quays. And they'd brought their parents and children or *their* friends, as well. After the great-cabins had been parcelled out to down-at-the-heels aristocrats and Royalist officers with families, the wardroom dog boxes going to families, and the warrant and mate's quarters assigned to people with children, he threw up his hands, and let refugees simply hang blankets from overhead beams, tack canvas to carline posts to partition off small areas of mess deck. As cold and drizzly as it was, Lewrie might have to assign people to the gun deck, with old sails stretched taut over the boat beams in the waist, and let people doss down between the guns.

Madame de Crillart and Sophie de Maubeuge already had his sleeping coach. Louis and Charles, with two other single officers, shared a stack of straw mattresses in the dining space, and the day cabins were awash in once wealthy or once titled humanity; mattresses, luggage and children everywhere one looked. He was crammed into the chart space.

Finally, after receiving two more miserable boatloads of Royalists (though not their piles of possessions) and a reduced company of the 18th Regiment of Foot, the Royal Irish, he had to beg off. There were nearly 300 people aboard, excluding crew, and he didn't have room or food for a jot more.

"Where do I quarter my men, sir?" the officer of the 18th asked.

"We've space below, on the orlop, sir," Lewrie informed him. "A stores deck, Lieutenant, uhm . . . ? between kegs and such, but . . ."

"Kennedy, sir," the wiry infantry officer beamed, one of those fellows, Lewrie could see at a glance, who was able to abide almost anything with a smile upon his lips. "Stephen Kennedy," he added, shaking hands jovially. "Yes, the orlop. We discovered all we wished to know, and *more,* 'bout the orlop, on our bloody passage here. Bloody hate a sea voyage. Now we're whittled down so, well . . . more room for the men below. Hoped to have the whole regiment t'gether, what's left of us, but . . . any port in a storm, hey, Captain Lewrie?"

"Indeed, sir," Alan smiled in reply. "Heard any more? How are things . . . ?" he asked, waving towards shore.

"Buggerin' awful, if you ask me, sir," Lieutenant Kennedy grumbled with a scowl. "Bloody damned Dons, bloody damned Dagoes. Cut an' run, they did. We were at Mulgrave, night o' the sixteenth? Frogs broke through the Spanish. Our Captain Connolly, he rallied us, and a prettier set-to a man's never seen, sir. Held as long as we could, but had to retire . . . down to the shore, and *creep* to Balaguer. An' would ya believe, when we got there, the buggerin' Dons that'd run into the place took God's own sweet time to let us in, sir?"

"So I gathered," Lewrie nodded.

"Latest now, sir," Kennedy went on, blowing his nose on a calico handkerchief. "We lost Fort Malbousquet and Missicy. Damme," he griped as a pack of children came tearing along the gun deck, hallooing and yelping, around and between them. "We were in town by then. That Artigues, and the Saint Catherine abandoned? Town, Malgue, and western forts was the new line. Well, the buggerin' Neapolitans, sir . . . just up an' ran! Nobody *firin'* at 'em yet, just didn't want to be last into a boat, I s'pose, but by all that's Holy, off they went, shootin' in the very air . . . at their own shadows, more'n like . . . yelpin' like hounds on a scent. Up and left Missicy. And 'thout Missicy held, the Frogs could march on it, and cut Malbousquet off. Get into the town, too, I s'pose. So, out we had to march. 'Least I'm *told* we toppled the guns before we decamped, them on the town side. Could have held another day . . .'cept for our . . . allies."

"So the French have the western forts, the powder mills, Fort Millaud and all, by now?" Lewrie speculated, thinking that anyone in mind to burn the French fleet was going to have a very hot time of it, with French guns and sharpshooters that close to the basin.

"Far as I know, they do, Captain Lewrie. But I doubt the Frogs will be that active," Kennedy chuckled. "Bless me, sir, but they've an eye, they see the writin' on the wall. Us packin' our traps, and away? All they have to do is sit back and cheer. No sense in killin' their own troops assaultin' Toulon, when it'll fall in their laps by tomorrow. And there's few soldiers I know who'll wish t'be the last man to die, just as the victory's won, d'ye see."

"So at least the fleet gets away safe."

"Aye, Captain Lewrie," Kennedy honked again into his handkerchief.

"*See* you're only a leftenant, but I learned to call the skipper of a boat Captain. Brevet promotion, hey?" he cajoled, getting chummy. "Now sir, when do we eat? I'm fair famished, an' so are me lads. Where's the officer's mess? And more important, *what* do we eat, sir?"

"Where, sir?" Lewrie had to smile. "Catch as catch can, sir. As for an officer's mess, we've not one. The great-cabins and wardroom are bung up with refugees. As for *what*, Lieutenant Kennedy . . . I sincerely hope the 18th Royal Irish is fond of salt beef, sir."

"You just *won't* set a good table, willya now, sir?" Lieutenant Kennedy boomed heartily. "No port? No biscuit nor cheese, ah well. Oh, dear God, now . . . there's a pair o' rare'uns. Oh, *tell* me I've a cabin, man! One tiny shred o' privacy!" Kennedy sighed, looking with longing over Lewrie's shoulder.

Alan turned. It was Sophie de Maubeuge with, of all people, the young Phoebe, on the quarterdeck above them, chatting amiably, almost in each other's pockets, peeking into a basket they bore between them.

"I hate to *further* disabuse you, sir . . ." Alan grinned. "But the red-haired one is a vicomtesse, and under the protection of her two male cousins. Meanest pair o' blackguards ever you did see. T'other . . . she is, hmm . . . mine."

"Oh, buggeration," Kennedy sighed again. "*Told* you I bloody hate sea voyages." He stomped off, bawling for his Sergeant, Rufoote, honking into his rag again, looking for a dry, empty spot.

Alan took time to ascend to the quarterdeck to join them, doffing his hat and making a formal leg. "Bonjour, mademoiselles . . . might I say des plus belles mademoiselles."

"M'sieur Lieutenant Luray, enchanté," Sophie beamed, dropping a graceful curtsy, though sharing an impish smile with Phoebe.

"M'sieur Alain, enchanté," Phoebe said, miming Sophie's graces. But laying subtle claim to him by using his first name. That tweaked one of Sophie's eyebrows in puzzlement. Lewrie compared the two, side by side. Sophie was fifteen, he knew, and Phoebe couldn't be any more than three or four years her senior, he thought, now that he had someone to compare her against. He cocked a brow as well, as if to caution Phoebe to mind her manners round Sophie, who probably was in total ignorance of her newfound friend's "profession."

"M'sieur Luray, nous sommes sur meesion of merci," Sophie said, sounding more excited and happy than she had when last he'd seen her. "You be so kin' a' Phoebe, maintenant, I 'ope you be kin' a' moi? Ve 'ave ze grand need. Voilà!"

She pulled the lid of the basket back to reveal kittens. Four kittens, about two months old, he estimated; blinking and mewing when the wan sunlight struck them.

"You mus' . . . espouse une chaton pour nous," Sophie giggled.

"Mademoiselle la vicomtesse, she tell me, wan you dine viz 'er famille, you say you 'ave le chat, le garçonet. Guillaume *Peet*? Mais, you read 'e nous a quittes?" Phoebe teased. "Pardon, eef zat mak' you sad mais . . . mademoiselle Sophie, she 'ave les chatons. An' le chaton new, peut-être, 'e mak' you 'appy, n'est-ce pas?"

"Well, I'll be . . ." Lewrie said softly, kneeling down to look at them, knowing his face had gone all soft and goose-silly. But he could not help himself. "Oui, I love cats. J'adore les chattes."

He stuck a tentative hand into the basket, wiggled his fingers at them. Two of the kittens were girls, he discovered as he toyed with them, mostly white, with pale tannish stripes or blotches. They shrank back to a corner, behind each other, little tails so very erect, and blue kitten-coloured eyes wide in fright. There was a male, mostly gray-tan tabby, just as scared. And there was the black one. There was white on paws and chest, white whiskers on his brows and chops. His chops were white, though his nose and under chin were black. And a white blaze tapering upward along the bridge of his nose to terminate between his bright yellow eyes. He was the only one intent on Lewrie's fingers, shifting his eyes and head back and forth faster and faster to follow, until with a manly little *mew* of delight, he pounced, tiny teeth and claws sinking in, holding on as Lewrie rolled him on his side, so he could break away and awkwardly pounce back.

"Ow, you little bugger!" Lewrie chuckled. "I dare you to do it again. Like the finger? Want a wood shaving to play with, hey?"

The kitten sat back on his haunches, front legs splayed clumsily, and licked his mouth, glancing up into Lewrie's face.

"Il ne comprend pas you, Alain," Phoebe chuckled, kneeling down with him, as did Sophie. "Eez le bon chaton Français. 'E ne parle pas Anglais."

"Oui, you 'ave to teach eem," Sophie laughed.

"You *adore* les chatons," Phoebe coaxed. "Quelles chatons préférézvous?"

Lewrie gently lifted the kitten from the basket and sat him on his upraised knee, atop his cloak, and began to stroke him, which elicited another tiny mew, as the kitten began to scale his cloak, up to bat at a corner of his cocked hat, almost fall off, dig in, and make another swat at it, from Alan's shoulder. He lost interest in that quickly, to nuzzle and prod under Lewrie's hair, to sniff at his neck, and go for an ear lobe as if it might be one of his mother's teats.

"I really can't," Alan sighed wistfully. "Once I rejoin my old ship, my captain . . . I shouldn't be tempted."

"Notre chat vieux, ze mozzer cat?" Sophie de Maubeuge told him as the kitten leaned far out to rub noses with him as he turned his head. "Elle 'ave 'er portée, uhm . . . comment, Phoebe? Merci bien, ma amie . . .'er *litter*, deux mont' ago? An' maintenant, ve 'ave ze familles to fin' for zem. Plais, m'sieur Luray? Vous espouse eem? You see? 'E eez déjà trés affectueux à vous. 'E . . . *like*' you!"

Alan almost relented, as the kitten rubbed his little chops on his chin and nose, pressed his side against his cheek and began a purr. "Well, we'll see. If he . . ."

The kitten slipped and fell, catching himself by one paw, deep-sunk claws into the rough wool of the cloak, turning a somersault.

"For now, I think he's best back with his brothers and sisters," Alan laughed, prying him off his cloak and putting him back in the basket.

"Le garçonet, 'e choose you, I save eem pour vous," Sophie promised as they all stood again. " 'E weel be you's."

"Oui, Alain, you mak' Sophie 'appy, mak' vous-même 'appy," Phoebe insisted. "An' mak' le chaton 'appy 'e 'ave ze 'ome. Votre capitain, phfft! *You* are un capitain, now, you canno' 'ave le chat eef you desire?" Her teasing pout took on more suggestiveness as she concluded in a softer voice. "Le capitain 'ave quelque chose . . . *anys'ing* 'e desire, n'est-ce pas?"

"Ahum . . ." Lewrie frowned, clearing his throat, hands clasped behind his back, quarterdeck fashion, with edginess. Sophie, by this time, had tumbled to his secret and was turning crimson to the roots of her hair, unable to look either one of them in the eyes.

"Pardon, ma amie Phoebe," Sophie said, with infinite inborn and noble grace, striving for a gay air. "Ve 'ave un chaton pour m'sieur Luray mais . . . trois bébés de plus." Switching to French only, she swore she could explore the lower decks and find some families who might wish to adopt the rest. Graciously, she excused herself, insisting that it would be a matter of minutes only, and that she would catch up with Phoebe later. They curtsied to each other and Sophie departed.

Phoebe tossed back the hood of her cloak to bare her head, and leaned on the starboard bulwark, arms widespread along the rails, to gaze off at the brooding, shrouded northern hills, taking a deep taste of harbour air, her head cocked back in pleasure, all unknowing.

"Uhm, mademoiselle la vicomtesse . . ." Lewrie began to explain.

"Ah, oui, Alain!" Phoebe bobbed as she laughed with delight. "La vicomtesse! She eez la ver' sweet jeune fille. Ver' charmant. Speak vis me beaucoup bonté . . . as eef I am bien élevé, uhm . . . well-born as 'er?

Ver' gracieux, mon chou. Avant, I nevair be connais vis someone si grand, vis pareil . . . to know someone so well-manner. Figurez-vous!"

"Aye, she is," he replied, stepping closer to her at the bulwark to speak more guardedly. She took his right hand under her left. "One hopes, though, Phoebe . . . Sophie is a very young girl, fifteen? Out of her convent barely six months, and that . . . forced out. Taken from the oven before she was fully baked, if you will."

He didn't think he was doing a very good job of this; Phoebe was chuckling at his statement.

"Innocent, Phoebe," he scowled. "Eager to think the best of anyone. A few moments ago, when you were so familiar with me, calling me Alan, 'stead of . . . well . . . she got an inkling of our relationship. And that's why she lit out, d'ye see. Off on her own. Embarassed."

"Mon dieu, j'ai marché dans le merde," Phoebe sighed, looking more and more stricken as she gathered his import. "Quel con, ma!"

"Maybe it's not as bad as that, Phoebe," he comforted, squeezing her hand on the rail. "Perhaps I took her wrong, and . . ."

"Non, I mak' ze emmerdement, encore," she groaned, near to crying. "I am ze paysan . . . un cul terreux. Wan' to be somebody, someday, an' 'ave non ze manners. Ze village girl! La *putain*, oui? An' now, you talk à moi, comme la putain. Tell me I do wrong."

"Phoebe . . ." he groaned, wondering if it was really worth it.

"Mademoiselle Sophie 'as tell me beaucoup concernant vous, mon cheri," Phoebe said in a flat voice, her face set against her misery. She turned to cock a brow at him and chuckle sardonically. "Zat you are marry? Zat en Angleterre, you 'ave le wife an' trois enfants?"

"Uhm, ah . . ." he groaned once more, gut-punched. Two nights in a row, now, they'd bedded together, and their one night aboard ship, crammed into the chart room and a narrowish fold-down bed cot, had been as maddening, as heavenly as the first, as inspiringly passionate and tender. No matter that he'd fulfilled his obligation, gotten her into a ship, and she could walk away as free as larks, her "debt" paid, too. He was sure he was going to miss that, painfully. "Aye, I do," Lewrie was forced to confess, slumping moodily against the bulwarks. "Phoebe, I know I have no right to rail at you, I'm *sorry*. I simply wished you might . . . for your own sake . . . be careful who knows about us. It hurt Sophie, I think. And it hurt you, if you wish to be her friend . . ."

"Pauvre Alain, mon chou," she laughed softly, half-turning towards him, taking his hand with both of her tiny ones. "You mak' amour comme le homme français mais . . . in you' 'ead, you are anglais. You are marry?" she said fondly, studying his sea-roughened hand, lifting her gaze to his face, her brown eyes huge once more, mesmerising and besotting. "Zen you are marry. J'comprend mais, je m'en fous . . . do not care. Ze jeune fille comme moi, she be viz beaucoup hommes 'oo are . . . marry. I do wrong. Merci bien, you correc' me. En public, ne pas encore emmerdements pour vous. Forgive me, I say you talk à moi comme putain, zat ees wrong. You correc' me, parce que . . . because you s'ink of 'er embarassment. An' my embarassment. Non on'y you' embarassment."

"Well . . ." he sighed. That wasn't exactly what he'd intended, but . . . if she wanted to take it that way, he'd be more than willing.

"You are good an' kin', trés affectueux vis me. I feel aussi à vous, Alain," she sighed, turning his hand over to peer into his palm. Then she laid his hand down firmly on the railing, slid half a step to the side, and crossed her arms on the bulwark to peer out, peeking at him from time to time, behaving with seemly public decorum.

"I do nozzing encore mak' you feel . . . honteux? Shame? But you mus' tell me. En private," she twinkled briefly. "Wan I be viz pauvre Barnaby . . . forgive, plais, mais . . .'e waz *non* le bon homme. I mak' eem anger, I ask concernant vous. Forgive, j'sais 'e waz votre ami, mais . . . eez vrai . . . true? An' toujours I weesh I be vis you, zat ees *you* wan' me, non eem. You seulement *talk* à moi, si gentil. You laugh, so easy? Mak' me laugh, aussi, an' 'appy wan you are zere. Now we are lovers, I know ze amité an' affection I feel au milieu . . . uhm, nous . . ." Phoebe paused, waving a hand to grasp the right word.

"Between us?" Lewrie supplied.

"Oui, between us, merci bien," she nodded quickly, rewarding him with another of her radiant smiles. "Zat eez so rare, en ze life I know. Avant you retourne votre ship, avant I retourne m'affaires," she sobered. "Am 'appy, *now*. 'Ow long ve 'ave, Alain mon chou? Une week, deux . . . ze mont', une année? Encore, je m'en fous. Long as you are mon cher ami. My loving frien'. An' I am votre jeune fille, an' votre amour. I demande nozzing more. I do nozzing more, mak' you be shame à moi, promesse! You weesh ze jeune dame, zan I be. En public," she concluded with a softly muttered leer and a shift of her hips.

"I'm sorry, Phoebe," Alan softened, knowing it wouldn't work— couldn't work, for very long, but . . . "I didn't mean to sound angry with you. Forgive *me*. Truth? Uhm, en verité? I *was* just as worried about what people would say about us. About *me*. Can't help that. God save me, I'm a horrid beast of a man. A poor excuse. God save me, again . . . with a gun to my head, this instant, I couldn't walk away from you."

"B'lief moi, Alain," she snorted in gentle self-mockery. "I know 'ow beas'ly men can be. You are non une of zem. Tu, je t'adore."

"Tu, je t'adore, aussi," he whispered, knowing he was throwing his mind away, and caring not one whit. "Long as no one gets hurt."

"Bien!" she laughed, suddenly girlish again, bouncing on her toes as if she wanted to fling her arms around his neck and kiss him in front of the entire world. "An' now I 'ave ma grand amoureux, comme amant tu crée partout, back, encore! An' monté comme un âne. Comme le Franchouillard, mais le plus formidable!"

"I'm what?" he chuckled. "Comment? Je ne comprend pas tous . . ."

She cut her eyes about the deck before stepping close to whisper, blushing with her daring. "I say, vous est ze mos' creative lover, like ze Frenchman, but more formidable, mon amour merveilleux. An ze, uhm . . . mon Dieu, so easy to say en français, mais . . ." She tittered into her hands, red as a beet, stifling a howl of laughter. "Equipé le plus, comme l'âne? Ze . . . donkey? La, mon Dieu, pardon . . . !"

"Ah?" he coughed sternly, though pleased beyond all measure. "Well, hmm . . . mean t'say!"

She coughed as well, flipped up her hood to partially hide her amusement and her embarassment. "I be good now, Alain mon coeur, I promesse. Jusqu'a ce soir. Until tonight, n'est-ce pas? Au revoir, mon amour. Au revoir."

"I would be most honoured, should you be able to dine with me, mademoiselle," he said, on public show once more, doffing his hat to her and bowing her away. She dropped him a rather good curtsy, then fled.

"Bloody Hell, until tonight, then," he crowed in a secret mutter, rocking on the balls of his feet. "Bank on *that*, ma cherie."

CHAPTER 4

The last diners had been served, the last families had slowly shuffled forward to the galley on the mess deck, with poor pewter or wood messware, soldier's issue tin plates and cups, or aristocratic china with sterling silver. Where they'd eaten had been their problem to solve, since there were too many for wardroom, midshipmen and great-cabin tables, for the petty-officer's messes. But they had all gotten a full belly of boiled potatoes, a quarter-loaf of crusty dry bread, a slice of cheese, and a portion of salt beef carved off hard joints. And a half-pint of vin ordinaire.

So much shipping had mustered round Fort Saint Louis that they had moved *Radical* in the late afternoon to a new anchorage close by the Cape Sepet peninsula, just under the battery named "The Brothers," waiting for the signal to sortie. Waiting for Capt. Sir William Sidney Smith and his party, and the Spanish under Adm. Don Juan de Langara, to begin the destruction of the French fleet.

There was not another inch of room in the Great Road. Seventeen Spanish sail of the line, and God knew how many lesser warships in attendance. Twenty-one British, plus frigates, sloops and brigs of war . . . and French warships taken from the basin.

Commerce-de-Marseille, the magnificent 120-gunned 1st Rate, the *Pompée* 74, and *Scipion*. The frigates *Arethuse–*40, *Topaze–*40, *Perle–*36, *Aurore–*36, *Lutine–*36, *Alceste–*36, *Poulette* and *Belette*, 28s; *Proselyte–*24, *Mozelle–*20, *Mulet* and *Sincère*, both eighteen-gunned corvettes, and the fourteen-gunned *Tarleton* brig-sloop. All crammed together in the Great Road, with a fingernail's grasp upon France, an anchor's flukes binding them to the ground. So many ships left behind, but certain to be destroyed; there simply weren't enough men in Admiral Hood's fleet to man them all, to provision them or overhaul them in time.

Crammed, too, those French prizes were, with French Royalists in their thousands. Over 14,000, Alan had heard from the flag lieutenant who'd

286

come 'round just before dusk, repeating the orders to be ready to weigh anchor once the fires were lit. And over 16,000 troops they had had. All off now but a handful, a rear guard at Fort La Malgue, soon to scurry down to Saint Louis at the base of the bluffs and take boats.

Lewrie and de Crillart stood on the quarterdeck apart from the other officers allowed on that hallowed ground; serving officers from Royalist units or the 18th Foot, a sprinkling of aristocrats or rich men who'd snuck up anyway.

"Beggin' yer pardon, sir," Will Cony muttered, coming to their side. "Uh, me an' th' bosun need t'speak with you an' Mister de Crillart, sir." Short-handed as they were, Alan had been able to promote Cony to a position as acting-bosun's mate. Porter came forward, hat in hand, knuckling his brow in salute.

"Yes, Mister Porter?"

"Ah, cap'm," Porter frowned. "Ya know that foot o' seep-water we pumped out'n 'er yesterd'y, right after we come aboard 'er? Well, sirs . . . h'it's back . . . some o' h'it."

"Good Christ, we have a bottom left at all?" Lewrie asked, dumb-founded. "How big a hole would that take, I ask you?"

"Not a 'ole, sir," Cony volunteered. "Maybe lotsa litl'uns. We sounded th' well 'bout half-hour ago, Mr. Lewrie, an' she come up wet. 'Bout three, four inch . . . deep'z a rum cup."

"Cony, she makes three inches in eighteen hours, why hadn't she already sunk at her moorings?" Lewrie gaped.

"Well, sir, my guess be," Porter stuck in, " 'long as she's light-draughted, she'd be fine. Suck in slowlike. But this many folks an' ton-nage aboard, full casks and all, she's back on 'er proper waterline . . . maybe an inch'r two over h'it. We laded 'er deep, sir."

"I see," Lewrie fumed, clasping his hands in the small of his back again and pacing off his sudden fretfulness. "Nothing much we may do about it. Can't go back to the basin and swap for another, can we, now? Is she wormed? And how badly?"

"Aye, sir," Porter confided. "First time we pumped her dry, we checked, and they's some soft patches, sure, but she was *mostly* sound. 'At Froggie bosun, 'e told us she'd been careened, breamed, an' copper re-done in May. *Thought* she'd weeded too fast, but I took that for sittin' idle, 'stead o' sailin' h'it off. An' then, we found 'ese. Show th' cap'm, Cony."

Cony offered them a handful of nails to look over. By the light of the binnacle lantern, Alan could see that some were copper and some were iron. Some were bent, as if they'd been driven badly, and pulled.

"Oh, Christ," Lewrie said.

"Sacre bleu," de Crillart moaned.

" 'As right, sirs," Cony agreed, with a disgusted expression over shoddy workmanship. "Aye, they recoppered 'er, but we foun' these all mixed t'gether, so we *think* . . . they got sloppy an' used iron nails, to drive through copper platin', when they laid on fresh stuff, sirs."

"But ev'ryone *know*, copper an' iron ensemble, in sea water, zey *eat* each ozzer," de Crillart cried. "Merde alors, I know ze peegs are lazy, mais non . . . non stupeed! Paysans connardes, cons comme la lune! Zut! An' now some of ze copper fall away, oui? Expose ze cloth, an'ze caulking? Zat eez ware ve leak, hein? Ils sont débiles!"

"Uh, yessir, I guess that'd be h'it, Mister de Crillart," the bosun nodded with an uncomprehending shrug to Charles's stream of invectives. "Uhm, 'bout th' caulkin', Mister Lewrie, sir? Been probin' down below. Like I say, ain't got no big leaks, just seepin', so slow we can't spot it. But some o' th' lowest down, 'long th' keel members . . . looks like h'it wuz a dirty job o' work, an' they didn' put much effort to h'it."

"Scrimped on oakum and tar, paying the seams, Mister Porter?"

"Aye, sir."

"Damn my eyes," Lewrie spat, putting a hand on his hip, staring aloft. Then realised how foolish he looked. "Right, then, we made four inches of seepage in . . . well, no, yesterday noon 'til noon today . . . and it's almost . . ." He pulled out his cheap replacement watch to add up the hours. But it had stopped. "Buggery, damned clock," he grunted, giving it a shake. "*French*, I ask you—oh, sorry, Charles."

The forecastle watch bell chimed; six bells of the second dog—half-past seven in the evening.

"Let's say, thirty-two hours to make four inches, that's an inch in every eight hours. Do we work the chain pumps for, say . . . one hour every eight, and should the seepage not get worse, pray God . . . we may be alright."

"The hands, though, sir . . ." Porter winced.

"I know, they've enough on their plates as it is. But we do have all this idle soldiery aboard. The Royal Irish, the French . . . ? Put it to 'em nicely, and we could use them on the pump levers. Charles, you're so much more diplomatique than I, especially with your fellow Frenchmen. Mm, perhaps you might be the one to spread the word? Quietly?"

"D'accord, mon capitain," de Crillart said with a wry look.

"Might let 'em drill a bit, too," Lewrie decided on a whim. "Get organised. That Major de Mariel in overall command, Lieutenant Kennedy and your brother as his captains? It might keep them out of mischief. And make 'em feel as if they're earning their passage. Appoint some as masters-at-arms, too. Sentries, like Marines. Especially on the magazine and such. Found children dashing in and out of there this afternoon, wild as red Indians. That'll spare our ordinary and able seamen, French or British, and our experienced landsmen too much work."

"Aye, sir," Porter agreed.

"I weel tell zem, mon ami," de Crillart agreed.

"Damme, leaks or no, I'll tell you all, it feels almighty good to be aboard a ship again," Lewrie smiled, revealing too much, being too open for a proper captain. But knowing that they felt the same way and would forgive his lack of august aloofness, for he said no more than any of them might, and thus spoke for them all.

Eight o'clock came and went. Full darkness. The skies were now clearer, the winds dryer, though still cold. They should be starting to burn the French ships, he thought, but there was no sign of that. Some brief firefly glitters on the hills around Malbousquet, from L'Eguillette and Balaguer, bright, brief little yellow sparks. Musketry, Alan imagined. A fire or two in Toulon proper . . . *sans culottes'* looting and revenge? Abandoned Royalists' homes being trashed? There were redder, longer-lasting sparks now, appearing to come from Dubrun or Millaud . . . a faint drumming. Light artillery, what the Republicans could man-haul to the shore. Musketry sweeping slowly forward like a grass fire towards the arsenals, the warehouses and the dockyards, downhill from Malbousquet and Missicy. From the heights above Toulon.

Nine o'clock, and still no signal to weigh anchors. Brisk little exchanges of fire, even closer to the dockyards. More light artillery winking amber from the shores.

"Ze end," de Crillart moaned at his side, suddenly. "Ma belle France. Pauvre France. I see 'er no more."

"We'll be back, Charles," Lewrie insisted grimly. "A year. We'll beat 'em, and then you can go back. The Vendée, up in arms . . ."

"Ah, a year . . ." Charles grinned sadly. "C'est dommage. I 'ave nozzing zere anymore. Ze France I know, she eez gone fo'ever. An' ze one een 'er place, I do not weesh to know. She be destroyed, beaucoup poverty, sadness. D'abord, we lose notre titles . . . ensuite, we lose our land. Our monnaie, phfft, perdu, mos' of eet. Now, we lose our country."

"There's still the Royalist French Squadron, Charles," Alan reminded him. "They'll need officers, captains . . ."

"Zere be no squadron, mon ami," de Crillart countered. "Votre roi Georges, 'e 'ave no need for nous. 'E 'ave eez own Marine Royale, an 'e canno' pay for bo'z. Englan', she pay monnaie pour soldats . . . for armies, not anozzer Navy. Non. An' no place for officeur français in you' Navy. I s'ink I am done viz mon service."

"Any plans, then?"

"I s'ink I like to go to America," Charles chuckled. "Oui, America, Alain! Wan I serve een Chesapeake, ware ve battle you an' I . . . I see beaucoup fin' land. Empty, America. Room for many. Maryland, I adore, mos' of all. We 'ave la monnaie, un peu, encore. Passage, an' ze bit of land. Work 'ard, save . . . mak' crops? Grow riche, encore . . . peut-être."

"Didn't think the Rebels cared for royalty, Charles," Alan warned. "Sure you're doing the right thing? And how would Louis feel about it? No one to call him Chevalier, over there, honour his bloodlines."

"Louis, oui," de Crillart heaved a heavy sigh, pulling his nose in Gallic fashion. " 'E may not care for America. So eager to fight . . . regain eez title? America may not care for eem, oui. Mon Dieu . . . ze famille! We may not chose zem, on'y abide? As 'ead of famille, I mus' do ze best for zem. But, Louis eez not boy, 'e mus' mak' eez own way, eef 'e disagree. C'est dommage!"

"You could come to England," Lewrie suggested.

"Pardon, Alain," Charles objected. "Nevair fit, zere. Live on ze charité, tolerated? Scorned? Nous sommes les Catholiques, et enemy ancien. Toujours, we be . . . suspect. An' remember, Alain . . . ze Comandant de Esquevarre, 'ow 'e say Toulonese are cold an' . . . 'tight-arses'? Not like eez Espagnole? Bien, I am French. To me, l'anglais are tight-arses. You, *non*, pardon, mon ami. You are not like ze ozzer anglais I 'ave meet. I sometime s'ink you 'ave made ze grand gentilhomme françcais! Sometime, I talk vis you, I am so amaze you are anglais, les bras m'en tombent, uhm . . . so amaze, my arms fall off!"

"You're not the first person to point that out," Lewrie chuckled, thinking of his past in English society. "French *or* English."

"Now, ze Chesapeake," de Crillart went on wistfully. "Ships an' boat-yards, some sea trade for us, n'est-ce pas? Maryland . . . ver' intéressant people, ze Americains, Alain. Ev'ryz'ing zer, new. Zey accept better? Maryland, she eez found' on freedom. You' Church of England . . . Catholique, dissenters, Moravians, ze Hughenots, even ze . . . Queevers?"

"Quakers," Alan offered.

"Oui, Quakers. Tous egal, all equal. Zere, no one say ze poor stay poor, illiterate stay dumb, 'ere are peasant, zere are nobles."

"Damme, Charles, but you sound like the very *worst* died-in-the-wool Revolutionary!"

"Ah, mon ami, remembre . . ." de Crillart laughed out loud, tapping his nose once more. "I waz een le États-Général, I *waz* ze revolution-naire! Not *zere* radical kin', on'y. An', someday, ve grow riche, peut-être? *Monnaie* eez title en America. Become success, et voilà . . . nous sommes l'aristocracie, encore! Peut-être, *not* riche? Zen, we be on'y bourgeois . . . a leetle land, a leetle trade. 'Ave *been* bourgeois, en Normandie . . . even wan ve *'ave* titles. All ze same, aussi. Build new, geef maman peace for 'er las' years. Fin' Sophie a fine 'usband, vis land, an' monnaie. Marry, moi-même, peut-être, once we 'ave securité."

"About Sophie, Charles, surely you must know she . . ."

"Ah, oui, j'sai, moi, elle adore, mais . . . eez child. Cousine, trop, too . . . close? Mon coeur waz tak' il y a longtemps . . . long ago? A neighbour en Normandie. Elle nous a quittes . . . she go away from us. Ze guillotine. I . . ." de Crillart hunched into his watch-coat collar and hat. "I no weesh to speak of 'er, s'il vous plaît, mon ami."

"Well . . ." Lewrie shrugged, into his own. So much for that, he thought. There was a story Charles wasn't telling, perhaps might never tell another living soul. But it was a closed subject. "Oui."

"Touchant petite Sophie, Alain . . ." de Crillart said, after some minutes of uneasy silence between them. "Une plus de emmerdement. You an' Phoebe?"

"Shit."

"Oui, mon ami," de Crillart snickered, sounding as if he enjoyed bringing the matter up. "C'est trés drôle. Louis, 'e eez furious vis you, zat you lodge Phoebe in ze great-cabins vis people of ze aristocracy . . . ze Quality, you say en Angleterre? Louis eez insult zat for ze voyage, ees cher cousine Sophie 'ave to associate vis *any* personnes à bas naissance . . . low-born, hein? D'abord, 'e warr-un Sophie, an' *order* 'er to 'ave nozzing to do vis Phoebe, tell 'er elle est sale courtesan. Zut alors, en suite, 'e tell maman. Et maman . . ."

"Christ, her, too?"

"Oui, aussi," de Crillart all but hooted with droll mirth, taking time to get his breath back, snickering and wheezing. "Maman she say eez no more zan she s'ought ze anglais man do, zey *all* 'ave no morals. Zen, maman eez furious vis me! Zat I associate vis *you*! Like eet eez catching? Ooh, la . . . zen *Sophie* eez ze furious. Sophie eez affectueuse vis Phoebe. S'ink she eez trés amusant et charmant? Merde alors, she eez scandalise, naturellement, but still *like* 'er. Not know what to do . . . *An'*, Sophie eez furious vis Louis, zat 'e *dare* order 'er 'oo she be vis. Louis say 'e weel not 'ave eez intended . . . besmirch? . . . and Sophie eez *more* furious . . . she say she eez *nevair* eez intended! Sophie eez furious vis you."

"Well, why not?" Lewrie chuckled. "Everybody else seems to be."

"Merde alors, mon ami . . . you 'ave ze wife an' enfants, but you couchez vis pauvre Phoebe," Charles further related, hugely amused by it all. "She eez egal furious . . . w'eech eez worse, zat you 'ave l'affaire adultère . . . *or* zat you are ze lapin-chaud . . . ze rabbit-'ot . . . but ze uncaring beast 'oo weel traiter quelqu'un comme . . . treat 'er like dirt? Promesse l'affaire de grand amour, mais . . ."

"J'suis dans la merde," Lewrie said of himself. "In English we call that 'to be up shit's creek.' Sans les oars," he added ruefully.

"Ah, oui, enfin . . ." de Crillart sobered a bit. "Enfin, Sophie eez furious vis me, aussi. Zat I am you' ami, zat *I* am not scandalisé. Merveilleux, now we are *bo'z* les sales bêtes . . . feelthy beasts!"

"Well, aren't you?" Lewrie asked. "Scandalised, I mean."

"Mon ami, you forget . . ." Charles confided chummily, tapping the side of his nose once more. "I am le homme français. Les Français, ve un'derstan' zese s'ings. Moi, I weesh you bonne chance. So ver' far from 'ome, so long . . . any man 'oo refuse to aid la jeune fille as beau as petite jeune Phoebe, 'e 'ave no 'eart. An' any man 'oo refuse 'er amour, c'est un *zero* . . . il as du sang de navet . . .'ave ze blood of ze turnip! En outre . . . homme go too long sans 'e couche avec la femme . . .'ave ze plaisir wiz girl . . . eez bad for you' liver. Ah, regardez!"

As four bells chimed forward at the belfry—ten o'clock in the evening watch—a matchlike tongue of flame appeared in the basin, at last. They were three miles or better away, with the northern headland of the Gullet between them and a clear view, but it soared up over even that, and the waters of the Little Road began to glitter like reflected candle flames. Through their telescopes they could espy tiny buglike rowing boats as black roaches scuttling over the Road, beyond the booms which guarded the entrance channel. Some, hung up on the booms, rowing furiously, yet going nowhere. More flames aroke, from the arsenals and warehouses. Sparks arose, borne on black-bellied columns of smoke from the slip-ways and graving docks where ships under construction were lit off like autumn bonfires.

As if awakened from slumber, the Republicans doubled, then redoubled their fire. The nearest hillsides, the basin itself, the headlands of the Gullet sparkled with tiny flashes from firelocks and gun barrels. Light artillery began an unsteady drumbeat. Near misses by the rowing boats frothed feathers of spray, and musketfire pattered a rainstorm about them. Now the fires were lit, the French had an open field of fire, and targets illuminated so well, so close within range . . .

BUH-WHOOM!

They felt that one in their bones; *Radical* shuddered seconds after to a shock wave so stupendous, as a massive fireball, a swelling and expanding miniature sun flashed into life inside the basin. The arsenal and all its powder, the powder removed from the forts, went off, sending debris and flaming embers soaring as high as the Heights of Pharon! And stupefying people close to it, friends or foes, into awed silence.

Guns fell silent, musketry winked out. All that could be heard for a time was the whooshing, crackling distant roar of a monumental fire that threatened to devour the entire city of Toulon, the rush of wind as it was drawn in to feed the flames. The fireship *Vulcan* was a torch put to the closely packed French ships of the line, laid across their sterns to set them alight. From the aftermost corner of the starboard quarterdeck, they could see rigging and yards aflame.

They should have been preparing to get underway, but the sight of an entire Navy being burned was too besotting. Gradually, the blazing fireball subsided, and smoke occulted their view, lit only with sullen smoulderings at the base of the smoke clouds. Yet as the light faded, the French guns opened fire once more.

"Well, then," Lewrie said, uselessly. "Mister Porter? Do you pipe 'All-Hands.' Soldiers to the capstans, topmen prepare to lay aloft, trice up, and lay out to make sail."

"Aye aye, sir!"

Soldiers and civilians breasted to the bars, began to trudge in circles—pawls began to chunk and clack in the well-greased capstans as the lighter messenger lines wound in, dragging the heavy hawsers to which they'd been nippered.

BARR-ROOOOMMMMM!

Another huge explosion, perhaps even larger than the first, hot wind coming from astern suddenly, shock waves rushing across the Great Road! *Radical* not only shivered this time, she heeled to starboard to the force of the explosion, rocked and dipped her bows!

Lewrie didn't think that'un had been planned, exactly. What in the world, once the arsenals were gone, contained that much powder? A pair of prizes, *Iris* and *Montreal*, had been filled with the gunpowder garnered from the French fleet and the Poudriere, the mills. But they were to have been sunk. Surely, no one in their right minds would *fire* them . . . would they? Thousands of barrels—not pounds of powder—*barrels* of gunpowder! It was the largest blast he could ever imagine.

"Short stays, sir!" Cony howled from the foc's'le, by the bower catheads. "Heave, you lubbers!" Gracey goaded the refugee landsmen.

Up and down, the bower cable bow-taut. A last heavy-heave and the anchor broke free of the holding ground. Pawls clattered like the rapid clopping of a trotting horse.

"Aloft! Let fall! Foc's'le! Haul away the inner jib!"

A land breeze, one of man's devising, the outrush of the fires, found her canvas; fore and main course, fore-tops'l, spanker and inner jib, enough to give her steerageway. Ebony waters scintillating with flame points chattered and gurgled about her cutwater, under her forefoot. Two knots at best she made, ghosting past Batterie la Croix and the headland bluffs, her shadow flickering like an errant moth's on the bare, crumbly land face. Out due east'rd to the Bay of Toulon, aiming at Cape de la Garonne, which could almost be seen as clear as daylight, ruddy-hued as twilight sunshine ahead. And an amber and rose-red glow astern, spreading and growing, an illuminated, tinted woodcut from some Germanic artist's medieval Hell. Or a glimpse down a volcano's seething throat.

Round Cape Sepet, sheering close as she dared to the shoals, clear of the ordered files of warships farther out in the channel as they made their southing, turning each in succession, in line-ahead, hulls gleaming with ruddy, linseeded sheens, buff gunwales bright as ivory, sails umber with the colours of a false sunset.

A sea breeze, then. A puff on the cheek, a luffing aloft, canvas drumming and fluttering. Squeals from blocks and parrels, as yards were braced about, pivoting on the masts, as sails filled on the opposite tack.

'Vast heaving, and . . . Belay! Well, the braces, well, the sheets! Do you hear, there! Larboard, tail onto the lift lines!"

Radical lifted her bows to the first scend of the proper sea, did a slow and regal roll to the first rollers that kissed her hull, a little forward of abeam on her larboard side. Creaking and groaning, timbers in adjustment, masts and stays taking a new strain as a second nightfall of 18 December 1793, found her. Stars appeared overhead, to windward and the south, thin rags of cloud far off simmered pale and indistinct and blue white. To the north, astern, they were red. Above Cape Sepet and the peninsula, there was red and amber, a pall which cut off starlight. And the Signals Cross stood on the highest hill, silhouetted on what appeared to be a tropical sunset, as stark as His on Golgotha.

"Well, the lifts, Mister Porter. Belay," Lewrie shouted down to his hands. He walked back from the quarterdeck nettings to the wheel, looking at the malevolence brewing astern like a witch's cauldron, glad to be away in one piece. To where, he had no idea, after getting this temporary command to Gibraltar. Turning his back on their doomed adventure, he faced forrud, leaned over to peer into the compass bowl.

"Quartermaster, steer sou-sou'west. Give nothing to leeward."

"Sou-sou'west it be, sir. Nothin' t' loo'rd."

It was dark before their bows, and a cold sea glittered and danced on the faint starlight. Wind-rush across the decks, a gentle keening in the shrouds and running rigging. A weary, deliberate movement beneath his feet as *Radical* conformed to winds and sea. The sluicing of ocean along her sides, under her quarter, a peaceful, soporific sighing.

The way things ought to be, Lewrie thought; for a time at least, it was peaceful. After such a dispiriting defeat.

CHAPTER 5

Radical was weeded worse than they had thought. She could not, for all her elegant length of waterline or finely moulded entry, make a goodly way. Weed, barnacles, algaelike green scum—a peek overside from the quarterdeck, hanging from the larboard mizzen chains, on the windward side, showed that her quick-work, which should have been smooth-joined copper and paint, was erose and irregular with Nature's sea-going pests. Weed waved like discarded rope in clumpy garlands up to three feet long. And all of it, save for the scum which thinned by morning of the 20th and no longer sloughed off as appetising morsels for the myriad of sea birds which swirled and mewed in her wake, was so firmly attached that a seething run with sails "set all to the royals" would not have scrubbed even a portion of it off.

A ship as long as *Radical*, with 100 feet of keel and waterline, should have logged nearly ten knots under plain sail; they were lucky to have averaged six. And the weather had been just boisterous enough to force them to shorten sail—first reefs in fore and main courses, second reefs in fore, main and mizzen tops'ls; forget setting stays'ls 'tween the masts, or freeing the gasketed t'gallants. They were too short-handed.

Plus, there were the unpredictably perverse currents in the Golfe du Lion, then there were fluky wind-shifts which had them at times close-hauled, beating into weather to make their southing, time lost in tacking to keep other ships in sight . . . neither Lewrie nor de Crillart could believe they'd made more than 180 miles to the good since leaving Toulon.

As for determining position, the skies had gloomed up again after dawn of the 19th, making noon sun sights impossible, and had stayed gray and overcast, rendering lunar or stellar sights hopeless, too. They'd fallen back on the old, and inaccurate, Dead Reckoning—by Guess and by God—estimating progress on casts of the knot-log.

The 19th hadn't been so worrisome, since there were many others in company, and if they followed along like lambs tagging after the bell-wether, they couldn't go very far wrong. So many captains and sailing masters, all slowly trundling along in the same direction simply *had to* know where they were headed.

By dawn of the 20th, though, they were almost alone. Slow the line-of-battle ships might be, sailing in rigid order, luffing or backing tops'ls to keep their ordained separation in line-ahead. But they were faster, manned well enough to take advantage of wind shifts.

There were two merchantmen astern about two miles off, a brace of hired transports crammed with refugees, wounded or troops, straining to keep up, flying more sail than the weather would really allow. Off to leeward on their starboard bows was another transport, an unarmed hired horse transport, with people in her stalls instead of chargers. Only one more ship was in sight, far ahead, hull down with only tops'ls and a lone t'gallant showing.

Making matters even worse, now *Radical* was upon the open sea, her seams were working worse than they'd feared, requiring a full hour at the chain pumps every six, instead of eight. Their music to celebrate what looked to be a Christmas Day at sea would be the mournful clank and suck of the pumps, and the irregular spurting gurgle of flood-water going overside.

Could be worse, Lewrie reassured himself at least once an hour—worse things happen at sea, right? Count your blessings! Two more days and we'll be in sight of Minorca, the Spanish Balearics. Fall off loo'rd and we're between them and the Spanish coast. Seamarks and charted positions again. Fishing ports to squeeze into, if the flooding gets bad. Maybe not Gibraltar, but . . . Another blessing, it's warmer. Clouds, or heading south . . . and this sou'easter out of Africa. And it isn't raining. Five more days, maybe, to Gibraltar? Money-draught from Coutts's and Mr. Mountjoy . . . letters from Caroline, new clothes and sea chest . . .

A slight change in *Radical*'s movements, a soughing wallow, with a slower rise of her bows to the next quartering sea. He looked aloft to see the coach whip of her pendant change angle, curl and falter. A change in the wind, not for the good, dammit!

"Pardon, mon capitaine," Lieutenant de Crillart said, coming up to him at the windward railings. "Ze wind eez drop, an' back un point astern. We . . . shake out . . . meezen tops'l reef? Main course reef? I 'ave you' permission?"

"Yes, Charles. Carry on." Lewrie smiled. Another blessing, he thought; to have at least one experienced watch officer aboard to share the quarterdeck with him, though they were forced to stand "watch-and-

watch" of four hours each. Definitely *not* a blessing, that schedule—
trying to eat, nap, scrub up . . . and pay proper attention to Phoebe, all
in a mere four hours. Porter and Spendlove, to make a third? Hmm.

Definitely a blessing, though: a girl willing to accomodate herself to
his horrid back-to-back hours, affectionate enough to be supportive in
those times when their privacy was interrupted. And wit enough to understand that he had two mistresses, one infinitely demanding, to which
she must take a back pew for a time.

Precious few able seamen aloft, topmen laying out to let fall a line of
reef-points. Landsmen and civilian volunteers on the gangways, tending
the braces, in the waist easing clews, hauling on sheets. For a moment
he wished he could dare let fall the t'gallants, but . . . should it come a
blow, and in the Mediterranean there was little time before squalls
struck, little warning. The wind was already trending more easterly. Another fierce Levanter on its way? No, they were doing the best they
could, with what little they had left to work with. He'd have to swallow
his impatience and tread on the side of caution. Overpowered by a
squall, they could lose the upper masts in a twinkling, broach her to,
roll her on her beam-ends. Or be driven under as too much canvas
cupped too much wind, and *Radical* exceeded her ultimate hull speed.

Damned galling, Alan thought moodily, testy with himself for lack of
sleep; here we are, one of the world's handsomest frigates, *crawling*
along like a snail, fair game for . . .

He looked around the horizon. Merchantmen were all he saw, tired
plodders, wallowing along short-handed, packed with humanity who
couldn't even begin to help their thin crews, landlubbers who'd more
than likely never set foot aboard a ship before, heaving their guts up,
helpless . . .

It struck him, suddenly, that they were the only warship present, no
matter how poorly armed, no matter how short-handed, or so crippled
by their own multitude of émigrés. One, just one Republican frigate,
could gobble up every ship in sight, fall upon them like a fox in the hen
coop and have them all in an hour. There were frigates, corvettes, even
74's which hadn't been at Toulon, scattered in ones and twos all over
before Toulon's surrender. In French ports west of Marseilles and Toulon, perhaps—now at sea, to see what they could eat, like a pack of
wolves on the hunt, falling upon the slowest, weakest, oldest of a deer
herd.

"That's us, by God," he muttered.

"Pardon?" Lieutenant de Crillart asked, now his task was done, and
he reported back to his temporary captain.

"Charles, I've been a fool. I've been remiss," Lewrie grimaced.

Feelin' too sorry for myself, he scathed himself, too defeated. Too busy bein' a ferryman, worried about leaks and weed to . . . *damme*, I'd more thought for another tumble with Phoebe than I had for being a King's Sea Officer! Countin' seconds 'til I can sleep again!

"Charles, does a Republican ship come across this miserable lot of barges, we're done for. They'd have us, sure as Fate, and take us as easy as a pack of sheep. We should be doing some drilling at the guns, organising volunteers, getting ready for a fight. Putting together at least *some* means of resistance."

"But, to offer bataille, mon ami . . ." de Crillart shrugged. "Ve are so weak. An', vis beaucoup femmes et enfants aboard, zey weel die uhm . . . during? . . . ze bataille, an' . . ."

"They stand a better chance fighting for their lives than they do surrendering and being taken back to Toulon to the guillotines, Charles," Alan said firmly. "Men, women *and* children . . . chop! Resist, though, well enough, and we might only lose a tenth. Not *all*. And get away. These other ships . . . easy meat. But us . . . too tough to chew!"

"Mmm, per'aps, mon ami," de Crillart nodded slowly, understanding coming to him.

"Look, we've Major de Mariel and what . . . about sixty soldiers?" Alan enthused. "They could be our Marines and sharpshooters. Gunners, yours and mine. Not enough hands to serve the guns *and* tend sail. But, we've all these civilian men. Work as landsmen at the braces and such. They're already doing that, some of 'em. Heave on the gun tackles, too, like landsmen in naval service. Run 'em out, overhaul. It only takes one gun captain, one experienced rammerman and loader per gun, the rest are strong backs, anyway. Bittfield and his yeomen below in charge of the magazine, plenty of boys aboard, to be powder monkeys and shot-fetchers. We put out a hot-enough fire, a foe might sheer away from us. And between Louis's men, de Mariel's, and the Royal Irish . . . and the rest of the male civilians with guns . . . should it come to a close-aboard fight . . ."

"Ze veapons, z'ough," Charles countered. "Ozzer zan ze troops, ve 'ave on'y un peu. Fusils . . . ze mooskets? I know beaucoup hommes 'ave pistolets, fusils de chasse. For 'unting? An' on'y les gentilhommes, ze bien élevé, 'ave épées."

"God helps those who help themselves, Charles. Verité?" Alan chuckled, clapping him on the shoulder. "Most especial, He helps them who got ready beforehand. Just in case He was short on miracles."

"Oui," Charles grinned. "An', eet tak' zeyr min' off 'aving ze mal de mer. D'accord."

"Mister Spendlove! Mister Porter! Cony!" Lewrie bawled suddenly.
"Come to the quarterdeck, if you please."

God, but it was disheartening. They had, beyond the muskets and infantry hangers, light-cavalry sabres and such brought aboard by the soldiers, barely enough cutlasses for the French gunners and his British
Jacks. There were no boarding pikes at all. Civilians owned light hangers,
hunting swords, aristocratic and elegant smallswords, some older heir-
looms among the elderly—rapiers and poignards, or a fencing master's
stock of foils and true épées doled out to others.

There were few French .69 caliber St. Etienne muskets, British Tower
.75 caliber Brown Besses, a handful of Mod. 1777 Cavalry musketoons
which fired a lighter ball. As for pistols, there were as many types and
calibers aboard as there were adult males. Most gentlemen, though, had
one or two pair, and those were allotted to those without.

Boys to serve as powder monkeys; that was no problem. Teens in
plenty volunteered, treating the whole thing like a lark. Men without
any personal weapons, commoners and shopkeepers, the poorer class
who had never hunted, served in the army, or dared aspire to fencing
skill—they went to serve the guns. Mild and fubsy tailors, chefs, cobblers
and domestic servants ended up with run-out tackles, train-tackles and
swabs in their soft hands. Or were taken over by experienced able seamen, "pressed" as landsmen on gangways or in the waist.

There was eight-pounder shot and twelve-pounder shot in plenty for
the quarterdeck, foc's'le and fore-and-aft guns. There were several casks
of powder below, but few made-up cartridges. There were several bolts
of serge for cartridge-making, but "impressed" silk shirts and gowns
were commandeered as well. Bittfield and his yeomen were delighted
to be in charge of a pack of women to aid them. Milliners, dressmakers,
housemaids and seamstresses, with a few elderly, near-sighted males
who had tailored for the Quality. Giggling, tittering, chattering as gay as
magpies, sewing neat, fine stitches—but taking as long with each cartridge bag as if they were running up a new gown for some very particular lady patron.

For the heaviest armament, though, the massive eighteen-pounders
amidships, there was only enough solid shot for about twenty rounds
per gun, shooting to one side only, before they were exhausted. Grape-
shot was almost nonexistent; they could double-shot the eighteens four
times at the most. Musket-shot and pistol ball was short, so they had to
satisfy themselves with scrap iron, bent nails (both copper and iron) and

the shards of broken bottles and stone crocks, tied up in spare stockings, in the eight-pounders only. *Radical* had no swivel guns, much to Lewrie's great disappointment. As the organisation wore on, he felt like kicking his own arse, time and again, for those things which had slipped his mind when they'd hurriedly outfitted. Or those things which he had thought of by way of armaments, but had consciously decided to forego.

Deep below decks, though, the French gunners had discovered some shot for the eighteen-pounders which had been neglected when *Radical* had been stripped, then abandoned; Chain-shot, elongating bar-shot, and multiple bar-shot, designed to take down masts and rigging. The French were more fond of it than the Royal Navy, it was their standard tactic; to cripple a foe at long-range first, destroying his motive power, and the ability to maneuvre or flee. Lewrie thought it a waste of time, and precious powder.

The results of the drills didn't enthuse him much, either. They worked without firing, since they had so little powder to waste, and it was a shambles. People tripping over ring-bolts in the deck, tripping over tackles, standing cunny-thumbed and unknowing in the bights which in action, when guns recoiled, would have had their feet off. Standing *behind* the guns, so please you, totally ignorant of recoil at all! One hour they'd drill, then rest for half of the next, whilst earnest gunners tried to explain, over and over again, how to do it safely and with the least confusion. Then, back to the guns once more, for another hour of drill, trying to cram three months' experience into their heads in a single day!

The soldiers were easier to deal with. They understood crouching behind bulwarks and letting fly by-volley, the bayonet, the mêlée. Few, however, were anywhere near marksmen. Their common practice was to line up shoulder to shoulder, three or four ranks deep, level their muskets in the general direction of the enemy, aim for the breastplates, close their eyes, fire . . . and hope for the best. To work in small teams aloft in the fighting-tops, firing at single targets, was too much to hope for. Thankfully, there were young aristocrats, too well bred to stand in the line (unless they were officers) who were also sportsmen, who took pride in their marksmanship with single-shot hunting guns or fowling pieces on a chase over their ancestral lands, and who could, with a few commoners who'd worked as gamekeepers, go aloft as sharpshooters and pick off a man in an officer's uniform. But they were painfully few.

They drilled for another hour, took another tutorial rest period, and then it was time to break and pump the bilges. Then serve dinner to all. They had two more spells of drill in the afternoon. Until it was time to pump the bilges once more.

Christ, it'll be hopeless, Lewrie thought, watching them traipse away for a lie-down or a sit-down, trailing their muskets or swords, more like walking sticks than weapons. They were beginning to get an inkling— but only the *barest* inkling—of what might be demanded of them. Like a brand-new warship just fitting-out, her crew as raw as a side of beef, nowhere near ready to up-anchor for weeks, engaging in a first day of sail-handling training—in the first hour of "river discipline." He crossed his fingers, hoping against hope that they'd not come afoul of an enemy ship. Their best would be pathetic, nowhere near enough.

Lewrie put his head down on his crossed arms, swaying against the quarterdeck rails over the waist, bone-weary. His little enthusiasm had cost him two spells off-watch, and it was properly de Crillart's turn to go below. It would be eight that night, end of the second dog, before he could let himself rest, or even close both eyes longer than a blink. Sure enough, eight bells chimed forward—four o'clock, and the end of the day watch.

He thought of staging one more drill before supper, but no . . . his "volunteers" were by then too tired themselves, too full of strange and new concepts not yet half-absorbed. More drill would put experienced, impatient sailors too much on edge, and the "volunteers" would rankle at the abuse which was sure to come, then. They'd learn nothing more this day. Might even bridle so stiffly, some of the aristocratic ones, that they'd have no more to do with it tomorrow. Or blithely "forget" the lessons of today. Let 'em rest, he thought. And dear God, let me!

CHAPTER 6

"Alain," a soft voice crooned in his ear. He smacked his lips, trying to ignore it, sunk so deep in a well of turgid blackness, echoing, swirling fever-dream deepness, both unable and unwilling to move a single limb. "Alain, mon cerf formidable. Arise, mon coeur."

"Oh, God," he whispered. "What's the time?"

"Almos' six?" Phoebe cajoled softly but insistently. "Ze aspirant, m'sieur Spen'loov, 'e sen' down pour vous."

"God," Lewrie reiterated, flat on his back, rubbing his eyes to pry them open. "There trouble, did he say?"

"Non, mon amour," Phoebe assured him, with a gentle kiss on his lips. " 'E say, eet eez ze ten minute aprés l'auroré. Ze dawn?"

"Uhmm," Lewrie sighed, trying to will himself to rise. Once he had come below, he'd fallen into an exhausted sleep, almost face down in his soup, gone back on deck at midnight, and had left orders to be wakened around dawn, no matter. He'd barely gotten his shoes and coat off before tumbling, giddy-headed, onto the bed cot, putting his arms about her an instant before total, dreamless sleep had claimed him.

"Maintenant, ze cinq minute 'ave pass."

"Right, then," he grunted, letting a leg fall toward the deck. He swung to a sitting position, head hung in weariness that a sleep of an entire night and day couldn't cure.

"I 'ave ze café! Trés chaud, et noir," Phoebe said, perkily.

I *know* she's bein' affectionate, supportive an' all, he thought, but *damme*, it's too bloody much cheerful, too early, for me!

She put the mug under his nose. His nostrils twitched, his eyes were, like a purloined letter, steamed open. He took the mug and took a sip.

"Bon matin, mon cheri," she said fondly.

"Bon matin à tu, aussi, ma cherie," he replied, trying to crack a matching grin. Damme, she call me a *serf*, just then? No, *cerf*. A stag? "Bon matin, ma biche," he added. "My little doe."

"Chatons, zey say 'bon matin,' aussi," Phoebe crooned, pointing to the black-and-white he'd ended up adopting after all—though just how that had come about, he still wasn't certain. The little bugger was just *there*, playing on the bedcot when he'd come off watch the day before. As was one of his whiter, lighter-marked sisters, whom Phoebe had also claimed. They were tumbling and pouncing each other all over the map table at that moment, too busy to say "bon matin." Scattering rulers and dividers, almost upsetting the inkwell . . .

"Uhm, thanks for the coffee, Phoebe," he said, as his thoughts began to trickle through his brain. "You must have gone forward, up to the galley? Very kind of you. Merci bien."

"Pauvre Alain, eez . . . leas' I do pour vous?" She sat beside him almost prim, though swinging her heels girlishly as they hung above the deck. "Ver' beau jour . . . nice day, I am s'ink. I weel non 'ave to worry concernant vous visou' you' cloak. Non as cloudy?"

"Good," Lewrie hurried to finish his coffee. "I'm sorry, Phoebe, but I have to go. They'll need me on deck. Thank you, though."

"Moi, need you, aussi," she chirped, full of good cheer, almost maternal. Yet seductive. "Wan we arrivons à Geebraltar, z'ough . . . Now, go. Speed oos zere. I let you' navire 'ave you, until zen."

With an offer like that, he could not depart without rewarding her with a passionate kiss and a grateful embrace. A moment's dally with the kittens, and he was off.

"Morning, sir," Mister Midshipman Spendlove reported crisply. "The dawn was at . . . half-past five, sir. Horizon clear. We logged six and a quarter knots, the last two hours, sir. Wind's veered more southerly, too, so it doesn't feel like a Levanter . . . I think, sir."

"And you let me sleep twenty minutes past dawn, when I left orders to be summoned at that time, Mister Spendlove?" Lewrie glowered, still too testy to be approached.

"Uhm, sir . . . we *tried* to wake you, me and the, uhm . . . mademoiselle Aretino both, sir," Spendlove blushed.

Who the Hell's *that*, Alan wondered? Damme, never even took time to discover her last name! Oh, well.

"My apologies for biting your head off, then, Mister Spendlove," Alan sighed. "Bad as one of Hercules's Twelve Labours, was it?"

"No error, sir," Spendlove grinned shyly.

"Where away, the other ships?" Lewrie asked, turning back to business.

"One ahead, sir, she's tops'ls down now. The horse transport down to loo'rd must have hauled her wind during the night, a point or so. She's about another two miles off, *almost* hull down. The pair astern are about where they were last night, sir. *Might* have lost some ground on us."

"Very well, Mister Spendlove. I'll—"

"SAIL HO!"

"Christ!" he said instead, wishing his bladder wasn't full.

"Deck, there! Two sail astern! Two points off th' larb'rd quarter! Hull down! T'gallants, all I see!"

"You and the bosun have the deck, Mister Spendlove?" Lewrie enquired. "Pray, do you keep it a few minutes longer." He took a telescope and went aloft the mizzen shrouds as high as the cat-harpings, to peer astern.

"Three sail! Deck, there, three sail astern!" the mainmast lookout shouted down. "Three sail, all three-masters! Two points off the larb'rd quarter!"

He could barely make them out, three sets of three t'gallants on the horizon, grayish-white sails bellied full of wind. *Radical* rose on a wave, giving him a slightly better view, then dipped once more, rising the horizon like a stage curtain. The strange ships rose and fell also. Too far off to determine their identity. But he could hazard a morbid guess. The ships around him had been at sea long enough for pale white canvas to go mildewed and tan. Royal Navy ships, wearing their working suit of sails, were usually amber or tan. These ships, though, had not been at sea much, hadn't exposed their t'gallants to the weather. They were nearly new, and pale. Weather nowhere near boisterous enough for the heavy-weather suit to be hoisted aloft, too gusty for the tropical suit . . . these were ships which hadn't been out of harbour in a while. And three, close together, travelling in a pack. Or a squadron.

He feared they were French.

"Bloody Hell," he sighed to himself. "*Now* what to do?"

He snapped the telescope shut, descended the ratlines, to land with a final short jump to the quarterdeck.

"Mister Spendlove, we'll err on the side of caution. Dig into the taffrail lockers and prepare a flag signal for the other ships," he directed. "First, Number Ten, followed by 'Make All Sail,' whatever that is, this month's book. There're Sea Officers aboard to read 'em."

"Number *Ten*, sir?" Spendlove gasped, eyes wide.

"Aye, Mister Spendlove. 'Enemy In Sight.'"

＊   ＊   ＊

Short, bluff-bowed, undersparred . . . and terrified, the merchantmen
and transports *tried* to make more sail. More than likely, they had one
poor, overworked Royal Navy officer aboard, assigned to a civilian master, who possessed as few crewmen as he could scrimp and still work
his ship, under Admiralty contract. They had guns, of course; no ship
put to sea unarmed. But to work them, to really fight back . . . always
sailing in large convoys or under close escort, they were there merely as
afterthoughts for most merchant ships in European water. *Supposed* to
man to something close to Admiralty standards, *paid* to, yet . . .

A prudent man would have let fall every reef, let fall every top-gallant,
and sail off and leave them to their own devices. Yet those ships were
so jam-packed, elbow-to-elbow with helpless civilians. Alan could not
abandon them. There was precious little he could do *for* them, either.
He couldn't fight *one* enemy vessel, really, and certainly not three. *Radical* didn't have the well-drilled crew to allow him freedom of maneuvre,
to dance with the approaching foes. And, he observed most bitterly, even
had he *attempted* to run away, he couldn't. *Radical* wallowed! She
couldn't pass seven knots in a full gale. And the ships astern were gaining.

Within an hour the three ships had sailed their tops'ls above the horizon; within another hour, the first sight of their courses as well. Stuns'ls
(which *Radical* lacked) spread snowy to either beam of their masts,
stay'ls between topmasts glittered fresh as new-boiled bed sheets. The
transports astern had caught up by perhaps no more'n a single mile,
strain as they might, their own topmasts appearing to bend forward
under the pressure of t'gallants and unreefed tops'ls. The horse transport
down to leeward had made better progress, now head-reaching ahead
of *Radical's* bows.

"Sail Ho!"

"God, not another one," Alan groused. "Where away?"

"Fine on th' starb'd bows!" came the wail. "Three-master! 'Er t'gallants only, f'r now!"

A fine trap they laid, Lewrie thought, massaging his brow in concentrated thought and fidgety frustration. Three to herd us, one downwind
to beat back, and cut us off? Horse shit! Didn't even know where we
were 'til *dawn*, when they spotted us ahead of 'em.

"Horse transport's hoistin' an ensign, sir!" Spendlove cried in wonder.
"And a private signal!"

"Of course, she's closer to the new'un. Maybe . . ."

"Deck, there! Strange ship t' loo'rd . . ." the lookout shouted with sudden glee. "Answerin' . . . private signal . . . !" He called off a string of code flags, that month's secret recognition between ships of the Royal Navy! Lewrie flipped through his slim signals book. They were correct! "Deck, there! White ensign! Royal Navy . . . frigate!"

White ensign . . . a ship of Admiral Lord Hood's fleet would show it, since he was a full admiral of the most senior squadron. Or a frigate on independent service would fly it, instead of the blue or the red of a lesser admiral.

"Mister Spendlove! Hoist our own ensign. *And* Number Ten," he roared, filled with immense relief. Help was at hand. If the strange frigate's presence didn't cow the French, then at least, should he be forced to engage, he would have more even odds.

"Number Ten, two-blocked, yonder!" the lookout bellowed. "She reads us, sir! D'ye hear, there?"

"Right, then," Lewrie dared smile and clap Spendlove's shoulder, glance at de Crillart and the rest of the military men who'd gathered together on the quarterdeck. "I think we're going to be fine."

" 'Nother hoist, sir!" the lookout yelled, calling off a string of flags. "Private signal!"

Spendlove opened his book, thumbing through the many entries. He had a short list of those vessels known to be in the Mediterranean, those further separated into Rates. Scanning 5th Rates took another fumbling moment to find the right hand-lettered page he'd diligently copied out.

"*Cockerel*, sir!" Spendlove informed them at last. "HMS *Cockerel* frigate. Come to *save* us, sirs!"

A cheer went up from *Cockerel*'s detached tars when that news was quickly circulated along the gangways, down to the waist and magazines. And for once, it didn't sound the slightest bit derisive. Closehauled though she laboured, within another hour, she could be up to them, with her thirty-two guns primed, loaded and run out. Just about the time the French squadron overhauled the fleeing merchantmen.

Lewrie began to consider coming about, then, to offer battle. He already flew a borrowed Royal Navy ensign, and *Radical* was a frigate, by God. At range-of-random shot, who was to say that she wasn't a frigate in full commission, proper-manned and armed? And spoiling for a fight!

"Quartermaster, helm up a point, no more," he ordered. "Give us a point free to leeward. Mister Spendlove, a signal to the ships astern of us. Direct them to pinch up aweather. We will interpose our vessel between them and the French."

"Aye aye, sir," Spendlove piped, seeing the plan at once, dashing aft for the flag lockers.

"Don't s'pose those are friendly, Captain Lewrie?" Lieutenant Kennedy inquired, hoping against hope, and nervous about fighting aboard ship instead of on land, where he knew what he was doing.

"Slow as we are, sir?" Lewrie scoffed gently. "And tag-end of the fleet? Hardly."

"Ve steel offer battaille, mon ami?" de Crillart asked from the other side.

"If we have to, Charles," Lewrie stated, turning to face him and the rest of the officers: Major de Mariel, the Chevalier Louis, and the senior gunner's mates. "Hopefully, we will make a demonstration of force, more than anything else. With a Royal Navy frigate to aid us . . . that might be enough. Now, gentlemen. Raw as we are, hmm? Let's not delay, and do things in a last-minute panic. Let us go to Quarters now. Uhm . . . aux armes, messieurs?"

An agonizing quarter-hour passed, as the decks were sanded, the water butts and tubs filled, slow match ignited and coiled around linstocks, coiled around the upper rim of the tubs. The galley fire was extinguished, the coals thrown overboard. Women and children trooped below to the safety of the orlop, low near the waterline, to huddle in between kegs and casks, boxes and bales, their chests and luggage. At least *Radical* would have an overabundance of surgeons; the Royalists were mostly people of the upper or professional classes, so they had no less than four surgeons, two physicians, a dentist, and several of those worthies' personal servants as surgeon's mates, experienced with assisting their masters' daily work. For loblolly boys to bear the wounded below, they had the least-useful older gentlemen, or the ones who simply could not grasp the fundamentals of artillery drill. And some few stocky older women, who were stronger than most of those men.

It was impossible to clear the mess deck, though, to empty that low-ceilinged cavern of junk. There were too many trunks and chests to carry below, out of harm's way, too heavy to tote quickly. There might be clouds of dangerous splinters flying there, perhaps, but with people at least herded below to the orlop, Lewrie thought, the noncombatants would not have to face that danger.

The boats *Radical* possessed, and those extra cutters Lewrie had brought along from their ferrying days, already were astern, under tow. For the simple fact that he hadn't had the labour available to retrieve them and stow them on the boat beams which spanned the waist. One less source of splinters, he thought grimly, though through no forethought of his own.

British troops of the 18th, the Royal Irish, to larboard along the gangways, Major de Mariel's infantry and Louis's light cavalrymen to starboard; red coats and black shakos on one side, and pale whitish-gray coats with black cocked hats, or blue-and-buff coats with plumed black-leather helmets on the other.

The bowsings for the guns were cast off, run-out tackles overhauled in neat bights. The guns were rolled back from the port sills, tompions removed, barrels checked for obstructions, touch holes cleared by the thrust of linstock ends sharp enough to puncture cartridge bags. Gun tools were thrust into shaky hands, and men stood atremble as if yesterday's drills had never occurred with stiffened rope rammers, rope swabs, crow levers, wormers used to scrape out clogging scraps of powder and the buildup of gun soot after a few firings, or to draw shot.

Nine men to each eighteen-pounder, seven to serve each twelve-pounder, and six for the lighter eight-pounders; those were the required numbers in the Fleet, though guns could be well served with slightly less. Under the circumstances, they would *have* to be. Still not enough, even with all the volunteers, to man both larboard and starboard batteries at once.

"Ve load, mon capitaine?" de Crillart called from the waist. He would be in charge of the gun deck, since most of the gun captains and volunteers were French. "Mon maître-canonnier, 'e sugges' ze chain-shot, d'abord. Non customary à l'anglais mais . . . ve are ver' good vis it. Zey are mos' esperience. Tak' down ze reeging, crac! An' ve are non ze maneuverable, n'est-ce pas?"

"Aye, Charles," Lewrie called back from the quarterdeck, thinking it made good sense to render a foe as clumsy as *they* already were, evening the odds. "D'abord, the chain-shot, bar-shot, all of it."

"Cartouches des poudre!" the grizzled master-gunner demanded, and a herd of boys emerged from the midships companionway hatch with wooden or leather cylinders which contained the powder bags. The artillery was charged, rammermen shoving the bags down the bores to thump against the rear of the breeches. From the shot-garlands, the gun captains picked shot. Blunt iron cylinders cast in two halves, linked by two bars between, with eyes hammered round each bar—elongating bar-shot, which would fly apart to their full extent upon firing. Longer, round-topped bundles of cast-iron rods, which would spread like spider legs to whirl through the air to rip away sails, rigging and light spars— that was multiple bar-shot. And chain-shot; loaded as what appeared to be solid iron balls, which became two hemispheres linked by a short chain. That, and the elongating bar-shot, were the heaviest, designed to take down a t'gallant or topmast above the fighting-tops, to shatter even the stout course-sail yards.

Alan had been on the receiving end of French artillery before, and had never been that impressed with the concept, never been aboard a ship really disabled by such ironmongery. But de Crillart and his master-gunner seemed confident about it.

"The enemy have hoisted their colours, sir!" Spendlove was quick to point out. All three ships had run up huge Tricolour flags, the one in the lead flying a smaller second one at her mainmast truck as well.

Lewrie lifted a telescope and went to the starboard rails. The lead ship was definitely a frigate, the other two . . . ? "Lieutenant de Crillart, could you join me on the quarterdeck for a moment?"

He loaned Charles the telescope.

"Don't happen to *know* them, do you, Charles?"

"Non. I do not reco'nise," de Crillart intoned soberly. "Mais, ze fré-gate eez ze trent-deux . . . ze s'irty-two? She weel 'ave twelve-poun' canon, an 'ze six-poun' canon de chasse et canon de gaillard . . . quar-terdeck? Ze ozzer two are ze corvettes. Vingt canon . . . twen'y, on'y . . . eight-poun', I 'sink."

"*Only*, the man says," Lewrie snorted, flexing his fingers on the wire-wrapped leather hilt of his smallsword. "They'll be up level with us in about half an hour. Range-of-random-shot? What's that with bar-shot and chain-shot? A mile?"

"Oui. Vis you' frégate out zere, z'ough, we not 'ave to bataille all at once. Mon Dieu, merci," de Crillart chuckled, though his mouth looked a touch compressed and white.

Alan took the telescope back, went to the mizzen shrouds again, and scaled them for a better view. Would they stay in a pack, he speculated? Or would the easy pickings encourage them to split up? *Radical* on a slowly converging course, to meet them on their windward, larboard beam, *Cockerel* downwind, but ready to slide along their starboard side, or cut across them to rake the leader . . . take us separately or together?

He couldn't suggest tactics to Captain Braxton, he was senior on the scene. And if he knew who I was aboard this barge, Alan thought in secret glee, he'd be even less willing to listen. No, he'll keep simplicity in mind, he's a cautious man. Eager to make a grand showing after all these years, yet he'll not do anything too rash, too risky. Pass them on the opposing tack, starboard to starboard, then tack around the stern of the last corvette in line, and rake *her*. Then line up behind *Radical* to make a battle line, he wondered? If Braxton thinks we truly *are* another Royal Navy frigate, he might.

Now . . . what would I do, were I the Frog commander, yonder?

Claw upwind, now, he was dead certain. Hold the wind-gauge on the British, and at the same time, sail nearer to those panicky merchantmen, threatening them. Force *Cockerel* and *Radical* to go about first to combine strength, *then* force them to beat up towards the three Frog warships to save the transports. All during that long, labouring approach, fire chain-shot and all, hoping to disable the British frigates before battle was really joined. The French would be faster, they almost always were, so they could out-foot them. And neither *Cockerel* nor *Radical* could point any higher to windward than they could, so it would turn into a long stern chase, with even more long range chain-shot. More chances to disable, then gobble up.

Hmm . . . he sighed to himself, rubbing his unshaven chin; maybe I ought to come about . . . go hard on the wind now? Be level with 'em, or hold the wind-gauge myself. Draw *Cockerel* to me. If Braxton wishes a name for himself, he'll follow along.

"Mister Spendlove! Mister Porter!" he bellowed from his perch. "Hands to the braces! Lay her full and by on the larboard tack! Close-haul!"

"Aye aye, sir!"

"Deck, there! *Cockerel*'s goin' about!" the mainmast lookout screamed, his voice cracking. A tone of wonderment in his voice which drew Lewrie's attention aloft first, before he turned to eye his former ship. *Cockerel* had been reaching across the wind, now out of the sou'-east, her bows pointing nor'east. To harden up closehauled would lay her just a little north of due east, should she remain on the starboard tack, with the wind across her right hand first.

Sure enough, she was foreshortening in the ocular of his telescope.

Should have waited, should have *waited*, Lewrie fretted, growing uncertain of Braxton's tactical skills. Harden up on the starboard tack first, *then* cross the eye of the wind to larboard tack, and beat up to me, cross their bows before they get anywhere near you . . .

This early tack would put him a couple of miles away, on the same course as *Radical*, but out of gun range. *Damme!* He'd done that before, hadn't he—last year, that Frog convoy, and that big forty-four-gun frigate . . . ! Lay off and be safe. *Appear* like he was doing something positive but . . . avoid action? The shrouds swayed as *Radical* leaned to the force of the winds, decks and masts angling to leeward as she hardened up to weather. Lewrie had to take both hands to secure his perch, to slip his arms in around the stays and ratlines for a firmer stance for a moment.

When he raised his telescope again, *Cockerel* had just completed her tack across the wind, sails luffing and spilling, shimmering like a heat wave in the ocular, like bed sheets in a stiff spring breeze out on a line to dry, before her hands could wheel her yards about, haul taut on braces and sheets. And kept *on* turning!

"No, you bastard!" Lewrie muttered in surprise. "Closehauled, at least, you . . . !" For a hopeful moment, he thought *Cockerel* was just clumsy and slow. Every ship usually fell too far off the wind for an instant upon tacking, before hardening back up to the proper course, as close to the wind as she might bear.

But, no. *Cockerel* kept on wheeling about, her yards going farther round until they were almost end-on to his view, courses, top'ls and t'gallants bellying taut and full, the profile of her low, sleek hull entirely presented. *Cockerel* had come about, aye—tacked since it was the quickest maneuvre—and was now sailing west-sou'west, not to join forces with him, not to stand off on a parallel beat, downwind and safe. She was running!

"Oh, you bloody man, you perverse, bloody man!"

Didn't matter, he grumped; me aboard this tub, nor anyone else. 'Least it ain't *personal*, the . . . ah! *He'd* never know who he abandoned. Couldn't care less!

All his plans in shambles, for the moment without a clue, faced with the prospect of fighting those three French ships alone once more. Let down by his own Navy.

"You filthy bastard!" he yelled, just for the temporary relief. "You bloody . . . *coward*!"

CHAPTER 7

Calmly, Lewrie thought, as he climbed down to the quarterdeck; calm and deliberate. They're not Navy, they're not used to my ways . . . Hands behind his back, chin tucked in low, eyes down in thought, pacing to the wheel to look into the compass bowl for a moment.

His natural reaction, so untypically English, as Charles pointed out, would be to curse and rave, gibber with anger, foam at the mouth or fall flat on the deck and pound upon it. Which would set off panic, by the bagful. And there would go any thoughts of resistance from all his already barely-willing volunteers.

What to do, then, he asked himself, scheming in a fury, conflicting notions at odds in his head. Hold this course, keep the wind-gauge? He turned to glower aft.

The two hired transports were astern, just a little left of dead-astern, still running with the sou'east winds large on the larboard side. Close hauling would make no sense for them. They were on their very best point of sail already, and to claw up to windward to try and escape made them slower, their capture even more certain. And sooner. Farther left and beyond were the French warships, astern of the transports, a little downwind of them, sailing only a touch closer to the wind, making rapid time, even so.

They hadn't gone closehauled? he frowned in puzzlement. Waiting another half-hour before they came level with 'em, passed them, really . . . before they turned up towards them, or tried to cut ahead of their bows and take them? Leaving it *damned* late, when they could do it now . . .

Another half-hour, and *Radical* would be so far to windward of the transports, and the French, no one could ever touch them. Though *Radical* would have abandoned them, letting them take the brunt of things, like a sledge in a Russian winter would throw meat scraps to slow down

312

pursuing wolves. Throw out servants, he'd read . . . yum, yum, hot and tasty!

Stacked almost overlapping from his angle of view, frigate in the lead, echeloned down to leeward so each would have clear air on her quarter. Why to *leeward*? he asked the aether. More speed, aye, but . . . for what purpose? Shouldn't they be rushing right at the transports, and at him, too? Beam-reach in line-ahead, and *still* have clear air, no blanketing . . .

"Damme!" he laughed of a sudden. "You greedy pigs!"

The transports were meat on the table, the French could scoop them up anytime. They were standing on, going for the horse transport and the tantalizing glimpse of that two-decker on the sou'west horizon far ahead. And suddenly it came to him—they would separate. With *Cockerel* running away, the lead frigate would dash on, overhaul the two-decker horse transport because she looked such a rich prize, and leave the corvettes to face off with him, *then* take the two ships astern!

"Bosum Porter?" he called. "Hands to the braces. We'll haul our wind. Quartermaster, new course, sou'west. Trim for a beam-reach."

"Aye aye, sir," Porter replied obediently. Yet sounding dubious, as if he was of a mind that sailing high upwind was much safer.

Radical came off her laboured beat, sloughing and slowing, yards reangled to cup the wind that now blew at right-angles across her decks. Those decks levelling as she sat down flat on her keel, on the easiest point of sail. And Lewrie waited, pacing aft to the taffrails, then to the starboard gangway ladder, over and over.

"Deck, there!" the lookout shrilled a few nervous minutes later. "Two chase goin' closehauled astern! Lead ship, standin' on!"

The frigate had left her consorts, stuns'ls and stays'ls still flying, t'gallants and tops'ls bellied wind-ful. The corvettes, though, had drawn level with the stern of the trailing transport and had turned upwind.

"Mister Porter, hands to the braces! Stations to closehaul!"

Radical had slowed on her beam-reach, the transports had made up some ground on her, still labouring, though, about a mile and a half astern, almost in line-ahead behind her.

Right, you bugger, *stay* greedy, he sneered to the distant frigate, standing on so swiftly, so effortlessly. Swung away as she was towards the wind once more, *Radical* would soon have her abeam of her last position. Up to windward of the transports. Two or three miles of hard distance between the more powerful ship and where *Radical* could be in ten minutes. And the corvettes would still be to leeward of him, too.

He waited a little longer, fingers fretting against each other, peering stoically at the frigate, which was now off his starboard quarter. Now? No, not yet. Wait a bit . . . breathe deep to shout? No . . .

"Mister Porter, stations for stays!" he boomed at last. "Ready to come about to the starboard tack! Mister de Crillart, secure your gunners, all tackles a'taut! Bowse the starboard battery secure!"

"Manned!" Porter screeched at last. Lewrie looked down to see de Crillart give him an assuring fist in the air.

"Helm alee! Rise, tacks and sheets!"

Slow, a bit "crank," indifferently balanced with all the civilian stores put aboard catch-as-catch-can, *Radical* swung up to the eyes of the wind, luffing and clattering, groaning and complaining. British men for the most part served the ship, men he'd drilled and trained, aided by raw landsmen who were terribly confused by sail-handling, much less the use of a foreign language. But she came about—crossed the wind. Reluctantly, she was about, on the starboard tack.

"Haul taut! Now, haul! Mains'l haul! Meet her, quartermaster. Nothing to leeward for now! Mister Porter, we'll haul our wind soon! Remain at stations!"

North by east she stood, running almost a reciprocal course to the transports, getting everything flaked down and sorted out, sailors still ready at the braces and jib sheets, driving for a moment within six points of the apparent wind. Rushing back towards the transports, their combined speeds hauling them near rapidly.

"New course, nor'east, quartermaster, helm up! Let her fall off four points, no more. Trim for a reach, Mister Porter! Then prepare to take in the main course."

Suddenly, after what had felt like hours of snail's pace, things were overlapping each other, almost too fast to be dealt with. Leading transport on the larboard bows, now, dashing to abeam in the blink of an eye, trailing transport coming up rapidly. French corvettes beyond, and still not near enough to ease off their beats to open fire, just beyond the range-of-random-shot. *Radical* slowing, as she lost the drive of the main course. The transports weren't half a mile alee. People cheering, waving coats and hats.

Haven't a bloody clue, he sneered. But thankee, anyway. Second transport, *huge* two-decker, working alive like a crowded anthill, awash in people, coming up fast, her bowsprit framed in the foremast chains, just over the larboard anchor's cat-head.

"Helm up, quartermaster, shave her arse! Ease her, Porter! Man for a gybe! Mister de Crillart, once we've gybed round the transport . . . be ready to open fire on the nearest corvette with the starboard battery!"

Radical pointed herself at the transport's sides, changing the cheers to cries of consternation for a moment. Abeam of her, passing close, jib boom aimed at her quarter-galleries and stern, the helmsmen judging it to a nicety of perfection to dash almost under her counter and transom . . . using them as a shield, a fence between *Radical* and the corvettes.

"Ready to wear ship!" he called. "Main clew garnets, buntlines, spanker brails, weather main, lee cro' jack braces . . . haul taut!"

The transport's stern was a pistol-shot away, before the mizzen chains. A second's more separation, then . . .

"Up, mains'l and spanker, clear away after bowlines, brace in on the afteryards! Up helm!" Lewrie yelled, on tiptoes with excitement.

Around *Radical* came again, balky and truculent, even slower than she'd been to tack, without the main course's power, yet trimming about, her crew throwing themselves upon the proper rigging from long training.

Round she came, until she lay with her bows due west, gun ports coming open, gunners hopping about to remove quoins below the breeches for maximum elevation, shimming them up again as they aimed, a touch at a time, preparing to concentrate their fire on the leading corvette, the one nearest them, about a mile away, still close-hauled.

"Préparez . . . *tirez!*" de Crillart shouted, waiting for the uproll.

Radical's starboard broadside went off as one; twelve-pounders firing solid-shot, the eighteen-pounders spewing disabling-shot. Gigantic gushes of powder-smoke wreathed her, to be whisked away to leeward, thinning out as her shot neared the target, shrieking and wailing as they flailed in the air, tumbling and spinning.

They threw themselves on the guns, to swab out, clear the vents, directing gawping civilians to keep their eyes inboard, on their work, for their very lives. Only the senior gunners knelt to peer out empty gun ports to see the results, linstocks at their sides, jammed in the deck by the sharp ends like ancient spearmen. Powder monkeys scampered up with fresh charges. Loaders hefted more disabling-shot.

"Well, damme!" Lewrie gloated as the corvette was struck; struck for fair! She seemed to quiver from mast-trucks to keel as that flailing, slashing ironmongery amputated her fore-royal mast, tore away her foret'gallant yard, sliced through fore stays and jib halliards, spilling everything forward of the mast into a sagging ruin! And tore gaping holes in her fore-tops'l and course, spilling their wind, those ravaged sails ripping open, tearing across as far as the bolt-rope edges!

"You *see*, mon ami?" de Crillart crowed. "Now, encore!"

Guns charged and shotted, run out through the ports, cartridges punctured and vents primed. Slowly, clumsily, guns squealing and complaining on their low trucks, tacklemen taking forever—one side of a piece hauled too forcefully, the other too weakly, jibbering them about before the ports as if they were iron mastiffs hunting for a scent.

The corvette had fallen off the wind—*had* to fall off, with her windward-driving jibs gone, all unbalanced. She showed her profile, but also began to display a line of open gun ports, parallel to *Radical*.

Quoins inserted deeper this time, lowering the aim of the barrels, gunners shouting and babbling, waving their hands to instruct their raw assistants to shift the lay of the guns with crow levers and handspikes to right or left. Then the excess crewmen were hustling away to avoid the recoil, the roar and the stink, after overhauling the tackles. A last onceover, then matches were blown on, lowered near the vents . . .

On the uproll. "Tirez!"

Another brutal clap of sound, another howling broadside! Guns rolled backwards to snub on the breeching ropes, making the stout bulwarks cry, rope groan, iron ring-bolts squeal. They juddered and they reeked, some slewed off-line, gushing thin trails of spent smoke. And their frigate, shaken to her heart by the force of the run-back.

A moaning in the air, a shrill shrieking, as round-shot returned toward them. Dull thuds, splashes alongside towering over the bulwarks, iron ball flying across the ship, sizzling sibilantly. Crisp bangs up above, where the furled main-course yard was struck, one end turning to a shattered stub as the ball glanced off.

The corvette twitched anew, her mainmast struck this time. More destruction rained down from aloft onto her decks, to dangle in her overhead boarding nettings. There was a hole in her spanker where barshot pierced it, a handful of men in her mainmast fighting-top spilled out by a whirling multiple bar-shot. Her main t'gallant mast above shook, then slowly leaned forward under the press of the wind, as upper shroud lines parted, the cross-tree braces shattered.

More fire was returned, raggedly. As if in retribution, a shot screamed over *Radical*'s quarterdeck, slapping a hole in her spanker . . . just over Lewrie's head. Forward, the starboard gangway bulwark caved in as an eight-pounder round-shot pierced it, making a rent about two feet across, and the air was awhirl with jagged oak splinters. Three French infantrymen standing behind the rent were ripped away, tossed over the rope railings into the waist, onto the gun deck, riddled with wood and iron shards. Another ball struck lower down, below the gunwale, with a dull *thonk*, creating wails of sudden terror among the noncombatants on the orlop deck. A third hit a closed gun port, behind which tacklemen were sheltering, waiting for orders to throw themselves on the guns once more. There were screams of pain and disbelief as two volunteers were cut down, cries from a dozen more throats as they beheld the ruins of men, twitching and thrashing bloody at their feet.

Lieutenant de Crillart and his senior gunners were there in an instant, to shout them down, shove them back to their duties, urging them to be brave . . . no longer gently tutorial. The time was past for that.

"Loblolly boys!" Lewrie shouted, directing the pasty whey-faces framed in the midships companionway hatch. "Help 'em, damn yer eyes!" The dentist appeared, seized the one at the top of the companionway ladder and dragged him out. They skittered fearful, as low as hounds to the decks, following him with a mess table turned into a stretcher. Three men were dead, abandoned round the base of the mainmast, while two who screamed and wept were carried below to whatever further horrors awaited them at the surgeons' hands.

The range had closed to about three-quarters of a mile. Alan took a quick look astern for the second corvette. She was coming on, still on the wind, bows pointed almost directly at him. There was a bloom of gunsmoke from her larboard forecastle chase gun. Still about a mile off, he decided; still time to hurt the other even worse.

"Hit her again, Charles! Rip her guts out!" he shouted. "Hurry!"

Shocked as they were, though, the gun crews hadn't much "hurry" in them. A well-served artillery piece could average three rounds in two minutes, in Royal Navy practice. These poor fellows were lucky to get off one in a minute and a half.

The corvette managed to fire again, a ragged, stuttering broadside. More shot coming for them, trembling volunteers flinging themselves flat on the deck to hide from it. *Radical* quivered as she was struck twice, thrice . . . then thrice again.

Not bad shootin', Lewrie thought, for a crew who'd been in port so long, without much chance for live-firing practice. Quivering in his boots himself, willing himself not to flinch or duck. Damme!

There was a crash above his head, a groan of rivened timber, and he looked up to see their mizzen-royal and t'gallant masts shot away, to come down in a spiral like a badly sawn tree!

"Ware below!" he shouted, scampering aft, away from its arrival. Jack-knifing upon themselves, the masts dropped, trailing rope rigging and furled canvas, yard ends flailing blindly, ripping across the face of the mizzen tops'l before the entire mess speared into the deck just at the forward edge of the quarterdeck, hung up by the broken spars on the nettings over the waist. Down with it had come two topmen, and one of the aristocratic French marksmen from the fighting-top.

"Cut it away, sir?" Spendlove yelled through chattering teeth at his side.

"No men to spare," Lewrie groaned. "No, leave it. But see to the men who were aloft."

"Aye, sir," Spendlove nodded, his eyes wide. But he dashed off on his errand, chivvying loblolly boys to their ministrations.

"Préparez!" de Crillart screeched from forward and below, ordering his spare tacklemen away to the sides. "Tirez!"

Slow they might be, quaking and gulping hot bile in near terror, but the gun crews were still slaving away, sticking to it like men. A broadside lashed out and away, ordered, controlled and well aimed by the steadiest older men. Eight-pounders yapping, twelve-pounders erupting in harsher barks . . . and the four eighteen-pounders bellowing, almost going off as one immense avalanche of noise, fired on the uproll, when the ship would hang pent for a breathless second of steadiness.

The French corvette took the brunt of it, as the sea beside her frothed with near misses and ricochets from the lighter guns. Heavier twelve-pound round-shot tore through her sides this time, flinging bulwarks and scantlings into trash, flicking planks into the air. And her mainmast was shot away completely! It was shorn off, halfway between gun deck and fighting-top, that massive trunk carved in twain. It jumped, hung suspended for a second upon the very air, then the shattered butt slid forward, and it teetered, half-turned and fell to starboard, and all above it came crashing down in disparate bits, the fighting-top to hammer itself onto her starboard gangway, crushing everything beneath its brutal weight! She showed her coppering as she rolled and rocked.

"Cheer, lads, cheer!" Lewrie shouted, encouraging his English sailors. "Charles! Vivats, vive . . . what you call 'em! Make 'em yell and cheer! Look what they just *did*!"

The poor, scared buggers, he thought. Aye, cheer, you bastards. Put some heart in yourselves, at last! You *can* do it, if you try!

For a moment, they gaped in total disbelief, then began to yell, to throw their hats in the air, clap each other on the back, embrace and buss in Gallic fashion, and exult.

Not Navy practice, is it, Alan asked himself with a smirk, but they needed that. Now maybe they'll have more confidence. Now, just where do we stand? he wondered, peering about. He went to the side to look out with his telescope, past the ruin of the corvette, which was sagging down to leeward, all her masts and sails trailing over the side and acting like a sea anchor. She wouldn't be going anywhere but round about in circles for awhile, not until they hacked all that loose. And without replacement upper masts and mainmast, nowhere very quickly for some time after, either, with only her mizzen standing.

The frigate! The most dangerous warship present had finally put about, taken in her stuns'ls and stays'ls, and was close on the wind on the larboard tack. But she was at least four miles down alee, and four more miles farther to the nor'west. To beat back to *Radical* where she was at the moment would be the better part of an hour, since she would have to tack first. And Lewrie was mortal certain he'd not be anywhere near his current position when she arrived.

The second corvette had fallen off, had hauled her wind, a little below the ruin of the first, as if she were about to go alongside to aid her. She was less than a mile off, still on *Radical's* starboard quarter.

No, not to aid, Lewrie saw—to shoot! Her gun ports were open, already blossoming with orange-y flashes and gushes of smoke! Feathers of spray leaped into the air astern, glass and transom wood shattered as round-shot lashed her stern. A portion of the taffrail went flying, and one of the lanterns burst asunder.

"Cease fire, cease fire!" he directed. "Mister Porter, lay us on the wind! Man the braces and sheets, ready to haul taut! Quartermaster, helm alee. Lay her full and by."

"Full an' by, sir, aye," the senior man grunted, already heaving on the spokes.

He'd whittled the odds down, thoroughly disabled one corvette—and most importantly, placed himself so advantageously that the frigate might have to spend the rest of the morning to catch him up. And closehauled, *Radical* would all the time be driving roughly sou-sou'west, to the Balearics, into shelter, into the patrol areas, perhaps, of Spanish warships which might aid him.

No, he thought; let's not be greedy ourselves. Get back up to windward, draw this last one after us, if he wishes. I think we might run him a decent chase. He follows us, the transports get clean away, too. If he follows.

With a shrug, he realised that the corvette and frigate might be more amenable to going to the aid of their crippled consort, or bagging the transports, after all, and letting *Radical* escape, too tough a bone to gnaw. Realising, too, that he'd shot his bolt, in essence. Fought and won, without getting his precious civilian charges slaughtered by artillery and sword-swinging boarders. Well, not too many, he amended.

Yet, what if they went after the transports, at least? Aye, I've saved most of my own, but those others are just as full of émigrés, just as packed with women and children. Can I turn a blind eye? Perhaps I must. Every man for himself now, and save what you can?

The corvette astern turned back onto the wind, barely a minute after *Radical* had altered course. This put her, from Lewrie's view by the wheel, just atop the starboard corner of the taffrail, bows-on to him, heeled hard over as she laboured for every last inch of windward progress. She got a gust, he saw, a puff of wind that he did not, and she pinched up higher as that gust backed, clawing out ten yards or so.

"Mister Porter, I think we're ready to send the topmen to loose the fore and main t'gallants," Lewrie ordered, then checked himself . . . aghast. "And let fall the main course! Let fall and sheet home!" He flushed with anger that he'd been so remiss, so muzzy without sleep!

As more canvas appeared aloft, *Radical* heeled further over and began to surge, hobbyhorsing over the waves, casting first her bows, then her stern towards the sky. Spray began to dash alongside, droplets wetting the starboard gangway.

"Mister Lewrie, sir," Cony called, appearing from below. "Got a leak, sir. Starb'rd side, forrud. Betwixt th' cat-head an' fore chains. Think we got hulled by one o' their shot."

"Bad?" he muttered.

"On this tack, aye, sir," Cony winced. "Suckin' water like a drain. Got a couple o' chair-makers down there, nailin' on a patch t' slow h'it down, but we need to fother a patch from over-side. There's nigh on five inch o' water in th' bilges now, an' it's climbin'. An' the seams're workin', o' course, but that's nothin' new, sir. But, I 'spects, long'z we beat t' windward, sir, they'll work 'arder. Need t' pump soon, sir."

A hole in her quick-work, starboard side, heeled over starboard, too— that would practically shovel water into her. And she'd flood forrud, when what she needed most of all, closehauled, was for the bows to ride high and light over the water, reducing the effort which went into beating. Should her bow end get too heavy, she'd slough in and snuffle, all the fineness of her entry and forefoot cancelled out.

"Tell Mister de Crillart to secure his guns for now," Lewrie decided after a moment's thought. "Work the forrud chain pumps. Maybe some will trickle past, aft. And tell Mister de Crillart to send men to the quarterdeck. We'll shift two of the eight-pounders right-aft to the taffrail, for stern-chasers. Maybe raise her bows a couple of inches, and take some pressure off the shot hole. Fother from inboard, spare sail and bosun's stores, once your . . . chair-makers finish their plugs."

"Aye, sir."

There was a rustling in the air, an atonal whistling that rose up the scales. Then round-shot cracked overhead, to sail past and hit far up to windward on the larboard side. The French corvette had her bow-chasers working. *Radical* heeled a little farther and slowed.

"Watch yer luff!" Lewrie said, rounding on the helmsmen.

"Wind veered ahead, sir. 'Adda bear off," the senior hand replied, working on a massive tobacco quid, gazing aloft, as he regained the spokes he'd lost, sailing most intently by his luff, and the Devil with the compass at that moment. Course did not matter; but the very razor's edge of the apparent wind, where lay safety in both speed and windward advantage, did.

Another shot from the corvette astern, this time pocking a hole in the main tops'l, as gunners loosed one of the quarterdeck eight-pounders from the breeching-rope ring-bolts, and laid on block and tackle to a fresh set, farther aft. Tethered like a trussed hog, the cannon must be restrained, moved gingerly from one lashing to the next, before being sited at one of the pair of stern-chase gun ports in the taffrail.

The French corvette reached the point in *Radical's* wake where the wind had veered ahead. She wavered, fell off perhaps a point, no more. And sailed through it, pinching up once more as the wind steadied. Pinched up higher, luffing up a touch, trading forward progress for another ten yards uphill to weather. She was head-reaching them.

And she was faster, Lewrie realised by the time the first gun was ready at the taffrail, and the second began to be moved. Larger, she loomed back there, framed now from the wheel squarely in the center of the taffrail. She'd gained about one hundred yards in a little less than five minutes.

Three-quarters of a mile . . . Lewrie's mind creaked over his sums. Two thousand yards to the sea mile, five minutes to make an hundred so . . . she'll have her jib boom over the rail in a little over an *hour*?

A horrible harpy-like ululation came up from astern. There was a crash forward, aloft. The main t'gallant yard shattered, lee side draping like a broken wing. Multiple bar-shot.

"Maybe less than an hour," he sighed softly, sensing defeat at last. "Goddamn fool! Could have *stayed* to windward, run, never took time to fight! Gave up a mile advantage to windward . . . for nothing!"

"Le canon, il est préparée, capitain," a French gunner called out, patting the breech of his eight-pounder. "Nous tirerons?"

"Oui. Tirez. Blaze away," Lewrie nodded, too spent to care.

The gunner directed his small crew to charge, to shot, to run-out. He knelt, hopped, fiddled with the quoin, had it spiked to the right a touch, then waved the men away. He primed, waited . . . then lit it off. With a sharp bang the eight-pounder reeled inwards. A waterspout leaped up to the right of the corvette's bows, close under her jib boom and bowsprit.

Lewrie watched, groggily detached and above it all. There was a chance, he was sure, that their stern-chasers *might* damage the French vessel enough to slow her, to rob her of just enough speed to reel out this pursuit 'til nightfall. Late afternoon *should* fetch Minorca under *Radical's* bows. Did God grant them just a *morsel* of luck . . . !

The corvette fired in reply; both her bow-chasers barked together this time, so near was she to being dead astern, framed on the very last vestige of his ship's foaming, spreading wake. One ball flew high, low above the starboard gangway, to smash into the forecastle bulkhead up forward. The second slammed into her transom again, low down, below the wardroom windows. There were muffled screams below. If the surgeons had been using the midshipmen's berth, the cockpit, as their surgery . . . ! On the orlop! Those were women's screams!

Just as easily, the corvette could pick her apart, too. Shoot *Radical's* rigging to lace and slow her down, rendering her helpless. Then surge alongside, cannon blazing point-blank, boarders ready . . . Strike the colours, he mused? Surrender to the inevitable?

Then those French boarders, those revolutionary, Republican men with steel in their hands and blood lust in their eyes, would murder everyone aboard, soon as they found out what his passengers were, and cheat the guillotines. British sailors could expect no better treatment, either. They'd butcher and slaughter as merciless as pirates, those victory-drunk, vengeful French Republican sailors, niceties of nationality be-damned.

For a stark moment of bleakness, Lewrie looked upon his death as a given, an inevitability soon to be realised. Outrunning them wasn't in the cards. One more well-aimed shot could end it all, and render his ship as crippled as that first unfortunate corvette.

God, a little help here, I'm runnin' out of options, he prayed. Haven't a bloody *clue* what to do next. Shot my last bolt? So weary I can't *think*! Got a storm in Your pockets? A slant of wind?

Another round-shot sighed in, singing a piccolo tune. Smashed into the transom again, blowing a cloud of splinters aloft from starboard as it demolished the wardroom quarter-gallery.

He surprised himself when he snickered aloud at that.

Thankee, God! Already scared so shitless . . . and here they just blew out the 'jakes'! Strike? Stand on, clueless . . . or fight?

"Mister Spendlove? Oh, there you are," Lewrie said of a sudden, turning away from his fell musings. "Right, then. Summon all the officers, foot, horse and Marine. We've some scheming to do."

CHAPTER 8

"We are too slow," Lewrie announced, amidships of the quarterdeck nettings, looking down into the waist at his assembled "crewmen." And Lieutenant de Crillart translated for him, phrase for grim phrase. "We cannot outrun her. We cannot strike our colours, either, and surrender. You know what that would mean . . . for yourselves . . . and your families."

As that was turned into French, he peered into their bleak-set faces, lips compressed and mouths pale. Women and children had come up from the horrors of the echoing, drumming orlop, drawn by the cheering, and the lack of dangerous noises which had followed, the absence of broadsides being fired, gun-trucks thundering and squealing. A bang or two now and then from far aft, the keen of round-shot from the Frog corvette was nothing in comparison. They, too, stood with faces grim. Some whimpered, cooed to vexsome, querulous children, dandled babes in arms who sensed what was to come, without waiting for a translation.

They stood with their men where they could, those who still had men, listening as Lewrie stood four-square above them, delivering what even he thought was a "whistling past the graveyard" peroration.

Roman Legions got perorated before every battle, to boost their fighting spirit, Alan recalled from translating so many of them in his school-day Latin classes—wondering if his was on a par with the ones delivered just before Lake Trasimeno, or Crassus's before his army was wiped out at Cannae.

"The Royal Navy frigate put about to summon help," he lied with a straight face, unable to tell them they were beyond aid. "The French frigate downwind yonder is too far away to matter. This last enemy vessel pursuing us is our greatest danger."

While Charles turned that into French, he looked alee, raising his eyebrows in perhaps the only delight he could discover. The enemy frigate *was* too far downwind, dithering. She'd come hard on the wind on the larboard tack for a time, clawing her way south, but had gone about to starboard tack, to take a look at her injured consort before hardening up once more. She'd abandoned her pursuit of the two-decker on the horizon and the horse transport, and was now approaching those two transports Lewrie had earlier used as shields, content with taking *something*, at least, after a frustrating morning's work. That put her five miles alee, instead of four, and a full hour away, even should the transports strike to her at once.

"Ahum," Charles prompted with a fisted cough, drawing Lewrie inboard once more.

"They have well-drilled gun crews . . . *we* do not," Alan continued, pointing astern. As if in punctuation, two round-shot droned overhead, making everyone duck and cringe. "We cannot stand . . . beam to beam . . . and trade shot with them. But!" he cried, leaning one hand on the net and light wood railing, above the tangle of fallen mizzen topmasts, and pointing at them with the other. "You have defeated one ship. And you will defeat this one! We will close with her . . . they will not expect us to do that. We will lash to her . . . and we will board her! We have men of the 18th Regiment of Foot, the fearsome Royal Irish, among us. Among us we have brave infantry, Royalist infantry . . . gallant cavalrymen. And we have hard-handed men of the French Royal Navy . . . and best of all . . . my British tars . . . shoulder to shoulder . . . with their cutlasses . . . they may cut and slash their way to the Gates of Hell, may the Devil himself take arms against them!"

Right, I don't believe it, either, Alan groaned to himself, seeing what little encouragement the French civilians felt to his bloodthirsty promises, his mounting harangue. They looked like bored voters.

"And when we board her," Lewrie concluded, "you courageous gentlemen of la belle France . . . you must strike them down! Sans merci! It is your blood or theirs. We must conquer them . . . or they will conquer you. When the time comes, fearless gentlemen of France . . ."

Bloody toady's what you are, me lad, he thought, in spite of all.

"Strike for your beloved, murdered monarchs! Strike for your nation! Strike for your honour! And strike," Lewrie softened from a hoarse shout to a voice they had to strain to hear, "for the lives of your wives . . . your children . . . your dear ones . . . strike to protect the helpless babes. Put your own lives at risk . . . and fight like true men. 'Stead of kneeling like whipped animals at the foot of the guillotine."

He paused, seeing some steel appear in their eyes, some heads up more erect. And some trembling like treed cats, with tears upon their cheeks, faces twisted with impending grief and fear into death grimaces.

"We dare all!" he called, loud once more. "We will fight! As men! If we die as men . . . we die on our feet, not on our knees! They . . . those Revolutionaries astern of us, have only their hatred to die for. Where are *their* families, where are *their* convictions? Be ready!"

The two stern-chasers went off with a close double bang, to end his peroration. And a thin cheer from the gunners aft, who'd finally hit something, said more than anything he could further compose.

He looked to Madame Hortense de Crillart beside her son Louis, trying to be as brave as a Spartan matron who'd send her children off to battle, urging them to come home "with your shield . . . or on it"— dead before dishonoured. Sophie de Maubeuge stood trembling with her, eyes wide in fear, eyes only for Charles. Phoebe Aretino, not too far away from them, among the lower-class dependents . . . and the few suddenly widowed or orphaned, therefore shunned, as if it was catching. "The ladies must go below once more, out of harm's way. See to your children and each other. Be as courageous as your menfolk will be."

Lewrie turned away, to stride to the wheel and look aft at his foe. She was up within a half a mile of them by then, edging even more upwind of *Radical*. He could see down her starboard side.

"Magnifique, mon ami," Lieutenant de Crillart said, coming to join him. "Ve Français . . . trés dramatique, hein? I add to you' speech, pardon . . . on'y un peu. Now, vot ve do to defeat zem?"

"Frankly, Charles, I haven't a bloody clue," Lewrie confessed.

"Ah."

The corvette would have to swing off the wind and lose all the progress she'd made upon them, if she wished to employ her main artillery. To swing up harder to the wind would put her in-irons, so it was not the starboard battery, which he could see, that would be the threat. She could fall off, haul her wind, slew about briefly, and touch off a broadside from her larboard battery before coming back to full-and-by. But that would sacrifice her slight, and hard-won, windward advantage. And perhaps an eighth of a mile of separation, which she would have to make back up.

"She'll stand on, as she is," Lewrie muttered aloud. "Quarter-hour more, and she'll be upwind of us . . . 'bout an hundred yards or so. And off our larboard quarter. That is, if they don't shoot something else away from our rigging beforehand."

"Ze wind an' sea . . ." Charles pointed out with a sour shrug: a drop in the wind, a calming of the seas. Neither vessel hobbyhorsed any longer, cleaving smoother paths. That was advantage to the French, they knew. They would have less wave resistance, could go faster to windward, and pinch up to gain even more windward position without a heavy quarter-sea butting against their bows when they did so. And it would make their fore deck a much less boisterous gun platform, so their aim would surely improve.

"Préparez . . . tirez!" one of the French gunners called out to his men. The larboard, upwind stern-chaser barked. "Hourra! Le coup au but!" he crowed in triumph.

"Oh, well shot!" Lewrie exclaimed. The eight-pounder round-shot had hit along the starboard side, fine on the bows, among the pin-rails for the jib sheets, right next to the starboard bow-chaser. Men had spilled wounded or frightened from the gun. And the corvette's jib sheets had been set free. The taut ellipses luffed and spilled wind, flagging to leeward, bulging flaccid, losing their knife-edge tautness. Inner and outer flying jibs and fore topmast stays'ls balanced a ship working to windward, gave her the fore-and-aft drive to lay her there, slicing the apparent wind. Without them, she would have to fall off. Square sails, no matter how braced round, could never drive a ship that close to the wind.

The corvette slewed, indeed, heeling farther to starboard for a moment, her helm down to keep what they had. For a second, it appeared she might round up higher, yielding to weather-helm. But she did fall off at last, as men raced to control those sheets, haul them flat-in, and belay them once more. But when she settled, under full control . . . she was dead-astern. Her windward advantage had been lost!

"A quarter-hour to close to musket-shot, but . . ." Lewrie grinned.

That close-aboard, dead in my wake, he schemed; let's say we haul our wind, give him the starboard battery, a point-blank broadside . . . no, he'll take it, then rush on past our stern. I'd have to fall away almost dead downwind to fire, and that'd lay our stern open for her to rake us . . .

That didn't sound promising. A stern-rake would expose everyone below, everyone on the gun deck, to round-shot bowling through the thin transom timbers, the great-cabins and wardroom, the orlop cockpit; an avalanche of iron, tumbling and ricocheting along her entire hull, the round-shot caroming from the thick hull timbers, contained within. There could be fifty . . . sixty dead and wounded in a twinkling. All his precious fighting men . . . women and children, too.

Best take it abeam, Lewrie thought; *Radical*'s a forty-gun frigate—built to take twelve-pounder fire. Reenforced to take eighteen-pounder shot? It'd make sense for them to stiffen her, to take the recoil of her new gun batteries, if nothing else. I can stand her eight-pounders a lot easier than her timbers could my shot, even hull to hull!

Or not take her fire at all? Bow-rake *her*! Let her stand on as she is, and . . . ! Lewrie almost squirmed with hopeful expectation.

"Quartermaster?"

"Aye, sir?"

"Let her fall off, slowly. Very slowly," Lewrie commanded. "A half a point, no more. Give it up, spoke at a time."

"Haul our wind, sir?" the helmsman yelped, turning to look over his shoulder at him for a dread, outraged instant, before discipline and years of training to concentrate aloft and nowhere else took over. "Aye aye, sir," he said at last, returning his concentration to the coach-whip of the pendant overhead, the luffs of the mainmast sails. He eased the helm a single spoke, then began counting to himself, under his breath, before he'd yield the second.

"Alain . . . pourquoi?" de Crillart demanded, similarly outraged.

"Why, to *have* the bastard, Charles!" Alan replied, almost gleeful. "To *have* the bastard! Mister Porter, come to the quarterdeck!"

"Aye, sir?" Porter said, hat in hand. "Leak, sir? They be nigh to a foot below now, if that's wot y'r askin' 'bout, Mr. Lewrie."

"Mostly aft?" Lewrie asked with a chuckle.

"Well, aye, sir," Porter rejoined, seeing nothing humourous about their predicament. "Wot got past th' forrud chain-pumps."

"That'll make her quicker to come about, the bows light and the stern heavier," Lewrie nodded, seeming pleased. "When I give you the word, Mister Porter, I want the hands to brace her round, like we were tacking. Before that . . . just before, I want everything aloft scandalised, brailed up damned sharp, in Spanish reefs. Then belayed, before every hand takes arms, ready for boarding."

He glanced astern, as the corvette's bow-chasers were got back in action, barking shrill as terriers.

"We might have about ten minutes, Mr. Porter. I wish you to be ready with at least four grapnels. Two light'uns, for tossing, when I give you the order. And two more on heavier lines . . . three'r four-inch manila that can take a strain. About half a cable each for the heavy ones . . . ready round the capstans, fore and aft. Got that?"

"Aye, sir, I *think* so. Scandalise, brail up . . . the first order. Stations for stays, the second. Two light grapnels, and two heavy, to the capstans. Then 'all-hands' to the gangways as boarders."

"Until the heavy grapnels are across, and a strain taken, leave a crew at the capstans, Mr. Porter. Three men each, even after, so we stay put. More important, *she* stays where we put her."

"Aye aye, sir," Porter agreed, though mystified.

"I'm giving her the wind-gauge, Porter," Lewrie explained, with a hand on the man's shoulder. "She'll take it, certain. Then, when we are too close and she's going to shoot us to flinders . . . we'll brail up and slow down like we just threw over a sea anchor. Tack right up, in-irons, across her bows, and grapnel to her. With *our* guns, Charles . . ." he said, turning to look at de Crillart . . . "with *our* guns aimed point-blank, in a bow-rake, and none but her bow-chasers able to bear upon *us*! And Major de Mariel?" he called, letting Porter go. "Then your sharpshooters will clear her fore decks, and we will board. My sailors first, with pistols and cutlasses. And the heavy grapnels . . . then, Lieutenant Kennedy, your company after us. Cover my men with volley-fire, whilst we affix the grapnels. After that, gentlemen . . . it'll be bare steel, and Devil take the hindmost! Then we all board her, over her bows, to support my sailors and Lieutenant Kennedy's 18th Foot. To *take* her, gentlemen. To take her, before she can hope to take us! A fight to the finish, toe to toe. And no quarter until we stand upon her quarterdeck . . . and cut her colours down!"

CHAPTER 9

Soldiers gathered to larboard, huddling below on the gun deck or hunkered down behind the bulwarks, on their knees. Aristocrats in the tops, cautioned to clear the enemy's foredeck; rifled hunting guns loaded and primed. Once again, Lewrie deplored his stupidity, dearly wishing he had but three light swivel guns aloft, one in each fighting-top, to spew clouds of pistol-ball or langridge.

Lieutenant de Crillart was amidships in the waist, his gunners low to the deck behind the guns of the larboard battery, which had been run-in, charged and shotted, primed, and run-out to the port sills, double-shotted with their few precious grape-shot loads atop solid-shot, with the powder monkeys ready with only one more cartridge bag, the gunners ready with only two more round-shot for a second double-shotted broadside, before they'd abandon their guns, take up small arms, and board.

It was a slender hope, he knew, a tenuous, neck-or-nothing act of desperation, no matter how enthusiastically he had couched his plan to the others. He paced to the windward bulwarks of the quarterdeck, studying his command, looking astern at the French corvette. She was now within two hundred yards of *Radical*'s stern, banging away with her starboard bow-chaser about once a minute, and employing her two forrudmost main-battery eight-pounders which could be crowed or levered about to bear. Whilst his own gunners had been reduced to the single twelve-pounder in the great-cabins of the larboard battery, and the lone eight-pounder stern-chaser to larboard, as well.

The frigate? He turned to look to the north, downwind. There she was, overhauling the trailing transport at last, gunsmoke shrouding her side, the transport attempting to shoot back. But too far off to even hear the reports of their guns.

The corvette, again—perhaps twenty yards closer, up to windward by about a single musket-shot.

"Quartermaster? Nothing more to loo'rd," he called. "Begin to luff *up*, spoke at a time. Very slowly."

He heard the clinking of bottles somewhere.

Damned good idea, he thought; someone's thinking. Liquor your boots for *this* madness. And wishing he had a glass of something, too.

"Sir?" Cony called to him from the waist.

"Aye, Cony?" He forced himself to grin, going forward to look at his long-time man. "Bloody Hell, Cony, there a dram left for me?"

Will Cony held an entire armful of squat port bottles, swaying a bit more than the sea demanded, as if he'd been into all of them. With him was an older French gunner, who bore a short, smouldering linstock with slow match coiled about its length, and laid in the top fork.

"Nary a drop, sir, sorry," Cony laughed. "Me an' monsooer Ahnree, here . . . sorta sampled it, like."

"Sampled, aye, you rogue," Lewrie scowled.

"Aye, sir . . . sampled. But poured h'it overside, mostly. Sir, do ya 'member Spratly Island, sir? Them pirates' wine bottles, an' th' whale oil we foun'?"

"God's sake, Cony, we don't wish to *burn* her!"

"Nossir, but Mr. Bittfield, 'e cut me some slow-match fusees, an' 'twixt us, 'im an' 'is powder yeomen, we made up some grenadoes. Oncet we're aboard, sir . . . thought they might come in 'andy." Cony chortled, quite half-seas-over after his "sampling," and full of cherry-merry bonhomie. "Mayn't kill too many, do they work. But they might put th' wind up 'em, yonder. Keep 'em from rushing th' foc's'le too eager."

"Cony, you're a godsend. Aye, good thinking," Lewrie praised. "Wish I'd had half the wits to think of 'em, myself! Go at 'em, man. And Cony?"

"Aye, sir?"

"I expect to see you among the quick, once we're done. I don't relish breaking in a new bosun's mate after all this time, any more'n you . . . well," Lewrie said, turning sombre. "God go with you, and all good fortune, Will Cony."

"Same t'yew, sir," Cony chirped. "B'sides, sir, z'much trouble I'm in back in Anglesgreen? I reckon the Good Lord knows a rogue and a weed when 'E sees one, Mister Lewrie. An' 'E jus' might get a laugh outa seein' me try t' wriggle, when we gets back 'ome."

"True enough," Lewrie laughed, turning back to his worries.

Dear Lord, You know Your weeds, don't You, Lewrie addressed his Maker silently; You know *me* for a rogue, already. I'm sorry 'bout my doin's in Naples. I'm sorry for . . . well, no, I'm *not* really sorry 'bout Phoebe. Plain truth, Lord? Started out of sympathy—pity for her. Now . . . God save me, I think I'm half in *love* with the little mort! I fall before the hour's out—thankee for Caroline, and the children. Look after 'em for me, as best You're able. And—thankee for Phoebe, Lord. You made a poor rakehell sailor damn' . . . *awfully* happy, for a few days. Don't let any harm come to her. I left a note, should I not be 'mongst the quick when this is over. Let 'em find it, so she could draw on my funds, start over somewhere. Not be . . .

He shook himself all over, lifted his head and took a deep lungful of air to clear his gloomy thoughts. There was the corvette, close now. Less than one hundred yards astern, less than fifty yards upwind. More of her starboard gun ports were opening as she ran them out to fire. They'd bear now, levered to the forrudmost rims of the gun ports. But even with quoins fully out, breeches hard on the carriages, she'd not be able to shoot high enough to damage rigging or harm the upper decks, as heeled-over as she was by the press of wind. Another advantage to be below her, he took time to gloat, the one thing he had over which he *could* gloat. These last few minutes of stern-chase they had not been able to fire at anything but his waterline or his stern. Up to windward, the lee guns were always canted too *low* for good gunnery.

He squatted down as the corvette let fly, even so. Four balls struck almost immediately, *thonking* into *Radical* below the quarterdeck. There were screams, womanly cries, grunts of alarm from men. But his ship had taken the corvette's best fire, and his frigate's timbers had proven tough enough to hold.

He stood back up, wincing as some French marksmen began to fire with their muskets. A ball whistled past his ears like a bumblebee. Alan ignored it, judging his moment. Lifting his arms slowly, taking in a breath with which to scream . . . wait for it . . . wait for it . . . !

Now!

"Porter!" he bawled, feeling faint and dizzy with the effort he put into his cry. "Scandalise her! Quartermaster, helm hard alee! Ready, the larboard battery! Troops on deck, muster in the waist!"

Round she came, luffing up to windward, yards crying and sails cracking like gun shots, masts groaning and loose gear coming adrift from aloft. The square sails were being brailed up, goosewinged by Spanish reefs, the foresails and jibs' sheets freed, the braces let ease. *Radical* slowed quickly, going from a painful struggle to flee to a weak surrender, the sort of rubbery-legged shudder a deer chased to exhaustion might display as it came to a halt at last, tongue lolling and ribs heaving to face the dogs, and its death.

The French corvette stood on for a startled moment, laid as full and by as she could lay, as *Radical* fetched up across her course, under her bows, almost at right-angles to her. She began to swing away, haul her wind, hoping to shave past *Radical*'s stern, within spitting distance.

But Lewrie's borrowed frigate had come up in-irons, dead in the eye of the wind, her square-sail yards purposely thrown all-aback, flat against the apparent wind, then against the *true* wind, as she groaned to a dead halt in a welter a of disturbed water, began to make a slight stern-board!

The corvette's bowsprit and jib boom came thrusting inward like a lance, soaring over the larboard side, steeved high into the air, almost as high as the main-course yard, just before the mainmast chains. Her sprit'sl yard, crossed beneath her bows but not deployed, tangled in the stays, ripping off, rigging lines parting like pistol shots, timbers moaning in agony as her elaborate beakhead rails were crushed back into her bows, as her cutwater slammed into *Radical* with a monumental, hollow booming that shook both ships like striking a rocky shoal at-speed!

Everyone was knocked off their feet—*Radical* shuddered—her side gave way to the impact of nearly four hundred tons of oak and iron striking her almost at right-angles!

"First grapnels, away!" Lewrie howled, getting to his own feet, even without looking. "Tireurs, there! You marksmen! Tirez! Charles, give her a broadside!"

Radical's gunners clambered back to their guns, opened their gun-ports, and ran out. Men teamed up on crow-levers to shift their charges to aim inward, aiming point-blank at oak scantlings mere feet away, the twelve-pounders far fore and aft laid so canted at their ports they'd snap their breeching ropes. Musketry aloft snapping and cracking, shouts of fear from the French gunners on the foredeck and foc's'le as lead struck about them, clawing at their wounds as they were picked off before they could get back to serving their guns. Or freeing the flung grapnels.

Then *Radical* fired her broadside. Twelve hundred feet per second, a ball flew when it left the muzzle of a naval artillery piece. Grape-shot . . . more like a sack of hard iron plums . . . and eighteen-pounder solid round-shot behind that . . . the corvette screamed! Wood cried out as it was blasted away, timbers flew, scantling planking whirled in the air! Thuds and thonks rose from her as *her* gun deck and mess deck were turned into a pair of bowling pitches, and heavy iron tore through tight-pressed men, overturning artillery on carriages, shivering masts as they struck on the lower trunks. Carline posts, scantling, decks, overhead deck beam timbers broke or were turned by caroming ricochets into jagged clouds of wood splinters, bits and pieces as big as bayonets, flicking quick as birds, quilling sailors and making them cringe or cry in terror.

Lewrie scampered to the larboard gangway above his guns, sword drawn. "Cockerels, to me!" he called, waving his tars to join him at the bulwarks. "Grapnel men? Boarders? Boarders, first! You, too, my man!" he shouted as he espied Cony and his French mate with their port-

bottle grenadoes. They came with muskets, pistols, and cutlasses bare
and brutally glittering. There was nothing subtle or scientific about cutlasses—they were choppers, not really swords.

"Now, Cockerels . . . ready? Follow me, lads!" he screamed, to left and
right. "Boarders! Awwayy, boarderrss!"

They surged across the narrow space, scrambling along the foot ropes
and bracing cables below the ruin of the corvette's jib boom and bowsprit, weapons in one hand and leaping from fore stay to fore stay with
the other. Some spryer topmen sprinted down the jib boom, as if running across a wide log footbridge, horny bare feet tough and sure on
pine spars and wound-rope doubling bands. All with a hank of white
cloth tied round their left biceps over their shirts or jackets, marking an
ally for the sharpshooters above.

There was a quick mélée among the survivors of the bow-chasers' crews,
those who had not already been picked off, or had fled. French sailors were
overrun in a twinkling, hacked down with cutlasses or axe heads, a fleet few
screaming in terror and scampering over the top of, around the sides of, the
petty officers' heads in the roundhouses of the forward bulkhead.

"Kennedy!" Lewrie shouted from the beakhead platform. "Bring your
men, now! Grapnels! We'll take 'em to the anchor cat-heads! Be ready
with pistols!" he said, drawing the first of a borrowed pair.

He climbed up from the beakhead platform to the foredeck, and the
abandoned chase-guns, shouldered into the bulkhead, and hopped up
for a view, trying to scale it. A French sailor was climbing atop it with
a musket in his hands. Eye-to-eye, not a single yard between!

He brought up his pistol cack-handed, snapping it back to full-cock
with his sword-hand wrist, leveled and fired. The man's forehead turned
plummy, and the back of his skull was blown out, flinging blood and
brains in a sudden rain behind him. His own dying scream was echoed
by the men who'd been in his rear, trying to dash forward to repel.

"Up, men!" Lewrie yelled. "Give 'em pistols! Point-blank!"

His men erupted from either side of the bulkhead and the roundhouses, shouldering into rough line and leveling their weapons. Guns
went off from both sides. A British sailor was flung backwards with a
howl. There was a sharp crack, a cloud of smoke from the far side, and
more howls among the French, followed by another light explosion, and
the air sang with lead and broken glass! Cony and his grenadoes!

Lewrie got to the top of the bulkhead, crawled across it and looked down
onto the forecastle. There were half a dozen dead below, a like number
writhing and shrieking . . . but a full two dozen running forward towards
him. Muskets crackled near his ears, making them ring, and a few of the
French skidded or tumbled to a halt, the ones behind tripping over them,

and coming to a stop. Lewrie drew his second pistol, glanced left to see a re-assuring flash of red uniform coat. The Irish had made it across!

The French took pause, confused by the sight of British Red, a heartbeat standing still. Then the corvette was quaking to a second broadside, and the men below were scythed away by raking fire, as more iron bowled and caromed the length of her gun deck!

"Take the forecastle!" Lewrie pleaded, turning to search for Lieutenant Kennedy. There he was! "Kennedy! Take the forecastle! Right to the railing! Volley and cover us!"

The Irish swept past him, bayonets winking, muskets presented at hip level; about twenty men shuffling into ranks whilst the first brave ten hurriedly reloaded to a clatter of ramrods.

"Grapnels, now! Set 'em to the cat-heads, behind the troops!"

He took the larboard side, Bosun Porter the starboard, trailing heavy four-inch manila lines across from *Radical*, heavy-barbed grapnels being carried by seamen. Skulking low, as the French got organized at last, as they picked themselves up amid a welter of blood and smoke, of sensible order overturned. Ignoring the shrieks of men torn in half by iron shards, those quilled like hedgehogs by splinters, or crushed and howling beneath shattered gun carriages, they were advancing, their numbers growing quickly. Musket fire began to buzz around them. Men went down. Lewrie lost his second hat, felt a brush against his scalp, and staggered, as a musket ball clipped the hair above his left ear.

But they had the grapnels set, two wraps about the projecting cat-head timbers, then driven deep into the bulwarks. Lewrie could see the strain coming on the lines, lifting them like snakes from the deck and turning them bar-taut. And a look forward showed him de Crillart and some of his regular gunners coming over, with French soldiers in a bunch along *Radical*'s gangway, clumsily scrambling for handholds.

"Hurry!" he shouted to them, waving Charles forward. "For God's sake, hurry 'em over! We can't hold long!"

Sure enough, there were men dashing along either gangway toward his outmanned boarding party. Porter to starboard had two pistols in his hands, seamen—Royalist French and British—at his back, ready with cutlasses or a few loaded muskets. Lewrie cocked his second pistol and leveled it, glaring down the barrel at the men running directly at him.

Hoping they might flinch. And his own body turned side-on, like a duellist. Hoping he wouldn't be shot!

"First rank . . . y'r lef' front!" Kennedy bawled. "Level! Fire!"

Ten men fired by volley, into the head of the pack facing Bosun Porter, taking down five and throwing the rest into confusion, which Porter exploited with a pistol or musket volley of his own.

"First rank, recover and reload. Second rank, y'r right front! Level! Fire!"

Lewrie shot first, taking down a French midshipman, an *aspirante* who had been brave enough to charge him, until he'd seen the pistol in a dead line with his chest. He'd stumbled to a halt, bringing up his own, getting bowled over by his seamen. The boy's waistcoat turned red as he was flung backwards by the ball, almost going erect again, before being trampled by the ones behind. Alan brought up his sword, matched blades with a cutlass-swinging petty officer who'd outrun the pack as Kennedy's soldiers tore gaping holes in the men who'd been slow to follow him. Screams of alarm, of disbelief as men realised they had been shot down, or that they'd been spared whilst a friend had not.

Two, three engagements, clashing steel against steel, high then low, to his left as the petty officer swung again, parrying him off to the right and over his head. Tripping him with his foot and shouldering the burly man off balance. A heartpounding gasp as he leaped back and ran him through, sideways, ducking as the cutlass came swinging at his head, backhanded. But the petty officer going down to his knees, with a death wound below his ribs.

No time to reload, no time to think! Another man, leaping the carnage the 18th had strewn on the gangway, confronted him, an officer for sure, with a smallsword. Up came his bloody blade to ring upon the foe's. But Lisney was beside him with a cutlass, at the head of the larboard forecastle ladder, making him spin away to confront them both. And Gittons beside Lisney, two more British sailors following them. The officer broke off, beginning to backpedal, glancing over Lewrie's head, as if to draw his attention off, now and again.

"Third rank . . . advance to the railings . . . cock y'r locks! And level!" Kennedy was shouting. And there were French shouts, too, of encouragement, coming from the beakheads and bulkhead behind Lewrie.

He advanced with a leap, sure he was being reinforced at last. The French officer was forced to meet his blade, begin the clashing of steel, the thrust, parry and anticipation amid the clatter of metal on metal as if an itinerant tinker band was repairing pots. Hilt to hilt, the Frenchman growling as one of his best overhand thrusts was averted. He leapt back, stamped his foot to advance, fencing-school fashion, and came spiralling in. Lewrie met his blade on the edge of his, about midlength. And the damned thing snapped!

His foe grinned as he cleared his arm for a thrust. Desperately, Alan was on him, right shoulder forward, brawling now instead of fencing, seizing the man's sword-hand wrist and jabbing him through the throat below his jaw with the ragged stub! Gave him another, lower down in the belly as he sagged against him. Nose to nose, looking into those dying eyes for an instant, jumping back to avoid the rush of gore from his mouth as he tumbled face-down. And taking *his* sword from him.

"Cockerels!" he bawled, waving his new weapon on high. "To me, lads! Kennedy, take the gun deck! Now! Don't give 'em time to think!" He turned about to see Louis and his cavalrymen mustering to starboard on the forecastle. "Louis! The gangway! Charge! Et . . . damme! Debarquement! The gangway! Clear it! Porter, show 'im!"

"We 'ave arrive, mon ami," Charles de Crillart said breathlessly. He shouted over his shoulder, ordering his gunners to join Porter and Louis on the starboard gangway, as Major de Mariel's first soldiers came up.

"Join Kennedy and de Mariel, clear the gun deck. I'll take the larboard gangway. Meet you aft, Charles. Bonne chance."

"Oui, bonne chance, Alain," Charles agreed, drawing his sword.

"Cockerels, let's go!" Lewrie shouted, advancing.

Kennedy's 18th Royal Irish, not waiting for de Mariel's men to take order in their rear, advanced, bayonets leveled, down the ladders to the gun deck, forming up before the foc's'le belfry in two long ranks across the deck. "Forward, the 18th! Up, the Irish!" Lieutenant Kennedy cried. And they charged. "Hoolooloolooloo!" they screamed, an ancient, pagan Gaelic war cry, full-throated, ululating hatred and slaughter, the wolves of Erin, who had never been conquered by Caesar's legions; these fierce rejects of that unhappy land. "Hoolooloolooloo!" they bayed. And foes shrank in terror before them.

A continual fusillade of pistol pops, musket reports, screams and wails, the tinny sounds of blades battering against each other. Mélée and mayhem, a swirling, twisting, nightmare dream of killing, of being killed, of narrowly avoiding death. Down went a man with a boarding pike to Lewrie's new sword, skewered through the belly. Another blade glittering as it descended towards his outstretched arms. Lisney there to fend it off, to hack the next foe down. Midshipman Spendlove under his arm, to dash forward, dirk in one hand, cutlass in the other, cutting right and left, horizontal. Sweeping the cutlass upward to tear a topman open, stamping and extending his left arm to stab another.

Lewrie sagged against the bulwarks, panting for air, wincing to a cut on his left leg he couldn't recall receiving, his mouth dry as dust. Looked to his left, saw Chevalier Louis at the head of his thrusting, swinging cavalrymen, popping off with musketoons and pistols. And saw Louis and the three men behind him taken down by a blast from a swivel gun on the quarterdeck! The gunner, leaning far out over the bulwark to fire down the gangway, was shot through the heart the next moment. Below, Irish bayonets jabbing, overhand and underhand, a French sailor with an Irish soldier by the throat, dirk stabbing, all the while his own body rising off the deck, hoisted by three more bayonets. A pistol going off near Kennedy's head, missing at point-blank range, and Kennedy hewing the shooter down!

Cony's grenadoes going off, far aft, lofted as far as he could throw them, waiting dangerously long as the fuses burned down, so that they went off in midair, at eye or waist-level!

And dragging himself back into the fray, as the French sailors began at last to give way, falling back as far as the main chains. Half the corvette was theirs! Slipping and sliding aft along the larboard gangway, stepping over dead men, the cruelly wounded, hacked and chopped open or apart by British sailors going through the whole brutal ballet of the full cutlass drill.

The next minute or so, Lewrie was too busy to ever recall what he'd done, as he slashed and stabbed, fired off a pistol, he thought, once, and took down a bosun's mate with a musket.

Then he found himself on the enemy's quarterdeck, a cutlass in his hand, from where, he had no memory. Facing off with an officer in a coat ornately trimmed in gold-lace oak leaves. Clash, slash, stamp . . . return to the balance foot, recover, then stamp and slash down and left, advance, back and right, balance and recover . . . his years as a midshipman and the cutlass drill had never left him . . .

And the man was throwing down his sword, backed up against the double-wheel drum, throat bared, panting hard, with fear in his eyes.

"Strike?" Alan gasped. "Amenez? Vous êtes le capitain?"

"Oui," the fellow wheezed, slipping to his knees.

"Amenez-vous? You strike?" Lewrie demanded.

"Oui," the man nodded weakly, eyes shut and filled with tears.

"Lisney?" Alan called out.

" 'E's dead, sir," Seaman Gold said at his side, gasping for air himself and bleeding from several scrapes and cuts.

"Take him, Gold. He's your prisoner," Lewrie ordered, filled with wonder. He strode aft to the taffrail, cutlass ready should any of the foemen huddled there present a danger. But they threw down all their weapons at his fell approach.

"Cockerels! Mes amis! Quarter! Merci! They've struck to us!" he shouted, turning to face the soldiers of the 18th, the Royal French infantry coming up to the quarterdeck. Then took hold of the flag halliard and set it free. Hauled in. And lowered the gigantic Tricolour battle flag to drape below the stern, trailing in the water, over the captain's stern gallery, in sign of her defeat.

"Cap'm, sir," Cony summoned, as Lewrie leaned against the taffrails, feeling utterly spent, woozy and weary beyond belief. "Mister Lewrie, sir? T'is Mister de Crillart, sir. Ya gotta come quick, sir. He's adyin', sir, an' 'e's askin' f'r ya."

Lewrie lowered his head to his knees for a second, took several restoring breaths, then followed. As cheers of victory began to rise, as men opened their mouths to yell to the heavens that they were still alive and able to yell . . . Lewrie found his friend.

Charles de Crillart had been blown almost in half, just as he'd begun to ascend the starboard quarterdeck ladder up from the waist, he had been the first man struck by a load of grape-shot from a swivel gun. His heels still rested over his head on the ladder, the rest sprawled awk-wardly . . . brokenly . . . at its foot. His head below his trunk, perhaps, was all that kept him conscious.

"Alain . . ." he muttered weakly, clawing at the deck in agony, as the shock wore off and the pain of his ravaged lower body sank in. His legs were both broken, almost amputated, his belly plumbed by shot.

"Here, Charles," Alan groaned when he saw him. He could not help sinking to his knees beside him. De Crillart reached out blindly, eyes wavering back and forth as if his sight was already slipping, and Alan took his hand.

"Maman . . . et, ahahh!" he flinched, trying not to writhe to his intense pain, yet having to, which caused even more. "Maman et Sophie, Alain. I am going, I canno' aid . . . ahhh!"

He had to bite his lip so hard to keep from crying out, and unmanning himself, that he drew blood.

"Alain, promesse . . . Louis . . ." de Crillart grunted.

"Louis is . . ." Alan said, wondering if he could lie to ease him.

"I *see*, Alain. I see eem fall. 'E eez . . . ?"

Cony gave his head a negative shake as Lewrie looked up at him.

"Charles, your brother . . . ils, nous a quittes. He is gone. I'm sorry."

"Maman et Sophie, zey alone now . . . you mus' promesse . . ." Lieutenant de Crillart insisted, squeezing Lewrie's hand so hard he felt his bones grate. He relaxed his grip as the spasm eased, his grip went flaccid, almost slipped from Alan's grasp for a moment, as his flesh grayed and his lips blued. "See zem to America . . . tak' care of zem for me . . . I beg you, Alain, plais? Promesse?" He demanded a little stronger, digging into his last reserve.

"I promise you, Charles," Alan intoned.

"Promesse, on . . . votre honneur!"

"On my honour, Charles, as an English gentleman . . . as a commission officer in the Royal Navy, I swear to you, I'll take care of them. I'll see them someplace safe," he croaked, blinking back tears.

"Bon," de Crillart sighed, shrinking away. His hand, as cold as ice, slipped from Lewrie's hand. "Bon," he said again, the breath his last, hissing out to rattle in his throat as his eyes glazed over. Alan closed them for him, crossed his arms upon his breast.

"Goddamn," he whispered, sitting back on his heels.

"Good feller, 'e waz, sir," Cony said in sympathy.

"So were a lot of men, just died," Lewrie grunted, chin on his chest. "God help me, Cony, I'm so weak, I . . ."

"Alluz are, sir, after th' battle's done. Help ya up, sir?"

"Yes, thankee, Cony." He got to his feet, swabbing his face on his sleeve. "Many others?"

"Fair number, sir. Mister Porter an' me, we're makin' th' list." They began to walk forward through the carnage, making a quick inspection. "*Radical*, she's beat up hellish-bad, sir. Stove in, an' leakin', I 'spects. Mister Porter's been below here, sir, says she come through in good shape, below the waterline. Jus' *looks* damn' bad."

There were bodies everywhere one looked, pulped, halved, broken and punctured, flopping in death throes, half-buried beneath overturned guns. There the doughty Major de Mariel, then another French soldier. A pair of the 18th, almost arm in arm as they died. A cavalryman hung over the starboard gangway. Men in civilian clothing, with their white armbands, strewn about like slaughtered game birds. But mostly French Republican sailors, thank God—hewn down, hacked down, scythed down by musketry, double-shotted iron, and cutlasses. Moaning, empty-eyed wounded clutching their hurts, sitting on the decks in shock.

There was a cannon shot, a deep-bellied roar.

"Oh, God, no!" Lewrie wailed, losing his rigidly enforced calm. "That bloody frigate!"

He and Cony dashed forward, leaping over obstacles, to ascend to the foredeck where they might have a view. There, close-aboard, was a warship, her pristine masts and yards towering over the two entangled ships. Flying a White ensign and "Do You Require Assistance." Lewrie waved to her, both arms wide. She was huge, bluff and tall, a massive two-decker 64. Where had *she* sprung from, he wondered?

"Sir!" Spendlove shouted from *Radical*'s quarterdeck, aft at her taffrails. "Mister Lewrie, sir! What signal do I send her, sir?"

"Send her 'Affirmative,' Mister Spendlove," Lewrie shouted back. "And I'm damned glad I am to see you alive, by the way, lad!"

"Makes two of us, sir!" the imp grinned, bloodied but whole. "I have her private number, sir. She's *Agamemnon*, Capt. Horatio Nelson! Beyond, there's *Mermaid*, 5th Rate 32, Capt. John Trigge," Spendlove prated on, even as he bent on the "Affirmative" to a signal halliard. "And *Cockerel*, sir. She really *did* go for help, like you said, sir!"

"Sir!" Bittfield, the senior gunner, was yelling, too, trying to draw his attention. "Takin' on water bad, she is, sir. Hadda get all the dependents up t' th' weather deck, sir. Best we get our people back aboard soon, we don't wish t' lose 'er, sir."

"Cony, fetch Mister Porter and all the men he can gather up," Lewrie ordered. "Patch what you can, until *Agamemnon* sends her hands to aid us. And get everyone, no matter who, working on the chain-pumps."

"Aye aye, sir."

Lewrie crossed over to *Radical*, working his way out the jib boom sideways on the foot ropes, to the bulwarks in which the corvette's bow was deep-sunk. Looking down, he could see crushed planking between two rows of vertical hull timbers. Perhaps that was the worst damage, none of it too far below the waterline, he hoped.

He gained the larboard gangway and looked down into the waist. Women and children milled about down there, weeping and wailing, crying to heaven. Surgeons moved among them, loblolly boys were fetching up more from below, on the orlop. Wounded women! Dead, lolling children!

Dear God, that last broadside she got off, just before we went up in-irons, he quailed. The collision, everything come adrift below . . . ! I killed 'em, winnin' my damned . . . victory!

He was at the head of the larboard quarterdeck ladder, about to descend, when Phoebe came rushing from the press to its foot, came up to throw herself upon him, laughing and weeping at the same time.

Thankee, Jesus, she's alive! Thankee! he thought, hugging her no matter who saw them. Stroking her hair as she babbled, one minute trembling and bubbling over with joy, the next instant bawling fit to bust—all punctuated by hiccoughy French tripped off so fast he couldn't catch a word in twenty.

"Calm, Phoebe, calm . . . I'm alright now. Calm," he shusshed.

"Oh, Alain, merde alors, ze canon . . . ! Beaucoup femmes et enfants, zey tuer. Keel! Si *trés* beaucoup . . . hurt!"

"Charles!" came a scream from below them. Sophie de Maubeuge scrambled up the quarterdeck ladder, blood on her gown. "M'sieur Lieutenant Luray, Charles . . . ?"

He let go of Phoebe, extended his arms to her. But she did not accept his embrace, but stopped short, paling, as she realised what he was about to say, by the expression of grief and sympathy on his face.

"Non, non, mon Dieu, *non!*"

"Mademoiselle vicomtesse, je regrette . . ." he said gently, taking her hands instead. "Charles Auguste, Baron de Crillart . . . ils nous à quittes."

Before she had time to take a breath for another hysterical scream, he told her the rest. "Aussi, Chevalier Louis de Crillart, ils nous à quittes."

God, how I hate that bloody phrase, he thought; nous à quittes . . . left us, gone away from us. Like it was *their* bloody idea!

Sophie let go of his hands, put them to either side of her head as if to tear her hair out by the roots, and screamed and screamed, as she sank to her knees. Had not Phoebe gone down to her, she would have tumbled to the base of the ladder, broken her neck. Phoebe cradled her head upon her breast, crooning to her, gentling her, while Alan stood, embarassed by his role and his slowness . . . his uselessness.

"Charles . . . Louis . . . ! Sophie wailed, gone white, with her eyes ready to roll back into her head in a faint. "Madame!"

"What?" Lewrie started, finally noticing the blood on her gown.

"Oui, Alain," Phoebe whispered as he went down to them, looking up with tears running free on her face, as bleak as if she'd lost someone, too. "Madame de Crillart. Ze murs, uhm . . . walls? . . . zey break open. Boulets de canon? Ze grande dame, elle est mort. Pauvre petite mademoiselle . . . she 'as lose 'er famille entier . . . 'ave no one, now."

"I . . ." he whimpered, turning away, overcome. And sure that it was all his own bloody fault! "Oh, bloody . . ."

"Go, I see to 'er," Phoebe urged. "You' ship, she . . ."

Lewrie staggered away across the littered quarterdeck, and his borrowed cutlass clattered to the deck as it slipped from his nerveless fingers. He fetched up at the battered taffrails by one of the stern-chasers which still radiated spent heat. Scrubbing his face with both hands, trying to deny what he'd done, wondering if he could have done something different, taken another course of action that wouldn't have gotten so many innocent and helpless slaughtered.

Off on the nor'east horizon a frigate was flying, pursued by a British ship. Near the transports, both fetched-to and looking as if they'd been knocked about, *Cockerel* cruised slowly. And the corvette he'd crippled had struck her colours, a Royal Navy ensign flying at her taffrail. How had the civilians fared aboard those transports, he wondered; had they suffered this much, after putting up token opposition, then striking? He feared they hadn't.

Damme, he thought; I could have stood on, just a few minutes longer, endured her fire, and help would have arrived, these French would have had to sheer off, soon as they saw our warships closing . . . !

He turned to the sound of tumult, saw wounded men being brought aboard, the healthy slowly crawling across the bulwarks as empty-eyed as the defeated, saw his mates and petty officers putting them to work on the chain-pumps after they'd embraced their families, and gotten a sip of something to relieve their dry mouths. *Agamemnon* fetching-to and lowering her boats—boats crammed with strong, helpful sailors to salve his ship and his prize. And saw men who'd faced battle and suffered come back aboard to find a loved one departed.

Shouldn't be like this, he groused. Hard as the aftermath of a battle is . . . shouldn't be like this.

Men could fall, be cruelly wounded and linger in their agonies among shipmates, in a tough masculine world where men could josh the dying, buck them up to go game or offer awkward comfort. And grieve for good friends departed, of a certainty, as their canvas-shrouded corpses were put over the side with round-shot at their feet. But to *hear* the lamentations of the orphaned, the widowed . . . 'stead of imaging some far-off bereavement, notified half a year later that the son, the father, the brother, the husband or lover was Discharged, Dead . . . !

"Shouldn't ought to be like this," he muttered, leaning on the taffrails for a few, last private moments, letting his own tears flow, choking on his own bereaved sobs before stern duty recalled him.

Phoebe had quieted Sophie de Maubeuge, last vicomtess of her lineage, turned her over to the care of another aristocratic family's women, and made her way back up the quarterdeck ladder to find him. She saw him far aft, leaning forward, head down, squeezing the rails, and her heart went out to him. She hitched up her skirts, ready to run to him, but Spendlove intervened.

"Ma'am?" he called, stepping in front of her, snuffling himself as the list of familiar hands who'd fallen accumulated in his ledger, as he recognised the bodies of friends and mentors and troublemakers from a full year's association. "Don't. Not now."

"M'sieur Spen'loove, 'e need . . ." Phoebe pled weakly.

"Ma'am," Spendlove objected gently, taking her nearest hand, "I know you an' Mister Lewrie . . . well, t'ain't my place to say, what's . . . but, ma'am? Do you care for him? Do you *love* him?"

"Vis all ma 'eart!" she declared, weeping anew at the force of her affection.

"Then, ma'am . . . give him a minute or two more, if you do," Mister Midshipman Spendlove dared to suggest. "He'll be back with us. For now, though, ma'am . . . let Mister Lewrie . . . let our *captain* have a cry."

L'ENVOI

Cessere ratemque accepere mari. Per quot discrimina rerum expeditor!

They have yielded, they have received the vessel on the sea. I find my way, now, through many a change in Fortune.

—VALERIUS FLACCUS
Argonautica, Book 1, 216–218

CHAPTER 1

Twilight at Gibraltar on the decks of HMS *Victory*, the fleet anchored about her, with glims and binnacle and belfry lights agleam, and lanterns strung by entry ports, poop and quarterdeck aboard the flagship. Wardroom and great-cabin lights reflected off the waters from over forty vessels. And from the transports from England: the ships that had brought, just a few weeks too late, the regiments of British Redcoats that might have made the difference, the ones held back too long by indifference, miscommunication. They'd put in to Gibraltar just days before Admiral Hood's ships had returned from the defeat at Toulon, as if in the worst sort of mockery. They had been held at Gibraltar, pending instructions from Hood to send them on to him, though he had no idea of their arrival at all, and was even then arranging for the hurried evacuation of Coalition forces.

Lewrie paced fretfully, turned out in the best that local chandlers could boast, now his packet had come from home; pristine new breeches, waistcoat and shirt, and a new hat. He'd clung to the Hessian boots, though—they seemed to be all the rage among Sea Officers lately—and, perversely, to the tatty older coat. He wore an elegant smallsword at his hip, taken from the captain of the corvette he had captured as prize, though he still longed for his original hanger.

"Lieutenant Lewrie?" a flag lieutenant called at last. "Milord Hood is now free, and may see you, sir."

Lewrie crossed the vast expanse of *Victory*'s quarterdeck, aft to the admiral's quarters under the poop—but was brought up short by the sight of Capt. Howard Braxton leaving those great-cabins. He seemed ill, as ill as he had in the days just after his recovery; spent and old, white-faced, the incline of his mouth to larboard even more pronounced.

"Sir," Lewrie said icily, doffing his hat properly in salute.

It took Braxton a moment to notice him. When he did, he turned even paler, almost dropped the bundles of log-books and ledgers he bore. Then his eyes flared before slitting in anger, and mottled ire coloured his cheeks. "Goddamn you, sir!" Braxton bleated in a harsh whisper. "Happy now, are you, Lewrie? Happy *now*? May God damn you to hell!" he hissed, before stalking away for the entry port.

"Hmm, well . . ." Lewrie shrugged to the flag lieutenant.

"Indeed, sir," that worthy rejoined with a sad, embarrassed moue.

"Lewrie. Good," Admiral Lord Hood grunted, as he mused upon the paperwork on his desk in the day cabin to which Lewrie had been shown. A festive display of linen, crystal, fine china and a sideboard buried in bottles he'd seen, in the dining coach and reception area. Evidently, the admiral would host a supper party that evening.

"Milord, so gracious of you to receive me," Alan replied.

"Take a pew, sir. A glass of something? Do avail yourself of a quite decent brandy, there, on the side table. Pour one for me, as well." Hood signed his name with a quill pen before rising to cross the cabin to join him. Hood accepted the glass Lewrie offered him and sat himself in the matching high-backed wing chair, crossing his legs as if ready to converse with a close acquaintance at his London club.

"Now, sir," Hood began, after a refreshing sip. "Read your account of *Cockerel*'s performance last week. And that report I requested of you, anent her past since her commissioning. Appalling, simply appalling! But . . . there will *be* no court martial, I have to tell you, sir."

"I thought . . . sorry, milord," Lewrie sighed, disappointed, a bit appalled himself at the reach of patronage and politics.

"Matter's been dealt with," Hood was quick to assure him. "Can't abide being lied to, either by omission or commission. Most certainly, I cannot abide a scoundrel who will not support a fellow captain brought to action . . . a total poltroon, no matter how plausible his explanations. Nor one, sir, who will falsify log entries in such fraudulent manner."

For a disconcerting moment, Alan thought Hood was speaking of *his* actions, wondering if Braxton had lied his way out once more, even if his words on the quarterdeck sounded as if he hadn't.

"Braxton, sir," Hood continued with a disgusted snort, "should never have had command of a harbour-watch cutter. Fascinating, really. Made all the appropriate noises 'bout fetching aid. Claimed he took your prize frigate, *and* that horse transport, can you believe it, for a brace o' warships, so he felt free to scuttle off, the situation being so well in hand! Changed his tune when pressed, though, said he could not accept battle against three *frigates*, could *never* be expected to do so . . . conveniently forgetting that he'd already misidentified *your* two ships, and was later amazed to learn that two foes were corvettes! Admitting, in essence, he'd put discretion above valour, and fled. Not only showing cowardice in the face of the enemy, but disobeying a direct order—from mine own hands, sir!—to safeguard the laggard ships to his utmost. What he *could* have done with a single 5th Rate 32, had he remained . . . your valiant action, sir, proved that most assuredly. As for lying to me, anent Naples . . . he and his clerk, most likely, rewrote portions of *Cockerel*'s log for that period. No mention of sickness . . . yet never thinking that I would have in my possession correspondence from Sir William Hamilton which proved him a complete liar, sir! Well!"

"Didn't think he'd go *that* far, milord," Lewrie replied, easier.

"Put it to him direct," Hood said with a wolfish grin. "Take a court . . . of mine *own* appointing, d'ye see, sir . . . take his chances with a board of seven post-captains. Or he could, for reasons of health, throw up his command, ask to be relieved immediately, and go on the half-pay list. Return to civilian employment. Resume his service with 'John Company,' lucrative as that is. But, I was quick to assure him, I would append to his letter of resignation, a letter of mine own to Stephens and Jackson, and our Lords Commissioners, that while he may be continued on the roster for post-captains—indeed, may attain, should he live; to the very pinnacle of that list—he should never have another appointment of any kind . . . seagoing command or sinecure ashore. And further, that even should Captain Braxton rise to the highest seniority as post-captain, he shall never . . . *never*, sir! . . . be 'Yellow-Squadroned' as a flag officer. I believe that takes care of that problem, do you not as well, Mister Lewrie?" Hood all but snickered.

"I do, indeed, milord. Most handily dispatched. With the very least harm to his son's career. Or to his family."

"I fully expect his letter of resignation aboard by eight bells of the morning watch. Failing that, well . . . !" Hood chortled, almost looking forward to a court martial. "Now, sir . . . *Cockerel*. She shall have a new captain aboard by eight bells of the forenoon, should Captain Braxton oblige me, and himself. Tell me all about her. Who needs weeding out. And explain this, uhm . . . mutiny which took place, sir."

For the next quarter-hour, Hood listened, having his flag lieutenant in to make notes. Nodding grimly, surprising Lewrie by laughing when he came to the mutineers.

"Aye," Hood said at last. "Mister Clement Braxton deserves a second chance. The midshipmen must be separated and assigned to new ships.

Under a new order of captains. Tell me, Lieutenant Lewrie . . . you ended up with most of those men whom your captain deemed trouble-makers. Did they ever cause you any grief, sir?"

"*None*, milord," Lewrie could state with assurance.

"Damme, loath as I am to turn a blind eye to an act of mutiny, or to condone the crime by taking no action against the perpetrators," Hood gloomed. "Terrible times we live in, Lewrie. *Rights of Man* and this spirit of revolution, a world turned upside down, as it were . . . time out of mind, we've kept our sailors in strict discipline with the lash, which they understand. Now, faced with two nations which have revolted against the proper, ordained authority of their betters . . . I fear your Captain Braxton may become a more common figure aboard our ships, in future. As our tars absorb the radical, levelling teachings of the American Rebels and these French we fight, we may all have to become ever more watchful and taut-handed to keep Jack obedient. I should . . ."

"Excuse me, milord, but . . ." the flag lieutenant interrupted. "Your guests should even now be arriving."

"Aye, enough for now, then. You will do me the signal pleasure of dining aboard as my guest, Lieutenant Lewrie?"

"With all gratefulness for your kind hospitality, milord!" he replied, stunned by the invitation.

It was hearty English fare. Portable Navy soup, local fish in a vinegar sauce, chicken with vegetable removes, then salad, and roast beef, of course. Lewrie was in heady company: Admirals Gell, Goodall and Cosby, Captain Elphinstone off *Robust*, Nelson off *Agamemnon*, and a dozen more distinguished officers, *Victory*'s Rear-Admiral Sir Hyde Parker and her flag captain John Knight, Holloway off *Brittania*, and Sir Thomas Byard off *Windsor Castle*, flag captain John Childs Purvis of Goodall's *Princess Royal* and Gell's Capt. Thomas Foley from the *St. George*, with a sprinking of commanders towards the middle of that groaning table, and a smattering of lieutenants who had distinguished themselves on detatched service at Toulon at its foot.

With the food came lashings of wine, a new one with every course—national origin be-damned—of which Lewrie took full measure, down near the token midshipman who served as Mister Vice at its far end. It was a convivial, very sociable supper, with many toasts made and drunk, and officers proposing individual "A glass with you, sir" duet toasts among themselves almost every minute. To observe them, it would have seemed hard to believe that these were officers who had just taken part in an appalling and embarassing defeat.

Finally the last plates were cleared, the linen and water glasses removed, and cheeses fresh from England, nuts and extra-fine sweet biscuit set out with the port bottles, which began to circulate larboardly.

Hood was prosing on from the top of the table, conducting a conversation concerning the material condition of the ships brought away from Toulon, and no one sounded exactly pleased, Lewrie noted, though a touch "squiffy." Few of those prize vessels sounded like they'd been exactly good value returned upon their investment.

"Lieutenant Lewrie," Hood called out, making Alan start in his chair and set down his glass of port. "That vessel you brought off . . . *Radical*, was she? Tell us of *her* state, sir."

He explained the weeding, the slovenly dockyard work done by the French, the iron and copper, and the further damage she'd taken.

"Milord, gentlemen . . . I fear she may require a full quarter of this next year in dock, to set her right," Lewrie concluded, queezy with all eyes upon him. "Decommissioned, though . . . a chance to rename her?" he said with a quirky and shyly ingratiating grin.

"Quite!" Vice-Admiral Cosby grunted. "Can't have a ship named *Radical* in our Navy."

"Nothing radical allowed, ha ha," said Sir Thomas Byard, quite amused (and half-seas-over with drink).

"And those two corvettes you fought, Lieutenant Lewrie," Hood probed on. "The, uhm . . ."

"Oh, the *Sans Culottes* and the one we disabled, milord, the *Liberté*," Alan replied, sitting up straighter, or trying to. "Both are in decent condition, milord. *Liberté* requires minimal repairs . . . new masts, spars and canvas, mostly. *Sans Culottes*, perhaps a month in the yards to repair battle damage. Other than that, fully found."

"Three warships, the gallant Lieutenant Lewrie has won for us, gentlemen," Hood announced. "Though with so many of our vessels 'insight' at the moment the corvettes struck their colours, I fear little in the way of prize money and head money as reward."

"Dare I say, though, milord," Captain Nelson posed, "that given the parlous state of his prize frigate, lightly armed as she was, and with so many untrained civilian volunteers aboard . . . to dare a full three enemy vessels, cripple one, and *take* a second . . . was an act of such conspicuous skill, not to mention pluck and bottom . . . that Lieutenant Lewrie's gallantry, and his victory, were the true rewards"

"Hear, hear!" they shouted, lifting their glasses high, pounding their fists on the table.

"And I suppose," Hood said with a twinkle in his eye, after the tumult had died down, "that we may avail ourselves of those two ships' time in dock to decommission them, and rename them as well. *Liberté*, perhaps, is innocuous, but . . ."

"Tradition is to keep the name of the captured ship, milord," Sir Hyde Parker countered. "In sign to our foes that the Royal Navy's to be feared upon the seas."

"If only our foes had the good sense and common decency, Admiral Parker, to christen their vessels with worthy *names*," Capt. Sir George Elphinstone of *Robust* rebutted with a chuckle, his comment raising a laugh among the others. "*Sans Culottes*? I *ask* you!"

"Quite right, Sir George," Capt. Sir Thomas Byard merrily said. "Why, given our tars' penchant for a baser humour, what would they make of *that*, I ask you, gentlemen? Eh, Lewrie?"

"Most like, Sir Thomas, they'd be calling her HMS '*Bare* . . . uh *Legged*', in a dog watch," Lewrie jested, quite happy that he'd caught himself from saying what first sprang to mind—HMS *Bare-Arse*!

"Worse than that, I fear, sir," Byard continued drolly. "Without breeches, it means, but . . . what state is that, hey?"

Encouraged by too much drink and the jollity of the assembled senior officers, Lewrie could not help himself. "You suppose, Captain Byard, that they might refer to a state involving another part of the anatomy, one more, uhm . . . *fundamental*, Sir Thomas?"

That set them off to another round of fist-pounding and laughing. Lewrie quite enjoyed his clever play on words. Until he noted that Admiral Lord Hood was most definitely *not* amused.

As the last chuckles died away, Hood spoke.

"Lieutenant Lewrie has always been, so I have gathered, quite the wag, gentlemen. Quite the witty fellow, indeed," Hood purred.

It sounded so much like censure that the others sobered.

Oh Christ, I've fucked it! Again! Lewrie groaned to himself. Damme, *and* my open mouth! *Never* know when to keep it shut!

"Aye, gentlemen, we'll rename our prizes," Hood announced as he poured himself a glass of port, a full glass. "As for *Liberté*, as I earlier stated, that is somewhat innocuous, though . . . it would not do to encourage her crew to dwell 'pon her name *too* closely. Before she's recommissioned, we'll think of something suitable. As for the *Sans Culottes* . . ."

Hood made a little moue, gave a tiny shrug.

"Our tars *would* make something of that, wouldn't they?" Admiral Lord Hood said with a brief smile. "So, gentlemen. Since she is the worst offender . . . Do you charge your glasses. I was struck, just now, with an inspiration, and I would be gratified were you to indulge me."

The bottles made their way about, full bumpers were poured and set before a multitude of thirsty fists in expectation.

"A double toast, if I may, sirs, gentlemen," Hood explained as he lifted his glass. "In the jocular spirit of this evening, allow me to propose . . . that the French national ship, the twenty-gunned prize corvette *Sans Culottes* . . . shall be bought into Royal Navy service, as His Majesty's 6th Rate sloop of war . . ." He paused dramatically, a twinkle in his old eyes," " . . . *Jester*. Sirs, gentlemen, I give you HM Sloop of War *Jester*. Proudly may she tweak the noses of our foes."

"HM Sloop of War *Jester*!" they repeated loudly, in a rough and manly chorus, draining off half their port and waiting, glasses pent at midchest for the rest of the toast.

"And to the jolly wag responsible for what little merriment we enjoy this evening, the provider of the one bright spot of cheer—and may I say, of glory—to illuminate our hopes for success and victory in future . . ." Hood beamed at last, looked down the table direct, and locked his eyes on Alan. ". . . and allow us to close the book upon our recent enterprise with an exemplary display of wit, courage, shiphandling and gallantry, in the finest tradition of the Sea Service . . . the young man who took her . . . *Commander* Alan Lewrie."

Jesus bloody . . . ! Lewrie gawped as they shouted his name, and his new rank. His glass sat between his shaky hands, as they tossed theirs off beyond "heel-taps." Head down in modesty; true modesty for once, it must be said, too surprised to do else but shyly smile.

"HM Sloop of War *Jester*'s new master and commander," Admiral Hood said as an afterthought, once the tumult had died down. "A captain in your own right, at last, sir. Use her well, and take joy of her."

CHAPTER 2

HM Sloop of War *Jester* stood out past Europa Point, hardening up to a land breeze from Spain on the starboard tack. Gun salutes had been fired, and the artillery secured. Sparse as Gibraltar dockyards were supplied, it had taken two months to set her right, more than the single month her captain had supposed.

Now she was off for England, with dispatches, to recruit and man, to replace French eight-pounders with British long nines, to add some carronades to her quarterdeck. There was a sprinkling of Maltese seamen in her crew, though the hard kernel of her experienced men were former Cockerels, those who'd served detached with him, and some who'd asked to turn over to her from their old ship after her new captain had read himself in. Plus those men separated from other ships who'd been with him from Toulon. A few more volunteered from *Victory*, *Agamemnon* (most graciously offered by Captain Nelson, though he was short-handed himself by then), and the other flagships. Enough to man her voyage home to Portsmouth, doubling Cape St. Vincent, along the Spanish and Portugese coasts, and lash cross the boisterous westerlies of the Bay of Biscay for Ushant, risking French warships.

But *Jester* was a fine vessel, no error, Lewrie thought proudly, savouring a first morning at sea, the fresh breezes, the warming climate of an early March Mediterranean spring day. She was well built of Adriatic oak, properly joined, caulked and payed, newly coppered, with quick-work as clean and smooth as a baby's bottom. And she was fast. He was certain *Jester* would get them all home safely and swiftly, sure his rising impatience would soon be satisfied.

To go ashore and visit Caroline, Seawallis, Hugh once more, and see how much little Charlotte had grown during his absence! Caroline had written that they'd coach down to Portsmouth and all be together during *Jester*'s brief refit. So long apart, so eager to see them, to hear their voices, touch them . . . to hold his dear wife once more. By the time of *Jester*'s landfall, the news of his battle, his victory . . . and his promotion would have made the *Marine Chronicle* and the London *Gazette*. He had not yet received Admiralty confirmation of his promotion, but surely that was a mere formality, with Hood speaking for him.

Beyond winning a fight against appalling odds, two-a-penny for the Public beliefs, he'd brought off women and children, rescued, then protected innocent lives. That made his official report, he was sure, the sort of fame beyond the normal. Even if he had gotten some of the innocent slain in the process, he groaned, reliving his errors again, trying to think of something he could have done better. He still felt guilty about those dependents who had died.

Admittedly, he felt rather guilty over his infidelities, too, of his failings as a proper husband. Though he felt drawn like filings to a lodestone, eager to rush home . . . he wondered if his sins would show in his face, if Caroline would know at the first instant of reunion.

Fearful, too, of his charge. Alan looked to starboard, over to where Mister Midshipman Spendlove was engaging in shy, clumsy repartee to Mademoiselle Sophie, Vicomtesse de Maubeuge, who was taking the air on the quarterdeck now the ship was secured for sea, properly chaperoned by an *émigré* Royalist French maidservant she'd taken on.

No help there, Lewrie thought sourly; Midshipman Clarence Spendlove was a year younger than she, of middling worth to begin with, and bloody hopeless as a swain. Now, Lt. Ralph Knolles, on the other hand . . . He turned to look at his first officer, fresh-plucked from fourth-lieutenant obscurity in *Windsor Castle*'s wardroom. He was of an age, about twenty-five, came of a good family, and had been very witty and charming when about the vicomtesse. Most swainlike, indeed! Hmm,..

Lieutenant Knolles felt his captain's intent perusal on the back of his neck, turned from his pose by the nettings forrud, and raised one quizzical blond eyebrow, wary of his new captain and their brief acquaintance.

"A good day for it, Mister Knolles," Lewrie grinned with false cheer, clapping his hands as if in pleasure. "Good to be back at sea."

"Indeed, sir," Knolles replied, relieved.

"Carry on, you have the deck, sir," Lewrie assured him gaily.

"Aye aye, sir."

Have to speak to the young swine, Alan told himself; dine them both in. *He* could take her off my hands, pray Jesus!

With no place else to go, no other living relations, and so poor in pelf with which to establish herself on her own, even if she could at her tender young age . . . Lewrie had been forced by that promise he'd made to Charles de Crillart, upon his very honour, that he'd look after the unfortunate Sophie de Maubeuge. There had been time enough for his letter to go to Caroline, and to receive a quick reply on a packet brig.

Caroline had been reduced to tears, both by the girl's piteous plight and her "dear husband's" tender and magnanimous promise to such a gallant, dying man. For the few years before Sophie was come to her majority, Caroline had insisted that the girl simply *must* come to live with them as their treasured guest, close as cater-cousins. Let her tutor the children in French, in poetry and such, music, of course . . . but raise her, and let her acquaint herself with a new life in England, safely away from city evils in the bucolic splendours of Anglesgreen!

And what the tender young Sophie de Maubeuge knew of her benefactor's amourous rantipoling, Lewrie most ardently hoped, Sophie might keep to herself . . . and from her benefactress! But dreading that someday, in a snit, perhaps, or an unguarded moment, the mort'd . . . !

Christ shat on a biscuit, he thought, massaging his brow; let's *please* marry the chit off, quick as we can. Damned fetchin', she is . . . a sweet, willing tit. *Hell* of a catch, somebody . . . titled an' all? What am I bid? And the worst part of it is, I can't caution her about it. Can't even *talk* to her 'bout keepin' silent! Jesus, let's hope poor Charles was right . . . she's French! Nun-blinkered or no, it's in the blood. The French'r s'posed to *understand* these things . . . about a man and a maid . . .'bout Phoebe.

Dear Lord . . . Phoebe!

Besides the cost of outfitting his new great-cabins (not that grand, really) with the bare minimums of comforts, of furnishings . . . which great-cabins he could not use since he'd been saddled with half a dozen nonpaying, all-eating, all-drinking passengers—live lumber!—of purchasing cabin stores, wine and such, plates and glassware, a new sea chest partially stocked with all which was needful, a new hat with proud gold-lace, and at least one new-pattern gold-laced uniform coat suitable to a Commander . . . there was Phoebe to lodge and support at Gibraltar.

Daft, daft, *daft*! he told himself yet again, turning his head to glance at the helmsman and the compass course. And discovering her scent on his coat collar, fresh from his very last shore visit of the night before, before taking *Jester* to sea at sunrise.

He inhaled deep, in spite of all his guilt, his fear and his misgivings, savouring her scent, his memory of her, and her passionate, kittenish, adoring *adieu*. Yet in spite of all, he could not help himself, could not force himself to let go of her!

All during *Jester*'s time in the docks he slept ashore with her, each moment snatched from duty a heaven-sent joy. And Admiral Hood had given him firm assurances that once his ship was ready, *Jester* would be returning to the Mediterranean, that Hood had written a specific request for his future services. There was Corsica to be taken to confound the French, after all. Royalist sentiments to exploit among the French on the island, separatist sentiments among the rather recently annexed Italian population, led by some fellow named Paoli, or something like that.

And, dovetailing so neatly with his enchantment with the petite and entrancing Phoebe was the fact that she herself was Corsican! Part French, part Italian, Mademoiselle Phoebe Aretino was. She knew every inch of the island, knew the people who mattered . . . and was well versed in her island's tumultuous affairs.

Besides being the most intoxicating, besotting, loving, amusing, exotically wee and clinging, yet so fiercely warm and passionate, a most cunning and beguiling, exciting, maddening little minx . . . !

Lewrie sighed, taking a surreptitious whiff of his collar again, still able to feel her soft lips upon his, see her huge waif's eyes as they peered up at him in total devotion. Daft or not, his affections and his soul were torn in twain. And he knew—feared, rather—that once home with his dear ones, like an antipodal lodestone, like a siren song, he would grow vexed for the feel of her, the taste of her, and be *just* as eager to put to sea, to hurry *Jester* back to Gibraltar. Hurry himself back to the arms of his tender young Phoebe.

He saw Bosun's Mate Will Cony by the fife rails of the mainmast in *Jester*'s waist, patiently tutoring some new-recruited landsmen in the identity of the maze of running-rigging belayed on the pins. And Alan smiled, in spite of all his forebodings.

Had it right, Cony, he thought; God knows His rogues when He sees 'em. I wager He'll be gettin' a *tremendous* laugh t' see us *both* wriggle . . . when we get back to Anglesgreen!

A black-and-white kitten, now four months old, came skittering on the quarterdeck from aft, shoveling a beribboned wine cork between his paws, arching, leaping and mewing as he pounced and footballed. He was turning out to be a horrid disaster, that kitten. Couldn't mouse, shied at the sight of a cockroach—and *Jester* had more than her fair share of *that* tribe aboard, at present. Loud noises drove him into hiding, in Lewrie's sea chest, hatbox, or behind the books on the shelves above the chart table. A pest for attention he was, too, all hours of the night— where he pawed and cried for stroking, butting insistently. When he did sleep, it was under Lewrie's chin, abed; or curled up in his hat. Yes, he was a perfect disaster. But amusing, and affectionate, for all that.

Which had, after much thought, suggested his name; a French name for a French cat.

"Here, Toulon!" Lewrie bade cheerfully. "Come here, Toulon!"

With a glad mew, Toulon bounded to his side in awkward hops, to scramble up his coattails and settle on his shoulder for a rub, thrusting his little nose into Lewrie's ear, clawing at his coat collar, and purring with ardour.

Too late to cure him of such sins, Alan wondered? Well, maybe he'll grow out of 'em.

Afterword

Even more disheartening for the allies of the First Coalition, who had been forced to evacuate Toulon, was the attempted destruction of the French fleet and the naval port facilities on the night of 18 December 1793.

French troops were already in the town and on the hills to the west, overlooking the basin. Nearly 800 convict labourers were free of their chains, and acting like patriots. The log and chain boom across the harbour entrance had been closed. The Spanish, however, and contemporary accounts refer to their desultory performance as "treachery"—of course these are *British* accounts, and they had their noses far out of joint when they wrote them—didn't appear to have tried very hard. Their work at the arsenals and warehouses didn't go well, and damage to the facilities was not as extensive as the fires might have made people believe. And instead of scuttling the *Iris* frigate, crammed with those thousands of barrels of gunpowder, they set fire to her on their hasty way out, which caused the tremendous explosion Lewrie witnessed, which blew the *Union*, a British gunboat nearby, to atoms.

Sir William Sidney Smith tried to enter the basin after firing docked ships and do what the Spanish had shirked, but was driven away by the volume of gunfire. He did burn two more French 74's, but they were condemned hulks, full of French prisoners of war, whom he freed. At last, as his party retired, having done all they could, the *Montreal* frigate, the other powder hulk, blew up with a blast even greater than *Iris*. No one is quite sure how she took light—a French patriot, some mistake by Smith's party, or another pyromaniacal Spaniard who rather thought he'd like to hear something else go "Boom!" that night.

Capt. Sir William Sidney Smith selected himself for the venture, and Capt. Horatio Nelson wrote of his failure to do more damage, saying,

"Lord Hood mistook the man: there is an old saying, *great talkers do the least we see.*" Though Captain Smith later distinguished himself in the Middle East against French troops ashore.

The basin and port were not destroyed, and the French regained the use of many of their ships thought burned. There had been thirty-one ships of the line at Toulon, some in-ordinary, in docks, or being built. Four were sailed away, and only nine of them burned. Toulon held twenty-seven corvettes, brigs of war and frigates. Fifteen were carried off, including *Alceste*, which the Sardinians lost to the French a few years later, five were burned, and seven left to the Republicans. Some ships on stocks were not burned at all, and the shipyards were back in business soon after.

The worst part of the defeat at Toulon, though, was the loss of civilian lives after the Coalition cut and ran, breaking their solemn promises to safeguard the Royalist sympathisers. The fleet did carry off 14,877 of them, but could not find places aboard ships for more.

At the last, as the rear-guard troops, British, Spanish and Neapolitans, broke and ran when French troops rushed forward, the thousands of people left behind, soldiers and civilians, dashed to the quays and the shores. They waded out, imploring the last boats to save them. They were cut down, shot down, or ruthlessly bayoneted by victorious Republican troops. Some accounts say hundreds, others thousands, died in the last hours, or drowned trying to swim after the boats or out to a ship.

General Dugommier protested, it is written, (though Napoleone Buonaparte did not) as the Republican deputies set up their guillotines, ending up exceuting, by their enthusiastic accounts, a brisk 200 a day. Toulon paid for its sin; in the end, it is thought, over 6,000 civilian Toulonese lost their lives one way or another. Men, women *and* children.

Joseph Conrad wrote a novel, *The Rover*, which concerned the fate of the Royalists, featuring a young girl driven mad by the Terror, the slaughter, the permanent exile of those unfortunate *émigrés* driven overseas to any port that would have them, like storm petrels, of families and loved ones forever separated by sailing on different ships to disparate corners of the earth. If you can find it in the classics section, read the tale of poor, mad Arlette, victim of the Revolution. And of Toulon.

Lady Emma Hamilton, indeed, could never resist a sailor. After he first met her in 1793, Horatio Nelson was perhaps more besotted by Emma than most biographers suspect—or care to admit. Did he, or did he not, that early? After his stunning victory at the Battle of the Nile, Emma threw herself at his feet, and he gladly picked her up. They remained lovers, public or professional opinions be-damned, until his death in 1805 on *Victory*'s quarterdeck at the Battle of Trafalgar.

Emma Hamilton was a sad case; she really did think of all those men, who'd used her then cast her aside, as her true, long-time friends and mentors. And we believe the depiction herein of this deluded lady is correct, especially Emma Hamilton's desire to tag onto the coat-tails of powerful and influential men and bask in their reflected, shared glories.

By the way—what Charles Greville paid for that Fetherstonehaugh would not was a baby, left in foster-care at Neston, and never reclaimed—by either parent.

There was a *Sans Culottes* in the French Navy, but she didn't keep that name for long. Originally the *Dauphin-Royal*, she was a 120-gun 1st Rate. Cooler heads prevailed at last, the wily politicians who took over the French Revolution from the wild-eyed radicals and might have been a touch embarassed by the earlier revolutionaries' fervour. She became the *Orient*, and served as the ill-fated Admiral de Brueys's flagship at the Battle of the Nile, where she burned and blew up in 1797, prompting that horridly sentimental poem, "The Boy Stood on The Burning Deck, whence all but he had fled" . . . or something like that. Imagine, if you will, a proud and noble forty-four-gun frigate of the fledgling United States Navy being christened USS *Tory Thumper*, and picture how quickly one might wish to thump the man who so named her up-side the head. Then get on to something more suitable, such as *Constitution*.

Lastly, before anyone gets exceeding wroth with the author and wastes postage or toll charges upon irate phone calls or scathing diatribes, allow him to plead dramatic license. Capt. William Bligh was still at Jamaica, having just delivered his breadfruit, at long last, in the Indiaman *Providence*. There was no way he could have been in London, nor at the Admiralty, to meet our boy Lewrie in late January 1793. You know this. The author, more to the point, knows this. But since mutiny, revolution and all were indeed the spirit of the age, Bligh's appearance in the tale neatly foreshadows that which came later aboard *Cockerel*, and in France and at Toulon. There, satisfied, now? Besides, it was a slow morning for the author, too, when he wrote that, and he couldn't help himself.

So, there is Cdr. Alan Lewrie, master and commander into a proper King's Ship, husband, father, lover, scared so bad he would not trust his own arse with a fart . . . ! What will Sophie de Maubeuge say to Caroline in future? How will he juggle wife and family on one hand, and the stunning Phoebe Aretino on the other? Will it last? Will the kitten *ever* stop nuzzling his ear, or catch a mouse? Will Alan retain the good opinion people seem to have of him, at the moment, anyway?

Most importantly, what sort of adventures . . . and troubles . . . will he get into next? We think we know . . . but we're not telling. Yet.